MW01152738

Renegade

The Spiral Wars, Book 1

Joel Shepherd

ISBN: 1-5239-8145-8
ISBN-13: 978-1-5239-8145-8

The Spiral Wars:

Renegade

Drysine Legacy

Kantovan Vault
(August 2016)

CHAPTER 1

Any thought of a leisurely homecoming from the war ended when *UFS Phoenix* entered Balise System. Nearly a third of the entire human Fleet was there — about four hundred ships, and nearly double that of merchanters and other vessels, mixing with the insystem runners and causing all kinds of confusion.

Approach to Homeworld was 'interesting' at the best of times, a moon in orbit about a ringed gas giant always presented navigational challenges, particularly when that gas giant was as magnetically active as Balise, and tried to flip all your instruments several times a shift. Add to that fourteen other moons, countless assorted asteroids and ice-chunks, and an entire ecosystem of mining runners, outpost stations and sub-light vessels ranging from transports to haulers to tankers and sweepers, and bridge crews were as busy on approach into this peacetime crowd as they were in any active hot zone.

Peacetime. The word crossed Erik Debogande's mind several times, but failed to register as something real. Mostly he was too busy. As *Phoenix*'s third-in-command, he was the junior command officer, and thus was responsible for all the things that Commander Huang and Captain Pantillo were too busy to deal with. That meant docking prep, and setting all the warrant officers to the task of getting *Phoenix* clean and presentable at dock. After a two year deployment in operational conditions, that wasn't easy, and there were galleys to clean, storage lockers crammed with worn and half-repaired gear, and an awful lot of junk to be jettisoned that now couldn't be because of the hazard in crowded space lanes.

Most nerve wrackingly of all, there was the matter of the upcoming parade. All through the ship, crew were breaking out dress uniforms from cramped storage that hadn't seen the light of day in twenty-six months. There followed the discovery of horrifying creases, of 'how the hell did that get there' stains, and a frantic dash to storage for spare shirts, shoes and ties to replace those damaged or mysteriously disappeared. Most crew hadn't been on parade since departure colours, and some couldn't recall basic formation procedures, having their heads too full of things that actually mattered in a war.

Erik was thirty-five years old, a baby by the standards of combat command staff, and for him academy graduation had been only ten years ago. And of course Captain Pantillo and Commander Huang *knew* he'd remembered all this stuff, and was always spotlessly presented in any uniform, so preparing the *Phoenix*'s entire crew for the biggest military parade in over six hundred years naturally fell to him. On top of which he had to sit the Captain's chair for eight hours a rotation on third-shift, while Pantillo and Huang were either sleeping or fulfilling other command responsibilities. After two days of crawling their way through the Balise System to Homeworld, Erik could only think wistfully of sleep and reflect that all in all, the war had been easier.

Occasionally he'd glance at newsfeeds from Shiwon, at the ridiculous crowds and the gathering of forces. All the human leaders were there, from hundreds of settled worlds and systems, all the politicians from the Worlder and Spacer Congresses alike, recalled in what would usually be a non-sitting period for both houses of government. Wealthy people were arriving on private or chartered vessels from a hundred lightyears away, and sleeping on their landing shuttles at various spaceports or open fields in the absence of hotels. There were stories of big ocean ships tied up in harbour for accommodation and charging fortunes by-the-hour, and tent cities in virgin forest where visitors were camping. Lots of the crew had families down there waiting, but trying to get messages through at this light-lag, and with Homeworld communications in knots with a hundred times the usual volume, was nearly impossible. Erik was not particularly worried that his family wouldn't have a good vantage to watch the parade. If Alice Debogande had to rent an entire city block to get a good view, she would do so.

The last few hours before dock were crazy. Erik reviewed the parade plans, consulted with warrant officers and lieutenants about details, ran short rehearsals in cramped corridors and comforted at least two tearful spacers who messed up the sequence of hands on rifle drill and were terrified they'd embarrass *Phoenix* in front of half-a-trillion watching people. Orders were placed ahead at dock for several missing hats, rifle-safety was reviewed for scan-techs who'd barely held a firearm in the last year let alone paraded with one, and meals were arranged on the run to spacers too busy to sit down and eat, who wouldn't get another chance during descent. If Major Thakur hadn't ordered her marine company to give their hapless spacer counterparts a hand, Erik was certain they wouldn't have been ready in time.

All six major trading stations for Homeworld orbit were full, with no berths even for perhaps the most famous warship of the United Forces First Fleet, let alone its accompanying seven cruisers, three haulers and four frigates. They held at parking orbit from Fajar Station, locked the crew cylinder and made a series of runs in *Phoenix* shuttles onto station transfer hub, where they crammed onto waiting Fleet shuttles that had been set aside for the purpose. Hats and other missing dress items were collected from floating station personnel at docking transfer, and then the shuttles took them down through the storm of orbital incoming and outgoing traffic from the atmosphere below. Erik then had several hours of absolutely nothing to do, and with no ability to influence outcomes anyway. He slept most of the way through reentry, waking only briefly when the Gs made it hard to breathe.

The military spaceport outside of Shiwon was nuts, with traffic that in recent times would have heralded a full planetary invasion. All the spaceport interiors were full, so *Phoenix*'s full complement of eight hundred and forty six formed up and waited in a huge empty hangar as endless vertical and horizontal takeoffs and landings shook the ground and filled the air with fumes. The crews of *Storm*, *Kapur* and *Fury* joined them, packing the hangar to capacity, while the poor bloody army units had to form up outside and hold their hats against rolling waves of jet-wash.

Erik took the time to form up the warrant officers again and practise. Rifle drill was the real problem, no one remembered what the hell to do and when — for most warship crew rifles were foreign objects only seen in basic or on parade. Again Major Thakur and her marine lieutenants helped, calmly adjusting rifle placement against shoulders, and giving tips on memorising hand movements and position with different commands. Usually marines would make fun of spacers for not knowing such things, and Erik was sure they'd be reminded later. But Thakur and company were nothing but helpful in a crisis. There was a standing bet amongst spacers for a lot of money for anyone who could make Major Thakur angry without breaking regs. Most didn't believe it was possible, but still no one had the balls to try.

Several times while drilling, Erik glanced to see Captain Pantillo by the hangar's edge, in deep conversation with several serious looking people in suits, their fancy black groundcars waiting on the shimmering tarmac with guards and drivers. Erik knew well that Pantillo had many friends in Spacer Congress, and had been overlooked for Admiral many times because of his politics. Some talked about political ambitions, about furthering the cause of the Worlders, always unhappy with their under-representation in the corridors of true power. Many Spacers had bad names for other Spacers who sided with the Worlders, but Pantillo was one of the greatest names in the whole United Forces — the most successful warship captain of the last fifty years, in command of one of the most legendary vessels of the entire Triumvirate War. He got a pass where others wouldn't, and no one would dare accuse him of receiving Worlder money for backing their side.

A group of chah'nas warriors ran by the hangar, weaving about the cars without breaking formation. Seven-foot-plus and four-armed, they ran with thudding, muscular precision, many arms swinging in unison, with a rhythmic chant on every fourth step. They were an imposing sight in full battle armour and weapons, as chah'nas had no such thing as dress uniform, only 'fighting clothes' and 'not fighting clothes'. Getting them to understand such things as parades had been a struggle in itself, as Erik recalled Commander Huang telling the crew all around a mess table one shift, having once spent a year as liaison officer to a chah'nas battle fleet. Now they were here to indulge this odd human custom, and fly the flag for their people on this, the great victory day for humans and chah'nas alike.   Humans had not fought this war alone, nor had they won it alone.   Were it not for the Chah'nas Continuum, all of humanity would have ended a thousand years before, at the hands of an entirely different enemy.   The chah'nas liked to remind humans frequently, and on this day in particular, most humans would not begrudge them that reminder.

Finally a convoy of busses arrived, and the assembled crews filed aboard.   Another long drive out of the spaceport, weaving through bus, truck and other traffic, and chatter increased as excitement levels rose.   There was no civilian traffic between the spaceport and Shiwon, just a long expressway reserved solely for the military, then some pretty suburbs, green trees and houses whizzing by below.   Above were formations of jets, fighter drones and gunships, then a group of assembled army dropships like giant, howling bees.   Crew peered from the bus windows to watch, then pointed and exclaimed in amazement as a mixed formation of craft roared by, assembled around a massive assault shuttle, like moths about an eagle.   All this activity was expensive and very loud, but today no one would be complaining.   Erik wondered if the whole event really was as expensive as a planetary invasion.   Just so long as the expense this time was only measured in currency, and not in many thousands of lives.

The expressway entered a huge tunnel under the great war memorial, where an entire low hillside overlooking central Shiwon had been converted to parks, walkways and pretty views about a series of monuments to the dead from a hundred and sixty-one years of war.   There were other, even grander memorials on Homeworld of course, to other wars that told the story of how humankind had ended up here in the first place.   But this memorial was to *this* war, Erik's war, the one that had been going for a hundred and twenty seven years before he was born, and that he'd occasionally doubted he'd live to see the end of even should he *not* meet some violent and glorious death in the cause of human freedom.

The busses queued in the long tunnels before finally disembarking their passengers and doing a U-turn onto the opposing lane.   Ahead were more endless rows of soldiers and spacers, forming up now with yells from their officers, a last minute check of buttons, hats, collars and weapons. As the *Phoenix* crew scrambled to make formation, Erik felt his heart thudding faster as a thousand thoughts and possibilities tumbled through his mind, things he hoped he'd gotten right and that wouldn't disgrace his ship and his family if they all went wrong.

The marines went first, by convention. Not a single spacer begrudged them that, recalling many times when enemy or otherwise non-compliant stations or ships had required capturing, and it had been marines who fought their way aboard through gunfire, booby traps and explosive decompressions, while spacers stayed safe and pressurised in their ship. Somewhere ahead the tunnel ended, and Erik could see over the heads of second-shift that Major Thakur's marines had left the tunnel into sunlight. There was a roar, and applause, and the echo of loudspeaker announcements up the road. The population of Homeworld were knowledgeable followers of the war, and knew their warriors like sports fans knew their football players.

Next would be Captain Pantillo, marching alone before first-shift. Then Commander Huang heading second-shift, then Erik himself leading third. It suddenly struck him that he was going to be marching here all alone, with no one at his flanks to provide the anonymity of numbers. The cameras would find him, of course. There goes Lieutenant Commander Erik Debogande, the commentators would say. The second-youngest-ever naval officer to make warship command. And on the legendary *UFS Phoenix*, of all the vessels to do it on, under one of the greatest Fleet heroes of the war, Captain Marinol Pantillo. Who could possibly believe that this promotion was earned, and not somehow political, given the extraordinary clout and finances of the Debogande family? Is this boy really that good, or did Mommy Debogande pull a few strings in senior command? Because really, given the sheer numbers of officers graduating from the Academy with exceptional scores, what were the odds?

Well. Erik himself sometimes wondered.

Rifle tucked to his shoulder, he took one final opportunity to look back and view his small line of third-shift officers. Most of *Phoenix* had two-shifts only, but the bridge alone had three. It meant that while Pantillo and Huang were marching before a formation of three hundred and one each, Erik had only his bridge officers and reserves — a little line of fifteen plus himself out front. They looked straight, and marched well enough, for spacers who hadn't been on a planet since leave on Tepi four months ago. Four months, and then the flanking feint on Thilum, followed by the secondary push to Moana Junction, then a month's regrouping before the final assault on Kattil Karam, on the very outskirts of the tavalai homeworld. Then the counter attacks, and Captain Pantillo's desperate flanking assault at the tavalai assembly point at Dhuvo, where *Prescott* and *Cutter* had been destroyed and a thousand lives lost. And then, a week later, news that the chah'nas had crushed an entire sard fleet at Trongkul, and the kaal were squabbling with the tavalai about surrender. And a week after that, news that the tavalai had finally caved, and were willing to surrender unconditionally.

Four months? It seemed like far more than four months. Sometimes the last few months seemed like years. And then at other times, the entire ten years Erik had been at war seemed to have passed in the blink of an eye.

Sunlight hit him with force, and he tried not to squint beneath the brim of his cap. Here before the tunnel mouth, the great plaza of the memorial hill came down to the roadside, with statues and steps and railings carved in old stone. Those were now gone, disappeared beneath a sea of people. They cheered and yelled, and the noise was like a shuttle's retros, shaking the air. Ahead, up the kilometres of straight Memorial Avenue, more grassy verges had vanished beneath a blanket of people. About them Shiwon's glassy towers soared against a warm blue sky, creating a canyon of noise. Ticker-tape fell in paper storms, sweeping the scene like some freak weather event of raining confetti. Loudspeakers struggled in vain to be heard above the millions of voices, as drones whined and jockeyed for overhead camera angles, and jets and gunships painted the sky above the towers with streaks of colour.

Erik marched, overwhelmed and focused only on keeping a precise distance with the rear rank of second-shift ahead. Here on the right came a viewing platform, a scaffold erected for old veterans of the war's earlier phase to see the parade. The command came through, 'shoulder left!', and hands shifted rifles in unison, five rhythmic steps from right shoulder to left. Then the next command, 'eyes right!', and all heads turned across as one. As the first rank drew level with the platform, 'salute!', and right arms snapped up, as the old vets saluted back, ranks and ranks of them atop their scaffold, and all proud and grey and happy.

"*Boys and girls, this is your Captain,*" came the uplink message from up ahead, as they resumed normal marching. "*You've earned this day, all of you. This day belongs to you, and it belongs to all our brothers and sisters whom we've lost along the way. March with your heads high, but please note — you are allowed to smile. That means you, Erik.*"

Though they did not break formation, Erik saw the shoulders of crew ahead of him shaking as they laughed. And then he was grinning, against all his better judgement.

"*Just one more thing,*" their Captain continued. "*Know that on all the ships in all the wars gone by, there has never been a captain more proud of his crew than I am today.*"

And then it felt like a load had lifted from Erik's shoulders. No longer was this parade something to be dreaded. It was a spectacle, no doubt one of the greatest in all human history. He was home, and though many of his friends would never return, there were many more who had. It was all over, the fighting, the dying. Final victory, for a species that had just a thousand years before been reduced to a meagre hundred million individuals, struggling to survive in the dark systems about their home star after their homeworld had been destroyed by unprovoked invaders.

It all culminated here, on this new homeworld, on this day, and he was somehow fortunate enough to be at the centre of it all, third-in-command behind perhaps the greatest warrior of the latest and hopefully last ever war. Now he marched proudly, and allowed himself to take in the roaring crowds, the great banners hanging from the towersides proclaiming thanks, the heartfelt memorials, the patriotic songs.   A little girl in a red dress jumped a barrier and ran to him with a flower.   He gave her a smile and a kiss, took the flower and pinned it in his lapel with a wave to the girl's beaming parents as she scampered back to them.

And just when he thought he was having fun, he thought again of all his friends who would have loved to be here and see this, but would never be seen by anyone again.   And suddenly he was in tears.

CHAPTER 2

After five kilometres of marching, the parade took a left exit and ended up in Victory Park. There MPs with loudspeakers urged everyone to disperse and head elsewhere, as the park couldn't handle more than fifty thousand people, and several hundred thousand would be marching today.

Rifles were collected, and goodbyes were said, as some folks wouldn't be seeing each other for weeks — *Phoenix* was now headed for perma-dock and half the crew had ground leave starting from now, while the other half would have to go up in a few days to prep the ship for long term stand-down. Erik had been expecting that he and third-shift would get the bridge duty, and was surprised that it went to Huang instead. Officers clustered beneath a huge fig tree, with handshakes and embraces, and Captain Pantillo went to Erik with a fatherly hug.

"Erik, good job these last few days. It all went well. I'm pleased." And that was worth more than all the medals that Fleet Command was rumoured to be about to pin on them.

"Thank you Captain." Pantillo was not a big man, tanned with Asian features that he claimed went back to someplace called the Philippines. His hair was greying, and he'd been alive for much of the war — one hundred and twenty seven standard Earth years, a very advanced age considering the reflexes required of a warship captain. "How does it feel, now that it's all over?"

"Over," Pantillo repeated, with a shrewd look. "Hmm. Well you know, something ends, something else begins. Give my best wishes to your parents, I suppose you're going to see them now?"

"If I'm not there in less than fifty minutes, Mother will be calling Fleet Command asking where I am," said Erik. Pantillo smiled. "She knows exactly how far a walk it is, she'll be timing me."

As it happened, he didn't have to walk — an uplink signal flashed on his inner vision, and told him that a cruiser was on its way to a local transition zone, ETA ten minutes. Courtesy of Debogande Enterprises, of course, and initialled KD. That would be Katerina Debogande, Erik's eldest sister and CEO of Debogande Enterprises. DE in turn accounted for slightly more than half of Debogande Incorporated — the core company, handed down in family tradition to the eldest child.

Erik rounded up two buddies from third-shift he knew had no family on Homeworld, plus one from Engineering second-shift, and ushered them toward the transition zone. As much as he looked forward to seeing his family again, a part of him dreaded it as well, and he did not want to be alone among the civilians. Besides, an invite to a Debogande family function could be a real boost to a young person's life in any career, and all three friends accepted eagerly. They exchanged some more embraces and farewells as they left, but before they could properly depart, Erik was halted by Major Trace Thakur herself.

"Got room for one more?" she asked him, eyeing his group of three.

"Um... sure, it'll be a big cruiser." To put it mildly. "Why?"

"The Captain feels you should have protection. Lieutenant Dale will accompany you." She glanced at Dale, who was tall, blonde and dangerous. The marine dress uniform did its best to civilise him, but Erik had seen the man bite the head off a live tulik in a drinking session. He was a killer bare-handed or with weapons, or with innocuous everyday items that could be used as weapons. His displeased expression suggested he'd much rather have gone drinking with his marines, and wasn't as thrilled at this invitation to party with the insanely wealthy as some might have been.

Erik gave Thakur a puzzled smile. "Major, I'm just going to see my family, I really don't think I need protection."

"The Captain feels you do."

Trace Thakur was a little below average height, had ethnicity going back to a more familiar-sounding Earth-place called 'India', and was kind of pretty but in no way delicate. Like all marines, she was the product of the best genetic engineering and bio-synthetic augmentations that money could buy. Unlike most marines, she was Kulina, the elite warriors from the world of Sugauli. Among other things, that meant she didn't drink or gamble, and as far as anyone knew, hadn't been screwing around either.

Some non-marines were surprised that a man like Dale could take a teetotaller seriously at all, but Erik had learned that if you wanted to make yourself physically unsafe around *Phoenix* marines, you needed only say something negative about the Major. Dale was a thirty year veteran, and had an impressive row of medals on his chest, yet despite 'only' ten years of active duty, Thakur's was larger. Foremost amongst them was the Liberty Star, the highest award the UF could give. Usually you had to die to get one.

Erik smiled. "Of course. Welcome aboard, Lieutenant Dale." Dale grunted. "And what about you, Major? Would you like to come too?"

"There are many things in this life that I would like to do, Lieutenant Commander," Thakur said cryptically. And she put a hand on Dale's shoulder as she left, in thanks. It seemed to cheer him, but only a little.

"Come on then," Erik sighed. "Let's do it."

The park perimeter was crazy with crowds, all the roads were shut to traffic, and the thronged pedestrians moved in a slow, shuffling sea, shouting, singing and shaking the hand of every uniformed person they saw. Erik's crew cleared the park's guarded exit just as the lights about the transition zone between road and sidewalk began to flash, and nearby pedestrians made room as the descending cruiser's field gens prickled their hair.

Erik scanned his ID and its doors opened to admit them — they could have fit another four at least, but Erik wasn't sure at his family's reaction if he turned up with half of third-shift in tow. Doors shut and the engines whined, and they rose past park trees and gleaming towers toward a cruising lane.

"Any idea where it is?" asked Lieutenant Dean Chong, who sat Nav beside Erik's command chair on third-shift.

"Somewhere with a good view," Erik replied. He glanced at Lieutenant Dale in the rear seat. "Lieutenant, did they tell you *why* I needed protection?"

"No sir," said Dale.

"Maybe worried you'll choke on an olive," suggested Ensign Remy Hale, who was from Engineering.

"I don't think my olive-swallowing skills have deteriorated that badly," said Erik. The cruiser reached an elevation where they could see past the towers to Memorial Avenue, cutting straight through Shiwon from Memorial Hill to the harbour like an arrow. Still the marchers marched, and the crowds cheered. No doubt it would go on for hours yet.

"I'm not sure even Lieutenant Dale could save you from a homicidal olive," said Second Lieutenant Raf Corrig, who sat Arms. "It doesn't seem his skill-set."

Dale glowered out the window. Erik nearly felt sorry for him. Spacer officer corp tended to be well educated from fine urban institutions. The marines were blue collar brawlers and proud of it. Lieutenant Dale, despite his officer's bars, had started off as a private after a rough childhood on a frontier world, and earned an officer's commission by still being alive after twenty years in the field. The two cultures were chalk and cheese, and here was Dale, stuck babysitting smart-mouthed spacer officers as they sipped champagne and exchanged witticisms, when he could be drinking with his buddies in celebration of something that truly deserved it.

"Pretty girls at the family functions, Lieutenant," Erik told Dale to cheer him. "Lots of pretty girls."

Dale raised an eyebrow. "No doubt, sir."

"Just don't touch the ones called Debogande, or there'll be trouble." And Dale actually smiled, just a little.

Almost immediately the cruiser began to descend, and the dash display showed its skylane curling down between towers to a middle height but hugely wide building that directly overlooked Memorial Avenue. As they drew closer, Erik saw that the entire top floor was a domed glass canopy, and it was filled with people. Upon the adjoining landing pad, lights were beginning to flash.

"Well Erik," said Dean, peering wide-eyed from the back seat. "Your mother's certainly outdone herself this time."

They landed on the pad beside the rooftop suite, holding their hats against the gathering sea breeze, and went to where guards opened the doors for them. Within were a cheering crowd of VIPs, and then Erik was swamped by his younger sisters Lisbeth and Cora, then with more grace, Deirdre and Katerina. And finally, and to even greater applause from the crowd, his father Walker, and mother Alice.

The rest passed in a blur, him introducing his shipmates to his family, his family to his shipmates, then speeches, handshaking, and far, far too many introductions. All he really wanted to do was go off somewhere quiet with his family and talk, especially with Lisbeth, whose entire engineering degree he'd only heard about through correspondence, and Cora, who was now running most of Debogande Incorporated's enormous arts and philanthropy program at the ripe old age of twenty-nine. Deirdre and Katerina's lives were still more or less the same as when he'd last had extended family leave, but Katerina's two kids were older now and eager to see their uncle, and Deirdre had racked up more travelling lightyears than he had lately with the family law firm, and there was so much to talk about.

But instead it was meet this corporate leader and dear family friend, and meet that Spacer Congress Senator and even dearer family friend, and darling *surely* you remember so-and-so from what-its-name... and Erik would nod with enthusiasm he didn't feel and shake another hand, or kiss another cheek. At least his friends seemed to be enjoying themselves — he'd cunningly introduced them all as 'single', with a pointed look around, and now each was suitably entertained by attractive women or, in Remy's case, handsome men. Even Lieutenant Dale had struck apparently civilised conversation with several of the promised pretty girls, though Erik happened to know that each was heir to city-sized fortunes, and not truly in the market for a square-jawed marine Lieutenant whose retirement might earn him a plot of working frontier land and a pension.

After an hour he managed to free himself for a drink on an outdoor balcony overlooking the parade. Still it rolled on, and still the crowds cheered and the aircraft circled in low formation. The sunlight on his face felt so good, after so long shipside. You could do it in VR, lie on a simulated beach, or climb a simulated mountain, but it just wasn't the same. The sea breeze teased a faint sweat off his brow, and that felt as good as a beautiful woman's kiss. He closed his eyes for a moment, and took a deep breath.

Someone came through the door behind, and stood beside him. "Unfiltered air tastes different," said his father. "Doesn't it."

Erik smiled. "It does. It's always the little things." Walker Debogande had also held a Fleet commission, in an earlier phase of the war. He'd been Walker Hussain back then, and the third child of Nilsen Hussain, head of one of humanity's more successful energy companies. As third-in-line he'd been grudgingly allowed to go to the war, but instead of being his end, it had been his salvation, as his parents and two elder siblings had perished when the sard hit the colony at Promise. His fourteen year service cut short, he'd returned to run the company, which became so successful it had begun making powerplants for the Fleet. That had necessitated working with Debogande Enterprises and its formidable CEO Alice, who was fulfilling another large part of that order for everything *but* the powerplants. The two had hit it off, and the marriage had folded the Hussain family into the Debogande, and Hussein Energy into Debogande Incorporated.

"I'm sorry we had to do it like this," said Erik's father. "Well... I tell a lie, we *didn't* have to do it like this. But you know your mother."

Erik sighed. "I know. It's okay Dad. We'll get time." His father put a rough arm around him, and squeezed. He was a strong man, not especially tall, but wide at the shoulders. His face was round, freckled and dark, with a grey-streaked beard and an energetic smile. A more African shade to Alice's light-brown. People still liked to try and designate skin-tones and face-shapes with corresponding regions of old-Earth, but after so many generations away from home, the human race was all blending together. There were still some purely white, black or Asian people left, but those were rare, usually living on some exclusively settled world where they didn't have to mix cheek-by-jowl with everyone else. Spacers, or those descended from Spacers during those long centuries where humanity had nowhere in particular to call home, were now various shades of 'tan', the exact details of which were usually customed in some gene lab prior to birth.

"We will, I promise," said Walker. "That last fight seemed pretty bad."

Erik nodded. "It was pretty bad. We lost a lot of ships."

"You think it was worth it?"

Erik shrugged. "Who gets to decide that? In strategic terms, sure. We won, the war's over. If we hadn't pushed so hard, right then, it might have kept going, and we'd have lost a lot more in the long run. But if some little kid out there decides to hell with strategic terms, he just wants his daddy back?" He looked at his father. "Well who could argue with him?"

Walker sighed, and leaned both thick elbows on the balcony railing. They looked out at the passing parade. "Yeah. Fourteen years was enough for me. Of course, I wasn't on the sharp end like you..."

"You were sharp enough. You know what it's like." Walker had sat Scan on a hauler. They weren't armed, but they often carried arms into hot spots, where god-knew-what was waiting for them. All in all, Erik was sure he'd rather be on a ship that could shoot back. *Phoenix* was certainly that. "Besides, I've only done three on *Phoenix*. The other seven years I was staffing, babysitting docks or serving on *Firebird*. The most action *Firebird* saw was the occasional solar flare."

"All valuable work." Walker patted his hand. "How are the tavalai taking it, do you think? Will the surrender last?"

Erik made a dismissive face. "Oh they've been sick of this war for decades. It should have ended fifty years ago Dad, you know that."

"Sure. But wars in space move slow." They did. The logistics alone took an incredible time. Anyone could strike a system from space, but the deeper you went into enemy territory, the harder it became to get back alive.   To hit deep into enemy space, you had to *capture* systems, not just skip over them.   That took huge time, energy and resources.   Doing it repeatedly, system after system, took decades.   It wasn't all high-energy combat and casualties, a lot of it was quite boring, months and years of preparations, skirmishes and reconnaissance, punctuated by huge explosions of terror and death.   It took a very stubborn people to do it for a hundred and sixty one years.   Until this surrender, it was thought that the tavalai were the most stubborn species in the Spiral. Now everyone knew better.

"Tavalai aren't warriors, Dad," Erik said tiredly.   "Their organisation is incredible, I mean, if only we could run logistics like they do.   But they're bureaucrats.   Their tech is good and they're tough and stubborn as hell, but they just don't go for the throat like warriors.   They aren't made that way.   You know what I mean."

"They aren't prepared to risk everything to win," Walker said sombrely.

"I used to hate them.   When they hit Valinta and New Punjab, I wanted to rip them apart with my bare hands.   But they hit military targets, they're probably better at avoiding civvie casualties than we are."

"The sard aren't.   Nor the kaal."

Erik shrugged.   "Sure, and we're allied to the chah'nas, so who's worse?"

Walker looked at him warily.   "Son, you know I respect your opinions.   God knows you've earned the right to hold them.   But I wouldn't be talking like that so loudly around here at the moment."

"I know.   I know."   It was the army infantry now out on parade.   Army were the biggest branch of the United Forces.   They occupied worlds, and pacified resistance.   It took a lot of soldiers, a lot more than manning ships.   But the technical requirements were also lower, and they used a lot more brute force than sharp finesse. Most marines didn't think much of them.   "I could kill sard all day and sleep fine.   Hell, if we could repeat with the sard what we did to the krim, I'd be okay with that.   The kaal... they're not as bad, but I can't lose much sleep over them either. It's just these stupid fucking tavalai Dad. They had no business fighting us and for the last sixty years at least they knew it. But they were just too fucking stubborn for their own good, and now it's cost tens of millions of us, and hundreds of millions of them. It just... pisses me off."

He'd gone aboard at Larakilikal Station, to help secure the facilities. Tavalai had fought to the last woman and man, their armoured bodies sprawled and blasted in the steel hallways, where Fleet marines had dropped them. A few had lived longer, their helmets off, their funny, frog-like eyes bulging, trying to get water on their skin to help the secretion process in healing. Some clutched religious artefacts, and others slate screens with pictures of family. He'd given a live one some water, and it had gurgled a thank-you, and patted his hand with clammy fingers. Sard would pretend to be dead, then blow themselves up to take a few humans with them. Kaal would like to, but lacked the nerve. But it never occurred to tavalai. In a century and a half of war, only a small handful of human prisoners had ever reported poor treatment at their hands. On Tirapik, the world below Larakilikal Station, some captured human freighter crews had been found living on a grassy compound on a hill. They were well fed and healthy, and demanded that their tavalai captors should be treated similarly.

"And then I hear what the chah'nas have done to some tavalai in their battles," he murmured. "And I wonder if we aren't fighting the wrong people."

"Now *that*," said his father, "is something you should definitely keep to yourself. Come on, we should head back inside. I think your mother's about to give a speech."

Alice Debogande was indeed about to give a speech, and someone had even brought an elevation for her to stand on, and be seen above the crowd. That wasn't all that had been brought in. Erik saw a pair of chah'nas towering by a wall, double arms crossed, in the coloured leathers that passed for formal wear among their kind. One of them saw Erik looking, and raised a glass in his direction — irony, because chah'nas metabolised alcohol so fast it was impossible to get them drunk on anything less than jet fuel.

Four-eyed with a massive underbite and protruding lower tusks, there was nothing gentle about chah'nas to the human eye.   Erik nodded back.

"Who's that?" he asked his father.   Chah'nas were usually as bored with human social life as human parades.   Most were direct to the point of rudeness, their social graces only saved by an abrasive yet undeniable sense of humour.

"E'tu'kas," said Walker, standing at his side.   "One of the new ambassadors."   On Homeworld, there were several.   One to the Spacer Congress, one to the Worlder Congress, and one to Homeworld itself, plus all their staff.   Then all the military attaches, and *their* staff.   It had occasionally been remarked to chah'nas that they should sort out exactly who was in charge, and give that person a title.   The chah'nas reply, with appropriate humour, was 'look who's talking'.

Being accused of multiplicity by the chah'nas was ironic indeed.   Chah'nas had dozens of castes, the purpose of which left most humans baffled.   Together they made a maze of ascending qualifications and specialities that chah'nas would spend their lives navigating and climbing.   What *was* certain was chah'nas used genetic engineering to differentiate specialities among themselves, like animal breeders selectively isolating desirable traits.   They did not try for species purity, but rather species complexity through caste competitiveness — which meant they tried to strengthen castes against each other in endless competition, as though to improve their species like some giant professional sporting league.   Certainly the chah'nas loved their sports to a degree that even humans found unhealthy.   Most were violent.   Erik had tried explaining golf to several, and been met with gales of laughter.

Against an opposite wall, Erik glimpsed the big, wide ears of a kuhsi... then a glimpse of the face, a short muzzle too canine to be feline, but too feline to be canine.   A flat, wide head, made wider by those amazing ears that went far more sideways than upwards. They weren't as tall as chah'nas, usually a touch shorter than humans, and so didn't stand out in crowds... until you saw the ears.

Kuhsi were humanity's contribution to species uplift — they'd been found near human space, on the verge of their own FTL flight, and so humans had hurried them on a little, needing all the friends they could get. Certainly the kuhsi had been pleased to be 'discovered' by humans and not krim, and humans had been good with them — letting them have their space, not interfering with local politics, giving them useful tech without asking anything but friendship in return. And kuhsi had reciprocated, not so much as to participate in humanity's latest war, but to offer moral and trading support, and even a few irregular volunteers.

People unfamiliar with kuhsi thought they were cute until they met the southern Scuti races, amongst whom the males grew as big as chah'nas, and far more deadly hand-to-hand. Kuhsi were comfortably the most athletic of the known sentient species, and probably the ones you least wanted a fist fight with, if only because of those awful three-fingered talons that would skewer you like meat on a stick. Kuhsi had only stopped duelling two centuries ago — just before human first contact — and a lot of traditionalists wanted the custom back. Erik also thought them a pack of misogynists who treated their women like shit. Cute with big ears wasn't everything.

"Friends," said Erik's mother above the crowd. She wore a red gown, her hair pulled back to a tasteful braid. One hundred and two years old, middle aged by the current human standard, though she barely looked it. Only a few crinkles about the eyes, which she could have vanished with treatments, yet kept for 'character purposes'. When you were one of the regularly voted 'ten most powerful' people alive, she'd told him once, you had to have a few wrinkles or they wouldn't take you seriously.

Now she smiled at them all. In all honesty, Erik didn't think she was a particularly great smiler. He'd seen her real smiles, and they were small, honest, private affairs. A careful amusement, well guarded and never abused. This was a big, 'I love you all so much' smile... and sometimes, when you knew someone this well, you just couldn't buy it, because you knew it was false. He didn't doubt that a lot of the others present also knew. The difference was that they didn't care.

"This truly is a fortuitous day," she said through that big smile. "It has brought my beloved son Erik back to me." Now the smile turned to him. Erik forced one of his own, all eyes temporarily upon him. "And it has brought a celebration of victory. A final victory, we hope, for all humankind, and for our valued allies."

She raised a glass at the chah'nas, who raised one back. Then at the kuhsi… Erik guessed he must be an ambassador of some sort also. A glass raised back. Hopefully the big-eared ambassador wouldn't drink too much — unlike chah'nas, kuhsi *did* get drunk, often alarmingly so.

"I'm sure our non-human guests are aware that it is customary on such grand occasions for the head of a family, or an institution, to recall the Great Journey. As I am both head of institution *and* of family — sorry darling," with a glance at her husband by Erik's side.

"No she's right," Walker conceded to the room, who laughed obligingly.

"Then this solemn retelling shall fall to me," Alice continued. "In the name of all that has been so that all may yet come, as we build the glorious future, amen." "Amen," echoed the crowd. There was no shortage of Destinos symbols among those gathered, the circle-and-crescent in earrings, pendants or on ties, the crescent rising behind the circle like a sunrise upon a planetary horizon, and pierced by a single line rising up to infinity. Many of the Debogande family's charities were Destinos charities. More a Spacer religion than a Worlder one, it was a statement of identity through faith for many Spacers, not to mention a networking opportunity through such institutions.

"Once upon a time," Alice began, "there was a race of people called humans. We lived upon a beautiful planet called Earth, and it had supported us as a species for more than three million years. Eventually we evolved to venture from our homeworld, but no sooner had we learned how to do so than our efforts were noticed, because faster-than-light travel is detectable far and wide. Humans learned that we were directly alongside the territory of a powerful race called the krim.

"We hoped that the krim could be our friends, but the krim were an evil and brutal race, who lived only to inflict pain on others. Krim invaded our beautiful world, and ravaged the resources of our solar system.   In desperation the humans called out to the other civilised peoples of the galaxy, whom they had only just learned to also exist. Humans fought bravely to save their homeworld, but they did not have the technology to match the krim spacecraft and weapons.

"But the galactic peoples were run by a greedy race called the tavalai.   They and their allies cared for nothing but their own peace and happiness.   The krim were powerful, and the tavalai agreed that each people should be allowed to do whatever they chose in their own area of space.   The human area of space was deemed to be krim space, and so the krim could do as they pleased, while the tavalai counted their money, and congratulated themselves on being such a peaceful and civilised people, that they avoided such trouble with the krim."

Alice read this line from her visual with scorn, and there were grim chuckles from the audience.   Human-tavalai bad blood was old indeed... though nowhere near as old as that between chah'nas and tavalai.

"Meanwhile the krim slaughtered the brave humans in their thousands.   But one of the galactic peoples did listen.   One honourable people did not think that it was right that the krim could rape and pillage a world that was not theirs.   These brave people took it upon themselves to defy the Tavalai Confederation, and smuggle arms and modern technology to the embattled humans."

Alice raised her glass again to the chah'nas.   "Our friends, the great Chah'nas Continuum.   Long may you prosper."   Loud assent from the crowd, and glasses were raised and sipped from. The chah'nas looked pleased.

"With their new weapons, the humans fought back against the krim, and began to do damage.   Humans left their home system and struck against the krim in the krim's own territory, now having the ships to do that. This caused the krim great consternation. For two hundred years did humans fight this guerrilla war from and around their occupied system, while the chah'nas argued the case for humanity with the Tavalai Confederacy."

She was taking liberties, Erik knew, by calling it that. There had been no Tavalai Confederacy — most species in the Spiral called it the First Free Age, and the tavalai claimed not to have been in charge of it at all. It had been the first equal time, they said, when all the sentient races could do as they pleased without having to answer to one powerful overlord. And to some extent, they were right. But allowing freedom of action had allowed the krim to make war on humanity without consequence. And for that, humanity would never forgive or forget.

"Finally the Tavalai Confederacy agreed to intervene. But instead of demanding that the krim leave humanity's home system, they sent a force of peacekeepers, to keep the *peace* between humans and krim." Again, the sarcasm was dripping. Old and often repeated history though it was, Erik could feel his blood boil at the telling. "But they found, of course, that there was no peace to keep. Humanity did not want peace with the krim — they wanted justice, and the krim to leave Earth, and Sol System, and all humanity alone forever. But the tavalai thought to make a deal between us, thereby to legitimise the krim occupation.

"This the humans could never accept, and so a new war began, the war between humans and the tavalai peacekeepers. Soon the tavalai tired of fighting these brave freedom fighters in a distant corner of the galaxy, and returned to their own worlds. The krim took this admission of tavalai defeat as an opportunity to end humans once and for all, free from tavalai interference forever. They destroyed the human home, the beautiful Mother Earth, and left none upon its surface alive. Humanity was cast adrift, a people without a home, and with no purpose left for living. No purpose, that was, except revenge.

"Once again, humanity's chah'nas friends nurtured us. Barely one hundred million strong, out of so many billions before, only those humans living off-Earth at the time had survived.

Humanity rebuilt its industry, in a hundred years of tireless work, out in the dark, in habitations of steel and stone, we rebuilt ourselves for the purpose of war, and steeled ourselves for battle.

"This time, when the humans struck the krim, we were finally at and past their military level. With nothing to defend, we knew only attack, and we drove the krim from one system after another. What we occupied, we turned to engines of industry to power our war machine, as the galaxy watched on in amazement. Again the tavalai intervened, right at our moment of triumph, to dissuade us from final victory. But by now humanity was too strong, and the tavalai dared not strike. The krim race ended there, killed to the last living vermin we could find, and today not a trace of them remains. Humanity made a statement, to all who would make genocidal war on us — we shall deal with you in kind. The galaxy heard us, and those who would make war on the weak and innocent have trembled."

Odd, Erik thought, that this telling had never bothered him before. This cheerful endorsement of genocide, this utter annihilation of an entire species, down to the last living child… to be sure, the krim deserved it, and that was no crude human propaganda. Nearly every species had been pleased to see them go — an evolutionary mistake, most agreed… with the possible exception of the sard, who were perhaps another such mistake themselves. But it did not change the fact that of all sentient species in the galaxy today, only one was responsible, and indeed happily revelled in, the successful genocide of another race. It was one thing to cheerfully recall that tale in the blood-curdling joy of just deserts. It was another thing to have seen mass killing in person, and to realise what it must have actually meant to do it.

"For five hundred years, we built our new spacefaring civilisation upon captured worlds and new technology," Alice continued. "But still the tavalai made us trouble. They blamed us for upsetting the old balance, with our new ships and weapons. They demanded that we disarm, as though we had not nearly been exterminated for that lack of weapons. They denied us membership of the ruling bodies. They blocked our trade routes, and intercepted our trading missions.   They harassed our shipping, and destabilised our worlds.   Their vicious allies, the sard and the kaal, launched many raids against us and our friends.

"Obviously this could not be allowed to continue, and so once again we joined with our chah'nas allies, and with our newest allies, the wise and powerful alo, to win our freedom and secure our rightful place in the galactic order."

Erik glanced around to see if there were any alo present, but predictably there weren't.   Alo were not sociable, and their manners made chah'nas seem paragons of etiquette.   They thought humans smelled bad, in more ways than one, but their combined wealth and knowledge was said to be more than all of human and chah'nas space combined.

"We three formed the Triumvirate Alliance, and today, one hundred and sixty one years from its commencement, this grand project has finally succeeded.   Let us raise our glasses in a toast.   A toast to humanity.   A toast to victory.   A toast to friendship.   The human race has been in space for fourteen hundred years, and we're just getting started!"

CHAPTER 3

The next morning Erik awoke to silken sheets and a distractingly comfortable bed. He was back in the family Homeworld residence — there were numerous, on all of humanity's major worlds, but this one was home, the place of all his childhood memories. The far wall was glass, so clean it seemed invisible. Beyond, a view of Shiwon from the high hills that surrounded it, a tall and gleaming city before a glorious blue harbour. Above the ocean horizon, Balise's huge crescent filled the sky, pale in the glare of daylight.

Erik lay for a moment and contemplated this change of circumstance. It didn't feel real. His life here, or his life on *Phoenix* — one of them had to be a dream. He just wasn't sure which. Why would anyone leave this? His shipmates had asked often enough. Exchange this room, and this house, for ten years of cramped Fleet quarters, dreary food, fake sunlight, and a final three years with the very real possibility of sudden death. Fleet hadn't desperately needed him, there was no conscription. He could have stayed here, like his sisters, and run the various family businesses in luxurious safety.

'What, can't rich people be idealists too?' he'd joked whenever one of his shipmates had pressed on it. It was a good way to deflect the questions, but even then, he hadn't been sure he believed it. An idealist about what? The need for human victory? Everyone was that, and five hundred years of war against the krim had pretty well ironed all the pacifist delusions out of the human race a long time ago. Humanity's spacefaring age had been born in fire, and the inability to fight well at the established galactic level had at one point cost ninety-nine percent of the human race their lives. They were all descendants of the survivors of that Holocaust, and when such descendants said 'never again', they meant it.

But Family Debogande had appearances to upkeep. A long tradition of military service, among the men of the house. No one had told him he had to go, but he'd felt it, that needling expectation.

And so he'd gone, and could not now for the life of him say whether it was a genuine passion for the cause, or the desire for the family to think well of him. Was that truly bravery, or cowardice — the seeking of favours and approval? Or was this onset of melancholy doubts just that he was tired, and no longer so enamoured of the war as he had been? And what kind of thinking was that anyway, to be doubting this last phase in humanity's war of survival just because it hadn't been as brutally hard as the first phase, and humanity had been winning for a change?

He sighed, rubbed his eyes, and rolled from bed to do his exercises. Then he went for a run, and the family security staff tailed him out the gate in big dark cars, but no one on these high, exclusive hill-top roads noticed or cared. He ran past mansion after high-walled mansion, up and down slopes, happy just to be out in the open air. Some spacers reported mild agoraphobia after too much time in space, but Erik loved the open sky, and the sense of freedom every time he rounded a corner to a beautiful, unobstructed road ahead, flanked by lovely green trees and alive with birdsong, was indescribable.

Time to get out of Fleet, perhaps? The war was over now. But there were vast new territories to patrol, and the defeated races weren't going to accept their new status easily. Some enforcement would be required for a long time to come. The new colonial age was beginning, and colonial ages required large fleets. A man with important friends and a strong service record could progress far in such an age... and the truth of it was, as much as he knew he must be insane for leaving this life, he truly didn't find the world of corporate management all that inspiring. It didn't *matter*, not like service mattered.

Or like politics mattered, he had to admit. If he wanted to go in that direction, Mother would back him all the way, and those pockets ran indefinitely deep. The way Spacer Congress politics worked, he'd need a longer and more distinguished service record than he had now. Three years on *Phoenix* was a start, but he'd held no combat command, and won no battles. Captain Pantillo was not in the business of career planning for his underlings, but he had let slip occasionally that he thought Erik could go far in Fleet, if he chose to.   Another ten years in service, perhaps even twenty... and then a political run?   With lifespans at two hundred years, he'd have plenty of time to enjoy the big houses and open roads when he got back.

The family were all up when he returned — one of those rare occasions with everyone together in the house, and breakfast was an entertaining talkfest in the big dining hall and adjoining kitchen with a similarly grand view as his bedroom.   No one asked him about the war, for which he was thankful, and Katerina's young children were fun and happy.   Her husband was a scandalously self-made man, builder of his own network business before meeting Katerina, and having no holdings beyond that.   But Mother had been pleased, surprising some, because her new son-in-law Diego was smart, skeptical and driven — something that those born into wealth too often lacked, she said.   'Your mother cares more about genes than portfolios,' Walker had explained to Erik in a vidmail.   'Diego's got those, and she's delighted.'

Erik was quizzing Lisbeth on her latest boyfriend (Mother disapproved) when the house minder alerted his uplink that Fleet Admiral Anjo would like to come and talk to him, would half-an-hour's time be suitable?   Erik put fingers behind his ear, the universal sign to indicate he was uplinked, and formulated an affirmative reply.

"Who was that, darling?" Alice asked when he resumed eating.

"Fleet Admiral Anjo wants to come and visit.   In half-an-hour, I said yes."   Because he'd really rather it was later, but you couldn't tell the third-in-command of the entire war that breakfast with family was more important.

"Really?" asked Diego, eyes wide.   "Fleet Admiral Anjo comes to you?   You don't have to go to him?"

"Of course," said Lisbeth, with droll humour.   "Who exactly did you think you were marrying?"

"Don't gloat Lisbeth," said Alice, helping her grandson Paul to butter his bread. "Erik dear, did the Admiral say *who* he was coming to see?"

"Me," said Erik.

"Oh," said Alice, a little surprised.

"She doesn't like that," Cora observed with a grin around her cereal.

"Oh stop it," Alice reprimanded, smiling. "Erik is a very important man now. I just thought, since we *do* build a quarter of all the Fleet's ships, he might have wanted to say hello."

"I'm sure he'll say hello, Mother," said Erik. "Now I'd better rush if I'm going to dress in time."

"Surely it doesn't take you half-an-hour to put on your uniform?" Lisbeth teased.

"It does too," Erik retorted. "I haven't worn it in so long, I'm out of practice."

Sure enough, Alice Debogande greeted Fleet Admiral Anjo in person before the lower doors of the big rear study, and Erik gave her the full five minutes to go through her list of concerns about ongoing projects. Then he entered, polished shoes clicking on the floorboards, and walked to the door to rescue the Admiral from his mother.

"I'm sorry about that Admiral," he said ruefully while inviting the man to sit. "She does like to do business in person, and she always complains about the lack of facetime with Fleet."

"That's quite alright, Lieutenant Commander," said Anjo. He was African-dark, broad but not tall, and no longer all that fit. With military augments and upgrades, you had to seriously abuse the diet to get rotund like that. It was the sign of an officer who hadn't seen line duty in a long time. "You Debogandes have it down to an art. But it's always a pleasure to speak with your mother."

They sat, while the Admiral's two aides waited in the garden outside, and a robot butler brought them drinks. Anjo admired its flowing, graceful movements as it poured green tea.   "That's an ANX-50 series, yes?" he said.

"That's right.   He's called Toby.   My little sister Lisbeth's idea," Erik explained to the Admiral's frown.   "He's been in the family about fifty years, so she figured he deserved a name.   Thank you Toby."   As the robot awaited instruction after pouring the tea, and now retreated.

"You've had him inspected?" Anjo asked.

Erik nodded.   "He's within parameters.   A long way from sentient, he doesn't have to do much more than pour tea."

"Yes, well just make sure he stays that way.   You hear these stories about rich families with pet AIs who think the laws don't apply to them.   It's a sad way to get a criminal record."

Sentient AI was illegal throughout the known galaxy.   The second-oldest known sentience in this quarter of the galactic spiral were colloquially known as 'The Fathers'.   They'd set up the precursor of the present galactic civilisation about fifty thousand years ago, until a poorly managed transition to new-generation AI had brought about a full scale robot uprising.   It had ended the Fathers, whose creations had decided their creators knew them too well, and were therefore a threat, and exterminated the lot.

The Machine Age had been the greatest horror the galaxy had ever seen, before or since.   Twenty three thousand years of terror, peoples enslaved, systems harvested, organic civilisations laid waste. Various rebellions had been ruthlessly crushed, until the AIs had begun fighting amongst themselves.   That disarray had finally opened the door for a successful rebellion, led by the parren, a warlike species whose primary positive attribute was the ability to suffer colossal losses without despair.   The parren had had a partner in their uprising — a junior species new to spacetravel at the time, called the chah'nas, and together they'd led an effort that ended the machines for good.   Eight thousand years after that, the chah'nas got tired of the parren and deposed them too, though somewhat less ruthlessly, to establish the also eight thousand year Chah'nas Empire, which had lasted until the First Free Age led by the tavalai.

Nests of those old surviving AI were still found sometimes, here and there, in deep space and far from the energy and resources they needed to thrive. Whenever they were found, species would drop whatever else they were doing and rush to exterminate the nest. Even humans and tavalai, in the midst of the last war, had on several occasions suspended hostilities to cooperate in those exterminations. The tavalai had continued the long-standing rule that banned sentient AI, and now that the tavalai were no longer in charge, no one even thought to question its continuation.

"So Lieutenant Commander," said Anjo, relaxing back in his chair. "Congratulations on making it back alive. Those last few months were some serious duty."

"All thanks to Captain Pantillo there sir," said Erik.

Anjo smiled. "Indeed. How does it feel to be home?"

"I'm not sure yet. Confusing."

"Have you had any thoughts on where you'd like to go next? Your sisters are all becoming very prominent in the running of Debogande Inc, surely your parents would welcome you back? I'd imagine with your Fleet experience, you'd be in an ideal position to oversee those contracts."

"Yes sir, I suppose that's possible."

Anjo looked at him closely over the rim of his teacup. "You don't seem convinced."

Erik grimaced, not liking to be put on the spot like this. Truthfully, he didn't know *what* he wanted to do next. But he could hardly object — most people would kill to have Fleet Admiral Anjo take such personal interest in their careers. "Actually sir, I was considering staying in for a while. Policing all of our new territory is going to take a lot of ships. It might be nice to do some deployments where not everyone's shooting at me for a change."

Anjo made a half-shrug. "Oh I wouldn't bet on that, I wouldn't trust the tavalai to make me a cheese sandwich." Which struck Erik as an odd thing to say — tavalai showed little sign of treachery. Indeed, many officers thought if they'd been *more* devious, they'd have done better in the war. "But yes. The new era promises some very active duty. You're seriously considering it?"

Erik took a deep breath. He'd put ten years of his life into Fleet, and he just wasn't sure he was willing to give that up yet. Because back here, in this house... well he had to face it, he was by far the least accomplished person here. He'd be starting from the bottom again, patronised by all. As much as he loved his family's company, that lowered status did not appeal to him.

"Yes sir," he said finally. "Yes I am."

Anjo smiled. "I'm very pleased to hear that, Lieutenant Commander. Very pleased indeed. Forgive me not getting to the point, I didn't want you to feel I was pressuring you into anything. But if you'd genuinely like to stay in the service, I'd like to propose something to you."

Erik blinked. "Of course sir."

"There are going to be a lot of new business opportunities opening up in the new territories. We have a lot of colonial possessions now, and once we've finished working out what now belongs to us, and what still belongs to the tavalai axis, there's going to be a lot of investment required to secure our holdings. Industry and private enterprise is the anchor that binds a new territory to human control. That is the lesson we learned against the krim. Military heroics alone did not win us that victory — it was industry, men and women like your parents, who built us the resources and capital needed to build the Fleet.

"Now we're going to do it again, on an even larger scale, and we're looking for officers well positioned to identify those opportunities and develop them. Given your background, I think you're the ideal man for the job."

Erik frowned. "I'm sorry sir... I'm a third-shift warship commander. I'm not sure I have the relevant experience to perform an industry liaison role..."

"Not a liaison," Anjo interrupted. "An administrator. We're planning to roll out industrial development on a grand scale across a number of key systems. Fleet will have to coordinate it because we'll have to guarantee the security of space lanes across those regions, and without those lanes, nothing happens. We need people in those positions who understand the bigger picture. Your performance reviews have been outstanding — Captain Pantillo can't praise you enough. I think you might be the man for the job."

"Well," said Erik, not really knowing what to think. Except that it sounded amazing, the kind of big-picture thinking missing from your standard corporate job. "That... that sounds like something far above someone of my current rank."

Anjo smiled broadly. "It does, doesn't it? There would be a significant promotion involved... bear in mind you'd be one of a number of people performing this role, the territories we've captured are vast. But we'd like to have people who'd like to build a longer career in Fleet, people who are young and ambitious, like yourself. And you know, this kind of thing would lead to some serious administrative responsibility, especially in another few years when it starts really rolling out. That kind of experience could be invaluable for someone seeking a political role in the future — you know Spacer Congress, they take hands-on experience above everything."

Well not quite everything, Erik thought. Money helped. Connections. Suddenly he felt uneasy, excitement fading. He was the son of one of the most powerful industrialists in human space. Family loyalties on one side, Fleet duties on the other. The perfect liaison between both, particularly as those interests did not always see eye to eye.

Anjo saw his uncertainty. "You've a question, Lieutenant Commander?"

"Yes sir. It's just that... am I getting this offer because of my surname?"

Anjo's jaw set. "Fleet's policy is to only promote the best, son. Do you think I'd circumvent that policy?"

"No sir. It's just that... well, surrounding my promotion to Lieutenant Commander in the first place. You know, there were rumours, people talked. About the son of Alice Debogande just happening to end up on the *Phoenix*, and... well, sometimes I couldn't help wondering if..."

"Well then listen, Erik." The smile returned. "Let me put your mind at ease. I've heard those rumours too — spacers talk worse than old women.   But hear this, straight from the top. Captain Pantillo asked for you himself."

Erik blinked. His jaw dropped slightly open. "He did?"

Anjo nodded.   "You couldn't be told before because the process behind each promotion is strictly confidential, of course. But now that the war's over, we're relaxing a little on that — he might even tell you himself, if you asked.   It was his request, Fleet Command had nothing to do with it."

Erik exhaled hard, and sat back in his chair. Ran a hand over his short, tight hair.   "That's... that's very interesting to hear, Admiral.   Thank you for telling me.   Because, you know, I shouldn't have questioned it... but being from this family..." he gestured about him, at the high ceilings, wide windows, the gleaming, cavernous wealth. "It's hard not to wonder."

Anjo smiled. "Completely understandable.   So Lieutenant Commander.   Can I take your response as a genuine expression of interest back to my superiors?"

Superiors.   Anjo only had two of those, in Fleet.   In Spacer Congress, only equals — the War Council placed elected civilians alongside Fleet Admirals in deciding the course of the war, but in truth, no one outranked Supreme Commander Chankow.   Who, Anjo was now suggesting, he would be reporting to on this matter.

"Yes," said Erik with a smile. "Yes Admiral, please do."

The thing with being very wealthy that a lot of less wealthy people didn't understand was that you didn't have to own everything yourself. As a Debogande, you could just make things happen with a call... like when Lisbeth thought Erik would like to go sailing, for the ultimate experience of wide expanses and freedom after so long in a cramped spaceship.   She called Aunt Michelle, who was a member at the yacht club, and soon enough a friend had offered them a catamaran for the day.

It was a forty footer, an automated monster that still left enough ropes and winches free to make you feel like a participant.

Lisbeth loved to sail having been taught by her dad, who came along with Cora and Diego. Everyone else was busy, but five was about the perfect number, Lisbeth captaining at her father's insistence while the men and Cora ran about the huge elastic expanse between hulls and got soaked by the chop exploding off the surface.

The wind was only moderate a few kilometres off shore, but the cat's huge wingsail converted every breath into motion and they skated across the heaving ocean at a good eighteen knots. Erik loved it, the fresh wind and the salty ocean on his skin, batwing flying fish leaping away from the cat's approach in flashing silver schools. Every now and then something fast and military would go flying over with a roar — Shiwon was still a hive of military activity, but out here with his family, Erik could almost forget that just a few weeks ago, he hadn't known if he was going to live another day.

They stayed out for hours, before grumbling stomachs told them it was time for lunch, and they turned the cat for shore. The yacht club was twenty kilometres up the coast from Shiwon Harbour, the hills rising green and lush beyond the shore, and tall houses behind the beach. They edged carefully between flotillas of expensive sailboats and motorised launches, the wingsail trimmed and keel brakes deployed to keep the speed down, and Erik was quite impressed at how certain Lisbeth was in charge, issuing commands at just the right moments, and never so forceful that she'd grate on the nerves.

"So how's Mum with the whole engineering thing?" he asked Lisbeth as they waited at the wheel for the others to tie the cat to the pier.

"Oh you know," Lisbeth sighed. Her hair was more African-frizzy than Erik's or Cora's. She took advantage by pinning it up and playing, and now it shone with water droplets. "It's not a thing for girls, she says. But Dad's fine, so she leaves it alone now. She doesn't like arguing with him."

"Still like to join Fleet?"

"Oh I'd love to! But Mum would really hit the ceiling, and I don't think even Dad would be too happy." She looked a little forlorn.

"Cheer up Lis." Erik put an arm around her shoulders. "You might not be able to serve on warships, but with your degree you'll end up working with Katerina in charge of making the damn things."

"Yeah but how much better a naval engineer would I make if I'd actually served on them, and know what they were like to operate from the inside? Besides, it's a dumb family rule. Only boys can serve, I mean it's not fair is it? It's not fair on me because I can't choose my career, and it's not fair on you because you've had to risk your neck while all us girls have been sitting at home."

In truth, Erik wasn't so sure. Fleet had been an eye-opener, not only to be around 'ordinary' people, but to discover that most of them didn't share Alice's notion of gender decorum. Alice had no problem with women being strong, but she *did* believe very strongly in the importance of traditional social roles. Women should organise and administer, she believed, and thus running a business was just a natural extension of what women had always done — organise families and households. But actually breaking a sweat in anything more strenuous than a game of tennis was man's work. From Academy onward, Erik had had his butt handed to him in physical pursuits by so many competent women that he'd concluded that his mother's opinions were slightly daft. But he couldn't deny that he still felt protective of some of his female comrades in a way that he didn't of the men... and the thought of his sister sitting post on some warship on an assault run through a hostile system made his blood run cold.

"I'm pretty glad you weren't out there with me Lis," he said quietly. "I mean really."

"Was it that bad?" Lisbeth asked earnestly.

"Not all of it, no. But the worst bits were... just awful. I wouldn't want you to go through that."

"But we all have, haven't we? As a species, we've all been through that. Or that's what the stories all say, how we've struggled as human beings together. Only we haven't really, have we? Some of us have suffered, while others of us have sat and watched. And applauded when the real heroes come home.   It's enough to make me feel like a fraud for ever having listened to those stories at all."

Erik smiled at her.   "I forgot you're the college debating champ.   That was good."

"Hah," she said with a roll of her eyes.   "That's just from arguing with Mother, I only joined the debating club because I thought I should put those skills to use."

"And it doesn't convince me that everyone should be in the fight.   It's not for everyone, Lis.   And it's for those of us who know we're good at it to do it well so all those others don't *have* to."

"You don't think I'd be good?"   With a hurt expression. Erik blinked at her, wondering how to try again... and realised she was playing with him.   "Scamp," he said, giving her a shove as she laughed.

They left the cat as tidy as they'd been given it, and walked up the narrow wooden pier between neighbouring yachts.   As they approached the shore, Erik saw two black marine uniforms waiting, one tall and one not.   Major Thakur and Lieutenant Dale, he recognised with surprise.   He waved cheerfully, and was surprised further that they did not wave back.   In fact, they both looked grim.

"Marines," Erik addressed them as he took the lead in his party.   A little self-conscious in his wet civvies, while they were immaculate in their dress uniforms.   He wondered what they'd been up to since he saw them last.   It didn't look like they'd been having any fun.   "What brings you here?"

"You need to come with us," said Thakur.   Her voice was cold and hard, and her words did not sound polite.   Off-ship she did technically outrank him, but still...

Erik drew himself up.   "What's going on?" he retorted, mindful of the audience behind him.

"What'd you tell him?" Dale snarled from Thakur's shoulder. "Fucking Admiral Anjo, what did you tell him?"

Erik was shocked.   "Lieutenant, that's no way to speak of a superior officer!" he snapped as command reflex reasserted itself. As Thakur held up a hand to stop Dale from speaking further.   From Thakur to Dale, a hand was all it took.   "Explain yourselves!"

"The Captain's been arrested," said Thakur.   Erik stared at her, not quite believing he'd heard that.   "Placed in detention prior to court-martial proceedings.   What did you tell Admiral Anjo?"

Erik stared.   "Court-martial?   For what?"

"We don't know, they won't say.   He's in isolation, no one's allowed to see him.   Huang's up at the ship, so you're now senior *Phoenix* command on the ground.   What did you tell Admiral Anjo?"

"I... I told him..."   That he'd be happy to accept a big promotion for a senior job in Fleet Command.   Anjo had to have known.   Court-martialing any senior captain, let alone one with the record and reputation of Pantillo, was a huge move.   Anjo would be in on it, no question.   And he'd just paid Pantillo's third-in-command a home visit that very morning, and not thought to mention it?   Fishy didn't begin to describe it.

And this offer of huge promotion and responsibility, to a relatively junior and untested officer... a coincidence?   To get him onside?   To drive a wedge between him and Pantillo?   Between him and the crew of *Phoenix*?   He looked at the marines' eyes, and saw hard suspicion... in Dale's eyes at least.   Thakur was as always unreadable.   Isolate the rich boy whose promotional advances to date everyone was already suspicious of?   Make sure Family Debogande wasn't in Pantillo's corner?

What the hell was going on?

"We have to go and see the Captain," he said.   "Now."

"They're not letting anyone see him," Thakur repeated coolly.

"Oh they'll let me see him," Erik muttered.   "Or I'll bring the fucking roof down on their heads."

CHAPTER 4

They went home first, to silence and concern from the family, while Erik put on the dress uniform, and the marines waited outside in the garden. No one ventured any of them any questions — Alice put a stop to those who tried. This was Erik's business, Fleet business, and he need not be troubled at this point by family concerns. Erik was grateful for it, and took a family cruiser to the city with Thakur in the passenger seat, and Dale in the rear.

"What did Admiral Anjo say to you?" Thakur asked again. Erik realised he hadn't answered her the other times.

"He offered me a job as a colonial administrator," he said shortly. "Helping to industrialise the new territorial possessions."

"That seems like an enormous promotion for someone with very little relevant experience," Thakur said matter-of-factly.

"Yes it does, doesn't it?" Erik muttered.

"What did you say?"

"I said yes." Thakur seemed to shake her head slightly, and gaze out the windows at the approaching city towers. "What would *you* have said?"

"They don't offer these things to normal people," Thakur answered. "That's the point."

"And you're a normal person, are you?"

Thakur's lips twisted slightly. "Relative to you, I'm positively pedestrian."

Erik felt his temper boil. Usually he was good at holding it, but today it was too much. "And so what?" he snapped. "Am I supposed to apologise for the conditions of my birth? I'm not in control of any of this, Major. I have no idea whether I receive favourable treatment or not, I certainly never asked for it. I can't go around apologising for every damn thing that other people give to me."

"No," Thakur agreed with measured calm. "None of us are in control of anything. We just go along as it comes. Your family in particular."

"You know, what the fuck is that supposed to mean?"

"It means that one day, Lieutenant Commander Debogande, you'll have to either grab the wheel, or admit that you just don't care, and go where ever your fortuitous life takes you."

"Well fuck you," Erik retorted. "I don't care what row of tin you wear on your chest. If you're going to accuse me of something, come out with it straight and stop insinuating like a coward."

"You watch that tone with the Major, boy," Dale warned from the rear seat.

Thakur held up her hand again, and Dale silenced. But she was smiling. "That's much better," she told Erik. "More like that, and we might just get through this."

Fleet HQ was located on the edge of southern Shiwon against the Feicui Hills, and could be seen from orbit with the naked eye. Erik, Thakur and Dale marched from parking across the huge central courtyard, large enough to land a squadron of assault shuttles on. It was centred by an eternal flame that burned within an inspired artistic scaffold, many storeys high. In concentric circles around it, inscribed in the acres of paving, the names of worlds conquered and battles fought, across the last twelve hundred years. There were thousands of inscriptions, some of them dating back to Sol System, and the krim invasion. Touring the courtyard was a ritual of all Fleet officer training on Homeworld — by the end of three years all cadets were expected to be able to march from one important battle to another, blindfolded.

They headed for one of the surrounding ring of glass towers, and were admitted past armed guards and automated security with their Fleet IDs. The circular, central foyer was awash with uniforms, striding, talking, pursuing various business. Hats off, Erik and the marines waited for an elevator, then rode it up to the twenty-third floor.

Then more halls and offices, busy with staff. Erik knew the way well enough — he'd done six months here straight out of the

Academy, learning how to salute while walking without bumping into things. And not much else, he thought sourly, entering the main reception for First Fleet Command. An Ensign glanced at him from behind her desk.

"Lieutenant Commander, can I help you?"

Erik walked briskly to front her. "Lieutenant Commander Erik Debogande, third-shift *UFS Phoenix*, reporting to Rear Admiral Bennet."

The Ensign glanced at her screen. "Yes Lieutenant Commander, she's currently in a meeting. Do you have an appointment?"

"Please tell her I'm here," Erik told her. "I'll wait." He turned on his heel, strode to a seat by the wall, and sat. Thakur and Dale joined him, not a word spoken. The baffled Ensign spoke quietly into a com.

"She doesn't know," Thakur murmured. "They're keeping it quiet."

"This is all kinds of fucked up," Dale muttered. "Court-martial for what?"

"The flanking jump to Dhuvo system," said Erik. Both marines looked at him. "It was irregular."

"It was brilliant," said Thakur.

"Yes, and irregular. Typical Captain. But he left the scene of the battle to hit the reinforcements before they came in. If someone's being a total ass hat, which seems increasingly likely, they might book him for leaving the battle without orders."

"Thus saving everyone's ass," said Thakur. "Captains always improvise, with light-delay in battle it's impossible to wait for orders in an unfolding fight."

"You don't need to tell me, Major," Erik said through clenched teeth. "I've flown the damn ship."

"And you're *sure* Fleet Admiral Anjo said nothing about a court-martial when you talked to him?" Erik just glared at her. It had no effect on Thakur at all. She looked at the file-pushers at work behind their desks instead, broodingly thoughtful.

The Ensign Erik had spoken to got their attention. "Lieutenant Commander? The Rear Admiral will see you now. Just you," as the marines made to follow him. Neither protested, and Erik continued down the hall.

Rear Admiral Bennet was in charge of personnel administration for all of First Fleet. Her office looked out over the huge courtyard and flame. From above, it looked like a solar system, with the flame at the centre where a sun should be, orbited by the many thousands of places where human Fleet had lost ships and lives. Erik walked in and stood to attention before her desk.

"Rear Admiral, Lieutenant Commander Erik Debogande reporting."

Bennet let him stand at attention, leaning back in her chair with a frown. She was a tall woman, with blonde hair pulled back in a bun, accentuating sharp cheekbones. "I did not order you to report, Lieutenant Commander."

"No Admiral. Fleet disciplinary proceedings manual, chapter five, section 23-D; in the event that a ship captain is court-martialled, junior command staff should report to the appropriate Fleet Command administrative officer. In this case, that would be you."

A brief silence from Bennet, as though she were checking that reg on uplinks. "Yes," she said, a little uncertainly. "Yes, that would be me."

"Admiral, I request to know on what charge Captain Pantillo is being court-martialled."

"I'm sorry Lieutenant Commander, that information is covered under wartime secrecy. I'm not at liberty to divulge it."

Erik stared at her. "I can't know what my own Captain is charged with?"

"That is correct. And neither can you discuss this case with anyone else, military or civilian, outside of this office. Should you fail to observe this restriction, you yourself could be up on charges. Do you understand?"

Erik blinked. "I understand, but..."

"This is a matter of operational review," Bennet continued. "No one can discuss Fleet tactics, past, present or future without clearance, least of all with civilians. The media can't touch this, and would risk prison time if they did."

Her eyes sought understanding from him. Erik felt incredulity battling cold disbelief. Bennet was worried about outside reaction... and so she should be, Pantillo was a hero. But she hadn't expected to see Erik here, that much was obvious. It felt like a rush-job, Fleet was a big institution and wires were frequently crossed, one hand on the thousand-armed-beast not knowing what the other nine hundred were doing. Probably she'd thought someone else had already dealt with him. That would mean this whole thing was cooked up recently, with little planning. Court-martials never happened like that. Never. Or at least, they weren't *supposed* to...

"Now I understand that Commander Huang is currently back on *Phoenix*?"

Erik nodded. "Yes Admiral."

"Which with the Captain in detention makes you senior *Phoenix* command staff on the ground. You are responsible for all *Phoenix* crew still on Homeworld until Commander Huang is ordered to return."

"Is there an ETA on that Admiral?"

"Not at this time. Now I'm half a mind to order *Phoenix* crew to barracks, but I'm advised that's not practical at this time. Whether the situation remains like that depends on their ability to keep their mouths shut. Do you understand?"

"Yes Admiral." Talk, and we'll lock you on base with no coms, that meant. "Admiral, I request JAG representation at this point, as is my right under Section 31-B."

Bennet frowned. "You haven't been charged with anything, Lieutenant Commander."

"My testimony in the upcoming court-martial will be integral to proceedings," Erik replied, still stiff and straight before the Rear Admiral's desk. "I am third-shift commander on *Phoenix*, I have commanded the ship before in combat, I know her capabilities and I know the Captain.   I also happen to know that he didn't do anything wrong."

"Noted," Bennet said coolly.

"And the regs say I'm allowed JAG assistance to help me prepare."

"Lieutenant Commander... I'm not sure that's necessary at this..."

"I'm not asking what you are and aren't sure of, Admiral," Erik said coldly, meeting her gaze directly.   "I'm informing you what *I'm* sure of.   And I'm sure that this is my procedural right. Denied that right, I will go higher."

Bennet glared at him.

The Judge Advocate General officer was Captain Sudip — army, young and quite wide-eyed about this crazy thing Fleet had just dumped in his lap.   They sat in a diner booth, one of dozens of restaurants about the base, but the booth provided at least some privacy.   The windows looked away from Shiwon, onto the low campus buildings sprawling up the green hills behind — the Admiral Shuan Academy, and bringing back for Erik a three-year rush of memories.

"It's been declared an S-1," Sudip told Erik and the two marines in a low voice beneath the hubbub of diner conversation. Sudip was thin, bookish and well spoken, the kind of guy who wouldn't have lasted a week on combat deployment.   But Erik had learned not to disrespect those kinds.   Not everything Fleet did involved blowing things up, and in those other things, officers like Sudip were often invaluable.   "That's the highest level of secrecy.   I wasn't aware they could even *do* that for a legal proceedings..."

"Who can authorise that?" Erik pressed.

Sudip swallowed hard.   "Well no one below the very top level.   I mean Bennet can't do it... I mean Rear Admiral Bennet, sorry... she's just a First Fleet administrator.   S-1 is like... like what you declare before you invade a planet or something, those battleplans are S-1. There's only three people at that level in the Fleet — Fleet Admirals Anjo and Ishmael, and Supreme Commander Chankow."

Erik, Thakur and Dale looked at each other.

"Word of this is going to spread," said Thakur. She ate a steak and salad with methodical precision. Erik thought the Kulina were supposed to have spiritual dietary requirements, but if so, that didn't appear to exclude meat. "They can't stop people from talking."

"Major," Sudip said earnestly. "I really wouldn't test those secrecy provisions. There are people in prison today, who were put there ten years ago, for doing that sort of thing. People who used to hold a higher rank than you do now."

"I didn't say *I* would talk, Captain," said Thakur. "I'm saying that people will. Pantillo is well known politically. His political friends will be wondering where he is, and asking Fleet for an explanation. They can't put both Congresses in prison."

"I'm sure they'd like to put the Worlder Congress in prison," Dale muttered. Dale was originally a Worlder, Erik recalled, living his entire childhood downworld before enlisting. Like all Fleet, he was registered as a Spacer, and could vote for Spacer Congress representatives only… but that didn't mean he forgot where he came from.

Humanity had two governments. Ninety percent of the population lived on planets. Each governed itself, with little interference from anyone. Those planetary governments in turn elected representatives to the Worlder Congress, which made collective decisions on the kinds of things that mattered to people who lived on planets.

Spacers, who made up the remaining ten percent, had their own governments, one per solar-system, or outlying settlements that were placed into system jurisdiction because they wouldn't fit anywhere else. Those systems then elected representatives to Spacer Congress, which represented the interests of those who lived and worked in space.

Humanity's great wars of the last twelve hundred years were almost entirely an affair of Spacers. After Earth had been destroyed, humanity had become for a time entirely a race of Spacers, without a single planetary body to its name. Survival had become about resource harvesting, mining, industry and Fleet operations. Spacer interests were all anyone knew, and were key if there were still to be a human race in years to come.

When humans had begun to claim worlds from the krim, it hadn't taken long for those newly colonised worlds to do what worlds did best — populate rapidly, and think primarily about themselves. Even before the krim had vanished, many of those planetary populations had settled into comfortable centuries of relative peace, content in the illusion that all was safe and well. Isolated from the harsh realities of inter-species politics beyond, they'd quickly begun to vote for withdrawal from conflict, expansion of social services, and other self-interested things.

Spacers had responded by cementing the primacy of Spacer Congress as humanity's singular, collective Federal Congress. Spacer Congress had the power to make foreign policy, which meant wars and trade treaties, that no Worlder body could legally stray from. All Worlder jurisdictions were also required to pay the Fleet Tax, just as Spacers were, which was adjusted by complex formula to account for individual circumstance, but averaged out at six percent of annual wealth. All of which led to the present situation, where the great affairs of humanity were conducted by those with ten percent of the total human vote, while ninety percent either applauded from the sidelines or were told to shut up and mind their business.

Most Worlders accepted this state of affairs — most did sympathise with Fleet, and most were not so naive as to think that pacifist isolation would ever work in a galaxy that contained assorted krim, sard and tavalai. But as the latest war had dragged on, against a race that most acknowledged were *not* krim-like in their goals and psychology, the disquiet had begun to grow.

"That has to be it," Erik muttered, picking at his salad. They looked at him. "It has to be something to do with the Captain's

Worlder ties.   He *should* be an admiral by now, we all know why he's not."

"Lieutenant Commander," Sudip cautioned with a careful glance around.   "That's really some very heavy speculation. Accusing your seniors of corruption really isn't helpful at this time, and could be very dangerous for you personally."

"It's not corruption, Captain, it's politics.   Fleet runs this war on its own, there is no civilian oversight from Spacer Congress, just a rubber stamp.   Nearly half of Spacer Congress *are* retired Fleet. Those are just facts, they're not accusations of anything."

Sudip took a deep breath.   "Look.   As your attorney advisor in this, it's my responsibility to advise you not to repeat those allegations too loudly.   That's all.   Besides which, there's no proof here of corruption that I can see — these kinds of crossed-wires allegations come out of post-combat reviews all the time.   Another captain sees Captain Pantillo doing something that he doesn't understand, and reports it as such, in isolation.   Further review usually clears it up, presuming the Captain does have good reasons for having done what he did, which to judge from what you've told me, it seems he does."

"Fleet Admiral Anjo paid the Lieutenant Commander a visit this morning," said Thakur around a mouthful of steak.   "At his home.   Offered him a promotion to colonial administrator in the new order."

Sudip blinked at her.   Then at Erik.   He opened his mouth to speak.   Then shut it again, looking confounded.   "Well that's... that's highly irregular."

"It's corrupt," Dale muttered.   "But that's the system."   His stare shifted to Erik, accusingly.   He'd said yes.   Erik looked down at his salad.

"And he said nothing about the court-martial?" Sudip pressed Erik.

Erik shook his head.   "No," he murmured.   "I think the conclusion's pretty obvious.   They offered me a big promotion to shut me up when they court-martialled the Captain."

Sudip shook his head. "Well, if we *are* going to entertain this line of thinking..." He took a deep breath. He was a lawyer, after all, trained to argue cases from multiple angles. "Then there's an even more obvious conclusion. They offered you a big promotion to shut your *family* up. You're nothing special..." and he held up his hands, "... no offence Lieutenant Commander."

"None taken," Erik said drily.

"But Captain Pantillo isn't the only one with known Worlder sympathies." With a meaningful look at Erik. Erik grimaced.

"I'm sorry," Thakur interjected. "I'm a little out of touch with this politics?"

"My mother has supported the idea of a constitutional convention before," Erik explained. "To reshape human politics. Give Worlders a bigger say."

"Are you guys even Spacer or Worlder?" Dale asked.

"Spacer," said Erik. "Debogandes have life citizenship. It's not subject to review based on current living conditions, like most Spacers. We can live anywhere and still be Spacer citizens. I grew up on Homeworld."

"The war's been winding down," Dale observed. "If either side was gonna try something, now'd be the time to try it. Because when peace is declared, logically, everything changes."

"And certain Spacer interests," Thakur added slowly, "with a lot of power to lose, start getting nervous."

The constitutional convention, Erik thought. Shit. Had his mother been pushing that, behind the scenes? Had her Worlder friends? Had Fleet noticed, and gotten worried? Had their Spacer Congress allies?

"Erik," said Thakur, observing his disquiet. "What is it?"

"Something Fleet Admiral Anjo told me," said Erik. "I asked him if I was receiving special treatment because of my name. He denied it. Because even people on *Phoenix* have wondered." Thakur and Dale said nothing. "But Anjo said that Captain Pantillo asked for me himself. That that's why I got the *Phoenix*. That Fleet Command had nothing to do with it."

"He could be lying," Dale said helpfully. Thakur gave him a frown. 'What?' Dale said with his eyes, defiantly.

"Which would mean the Captain might have seen this coming." And would also mean that he *hadn't* been selected for this duty purely on merit. That scared him nearly as badly as the Captain's court-martial. These last three years on *Phoenix* had been hard, but they'd come to mean more to him than anything else in his life. He thought he'd done a good job, and earned the respect of his peers. Surely he deserved to be here?

Across the table, Lieutenant Dale was all skepticism.

"I have to talk to the Captain," said Erik.

"Well you can't," Sudip replied. "No one can."

"Then that's the first thing you have to work on. There's got to be some legal angle on this. Get us some access to him, find a way."

Sudip nodded nervously. Worried, but thinking hard. Professionally a case like this could see him crash and burn... or skyrocket into high orbit. If Sudip was the kind of person who thought about such things. In all his time in Fleet, Erik had only known two people who weren't — one was currently in isolation awaiting court-martial, and the other was munching a steak at Erik's side in the booth.

"I'll get on it," said Sudip. "No promises. But I'll see what I can do."

"Make a lot of calls," Thakur suggested, with a sip of water. "You're not breaking secrecy provisions, you're a lawyer doing your job." Sudip nodded warily. Spread it around, she meant. Get everyone talking, the only way they legally could.

"And I'll talk to my mother," said Erik. "She doesn't like talking politics at home. This time I'll insist."

Lieutenant Commander Debogande called on uplink just after dinner. Trace Thakur sat in cross-legged meditation before her view of the beach, and listened. He said that his mother denied pushing any particular support for the constitutional convention, or that she supported the Worlders' cause in general. Yes she had friends there, but Debogande Incorporated was huge, and a well-maintained network of political friends was essential for good business.

Beyond that, she sounded a little vague. Or he did. Trace didn't know which. She'd served with Debogande for three years, but didn't know him that well. It wasn't his fault, or hers — as *Phoenix*'s marine commander, she timed her onboard shifts to Captain Pantillo's, which meant that unless they were on combat alert, she was usually asleep when the Lieutenant Commander sat the command chair. He was the night shift, she the day, and despite the close proximity of *Phoenix*'s bowels, marines and spacers ran vastly different routines. Usually she saw him at command meetings, which happened on average every few days, but there Debogande would listen and say little, as befitted the junior command officer.

Fleet Admiral Anjo might have been lying when he'd said the Captain had picked Debogande personally for *Phoenix* command, or he might have been telling the truth — it did not particularly matter to Trace. She might not have known Debogande, but she knew the Captain, and the Captain would never have selected an officer for third-shift command if he wasn't qualified. And properly qualified too, on all the indices that actually mattered, rather than just having shiny boots and pleasing instructors at the Academy. Debogande had *very* shiny boots. Among *Phoenix*'s marines, whose boots were rarely shiny, it had only increased skepticism of how Debogande got the post. *Phoenix* spacers were less skeptical, particularly the officers on bridge third-shift with him. Several times in the past three years, *Phoenix* had run into trouble so fast the Captain had not been able to assume the chair, leaving Debogande in charge in combat conditions. He'd done fine, though again the skeptics had muttered that any dozens of other young officers could have done as well, but *they* weren't given the *Phoenix*. Trace had shut it down on several occasions — all soldiers liked to bitch about their commanders, and needed enough space so they could do that and let off steam, but it was her job to recognise when that bitching crossed the line from harmless to harmful.

She wasn't about to tell Debogande that she did not actually doubt his ability, however. If she knew anything from her meditations and teachings, she knew that all people needed to find and draw their strength from within. Relying on the praise of others could become a habit, and those in the habit would seek that praise like an addict and his drug. Strength came through self-belief, and the belief of others without belief in yourself was useless. Chalk was still chalk, even surrounded by granite.

She sat in her loose pants and shirt long after Debogande's call had ended, on the small footrest she used as a meditation stool. The sound of waves on the beach was soothing, nothing at all like the sounds of her homeworld, or the sounds of the *Phoenix*. She'd used to meditate in her small room in The Perch, the Kulina Academy, halfway up a mountain and listening to the howl of freezing wind across the sheer, rocky cliffs. That was a peacefulness too, of a sort. But she had to admit, the beach was nicer.

Some marine commanders stayed with their troops, on long downworld leave. Most found officers of similar rank to socialise with, to maintain a proper command distance, and to let their men get their kicks free from higher supervision. But both higher and lower ranked marines would then indulge in much the same thing — drinking, fucking, sometimes even fighting... as though they hadn't had enough of that on deployment. Trace would join with them sometimes for interesting excursions, to see sights, climb mountains or dive reefs. But the rest of it disturbed and depressed her. She could not meditate in such surroundings, and deprived of her outlet for rage, pain and grief, she suffered.

And so on this momentous leave, she'd sought this place — a small hotel by the beach, well down the coast from Shiwon, to sit with a view and meditate to the sound of waves. And she struggled, as she always had of late, to find any particular peace of mind. But here at least, she found far more than she would have, in other surroundings.

There was a knock at the door.   Trace unfolded herself and went, taking the pistol from the table on the way.   An uplink view of the outside balcony showed her marine uniforms at the door, and a familiar face raised to the camera.   Trace smiled and unlatched the door, tucking the pistol into her waistband so she could namaste the visitors, both palms together, pointed fingers at her chin.   They replied in kind, all three of them.

"Friends," she said.   "Svagata mitraharula.   Please enter."

"Bahini," said marine Colonel Timothy Khola with a smile. "Good to see you.   These are Majors Naldo and Kriti, from the warships *Glory* and *FarReach*."

He entered, presenting the two majors behind him.   "Yes I have met Major Naldo," said Trace with another namaste, "we served at Pacamayana together."

"Bahini," said Major Naldo, "good to see you again."

"And Major Kriti, I have not had the honour."

"Third class of Capricorn," said Kriti behind pressed hands. "Fifteen years ahead of you, yet only the same rank."

"It is as nothing," Trace gave the usual reply, with a dismissive wave, welcoming them both inside.   "Forgive my informality, I was meditating.   Can I make you tea?"

"Tea would be perfect," said Colonel Khola, removing his shoes and placing them in the hall, as the majors did likewise.   "We shall join you.   A pity we do not have time to meditate together, but from what you have told me, we have much to discuss."

Trace made her three fellow Kulina tea, while they sat shoeless on chairs that did not make cross-legged sitting easy.   The posture was in breach of all marine protocol in uniform, but for Kulina the marines had long ago learned to make allowances.   Tea presented, Trace retook her low seat before the windows, and sipped.

"And how goes the meditation?" Colonel Khola asked her. Khola was pushing eighty, still young and fit.   He'd seen more combat in the war than seemed reasonable even for a Kulina legend. These days he taught at Fleet Academy on Homeworld, and had declined further promotion as it would take him too far from his greatest love — the mentoring of marine officers, and Kulina in particular. Of only eight living marines to hold the Liberty Star, half were Kulina, and half of those Kulina, between Trace and the Colonel, were here in the room. Kulina made up barely one percent of total marine officer strength, but no one was surprised that they won nearly half the top combat awards. That too was tradition, nearly a thousand years old.

"Not so well," Trace admitted. It was so good to talk with fellow Kulina officers. Here she could be honest, and be sure they would understand and not judge. "It is hard to fight a war without rage or fear. But we strive."

Khola smiled. "Bahini, one cannot fight in a war such as this and not expect sleepless nights and peaceless meditations. If our paths were easy, we would not need to meditate at all."

"I saw the combat reports of the Moana Junction action," said Major Kriti. She was tall and lean, hair trimmed short like Trace... fifteen years older, she'd said. That would make her forty-seven. "That was some impressive fighting. Paralim Station is a monster, you took it with minimal damage or losses."

"That station was defendable," Trace said sombrely. "If the tavalai had been prepared to booby trap it properly, and lose parts of it to save the whole. They were not. It was an important facility for them, and they do not like to destroy what they have built."

"I once saw an infantry squad of tavalai die to defend a temple," Naldo agreed. "I suppose they did not mean to die, I think they thought they could defend it successfully. But they did not realise we were marines on the ground, not army. And they did not retreat once they realised their mistake."

"It is easier fighting sard," said Trace. "Against sard, one is certain. Against tavalai..." she took a deep breath. "Well. One regrets. Too much, I think."

"Never forget that tavalai chose the sard for their allies," Khola cautioned. "Cultivated them in fact, for many, many centuries, to do all their dirty work. The sard have earned their reputation well, and every time it was a tavalai hand holding their leash."

Trace nodded reluctantly. "As you say."

"Now tell us about your Captain's predicament," said Khola. "We will see what is to be done."

Trace told them. That she'd been specifically ordered not to talk about it barely occurred to her. She was Kulina, and these were her people — the elite club within the elite club of marine officers. Theoretically she could have been court-martialled herself for this breach, but if Command were going to start disciplining Kulina for behaving like family, then Kulina everywhere would resent it. For Fleet, that was not a happy prospect. When Trace had finished, all three of her visitors looked concerned.

"And you are certain that Captain Pantillo did nothing wrong?" Major Kriti pressed in the lengthening silence. At Trace's back, the sun was setting, turning the ocean sky orange and red.

Trace felt anger, and emotional certainty, and forced it down. To seek peace was to seek objectivity. She could not allow her attachments to rule her. "I'm a marine commander," she said. "Space warfare is not my speciality. If the Captain's accuser is another spacer captain, I would be unlikely to prove a good witness for the defence, as my expertise is infantry combat in space facilities.

"However, I didn't see the Captain do anything wrong. On the contrary, I thought his action was exemplary, and contributed greatly to our victory."

"Do you consider it possible that another captain may have misinterpreted?" asked Khola.

"Yes." Trace nodded. "As I said, we left the battle. Tavalai reinforcements were massing at Dhuvo. If they'd been allowed to gather unmolested, we'd have been flanked, and taken heavy casualties. Captain Pantillo broke them up before they could hit us. It was unconventional, but that is his style. He's done the same thing a hundred times before, and been commended for it. Now this."

She could not keep the anger and frustration from her voice. It was an effort just to hold her pose on the footstand. Small muscles tensed and twinged, that should have been calm.

"This is troubling," Khola admitted. "But misunderstandings do occur in battle. To presume that it is corruption seems a stretch, despite the Lieutenant Commander's concerns."

"Colonel," said Trace, attempting patience. "Let me be blunt. Command's actions regarding Captain Pantillo have been unjust. The offer of promotion to the Lieutenant Commander just that morning was highly improper, and beyond suspicious under the circumstances. Now it appears the Captain is even being denied due process, despite all his service to the human cause."

"Major." Colonel Khola held up his hands, calming. "The process has only just begun. Fleet makes mistakes, it's a big organisation and often a flawed one, run by flawed human beings. Let us await an outcome before judging this or that."

"We must assist the Captain in getting a fair hearing," Trace insisted. "He's certainly not getting one now."

"I'm not sure that's yet been established," Major Kriti cautioned.

"They won't even tell us what he's charged with!" Trace retorted. "It's unheard of, our JAG Captain Sudip says that in every preceding case with a court-martial of this rank and magnitude, they've always declared the charge so that the defence could prepare."

"Major," Khola said calmly. "Major you are upset."

"Yes I am," Trace said shortly. She swallowed hard. It would not do to lose her cool completely, and show her comrades just how far her control had slipped. The Captain had entrusted her with things that he had not entrusted to others. She could not let him down. "I owe that man. All humanity owes that man, whether we are aware of it or not."

"Major the Kulina exist to serve," said Khola. "Our founders made a decision, a thousand years ago, that humanity required selfless sacrifice to survive. We are the embodiment of that sacrifice. We do not fight for blood lust or revenge, we do not thrill in the kill, we do not seek glory and remembrance. Our lives have meaning only in that they are currency, to be spent in the service of all humanity.

"Now we all gave that oath, and we gave it to Fleet. We knew Fleet's imperfections when we gave it. Fleet has done far worse than accuse an innocent man before, Fleet has made a mess of assaults, has let complacency and poor judgement lead to the deaths of... well, of millions, depending on the incident. Yet our oath stands, Major, because Fleet is all humanity has."

"Will you assist me to get him a fair trial?" Trace asked, attempting calm. "The Kulina are influential."

"Captain Pantillo is not Kulina. We use our influence with High Command sparingly."

"And we would deny a warrior as worthy as Captain Pantillo our assistance, because he does not hold membership of our club?" Trace retorted. "Colonel Khola, this sounds like Kulina ego."

"It is pragmatism," Khola said calmly. "Ego is that we intervene at all. Pragmatism says we do so very sparingly."

"We spend of ourselves as the need of humanity requires," Trace insisted, her voice hardening. "That is what I was taught. That is true peace, to place aside personal need to do what is necessary for the whole."

"Even Captain Pantillo is not the whole. He is just one man. Fleet is the whole."

"And Fleet without Captain Pantillo would still be another five years at war. You know it, and I know it. He won us several battles just that important, single-handedly. He saved us that many years of war. How many lives must a man save before the Kulina will bend a single precious rule to help him? And what is this stubbornness if not pride?"

Colonel Khola took a deep breath, and glanced at the Majors. Their looks were guarded. "I will have a word with High Command," he said finally. "I will express our concern, and our interest to see that the Captain is treated fairly. More than that, I cannot do."

CHAPTER 5

Erik's morning run was a little odd with Lieutenant Dale and six security guys, two in a groundcar, the other four in pairs ahead and behind. Erik had protested, but they were under orders from 'the boss', who was off at some meeting and currently unreachable. Happily he wasn't breathing any harder than the Lieutenant when they returned, and settled into breakfast after a shower and a change into uniform. Dale protested that he'd eaten, but Erik made it a non-negotiable offer.

No doubt Dale thought he'd be uncomfortable at the Debogande breakfast table, but was astonished to find the long dining table a less formal affair, with family working at the table, talking across each other and the food that waiters brought from the kitchen. He was most astonished to find the security they'd just been jogging with already changed and eating, while watching the news screen and talking together about the day's schedule. He'd expected the rich folk to eat alone, obviously, but the Debogande household functioned as a single, working entity, at Alice's insistence.

"It's the Debogande way," Erik explained to Dale as he took some cold meats, eggs and a smoothie brought for him, dodging a noisy niece and nephew scampering past his legs. "Organised chaos."

"Can see why you like Fleet then," Dale admitted, forcing a smile and a nod at various Debogande sisters who greeted him.

"Well something's changed," said Deirdre, coming to give Erik a morning kiss on the cheek, coffee mug in hand. She nodded at the news screen. The feed showed Captain Pantillo, and a choice of various ongoing discussions about his arrest and impending court-martial. It had been going since last evening. Apparently all of Homeworld knew, and Fleet weren't arresting anyone for talking about it. Yet.

"They saying anything new?" Erik asked around a mouthful, not bothering to sit. Seats at a family breakfast were always optional, everyone preparing their affairs for the day.

"The usual, the charges are dereliction of duty and disobeying orders, that hasn't changed. There's not a heck of a lot of speculation, everyone's being very careful."

"Not on the underground nets they're not," Lisbeth added from her seat, looking up from her screen schedule. She still wore her bathrobe, hair tousled and a lot of neck and shoulder bare, Lieutenant Dale pointedly not looking too hard. "They're saying it's…"

"Lisbeth," scolded Cora, "don't talk about that unpatriotic nonsense in front of the Lieutenant. You'll embarrass us."

"I'm quite sure a man who's been shot at as many times as the Lieutenant isn't going to be bothered by some stupid news channel," Lisbeth retorted. Dale smiled and nodded with his mouth full, uncommenting. And stood back in further surprise as some servants came to eat from the standing plates on the table.

"What do you think changed?" Deirdre asked Erik.

"I don't think they could ever keep it an enforceable secret for more than a day or two," said Erik. "I mean who are they kidding — court-martial one of the war's biggest heroes without anyone talking? On Homeworld?"

"Which means they were stalling," Deirdre said thoughtfully into her coffee mug. "Buying time to set up their case."

"Stitch up, more likely," Dale muttered.

"I don't think that's all that happened," Erik added. "I think Major Thakur talked to the Kulina. She said she would."

Deirdre raised an eyebrow at him. "The Kulina have that much influence with Fleet?"

"Kulina don't pull weight with anyone," their father said, entering in a suit and tie, briefcase in hand and accepting with thanks a coffee mug that a servant handed to him. "That's the remarkable thing with Kulina, they don't ask anything for themselves, not even a marked grave. Lieutenant." With a nod to Dale.

"Sir," said Dale, with what Erik was sure was respect more for his veteran than his civilian status.

"If they've intervened on your Captain's behalf here," Walker continued, "it'll be something amazing, the first time I heard of it."

"Major Thakur can be persuasive," said Erik.

"How did she win the Liberty Star?" Lisbeth wondered. "I don't think I heard that one." Cora glared at her younger sister — it wasn't an appropriate time to ask, but Lisbeth had that habit of just wondering odd thoughts aloud. Everyone looked at Dale, expecting some discomfort. Instead, Dale put his plate of cold meats aside and got into pub-storytelling-mode.

"Right," said Dale. "So it's four years ago, before the Lieutenant Commander's time. And we hit Toji Station, at Trailak Major, and we gotta hold it because the freighters are incoming and if they don't have a place to dock, they're stuck out-system and sitting ducks for the tavalai sweepers jumping short and cutting our resupply to pieces. Tavalai have this damn station booby trapped to the eyeballs, we find out there's about three times more of them defending the place than intel suggested... all of them hiding.

"Anyhow, long story short — we get aboard on assault shuttles, all hell breaks loose and we get cut up and pinned down. Different units in different parts of the station, we're supposed to rendezvous in the middle, but now we're trapped. And Delta Platoon, they're getting smashed, cut off and pinned against the bulkhead, lots of wounded, can't move 'em, can't get out. And we're now getting jammed to hell, so we can't talk, got no idea what each other's doing — usual situation for us, defenders communicate using hardlines, which we ain't got.

"And I'm in Alpha Platoon with the Major... and we're defending our beach head on the docks, we can't afford to move or we'll loose it. So the Major, she puts me in charge, and she takes four guys, and she goes to get Delta Platoon. Across half-a-klick of the worst, tavalai infested station corridors you've ever seen.

"She's the only one who gets there alive. Once she reaches Delta, she sees all their wounded, so she tells them to stay and defend them. Then she comes back. Alone. Must've killed about thirty froggies on the way, I don't know how anyone could survive twenty meters on their own in that, let alone five hundred. But she does. Once she's back we grab a shuttle off the rim, and go and get Delta Platoon from outside, cut through the hull to extract them, right where she said they were. Saved twenty guys. Lost the station, had to pull out, whole thing turned into a giant mess and Fleet lost another three ships in the extraction. I filed the report myself, got everyone to sign it. Two months later, Liberty Star for the Major. Takes a while, with space distances. Captain Pantillo pinned it on her himself."

There was near silence at the breakfast table, save for the chattering news screen. Even the servants had stopped to listen.

"Wow," said Lisbeth, wide eyed. "What an incredible woman."

"Most incredible part?" Dale continued. "She hates that damn thing. Most miserable I've ever seen her, when the Captain pinned it on her. If she could toss it out an airlock, I'm sure she would."

"Why?" Cora exclaimed. "Isn't she proud?"

Dale smiled at her crookedly. "You don't know any Kulina, do you miss?"

"Pride is ego," said Walker. "Ego is a barrier to inner peace. She did it because it needed to be done. That's all."

Dale nodded at Walker, and raised his coffee mug to him.

"Erik," said Walker. "You're going to see your Uncle Thani today?"

Erik nodded. "If there's leaning to be done, I figure he's the guy to do it."

Walker raised an eyebrow. "Just be careful. Don't lean too hard. Most things this family leans on will bend, and we try not to abuse that. But there are some who actively resent it. They lean back."

"So Lieutenant Commander," said Dale around a mouthful. "What does Uncle Thani do?"

"He represents three billion people in Endeavour System and New Dakota, and he heads the Spacer Congress Commerce

Committee," Erik said innocently. "Making him probably the third most powerful politician in all human space. Why do you ask?"

"Ah," said Dale. "Thani Gialidis. Even a dumb grunt like me's heard of him." With a wink at Lisbeth. Lisbeth grinned.

Family security took a second cruiser with Erik and Dale to Spacer Congress. The Congressional complex was in north western Shiwon, tucked in the Jin Valley between hills. Traffic Central queried their flight route on the way in, then Congress security queried their ID as they approached.

The complex grounds were two huge, circular podiums, surrounded by and integrated with a series of gleaming glass towers. Traffic put them in a slow approach amid a number of other incoming vehicles, as suburbs gave way to green gardens and security barriers, and lots of staff and visitors walking the paths below. Dale craned his neck to look up at the towers — the architecture was famous, as were a number of sculpture memorials about the grounds. Odd, many remarked, that the Spacer Congress was not actually located in space... but the administrative requirements were huge, and this many bureaucrats became expensive when air was not free. So much transit to and from the gravity well was even more expensive, given the need to deal with all kinds of ground-dwellers, and even Spacers were forced to admit that permanent gravity had its advantages.

"Ever been here before?" Erik asked Dale.

"Nope," said Dale.

"It's pretty cool," said Erik. "Just watch your wallet." Being from a frontier world, where cash currency was still used, Dale would know what a wallet was. "I still think it's odd that Chairmen Ali and Joseph weren't here for the parades. You know how politicians hate to miss big public events. You'd think the two most powerful politicians in Spacer Congress would make it a point to be here."

Dale shrugged. "They got home constituencies, yeah? Gotta get home sometime, they're the ones who vote for them."

They bounced on a transition zone, rolled to security for a full check inside and out, then into underground parking. As serving Fleet with a ship at dock and a registered appointment, they were allowed to keep their sidearms, as were the security in the second car. The cruiser parked near an elevator, which the marines plus two of the house security took up to podium level, then walked along polished hallways filled with busy staff to a tower elevator.

"How close an uncle is he?" Dale asked, adjusting his tie. Erik thought he looked a little nervous. Humanity had no single President, as such, just a series of committees that ran things like security, finance and commerce, in that order of authority. The heads of those committees were referred to as 'the leadership'. Thani Gialidis was the Commerce Chair, but was senior on the other two big committees as well. Security Committee was top, of course, and sometimes called the 'War Council', as that more correctly described what it did. It was co-chaired by Supreme Commander Chankow. Chairman Ali was the elected co-chair, but no one was going to call him President Ali when Fleet had veto in the form of the Supreme Commander, and Ali did not. Chairman Joseph headed Finance. And with both of them offworld on who-knew-what business, that left Chairman Gialidis as the most senior politician on Homeworld.

"Great great uncle," Erik admitted. "My mother's mother's uncle. He's a hundred and fifty six, so he's seen nearly the whole war."

"So who gets to be a Debogande?" asked Dale. "The family's been rich a long time, that many generations can't all live like you. There must be hundreds."

"Thousands. But thousands can't inherit the company, that goes to Katerina, the rest of us siblings will squabble for the smaller companies. Various cousins can get jobs if they're qualified."

"Damn feudal monarchy," said Dale. "So much for merit, huh?"

Erik smiled, unbothered by the Lieutenant's needling. "Sure. Like Fleet Admirals. All the quality gets promoted while under-performers like the Captain tread water." Dale snorted. "Thing with having lots of money, you can buy education and corporate experience, so the people in these jobs are actually very good. With genetics and augments like they are, you can even buy talent. Just not wisdom."

"Gotta join Fleet for that."

"Exactly."

"Woulda got more if you'd joined marines."

"Yes, but you only inherit if you're still alive," said Erik. A couple of female staff in the hall turned to look at the passing officers with smothered smiles. Erik overheard the phrase 'officer hotties', and nodded to the ladies as he entered the tower elevator behind his forward security. They smiled back, and waved suggestively.

"Don't bother LC," said Dale as the doors closed. "They weren't looking at you."

"I'm pretty sure they were."

"To tuck into bed with a glass of milk and a bedtime story, maybe."

Erik gave him an incredulous look. "You know if I'm ever commanding combat ops, *Lieutenant*, and we have to deploy into something hot, you'll be on point."

"Hooyah sir."

The elevator let them out at the top. Staff bustled about, and one came to Erik immediately, and ushered them to a waiting room, with apologies. Ten minutes later some important looking people emerged from the main office. A staffer beckoned to Erik, who stood.

"Lieutenant, come and say hi at least. Pity to make the trip and not get to meet Uncle Thani." And he further enjoyed Dale's nervous tie adjustment, jacket adjustment, button and fly check. "Relax. And remember he's a civilian, you don't stand to attention." Because some soldiers forgot.

The office was wide atop the tower, with a glass wall overlooking green hills and surrounding towers in a blaze of tinted sunlight. A dark haired man with a photogenic face broke from a conversation with a staffer to give Erik a beaming smile. "Well well! Lieutenant Commander Debogande!" They embraced. "So good to see you home safely."

"Good to be home safely, Uncle Thani," said Erik. They parted, and Erik indicated Dale. "This is Lieutenant Dale, he runs Alpha Platoon under Major Thakur."

They shook hands. "And what's life like under the legendary Major Thakur?" Thani asked him.

"Interesting," said Dale.

"I'm sure. I'm so sorry to hear about your Captain, both of you..." and his eyes narrowed at Dale. "You're Erik's security?" So he knew something was up, Erik thought with relief.

"Something like that."

"And I'm sure as a marine officer you're thrilled to be made into a bodyguard?" With a smile.

"Well you know sir," said Dale, with a sideways look at Erik. "Some people need more looking after than others."

Thani laughed. "And it had to be someone with your natural class and refinement, of course."

"He hasn't tried to hump my sisters' legs yet," Erik conceded. "Which is more than I'd expected." Dale gave Erik a look that promised amusing things to come, of the kind that only marines would find funny.

"I'm sure you're doing a fine job, Lieutenant," said Thani.

"Thanks for the vote of confidence, sir. LC, will you need anything else?"

"No Lieutenant," said Erik. "Try not to kill or impregnate anyone while you're waiting."

"No promises LC," said Dale as he left.

"Wow," said Thani after he'd gone. "A *real* tough guy, huh? Not like the wannabes around here."

"Total pain in the ass," said Erik, taking the seat Thani indicated. "But a hell of a marine. One of the best."

"And little Major Thakur orders men like him around with no problems?" asked Thani, sitting behind his desk.

Erik smiled. "She doesn't even raise her voice. There was a Sergeant on the last port call, tougher guy even than Lieutenant Dale, he got rowdy with a couple of girls in a bar, too much alcohol, the girls were upset. The Major heard about it, had a quiet word to him when he got in. She said he'd made her unhappy. That's it. Poor guy nearly cried, didn't touch a drink the rest of the stop. Found the girls from that night and apologised, the works."

Thani nodded slowly. "And now I hear she's gone and leaned on her Kulina superiors to lean on Fleet HQ."

"Seems that way," said Erik. "What can you tell me about it?" As a staffer entered with some tea, which both men accepted with thanks.

Thani sipped, and pursed his lips. "Okay," he said finally. "Let me tell you this. When Fleet is about to do something big, generally I'll hear about it first. I've got staff who keep track of Fleet, they've got contacts inside, a lot of them are ex-Fleet."

"A lot of this whole building," Erik agreed.

Thani nodded. "Exactly. Spacer Congress is a giant Fleet echo chamber. Whenever Fleet makes a noise, this place rings like a bell. So usually, if they were about to do something stupid, which Fleet will too frequently do... something like put their greatest war hero under arrest on charges no sane person could believe... we'd usually hear about that in advance. Not exactly what was going to happen, mind you. We'd just get wind that *something* was about to happen — there'd be secret meetings, odd comings and goings, Admirals rescheduling Committee appearances, etcetera. And we'd all look at each other and say, 'something's up.'

"This one? Nothing."

Erik frowned. "So what does that mean?"

"It means that they decided to court-martial Captain Pantillo with very little warning, and very little deliberation. It means that only a very few people knew about it in advance, and the way that Fleet works, you know which people they'd have been."

"The Big Three," said Erik.

Thani nodded.   "Because the only part of the command pyramid that can make executive decisions with no deliberation is the very top part.   Fleet Admirals Ishmael and Anjo, and Supreme Commander Chankow.   That's it."

"But that doesn't make sense," said Erik.   "Fleet deliberates on *everything*.   It's a fucking bureaucratic mess, no one wants to make command decisions on anything politically controversial because all the top commanders are into politics themselves.   If they're going to railroad the Captain, they'll want to make damn sure they've got a base of support behind them, and that means all kinds of meetings and number crunching, the kind of thing you'd hear about."

"So here's the thing," said Thani, very seriously.   "The Tanok Offensive.   We heard rumblings about that two years in advance.   Didn't know what it was, of course, though some of us guessed."

"Right," said Erik, "well it takes years to plan a big offensive."

"But then there was the Sherin Offensive.   And we didn't hear boo about that.   It just fell out of the sky on our laps, and that was just as big."

The Sherin Offensive was forty-two years ago, but Erik had studied it well.   "Yeah, but that was to relieve pressure on the chah'nas flank after they got whacked at Pou-duk.   We had no time to plan."

"Sure," said Thani.   "It came from a non-human source."

"Well no, we still had to do most of the planning ourselves..."

"Yes, but the motivation to do so came from a non-human source.   In that case, the chah'nas."

Erik stared at him for a long moment.   "Are you saying that... that the Captain was court-martialled at the say-so of our *allies*?"

"No," Thani said carefully.   "I'm saying this.   Whenever something happens in Fleet HQ, that Spacer Congress doesn't get a whiff of in advance, it's come from outside.   I'm *not* saying that aliens commanded it. I'm just saying that it has to *do* with aliens. Fleet HQ often doesn't deliberate on that at all. That's one for very High Command only. That's my guess."

"Well," said Erik after a long pause. "I'm not sure that helps me very much. No idea *what* to do with aliens?"

Thani shook his head, and sipped tea. "Erik, there's peace coming now. That scares a lot of people as bad as war did. Some of them worse, because war's all they've known. They're used to war. War made them powerful. Lots of people are about to be downsized. Not all of them are thrilled about it."

"Well Fleet will still be powerful. All those colonies will need patrolling, and worlds occupying. Takes a lot of ships. Army units too."

"Yes," said Thani. "And a lot of those ships are chah'nas technology, or alo technology. They call it the Triumvirate War because there's three of us, in one big alliance. Now I see chah'nas every second day, but I'll see an alo maybe once a year. There aren't many people in humanity who know more about that alliance than me, but I'll let you know this for free — most of us really don't know what the alo are up to, or why they joined this alliance in the first place.

"Chah'nas, sure. They want their empire back. It's not the most wonderful motivation, but it suits our purposes — the tavalai used to be their administrators in the old chah'nas empire, but they got uppity. Chah'nas want the tavalai back in their box. Chah'nas are complicated, but their motives usually aren't. Alo…?" He shrugged expansively. "How much of the tech we use every day actually came from alo originally, and *they* gave to the chah'nas? Nobody knows. Alo are a damn sight smarter than chah'nas, smart enough they've got everyone else doing their fighting for them.

"There's so much going on outside of human space that no one knows about, Erik. Stuff I can't speculate upon with you because it would cost me my job and land me in prison. We've been in space twelve hundred years — with FTL, anyway. The first three hundred of that we were stuck in a small corner of krim space, fighting for our lives. Then we took krim space. Now we've taken half of tavalai space, and some of sard and kaal. There's still a lot out there beyond the Spiral boundaries, all the way through the inner reaches. Those places have had sentient, spacefaring civilisation for fifty thousand years at least. More, if you count the Ancients. We're just the kids out here, the newcomers. All these older species might have learned we're damn tough to beat in a war, but they still think they can play us for fools, and they might be right.

"You've been understandably preoccupied with the war. But here in this office, I spend much of my days thinking and worrying about all that other stuff beyond our reach. And to me, it looks like Captain Pantillo got screwed over because he got in the way of something between Fleet HQ, and some other alien race we've got dealings with... and trust me, there's a lot more of them than just chah'nas, alo or kuhsi. That's all I can tell you."

Trace found her marines on the beach, playing volleyball, swimming and surfing, or lazing on the sand with food and drink. She strolled from the cab, sidearm and details in her small pack — being out of uniform was an inconvenience that way, she couldn't wear the gun openly. But she felt safe enough here, on a lightly-trafficked road with a line of shops and cafes... despite the car along the parking line with two people in it, plainly watching.

Her guys didn't recognise her immediately — there were about twenty, less than ten percent of the *Phoenix* company, all buff and lean in their swimwear, and drawing no few looks from the civvies around them. Then Carville saw her, sitting up from the sand by the volleyball game, about to call out but she shushed him with a finger to her lips, and took a seat beside him and three others.

"Hey Major," said Carville, genuinely pleased to see her. "Didn't recognise you in civvies, nice look." She wore tight swimshorts and a short top over a bikini top. Dress for female officers around those she commanded wasn't quite as simple as for male officers, and this was as much skin as seemed wise, on a beach, trying to blend in.

"Thanks Benji," she said.   "You look like you've been looking after yourself this shore leave, I'm impressed."

Private 'Benji' Carville grinned, delighted as they all were when she used their nicknames.   He was Alpha Second Squad, like were they all.   "Well I may have had one too many last night," he admitted.   "But only one."

"PT this morning?" she pressed.

"Sir yes sir!" said Kaur, and they laughed.

"Three klicks run on soft sand and full workout," Carville assured her.   "You'd have been proud."

"I'm always proud Benji.   I don't know if I believe you, but I'm always proud."   More laughter.

"You here for the day Major?" Aram asked hopefully.

"Couple of hours," she said.   Truthfully, she *could* have spent more R&R time with them — they weren't always drinking and being rowdy.   But those that weren't, tended to be the same ones, and if she spent all her down time with the same guys, the others would feel aggrieved.

"Any news on the Captain?" asked Kaur.   She'd had to order them to go to the beach, have fun, and keep doing all the usual things they'd do on downtime.   Because they were all upset, and when marines got upset, sometimes people got hurt.   That was the last thing anyone needed now, the Captain least of all, so Trace had ordered them all to continue recreation as usual, no exceptions, and she'd tell them when anything changed.

"Nothing more than you've heard," she told them. "Commander Huang's down from *Phoenix* now, she's in talks with HQ."

"She's got family contacts in HQ doesn't she?" Aram pressed.

Trace nodded.   They all looked so hopeful.   But she made it a rule to always tell them straight, on anything that might affect their safety.   "Honestly, I don't hold much hope for Commander Huang. She's a great commander, but that family she has at the top levels is a liability in this situation.   I spoke to her briefly, and I got a distinct lack of urgency from her."

"She's ditching us?" said Carville, eyes darkening. "She's ditching the Captain?"

"She's caught between this family and blood family," Trace corrected firmly. "Don't judge her, it's not her fault. But don't expect much either. The one who *has* been raising holy hell is the LC."

"Debogande?" said Kaur. "Seriously?"

Trace nodded. "He went to see his Great Uncle Gialidis this morning." Eyes widened, everyone knew who *that* was. "Dale told me, said the LC was real serious, and real pissed. And just now Huang called me, told me to tell the LC to cool it a bit, apparently HQ's getting jumpy. Huang told the LC to cool it herself, the LC told her it was a family visit and mind her own business."

Surprised laughs from the marines. The standard assumption with LC Debogande was of an okay officer who couldn't be much special because he couldn't possibly deserve the post. Certainly no one thought he was the guy who came out swinging when the bigwigs pushed them in a corner. Most marines thought Debogande *was* a bigwig, he sure shined his shoes like one.

"So here's the thing," Trace continued. "I want us to start moving back to *Phoenix*. We're being watched, for one thing."

"That car in the parking line?" said Carville. "Yeah, there's always one. There was a guy in the bar last night, another at a restaurant."

"Exactly. I don't want anyone getting paranoid, they might just be checking that nobody's witness tampering before the trial. But I feel vulnerable down here, and I've requested to the Commander we start moving back to *Phoenix* before someone starts some incident, creates more trouble, etcetera. If they're trying to stitch the Captain up, they might try to stitch us all up, we just don't know what this is yet."

Grim nods. "When?"

"Tomorrow. Commander's arranging it."

"What about *Phoenix* crew?"

"I'm not sure," Trace admitted. "Not my area. But something similar seems wise. I'm sure the LC agrees with me. The Commander, not so much."

"Yeah but Major," said Aram. "I don't like leaving the Captain alone down here. It's a bad look."

"There's nothing we can do for him here," Trace said firmly. "This isn't our environment. It's in the hands of the bigwigs now, and if any of us have to testify at the court-martial, they can fly us back. Until then, the best we can do is avoid making extra trouble."

Reluctant nods. "You want us to tell the others?"

"Just rotate everyone else back through here," said Trace, finding a comfortable seat on the sand. "Nothing suspicious for our watching friends. I'll tell them myself."

Two hours later, after some sun, some lunch, some swimming and even a bit of volleyball, she'd briefed all twenty-three of them in depth. That gave her confidence that the message would spread to the entire two hundred and twenty-eight strong *Phoenix* marine complement verbally, without too much distortion. She didn't dare do it on any communication net on this planet — she was no network genius, and was certain Fleet HQ had plenty working for them who were. If she encrypted it, they'd break it in minutes.

She was playing volleyball when her next meeting showed up, strolling along the beachside path in a short pink skirt and blue top, brown-limbed and frizzy-haired with four casually dressed security guards in tow. Lisbeth Debogande waved, and Trace waved back.

"Sorry guys," she said, tossing one the ball. "Business appointment, have a nice ride up if I don't see you before."

"Hey, just when she was losing too!" came the predictable catcalls. She climbed stairs from the beach with a middle finger raised to her marines, who fell about laughing.

Lisbeth looked quite awed as she approached, and Trace raised her sunglasses and smiled so she didn't look quite so scary. "Hello Lisbeth, lovely to meet you finally."

"Hello Major Thakur!" With wide-eyed worship, as Trace kissed her cheek. It was surprising, this reaction from a pretty young girl like Lisbeth Debogande. Trace hadn't thought a young woman with this much money and power could be awed by anyone, least of all a marine major with barely a cent to her name. And she knew that the women in Erik's family were not the military sort. Or most of them.

"Shall we get a drink?" she asked Lisbeth. "I'm kind of thirsty."

They sat on a bench on the green lawn overlooking the beach, Lisbeth with a milkshake, Trace with a fruit juice. Lisbeth's security went to the watching car and talked to the occupants, who looked quite annoyed. They also went to an older woman with a baby in a stroller, and talked to her too. She took the stroller and left. Wow, Trace thought. She hadn't picked the woman for a watcher. This really wasn't her environment. The sooner she was out of here, the better.

"You're being watched?" asked Lisbeth, watching proceedings.

"Won't they get in trouble?" Trace replied, nodding to her security team, still fanning across the beachfront. "Those are government agents they're questioning."

"Oh we have this debate all the time," Lisbeth sighed. "Government security versus Debogande security. We usually win — most of our guys are former government agents, we pay them five times more and they know all the tricks."

"Your family's like a state unto itself," Trace observed.

"I can't argue," said Lisbeth. "Were you really losing at volleyball before I arrived?" She seemed cheerful and curious, and was disarmingly friendly. Young, but not especially naive, and very far from stupid. She looked quite a lot like Erik, save she was a little darker, and her hair was bigger.

"Yes," said Trace. Lisbeth looked astonished. Trace smiled. "There aren't many similarities between volleyball and combat ops. A lot of these bigger boys would rather be my size under fire, I can tell you."

"I'm sorry," said Lisbeth, fascinated. "You must think me painfully silly."

"Not at all. If I ventured into your world I'm sure I'd be lost as well."

"I very much doubt that. Please let me thank you for being such a good friend to my brother. I love him so dearly, and although I know your job and his are very different, I'm sure that him returning safely must have something to do with you. So thank you, truly."

Trace felt uncomfortable. She'd never held the poor opinion of Erik that some of her troops did, but she'd not been completely convinced, either. Had that been wrong? Certainly his actions had surprised and impressed her, these last few days. Had she been prejudiced in her assumptions toward him? Even Dale reported, very grudgingly, that his family actually weren't too bad. And now Lisbeth... if ever there was a girl who was set up to turn out poorly, with her wealth and privilege. But instead she was proving quite charming. Prejudice was the sign of a peaceless mind, when objectivity was her goal. Was she failing at this as well?

"Your brother has surprised me," she admitted. "I've never had money. Those of us without it often don't know what to make of those with so much. Sometimes I think we see only the money. But Erik has shown me the man, and the man is impressive."

"Mother always tells us that we'll have to work twice as hard to earn true respect," Lisbeth said solemnly. "Because so many people will assume we just get handed everything on a plate. She also taught us not to resent it, because we are very fortunate and all good fortune naturally comes with a downside."

"Karma," Trace agreed. "Kulina believe the same."

Lisbeth smiled. "So. You said you had something to discuss with me?"

Trace nodded. "I'm arranging for all of my marines to head back to *Phoenix*. There are a lot of frayed tempers and hot heads, I think it's safer if we remove ourselves from a volatile situation, for everyone's sake."

"I think that sounds very wise."

"But I only have command authority over marines. *Phoenix*'s spacer crew are under Commander Huang, and she is less inclined to do the same with her people.   Your brother agrees with me, however.   Now, I always like to have emergency contingencies, for all *Phoenix* personnel.   At the moment, if we were to need to get back to *Phoenix*, we can't guarantee enough transport to do it quickly."

Lisbeth frowned.   "*Phoenix* has her own shuttles, doesn't she?"

"We have four, but only one is currently grounded, and using them to come down to Homeworld requires Fleet HQ approval.   If I had to move them *without* Fleet HQ approval, that could be problematic."

Lisbeth stared.   "Do you think that's likely?"

"No.   This is why they're called emergency contingencies. However, I am on the lookout for other methods of transport back to *Phoenix*."

"Well that's not so hard," said Lisbeth.   "The family's got shuttles.   We own an entire spaceline here on Homeworld, Allied Transit.   It's got nine shuttles, we use it for a lot of cargo operations and vertical integration with various companies, and VIP transport of course."

"Can you authorise the use of those shuttles?   On short notice?"

"Of course."

"And could you keep this request a secret?"

Lisbeth smiled.   "Well I was going to say… I think I'd better keep it secret, because otherwise I'll get questions.   My father and Erik can get… protective."

"Well look," said Trace.   "I don't want you to put yourself into any trouble."

"Oh pish," Lisbeth said dismissively.   "You've risked your life for soft civilians like me so many times.   You all have.   This is the very least I can do."

CHAPTER 6

Erik arrived at the detention level beneath the HQ towers just as his mother called.

"Hello Erik, I just wanted to check where you were."

"Hello Mother, I'm just heading into HQ detention to see the Captain." He handed his sidearm to the guard at the first secure door, and had it scanned and registered for collection upon return. Then he stepped into the body screener, arms raised.

"So your JAG officer got you access finally?"

"Yes, it came through this morning. Commander Huang would have gone, but apparently the Captain's asking for me specifically. Where are you, Mother?"

"Erik, I'm hearing a lot of noise from various quarters. Something's going on in Fleet, and I don't like it at all."

Well anyone could have made that observation, but it was a different thing if Alice Debogande made it. He'd barely seen her since that speech upon his homecoming. Given her usual schedule, he'd known better than to ask, or risk seeming miffed that she couldn't make time for him, knowing well the lecture he'd get about responsibilities and duties above all else.

"Mother what noise are you hearing?" The security guard waved him through, took his ID and scanned him through the outer door. A guard on the far side opened the second door, and pinned a visitor's badge on him.

"Just noise. Erik, I don't think you should go to see the Captain today."

"Well I'm already here, Mother. Why don't you tell me who you've been talking to?"

"Darling you know I can't do that." This call was being routed through Fleet HQ servers, that meant. *"But there are corporate troubles, and I'm not entirely sure that this whole thing isn't aimed at our family. In which case your Captain might just be collateral."*

Erik was not particularly surprised — it had occurred to him. A guard arrived to escort him, and he followed down the white, bare corridor. *"Well I wish you'd mentioned this a few hours ago. But I'm here now, and I'm not abandoning the Captain, he's had no outside contact for two days and he'll be wanting to speak to someone. Plus I might finally get some answers."* About more things than just this court-martial.

A silence on the other end. *"Very well. Erik, just be careful. Love you, we'll talk when you get out."*

"I love you too Mother." Damn the timing, he thought as she disconnected. He'd just been thinking about all the questions he needed to ask the Captain, and now this major distraction. It deserved a lot more thought, but discussion with the Captain on serious matters required a very sharp brain — junior officers unaccustomed were known to take stimulants and spend advance hours studying before such sessions, so formidable was the Captain's reputation. No one wanted to be caught without an answer when he asked a pointed question.

They passed a corridor junction, then stopped at a nondescript door along a row of nondescript doors. The guard IDed the door, and Erik went in. The cell was partitioned by a transparent wall of hard plastic. There was a chair here, opposite speaker holes, where visitors could sit and talk to inmates without contact. But Erik had been promised proper contact, and waited for someone watching via monitor to open the second door. The Captain lay on his bunk, hands folded, calmly waiting. Erik smiled. He didn't imagine the Captain had been doing much else, other than exercising. Surely they'd let him have reading materials. He loved to read, had often passed his occasional spare time with Erik or another officer, discussing this or that amazing book, often about old, lost Earth. And then Erik had been obliged to read that book as well, if only so he could properly join the conversation. He'd lost a lot of sleep that way, catching up on the Captain's reading list.

The door behind closed, and the one ahead opened. Erik entered, pulled up a chair to the Captain's bedside, and sat.

"Captain. How've you been?" The Captain said nothing. He seemed to be sleeping, eyes closed. Erik frowned. "Captain?"

He reached, and shook the uniformed arm. Nothing. The Captain was very still. Suddenly Erik felt fear unlike anything he'd known before. The fear that recognised a moment when a life was changed forever.

"Captain Pantillo!" He put an ear to his mouth, but neither heard nor felt a breath. Fingers to his neck, clean shaven, but no pulse. "Oh no no no, hey!" He yelled to the room monitor. "Hey, send a medic! I need a medic right now!" He tilted Pantillo's head, mouth open, ready to apply CPR... and saw the blood on the pillow, hidden by the previous placement of the head. So neatly done. His posture all perfect on the mattress, not a sign that anything could be wrong.

Erik rolled the head aside, somehow knowing what he'd find, but not quite believing it. A single hole, hair matted with blood. Execution style to the back of the skull. Not heavy caliber, the damage wasn't that great. But high enough to kill instantly. His heart thudded as the room swam with disbelief, further appeals for help frozen on his lips. He knew who'd done it. It was that obvious. But if it was that obvious to him, it would be to everyone else, so how could they think to get away with it? Unless they'd already made plans to cover their tracks.

A low caliber weapon. Fleet didn't use those, even sidearms did much more damage than this. This would have come from the kind of weapon that could be concealed. Slipped past security. Or planted on a person without them noticing. His hands reached for his jacket pockets, and sure enough, there was something in the right one. He pulled it out — a small plastic tube, it looked like a pen but it smelled of recent explosive discharge. And it now had his bloody fingerprints all over it. Smooth Erik. Real smooth.

He slumped back into the chair in disbelief and shock. He felt chills and nausea, like the time he'd badly broken his arm in Academy training. Horror at the sight of the disfigured limb, the bones protruding in a nasty lump. The brain struggled to process such things. He thought he might throw up.

The guards would be in through the door any moment, to catch him red-handed.   Then a trial, and more scandal.   Maybe they'd even find a way to knock him off as well... though that would be stretching it, even for these guys.   Lots wouldn't believe them, but Family Debogande was not universally popular, and lots would believe Fleet, for no better reason than ideology or spite.   Possibly he'd get off, Debogande family lawyers were good, but even more likely he wouldn't, not with Fleet HQ itself behind this stitchup, and all the resources at its disposal.   Either way, scandal stuck to the politically involved, and he'd be untouchable forever.   His family would be too.   Possibly even Uncle Thani, and others who relied on Debogande money to get reelected.

Then he realised that his Captain, the man he admired most in all the world, was dead.   And here was poor little LC Debogande, thinking only about himself.   He leaned over the body, not wanting to touch more in case bloody fingerprints only incriminated him further.   The Captain looked peaceful, as though he might be sleeping.   Surely he'd not given them the satisfaction of fear or begging.   He wasn't that sort of man.

Erik's eyes filled with tears.   "I'm so sorry Captain.   I wasn't fast enough.   I thought I did everything I could.   I failed you."

Something he'd just thought kept replaying over in his brain. Wouldn't give them the satisfaction... the Captain would have faced his death without surprise.   Certainly he'd known a heck of a lot more about what caused it than Erik did.   Seeing his death approaching, he would have... would have what?

Erik quickly went through Pantillo's uniform pockets, uncaring about fingerprints now.   In the breast pocket, he found a small plastic square — a memory reader, not a commercial civilian one, but an implanted military one.   It looked like it had been dug out of some other device.   A smart man could keep it concealed, perhaps, in a place like this.

The outer cell door crashed open, and armed guards rushed in.   They'd strip him and confiscate everything, Erik realised.   He put the chip in his mouth and swallowed. Guards crashed the second door and levelled weapons at him.

"Lieutenant Commander Debogande, you are under arrest!" The head guard indicated to the Captain. "Check him!" Another guard rushed to do that, with genuine alarm. They didn't know, Erik thought. They genuinely thought he'd done it. Certainly it looked pretty bad, him sitting here with the smuggled murder weapon and the Captain's blood all over his hands. It didn't even occur to him to protest his innocence. Against Fleet HQ, what was the point?

"He's gone," said the guard examining the Captain.

"You son of a bitch!" said the first guard, pistol levelled at Erik's face. "Get on the floor, face down, right now!"

Trace was calmer than she'd expected when they came. She sat on her footstool in cross-legged meditation, and did not open the door when they knocked. If she couldn't use weapons here, she wasn't opening any door for armed soldiers. If they were going to make any kind of armed entry into her room, they'd find her non-confrontational and meditating with her back turned — face to face in a narrow doorway was just asking some hair-trigger fool to panic.

As it happened they didn't bust the door down, but came around the back and climbed onto the balcony. Seeing her there, unarmed and eyes closed, there were shouts to open the door, and raps on the glass. Ignoring them was easy. She never truly heard them in the first place. Finally one of them got the hotel key to the front door and came in sensibly. Still they did not touch her, nor force her, but told her that they were under orders to bring her, and now. None were game to be the first to lay a hand on her. That was probably wise.

She kept them waiting for a good five minutes, while they stood around her in light armour and weapons and wondered aloud and to their commanders back at base what to do with the Kulina marine commander who refused to acknowledge their existence. Finally when she was ready, and had finished her various uplinked conversations (which the intruders had unwisely not jammed) she unfolded herself from the footstool, and informed them that she'd get changed, then accompany them.

They took her weapons first and put a guard on the balcony outside the bedroom window, but she had no intention of running. She put on her uniform from where she had it neatly hung in the closet, collected her necessary ID and documents, then went with the armed men to one of their waiting vehicles. Half were MPs, the other half were army commandos. Evidently someone wanted her in custody very badly. She wondered what they'd have actually done if she'd resisted. But then no one would ever expect a Kulina to resist. Kulina were not only brave, but loyal. These men had not made a hard entry, and now did not put restraints on her, or point weapons at her. Partly it was respect, she thought, and partly it was fear. But mostly, it was that Kulina always did what Fleet told them, and put all other concerns aside.

She watched the newsnets on uplink vision on the way in. She was better at that than most, having mastered the art of relaxing her mind and simply seeing the artificial image projected upon the inside of her eyelids. The newsnets told her that Lieutenant Commander Debogande was under arrest having been caught red-handed in the murder of Captain Pantillo. News had gone out very fast, she thought. It had even beaten the armed team who'd arrived at her hotel, giving her plenty of time to prepare. That was poor planning, and it spoke of haste, and perhaps desperation, from someone in HQ. Someone who wanted the Debogandes silenced as fast as possible. Or someone who was distracted with more pressing matters, and wanted this to go away fast.

Her calm now as she considered it all in the rear seat of the MPs cruiser surprised her too. The Captain had been like the father she'd never truly had. But his death was not surprising. In fact, it was clarifying. She knew now what she had to do next, and suddenly all the doubt was gone. As though the Captain himself were speaking to her, with that wise and kindly smile, and showing her the path ahead. What he told her was that all choice was illusion. The things that happen, happen. To ponder these choices was to open yourself to selfish desires, to weigh possible outcomes upon the scales of want and need.   Remove all choice, and both want and need went slinking back into the shadows from which they'd come.   Certainty took root, and with it, peace and calm.

It was a lesson she'd learned on Sugauli, as a young teenager climbing the Rejara Phirta Range in mask and suit, on ropes and clamps that you placed yourself in the little gaps and crevasses in the rock.   They only gave you a small amount of rope, which you had to constantly recover and reuse, while the howling wind blew, and the methane squalls ripped your icy fingers from the ropes that kept you anchored to the cliff.   Retreat was nearly impossible, the rope below was gone as soon as you recovered it.   Ahead and upward was the only choice, and the more frightened you were, the more your hands would shake, and the slower you'd be.   Control your fear, and you'd make the summit faster.   Shake and tremble, and you'd still be climbing after nightfall, as the temperature plummeted and the rock turned to featureless blank slate before your eyes.

Climb it often enough, and you came to realise that fear was itself the enemy, the thing that would truly kill you.   The cliff itself was indifferent to your fate — only fear would grasp your throat with treacherous fingers and squeeze until you died.   Facing such things, soon fearlessness became a habit.   With meditation and training, the elders insisted, it soon became possible to forget why fear was even necessary in the first place.   Too much choice was frightening.   Those who were happiest were those who realised that life was like the climb — an endless effort, against wind and gravity, with no hope of return.   Accept your fate, abandon all hopeful desires, and be still.

The cruiser landed by a main tower and rolled through checkpoints into a separate carpark.   Trace ignored it all, and watched the newsnets chasing various Debogandes at work and home, reporters shouting questions, then shut down by security guards.   Apparently journalists were allowed to ask all the confronting and nasty questions they liked so long as they didn't ask them of Fleet.   A lawyer read a statement from Alice Debogande. 'Innocent of all charges', was the gist of it.   The implication was not spelled out — that the whole thing was fixed. No doubt the lawyers would tell Madam Debogande that such statements were not wise at this time.

The cruiser rolled to a halt, and Trace got out with her escort. They passed security getting into the carpark elevator, then more security when they got out at the detention level. Big double doors and body screens got them into the shiny bland corridors beyond. They'd be keeping Erik down here somewhere. As they'd been keeping the Captain before him. If HQ wished it, Erik could easily meet a similar fate.

They took her to an interrogation room, bland and featureless, save the big one-way mirror and cameras at the ceiling. There she sat for half an hour, unmoving with her eyes closed, until an interrogator entered. He was an army Colonel, Trace saw as she opened her eyes. She didn't recognise the name, nor cared to recall it.

"Major," he said, taking a seat opposite, a slate screen on the table between them. "Do you know why you're here?"

"Yes," said Trace. Perhaps he was uncertain, given that she was meditating, and neither particularly cooperative, nor particularly involved. Some might view that as guilt. Possibly quite a few of these people did not know that it was all a stitchup. They believed the LC was guilty because HQ had set it up that way. But she doubted the Colonel would be so naive. HQ would make certain one of their own was sent to interrogate her, to find out the score, and how much trouble she was likely to make. If he deemed 'a lot', then they'd have to find a way to deal with her too. Only how did you blackmail a Kulina, who desired for herself not even safety?

"And why *are* you here, Major?" pressed the Colonel. He was a big man with a big neck that swallowed his chin. Trace wondered what compromises such men made with their lives, to wear that uniform, yet to participate in *this*. And once begun, where those compromises would stop, if anywhere.

"To find the answers to questions," Trace answered honestly.

"Which questions?"

"My own questions."

The Colonel considered her for a moment. Trace wondered if he were uplinked, being fed questions from outside. Perhaps from behind the one way glass. "Look, Major," he said, with a kinder, more conversational tone. "This is an unfortunate situation." His pause invited her to agree. Trace just looked at him. "We all know the loyalty of Kulina officers to Fleet. But we also know the loyalties that develop between officers on the same vessel in wartime. What I'd like to do in this briefing today is establish some facts about Lieutenant Commander Debogande, and then see where you stand after that."

"My loyalties are absolutely clear," said Trace.

"Really?" said the Colonel. "Please continue."

"And my goals are also absolutely clear," she added. "To me at least."

"And?" With the faintest trace of impatience.

"To get here," Trace explained. "In this room."

The Colonel frowned. "To what purpose?"

"To do this." She grabbed him across the table, yanked him over it, and broke his neck with a twist. Then she hurdled the table, smashed one guard to the midriff, then judo-threw the other over her shoulder as he grabbed her, depriving him of a weapon in the process. The first guard went for his own, so she shot him, then put a spread of five shots through the glass. The window was tough, but the bullets made holes big enough for a uniformed arm to smash the rest without injury, revealing several officers sprawled and scrambling on the floor.

One had her pistol out so Trace shot her, side-kicked a spacer captain into a wall, then grabbed the Admiral off the floor and shoved the gun up under his chin. "Where's LC Debogande?" she asked him.

"You fool!" he hissed, eyes wild with terror and disbelief. "Don't you know who I am?"

"I know exactly who you are, Admiral Kennet," said Trace. "But karma rules us both at this moment, and one more dead officer hardly weighs the scales. LC Debogande, where is he?" No reply.

Trace shot him in the foot, then put the hot muzzle back under his jaw as he screamed. "Where?"

"Level two, C-21!" he hissed between sobs. Trace smacked his head against the wall and dropped him. Then she opened the door to the observation room, and ran out. Alarm klaxons were howling, and lights flashed red. Immediately there were two armed guards up the corridor coming to a halt and raising pistols at her. Trace opened fire, fading her stance from high right to low left and a shoulder crouch against the wall. She'd been good at that since age nine, and with both her targets down, she took off running once more.

Across the next corridor too fast for anyone to shoot at her, then left down stairs and hurdling the flight across to the lower level. She landed two steps up and rolled to avoid snapping her ankle. Broke her fall with a free arm and looked right then fast left from the floor. Another couple of guards tried to aim at her and she shot one, backrolled to her feet and pressed against the corridor wall, moving one way while aiming back the other. The other guard wasn't reappearing, so she ran ten yards then pressed to the wall again… sure enough the sound of running footsteps brought him out for a clear shot at her back, only to find her braced against a wall and putting two through his chest.

The speaker system was now announcing something, calling her name, telling her to stop in the vain hope she was stupid enough to listen. As though stopping now could possibly stop them from executing her if they caught her. And probably the LC too, now that she'd started shooting they had a perfect excuse to get him caught in the crossfire. But using the speakers was stupid of them, because now every guard in the complex knew exactly who they were chasing. Many would probably stop trying very hard to find her.

Another guard she predictably found sheltering at a corner ahead… but too close, shooting at point blank against an expert was even harder than shooting at extreme range. She went around him, took his leg with an arm to his chest and crashed him to the ground hard enough to stun. She grabbed his collar, dragged for several doors, then propped him upright with an armlock before room C-21.

"Key the door," she told him, and he did that.

"Please don't kill me!" he gasped.

"That's out of my hands," Trace told him. She pushed him first into the doorway, and was now in the plastic-partitioned half of a detention cell. There were two guards on the far side, pistols out and yelling at her to stop. And LC Debogande, in wrist and ankle restraints on the bed, looking otherwise unhurt. Trace kicked the chair into the doorway, to block the door in case someone closed it by remote. The doors weren't heavy enough to break a chair, this was light detention, not maximum security. "Key the door," she told her prisoner.

"Don't do it!" yelled a guard on the far side, pistol trembling. "Don't you do it!"

"Key the door or I'll start blowing holes in you," Trace told him. He reached his trembling palm to the reader, ID card in hand. "You two, shut your mouths and put your guns down or I'll kill you."

Fear on both faces, battling with duty. And possibly pride, given there were three of them, all told. "Okay!" said one, raising his hands. "Okay, we're putting our guns down!" They did it very slowly.

Trace didn't have time to wait, every second in this room was getting her trapped, if someone worked up the nerve to come up the corridor behind. Unlikely for a few moments at least, lesser soldiers always froze when people started dying. The plastic door opened, and Trace pushed the guard ahead of her as a shield.

One of the two inside abruptly changed his mind and dove sideways, angling for a shot. It surprised Trace not at all, and she shot him halfway through the move. But her response exposed her to the second man, who also aimed. Trace threw her shield at him as the gun went off. The shield-man fell, exposing the remaining guard for a desperate second at Debogande's bedside. Trace blew his head all over the wall, then knelt in the mess to retrieve keys and unlock the LC on the bed.

Debogande was swearing and shaking, badly shocked and spattered with gore. "Oh good god," he muttered as Trace removed the restraints and gave him a gun and ammo from a dead guard. "Major what have you done?"

"Do you want to live?" Trace asked him, pausing for a hard look in his eyes. "Then do exactly what I say, when I say it, and kill anyone who tries to stop us. Let's go."

There wasn't time for anything more. All spacer crew knew basic close quarters combat, but few had actually done it, and none of those by choice. Worse, they didn't have a marine's combat augments or gene-mods — a pilot like the LC would have reflexes every bit her equal, but total physical coordination was a different thing again. He was definitely going to get in her way, and she'd have been much better off alone, but Trace didn't make a habit of worrying about things she couldn't help.

She cleared the corridor first, then set off running with the LC behind, keeping 45-degrees ahead so he wouldn't block her view back. A fist up at the next cross-corridor, and he stopped, but on the wrong side of the corridor instead of behind her. She cleared the corner with a fast look, then ran on and angled left for the next stairs... someone dropped a stun grenade from above, and the LC might have panicked but she grabbed him and spun him neatly about the next corner, and had time to clear both ways before it exploded.

She put her gun around the corner to fire blind up the stairs at whoever might be thinking of following that grenade, loaded a new clip and ran up the next corridor to the security entrance, gesturing the LC to keep low as they approached. Sure enough the guards on the far side saw movement and opened fire with assault rifles, big rounds exploding windows and kicking open doors. Trace scrambled on all fours where the thick wall gave better cover than the windows, and put her back to a security scanner.

"We have to go around!" the LC insisted, wide-eyed and terrified as she'd expect from someone unaccustomed to firefights, but holding his nerve despite it. Trace ignored him... there were only two well armed troopers, they just made a lot of noise with those rifles, and the one on the left was exposed in the wrong spot by the outside wall. Trace rolled through the open first security door, crawled to the second, waited for a pause in fire, then pushed the first door open enough to show the left-side trooper, but not his friend.

One shot put him down, his buddy fired on panicked full auto until his gun clicked empty, whereupon Trace swung fully around the doorway and shot him too. Then she ran quickly, got a better weapon and more ammo, handed the other to the ashen-faced LC as he followed, then hit the elevator call button.

"We're taking the elevator?" Debogande asked in disbelief.

"Yes."

"Could use a fucking grenade." He checked his rifle with shaking hands.

"Do you see any grenades?"

"No."

"Then be quiet."

The elevator arrived — empty, and Trace got in and hit the parking level. Debogande leaned against a car wall, breathing fast and hard as the doors closed. "You don't think they'll slaughter us at the parking level when we get out?" he asked.

"We're not getting out at parking level." She hit emergency stop and shouldered her rifle. "Boost please." The LC got the idea and she stood on his hands to open the emergency access hatch above, then wriggled out. Helped the LC up after her, then grabbed the shaft cable and climbed fast. If someone overrode the emergency stop beneath them, they'd be in trouble, but she didn't think they were working that fast, or that the elevator would work with the top hatch open. The higher she climbed, the better her uplink signal became.

"*I'm here,*" she said as the connection came clear. "*Let's go.*" And she waited, hanging on the cable opposite the doors two levels above the main parking level. The LC hung on grimly beneath her, thankfully breathing too hard to make more useless suggestions.

A massive crash from outside the elevator doors, and yells. Trace leaped to the doorway and pulled the doors open — with augmented strength it wasn't hard. On the far side was the main lobby to one of the big HQ towers... only the glass wall was in shattered ruin all over the polished marble floor, and people were running everywhere for cover. The cause of it, a civvie cruiser, sat waiting for them on the marble, doors open and two armed marines covering with pistols. Trace and Erik ran, threw themselves in as the marines bundled after, and the driver powered them up and out the shattered glass wall.

The driver was Lieutenant Dale, and he kept them low, howling across the memorial yard toward the distant Shiwon towers at head-height in case the defensive emplacements were active yet. It was early evening, the grounds still full of uniforms despite the fading light, and Trace didn't think they'd shoot so low over everyone's heads.

"LC, you okay?" asked Private Tong in the rear seat. Because the LC was still covered in blood and bits of brain. He hadn't fired a shot, Trace noted, and that was just as well, given he could have hit anything, her included.

"I'm okay," said Debogande. "Holy fuck. You're all in on this?" As the cruiser rocked a turn, accelerating and now climbing for some altitude as they howled over suburbs.

"Major set it up," Tong confirmed. "Put us on standby when you got arrested."

"You saw this *coming?*" Debogande asked incredulously.

"They're called emergency precautions," said Trace. "Something's always coming."

"That's why she's the best," Dale shut down the argument. "What's the damage Major?"

"Killed a bunch of them. They tried to stitch me up too."

"Was it necessary?" Debogande asked, still trying to get his head around it. As though still in a daze, and expecting himself to wake up at any moment. "Major, you killed all those people! Fleet people!"

"Hey asshole!" Dale snapped. "Those Fleet people just declared war on us, you get that? They declared war on *you*, on your family, on our Captain, on all of us. They murdered the Captain!"

"Are we right to go at the spaceport?" Trace asked Dale, not especially interested in the LC's distress.

"We're rolling," Dale confirmed.   "We'll be there in five minutes and just hope they don't shoot us down first."

"Over the suburbs, I don't think so," said Trace.

"Hey LC," said Tong.   "You really *didn't* kill the Captain, did you?"

"Oh that's great Private," said Dale.   "Real useful time to ask."   Tong shrugged and handed Debogande a cloth.

The LC wiped himself down.   "We won't make the military spaceport," he muttered.   "They'll shoot us down over the tarmac, those air defence systems can kill a fruit fly at two klicks."

"We're not going to the military spaceport," said Dale.

"You've got a civvie ride?   Up to *Phoenix*?"

"Yep."   The Shiwon skyline shone in the night to their right. They were headed north-west, past the main city, heading for Lei Quan Spaceport.   Down below, the main freeway from the military port to Shiwon central, that they'd come along on the way to the parade.   To their right, a circle of lights marked Memorial Hill, directly above the freeway.

"What about *Phoenix* crew?" Debogande asked, scrubbing the worst of it off his uniform.   "What about Huang, is she in on this too?"

"Nope," said Dale, searching traffic net for signs of pursuit. "She made it clear early she wasn't interested.   All marines 'cept for us went up yesterday.   Second-shift crew's still up there, some of first and third went by civvie lift as well to Fajar Station."

"Without telling me?"

"After you got arrested," said Trace.   "Docked at station just a few hours ago."

"How... how do you get *Phoenix*'s crew off Homeworld on civvie transport?   With HQ locking everything down?"

"Your sister helped."

"Which one?"

"Lisbeth.   Allied Transit, your local hauler.   She chartered one for us.   Well, two, actually."

"And HQ didn't try to stop you?"

"Four hours ago getting *Phoenix* crew off Homeworld probably sounded like a good idea to them. No media on *Phoenix*, no politicians, it's quarantine. They'd thought."

"And what is it now?" said Debogande, disbelieving.

"Well I don't know about you," said Trace, checking her rifle mag as the bright lights of the civvie spaceport lit the horizon ahead. "But after what we just pulled to get you out, I'd suggest we run like hell."

"Oh great," he said tiredly. "You needed a captain. With Huang out, I'm the only command level pilot left. That's why you busted me out."

"Yes," Trace admitted. "That, and you're our last remaining command officer, and we'll need you if we're ever going to get to the bottom of this."

"And root out the fuckers who've planned this whole mess," Dale growled, "and kill the fucking lot of them."

"The way this is starting to look," said the LC, "I think that might take a revolution. Or a civil war."

No one in the cruiser had anything to say to that. A few days ago, they'd thought the war was over.

CHAPTER 7

The Lei Quan Spaceport was a huge, sprawling facility with four main terminals around a central traffic island, all joined by freeways and maglevs. It was busy tonight, traffic crowding the roads and big shuttles rolling upon the taxiways, or locked into the big, covered gates for refuel and reloading.

Dale flew them at the far perimeter where the cargo vessels waited aside from the main terminals, as the cruiser's navcomp squawked perimeter warnings and threats of action against airspace violation. But here along a line of waiting cargo vessels was a big shuttle with running lights flashing and thrust nozzles angled down. Dale put coms on speaker and then they could all hear the ongoing shouting between Spaceport traffic control.

"*AT-7, you have no clearance for departure, I repeat, no clearance for departure! Turn off your engines and stand down immediately!*"

"*Lei Quan control, this is AT-7, we are leaving in three minutes, either make a space for us or expect it to get very tight and crowded.*"

Erik's heart stopped at the sound of that familiar voice. "That's Lisbeth! What the hell is she doing here?"

"She got us the ship," said Trace. "I told you."

"You said she *arranged* it! You didn't say she was *on* it!"

"She's a grown woman LC, she can do what she wants."

The perimeter fence flashed beneath them, the cruiser slowing even now as it came alongside the row of transports and flared toward a landing at the shuttle's angular nose. They touched, doors open in the warm Shiwon night to let in an earsplitting howl of engines, as the marines and Erik all clambered out. Several yellow vested groundstaff ran to them, yelling and waving them off, then changed their minds at the sight of levelled rifles.

Erik ran up the ramp and into the empty shuttle hold, then into the left access and up the narrow, curving staircase that circled the forward starboard mains. Then ducked out of the low doorway and into cockpit access, finding two marines strapped into engineering posts and awaiting takeoff. Past them was the cockpit, a narrow arrangement of pilot and co-pilot one behind the other, the pilot offset so the co-pilot could squeeze past.

A slim figure squeezed out of the pilot's chair and flung herself at him. "Oh thank god!" Lisbeth gasped. "You're okay! The Major got you out, I knew she would!" With a young civilian's innocence of the horror that entailed.

"Lis." Erik hugged her back. "Okay Lis, out. We're leaving."

"I'm coming too!"

Erik stared. "No you're not! Lis, we're fugitives! We have to…"

"Yes you're fugitives!" she exclaimed. "And they will blow you out of the sky without me! If I'm on board they won't dare!"

"Guys, we have to go," Thakur said urgently at their backs. "LC, Lisbeth's our willing hostage for the moment, it's the only way we'll get out of here. That's the plan."

Erik wanted to hit something, but everything was so crazy and the time for violence was past. And hit who? Lisbeth? He'd rather hit Thakur, even though it could be his last use of that arm for a while.

He swore and pushed past her into the pilot's seat — a fast glance over controls and systems showed the pre-flight was all done and they were ready to go. He buckled in as Lisbeth pushed past into the co-pilot's seat up front. She was licensed on family shuttles, one of the first perks she'd insisted on to go with her engineering degree.

"When was your last launch?" Erik asked her.

"Um, I did a run with Trioli last month to Fajar Station as co-pilot, he gave me an A-minus."

"So where the fuck is Trioli? He's our damn pilot, why isn't he helping?"

"I had to leave him in the dark," said Lisbeth. "He wouldn't have gone for it Erik, he'd have told Mother and she'd have grounded us."

"Dammit." Erik powered the thrusters, and watched the redlines build. "Well my shuttle flying's so rusty we'll be lucky I don't put us through the control tower." He pulled on the headset, and activated full coms. "Everyone buckle up, we're leaving."

Lei Quan control was still issuing terse instructions. "Lis, talk to them would you?" And now navcomp was showing him some nasty-looking traffic at high speed coming from the military spaceport. "And make it convincing, because it looks like they've just sent gunships after us."

"Hello Lei Quan control," came Lisbeth's voice from behind him, "this is Lisbeth Debogande. I repeat, this is Lisbeth Debogande. I am a willing passenger on shuttle AT-7. Please rebroadcast this to all Fleet vessels, I repeat, I am a willing passenger on shuttle AT-7. If we are shot down, Fleet will be at war with the entire Debogande family. Tell them that."

A perplexed silence from coms. The poor tower controllers would have no idea what was going on, only that an Allied Transit shuttle was leaving recklessly without authorisation, and Fleet were telling them to keep it grounded or else.

"They'll know," said Erik. "Fleet will be patched in and listening to everything whether control want it or not." His eyes flashed across mains indicators, control systems, nav, coms, all on the display before the forward windshield. Nothing like as advanced as Fleet shuttles, his eye had to move a lot more between dash and HUD to find the relevant data... but everything checked green and they had to move.

He powered thrust and they lifted with a shuddering roar, any groundcrew not yet clear now scampering to become so as massive jet-wash blasted the apron. He wondered if they should kill running lights, but decided no — with this traffic around they might need it. A slow pivot atop their axis of thrust, you couldn't rush anything when hovering three hundred tonnes atop a column of hot air. Then facing out toward the suburbs, he violated every rule traffic control had and swung thrust forward.

More alarms on the nav screen, and squawks in his ears from the tower, but they accelerated fast enough that as they passed over the perimeter fence the thrust was already angling behind them, and cars and houses were spared the low altitude blast, though not by much. "Lis, get me *Phoenix* position, where the hell are we?"

The gunships were curling around to target them — whether they were locked or not he couldn't tell, the civvie shuttle had no military systems, nor any form of countermeasures. If the gunships fired, they'd know about it when the missiles hit. Though bringing down a three hundred tonne shuttle over suburbia didn't seem likely.

A course-plot came up on nav as Erik poured on power and altitude. "Well crap," he said conversationally. "*Phoenix* is on the other side of the damn planet. Good timing Major."

"*Stop whining,*" came her reply from the back.

"Lis, orbit will be variable, I'm going to shave as much time off as possible but it'll be hard and nasty, we'll break every orbital lane code there is."

Lisbeth's projected trajectory began out over the ocean, but if staying over populated areas was going to give Fleet another reason not to shoot at them, Erik would use it. He powered up full as they passed a thousand meters and thrust locked into full forward, and the shuttle thundered and shook. The speed wasn't actually so great, the very earliest chemical rockets in human spaceflight's infancy accelerated faster and were a lot more aerodynamic. But mobile fusion meant you didn't run out of fuel for nearly a full day's burn if necessary... and you could get to orbit at walking acceleration if you had unlimited gas. Soon they were climbing hard, cloud layers flashing by and falling behind, acceleration increasing as atmospheric pressure dropped.

"Lis, you got that orbital feed?" It came up, a display of all the orbital traffic across their path... and good lord it was tight. Most of the long-term stuff was parked in higher orbit, he'd have to keep it low. Nearly everything orbited spinward, by long tradition even now that propulsion technology made it no longer necessary, but with *Phoenix* currently on the planet's far side he was going to do a polar route that was going to cross an awful lot of higher orbits. "Well that looks interesting."

He rolled them onto their backs in the upper atmosphere, heading north along their plotted course as their velocity passed mach four. *"LC, status?"* asked Thakur. On a civvie shuttle without her familiar uplinks, she was blind back there.

"Quiet," Erik told her, to see how she liked it. "Lis, that thrust alignment seems a little off, run the diagnostic please."

"I see it," she said. "I think it's the number three gimbal hasn't locked out entirely, just watch it."

They left the atmosphere completely, and now the acceleration truly started. In a few minutes they were passing mach 24, orbital velocity on Homeworld. Erik kept the thrust maxed, and they began building plus-orbital speed, which would throw them out on an elliptical orbit if he didn't correct. He did, pushing the nose down at ever-increasing increments as the thrust continued, sliding them around the planet sideways like a teenager drifting a car on a gravel road. The acceleration remained a constant 4Gs, and in minutes they were speeding far beyond safety requirements for heavily trafficked orbits.

"We've got company," said Lisbeth in a strained voice as they approached Homeworld's north pole, and the first sunlight glinted upon white icecaps along the horizon rim. "Combat shuttle on high-G approach behind." As navcomp identified it for Erik to see — sure enough, while everything else was whizzing by on previous orbit, this one was trailing them, and apparently burning much harder than the civvie shuttle could.

"They don't need to be tailing us to shoot us down," Erik replied. "A long range missile would do it." Sunlight grew to a glare as they passed the pole, the forward view polarising to shield their eyes. At the turnover point Erik kicked the shuttle's tail around and over, still thrusting to slow them while skidding them around onto a new orbit, chasing Fajar Station and *Phoenix*. Barely fifteen minutes at these velocities, approaching at plus twenty thousand kilometres an hour.

Five minutes later, *Phoenix* called, in the form of Lieutenant Shilu, second-shift coms officer. "This is LC Debogande," Erik replied. The signal was bounced off various remote coms in orbit, there were so many up here that Fleet couldn't jam them all without shutting down all orbital coms — a dangerous proposition in a system this crowded. "How is everything with you, *Phoenix*?"

"*Full complement of marines aboard,*" came the reply. "*Elements of first and third are coming aboard now, they're commandeering various vehicles from Fajar Station to do it.*" Erik wondered if that meant they were doing it at gunpoint. There were other uniformed and armed personnel on Fajar Station, it didn't seem a safe situation. "*Sir we're locked in standoff with several nearby armed vessels, we've got full weapons lock and engines active. We could come and get you if you liked.*"

"No, you need to stay close to station to pick up our crew and gain protection in their shadow. We'll be there in ten. What's the situation with our crew on station?"

"*Sir, anyone stopping them will be committing an aggressive act against Phoenix. We've told them.*" So *Phoenix* was threatening to fire on station. Dear lord. Firing on a crowded civvie station was what the bad guys did in the movies. If HQ didn't have enough to demonise them before, they sure would after this. "*We've got a shuttle at the hub, it's getting the last of them. Sir, a lot didn't come up. We're short about a hundred crew, even if we get everyone aboard.*"

It was actually more than Erik had thought. They were being asked to go renegade. Most probably just wanted to go home to their families, and now to sacrifice everything on the say-so of Major Thakur and LC Debogande... Well the marines would go. Thakur said all her marines were aboard and that wasn't surprising, they'd charge into a star if she told them to. But while spacers respected her, Thakur was still a marine, and spacers didn't take orders from marines unless bullets were flying. Most of third-shift would probably do it for LC Debogande, he thought — but third-shift was just twenty people, all bridge crew and reserves, compared to about three hundred each for first and second-shift. Third-shift commanders were often teased as 'Captain Appendix', because compared to the vital bodily organs of first and second-shift, that was what third-shift was.

But all shifts had loved the Captain. And now Major Thakur was telling them the Captain had been murdered by HQ — unthinkable if anyone else had said it, but Kulina never lied about their age, let alone anything serious. Lots of them would have been asking themselves which loyalty was superior — the loyalty to Fleet, or to the Captain. Most would decide the latter, but even then, to throw one's life away just on the brink of peacetime, for a cause that had nothing to do with them and everything to do with the powerful, connected officers who commanded them...

Damn right they were short a hundred. And Commander Huang's second-shift had been posted to *Phoenix* for docking duty, before any of this mess had happened. If they were given the option, probably a third of them would get off right now if they could. Which raised the question — should he let them?

They approached Fajar Station tail first with thrust blazing, and now station traffic control was squealing at them that this was most unsafe, and legal action would follow. Erik wondered exactly who they thought they'd prosecute — his corpse? Or his mother's still very-living body, with her army of powerful lawyers and pockets so deep they accessed alternative dimensions?

Fajar Station was quite a sight — five kilometres wide with its rim docking gantries full of weight-supported ships, nestled up to station in a nose-first ring as the station spun. But all traffic was now halted, save for a few runners and shuttles, because here parked barely a kilometre off the enormous spinning twin-wheel was *Phoenix* — four times the size of any standard freighter, two-thirds engines and jump-lines, the remainder a cage-like shell for a rotating crew cylinder, while the shell itself bristled with weapons, external pods and combat grapples for attached shuttles and aggressive interceptions. Even at zero-V that armament could shred a big station in minutes, and ships in seconds. Thus no one in the general vicinity so much as twitching.

"Whoa," said Lisbeth as they got close. "I just... the com feed just got taken over, I think... is that *Phoenix*?"

"Just put it through," said Erik, watching the mass of stand-off traffic now either leaving, or holding position so as not to risk

Phoenix blowing them to bits.   There in close parking orbit was *Annalea,* a strike cruiser with half *Phoenix*'s complement and a quarter its firepower, yet deadly enough at these ranges.   Also *Reggio* and *George F Latz,* fellow Alpha Squadron Firsters. "*Phoenix* this is the LC, who's in command on *Annalea, Reggio* and *Latz?*"

"*Um... one LC and two commanders, all three captains are downworld.*"   Good news at least when they ran — these three would be reluctant to follow without their captains, and most of their crew.

"Anyone up here have full crew and command staff?"

"*I'm sorry sir, we don't have full records on everyone.*" Because Fleet, of course, didn't tell lower ranks shit. And outside of combat ops, ships tended to mind their business. "*We're just asking around, getting the gossip.   It's likely some of the outsystem ships have full crew.*"   Because, being located in the outer system meant they were doing security, and hadn't participated in the parade and celebrations.

"And no one's talking?"   It was hard to speak, flat on your back at 4-Gs for the past thirty minutes.   His augments helped, keeping blood in the brain and muscles from cramping, but still it was exhausting.

"*No sir, not a word.   We're not in the loop of whatever HQ's saying, but we broke into their channels — they're talking a lot about you murdering the Captain, and nothing at all about how you escaped from custody.*"   There was a hopeful note to Lieutenant Shilu's observation.

"That's because Major Thakur busted me out personally, and my guess is they don't want it known." Because Major Thakur was known to be incorruptible.   Any number of people would believe he'd murdered the Captain, because he was a Debogande with all the shady big-power interests that brought into play.   People would always buy conspiracy theories about well-connected power players. But if it were widely known what Major Thakur had done to get him out, a lot of people would start doubting HQ's version.

"Sir. Should we broadcast that? We've got an audience out here."

Heck of a thought, Lieutenant Shilu. But there was that shuttle, docked at Fajar Station hub, loading the last of their crew, and very vulnerable to Fleet's sudden whims. "Let's wait until we've got the rest of our people aboard, Lieutenant."

"Aye sir. We've got you on near-scan now, confirm your current approach as within combat parameters." Meaning he wasn't breaking any rules according to the kind of rules *Phoenix* was accustomed to running by. *"Sir, what is your manifest?"*

"Myself, my sister Lisbeth, Major Thakur, Lieutenant Dale, Private Tong, Private Carville, two marines I didn't get a good look at, and... Lis, you bring anyone else?" Because he'd gone straight past upper level crew without looking.

"My four personal security," Lisbeth said weakly, her voice strained. It was at about this time, in Academy runs when recruits did a 4-G push for the first time, that you started wishing you'd black out and wake up when it was all over. In a pilot's chair, that wasn't recommended if you wanted to graduate.

"Copy that, four more civvies plus your sister." God knew what they'd make of *that.*

At three klicks out Erik cut thrust and flipped them end-over so they could see where they were going. Homeworld glowed blue and white to one side as they approached the night-side once more, while Balise glowed huge and red on the other. The colossal steel bulk of Fajar Station rotated slowly by, twin wheels affixed to a central axle, fifty berths to each wheel-side, two hundred in all with smaller vessels squeezed in the middle between the wheels, larger on the outer rims. Fajar had over three million people at any given moment, a lot of them transitory from on and off those vessels.

Phoenix's com feed now linked into nav, and gave him ship names, mostly civvie and mostly human, though three of the two hundred were chah'nas, and another two kuhsi. In parking orbit nearby, another hundred and seventy one, and quite a bit of that was military. Insystem freighters were thankfully few, they mostly used the smaller industrial stations that processed the bulk freight most insystem traffic dealt in. But some of that was Debogande-owned...

"Shuttle's undocked," said Lisbeth, and Erik looked and saw that with his own eyes, a tiny silver speck lifting from the station axle's huge protruding docking cone. "I think they're going to beat us there."

Manifest came through on the shuttle — Lieutenant Chia was the pilot, one of the shuttle specialists and very skilled. The rest were mostly first-shift plus a couple of his third-shift crew... Dean Chong was there, his buddy who'd come to the Debogande party after the parade. Several others, all he'd be very glad to have back.

And then Chia was on coms. *"All Fleet ships, this is Lieutenant Chia commanding shuttle PH-2. We are commencing flight return to Phoenix with thirty-six Phoenix crew aboard."* It was *general* coms, Erik saw — Chia was talking to everyone, on general frequency. *"Request that you do not point guns at us, we're all friends out here, and if you seriously think LC Debogande killed our Captain you've got rocks in your head."*

Erik's blood ran cold, and his heart nearly stopped. "Oh god no Chia, shut up!" But he dared not broadcast it.

"Our traffic is that Major Thakur busted our LC out of the brig herself, and if you think she can be bought by the LC's money you've got even BIGGER rocks in your head..."

A flash came from station. The silver dot departing the docking cone vanished in a bright flash. All transmission stopped.

"LC this is Phoenix!" Second Lieutenant Shilu yelled in shock. *"They fired on PH-2, she's hit!"*

"*Phoenix* this is your commander!" Erik replied. "Find who fired that shot and destroy them! That is a direct order!"

"Sir... sir, I think..."

"LC this is Shahaim," came a familiar voice — Lieutenant Suli Shahaim, first-shift Helm, technically fourth-ranked on Phoenix, and acting captain. *"We fix that shot came from a docked ship, Berth 30, that's Gloria out of Halifax, armed Fleet merchant."*

"Lock a viper solution and strike with terminating round."

"Sir, target is affixed to station..."

"I fucking know that Lieutenant! Either you kill it, or every docked ship under Fleet control will assume they can fire on *Phoenix* vessels without retaliation and then this shuttle is dead, and *Phoenix* will be under fire shortly thereafter!" He flipped channels to general broadcast. "This is LC Debogande of *UFS Phoenix*, unarmed *Phoenix* shuttle PH-2 has been destroyed by a shot from Fajar Station, you all saw it. This is how HQ deals with anyone who speaks out of turn — first Captain Pantillo, then me, now thirty six innocent Fleet lives. Let this stand and you'll all be next. Advise Fajar Station in proximity to Berth 30, brace for impact." And he just hoped to god that Shahaim did actually fire, or he'd look like the biggest idiot possible.

A small flash from *Phoenix*'s side, and a small missile flew. A tiny fraction of *Phoenix*'s arsenal, arcing out wide as it acquired the plotted trajectory. "We're moving," Erik advised them, and hit thrust hard. "*Phoenix* we're coming in hot, prepare to leave, don't wait." Because however justified, they'd just fired on station, and in spacer moral code that was like punching your grandma. Of course, grandma wasn't supposed to stab you in the back with a steak knife either...

The gradually approaching warship suddenly came up real fast. Erik stared at the tumbling wreckage of PH-2 as they passed it... there were only fragments, it had been a mag-rail shot and at these ranges and velocities there wasn't much a shuttle could do about it. Thus his haste.

"Lisbeth!" As the shuttle hit midway, and he cut thrust once more and rolled for braking. "Get your mask on girl!" A flash on station, the missile striking, and the offending freighter lost a good portion of mass, and probably most of any lives aboard. "Get your mask on and give full control to your environmentals, we're not going to have time to make the bridge, we're going to have to ride out the run in the shuttle, you understand?" Because at 10-G thrust the body acquired all the utility of wet jello, and even blinking was an effort. And so was breathing... oh fuck. "Lis, when you took the shuttle course, you augmented for Gs, right?"

Thrust thundered them back in their seats once more, Erik squinted hard as he matched the cross-hairs on nav to what he saw via uplink in his head — *Phoenix*'s number-three docking grapples, back from the crew cylinder amid-ships before the engines.

"Yes!" Lisbeth said shakily. "Full G-augments, Daddy insisted!" Thank god. The human body wasn't designed for 10-Gs for more than a minute or two — at prolonged stretches it would kill an unaugmented person via unconsciousness and suffocation.

Crosshairs matched, Erik hit thrust for a final 6-G shove as they came in too fast, then cut, and the grapples clanged. "This is AT-7, we're aboard, grapple readings good!"

"This is Phoenix, we read green grapples on this side too."

"Punch it!" That was Shahaim, and *Phoenix*'s mains hit them with a hammer blow that made the shuttle's thrust feel like child's play. Erik thought someone was shooting, but his vision compressed in the Gs and made it hard to tell. He closed his eyes and fought for breath, short, hard gasps with muscles tensed head to foot. This was why all spacers loved uplink visuals — with his eyes closed he could see all main systems like a head up display, in high-G push it was priceless. But though he had a good feed, he didn't have command feed, and he couldn't see projected trajectory, or armscomp, or nav assessment... and damn he hated that. He hadn't even liked it much when Captain Pantillo was flying, and while Suli Shahaim was good, she wasn't the Captain.

There was a thud and lurch, and for a second he thought the grapples had broken — it was nearly impossible, but AT-7 was a civvie shuttle of slightly different configuration. Then a flash outside the windows, then some more... that was countermeasures, someone *was* shooting, but he didn't know if they were shooting back. Nav showed them already fifty klicks from station and accelerating fast... they couldn't pulse until about fifty thousand, the physics of FTL were brutal to ships that pulsed too deep in the gravity well. At 10-G, fifty klicks turned into fifty thousand in no time at all.

"Oh my god!" That was Lisbeth, in panic and pain. Ten-G at length was horrifying if you'd never done it before. You wanted to die, but couldn't lift a finger to kill yourself.

"Lis! Lisbeth, listen to me. I'm right here, you're going to be fine." Uplink vocals were just as important as visuals now, because even if you could move your jaw, you couldn't get a proper breath to push air through your larynx.

"How much longer?"

"A few minutes Lis, then we'll pulse and the thrust will come down a lot, I promise." Actually it didn't come down a lot, it came down a bit, but if lying to your sister was ever acceptable, it was acceptable now. *"We have to get clear of Homeworld and Balise's gravity both, you understand? We can't pulse until we're clear."*

Balise was only average-sized as gas giants went, but Homeworld was only its second-biggest moon. And now nav was showing a storm of insystem traffic, all of them cutting thrust and just hoping *Phoenix* would miss them. There were also a lot of rocks out here, and dust clouds and other very good reasons to approach insystem navigation a lot more cautiously than this. *Phoenix* was pretty good at vaporising small rocks, but at these speeds the auto-countermeasures didn't distinguish much between rocks and small ships.

The grind went on and on, and then everything inverted as the world caved in on itself...

...Lisbeth at age seven, at Academy graduation. Erik was in his dress uniform straight from the final parade. The families were assembled in the function room, everyone giving the Debogandes and their security a wide berth. But little Lisbeth had run to him, and he'd picked her up, and taken the little kuhsi doll she gave him. The doll fit in the palm of his hand, was cute and furry with big ears in a Fleet officer's uniform. For luck, she'd said, when you go to fight the tavalai. And had been a little disappointed that he wasn't going *immediately*, and that he'd still have another three years of training before they allowed him anywhere near a starship's controls...

…and out again, a blurring disorientation of everything coming back together, but not quite where it had been.

"*Pulse one,*" he said back to the others. "*Lisbeth, you okay? Lisbeth?*" A cockpit camera showed her unconscious, and probably just as well, as Gs were still 8.5. Nav showed them hurtling now, jump cycle having traded energy for velocity, over one percent of light and building. Hitting anything bigger than a grain of sand at this speed would kill the ship. *Phoenix*'s scanners were very good at spotting and evading all such grains, and countermeasures even better at evaporating anything they'd missed. In deeper space the odds of even grains of sand were astronomical, but this close in it was never safe…

…Lisbeth at age nineteen, crying before his deployment to *Phoenix.* Because somewhere in her teenage years the realisation had set in that her big brother wasn't immortal, and lots of people's big brothers and sisters weren't coming back. 'Don't worry Lis', he'd told her. '*Phoenix* is a legend, and Captain Pantillo's a genius. There's barely ten ships in the whole fleet as advanced as *Phoenix*. The tavalai won't know what hit them.'

…"*Second pulse!*" as they came back in. Shuttle's civvie nav was struggling now to display velocity, not equipped to measure at this scale. *Phoenix* feed showed them seventeen percent light, streaking into deep space beyond Balise. Gravitational detach approached, jump engines straining against the mass that kept them anchored to this particular piece of space-time fabric. Everything rattled and shook, and the light that he could glimpse through G-strained vision looked an odd colour… at this speed everything dopplered, light itself conceivable on a spectrum humans rarely saw. It occurred to him vaguely that Lieutenant Shahaim had never made a combat jump before, and that Phoenix's bridge crew was missing some of its usual members. If they'd been hit, as seemed likely, and something broke in mid-jump strain…

CHAPTER 8

"Pulse three!" The Gs were gone. His mouth was impossibly dry, and his vision refused to come clear. Like waking from a long sleep, aware that much time had passed, and looking for the time, or a window, to see if the sun was up, or some other indication of just how late it was. Uplink visual gave him time, but it was hard to focus. Without access to bridge nav he wasn't even sure where they'd gone, and hadn't the mental energy now to try to figure all the possible routes. Where the hell were they?

A velocity reading, much clearer on his uplink visual than normal vision — straight out of jump you always saw more clearly with your eyes closed. Point thirteen light... dammit Shahaim you're too fast! He patched into bridge coms with a conscious effort, he couldn't start directing them from outside, Shahaim had to be in full command, but point thirteen meant something was badly wrong...

"Helm, correction! Helm!"

"We're off! We're off! Nav, I need realignment, where the hell are we?"

"Scanning, all readings negative!"

"Engineering! Engines status!"

"Sir, I... I got red lights everywhere! We're not... jump lines not getting traction, we are not charged!"

And now Erik's heart was thudding harder, because if the jump engines were damaged and they couldn't dump velocity, the only hope of rescue was another FTL ship that could chase and rendezvous, and at this speed with no warning that was hard at best. And who the hell would want to rescue *them?*

"Navcomp says we're in! Argitori System, positive fix!"

"I'm not getting that fucking navbuoy, where is it? Oh hang on, I got it... we are five point three nine offline, we must have come out of that fucking thing sideways!" That was Shahaim, and she sounded panicked. When you were in flying a warship through combat jump at sizeable fractions of light speed, panicked wasn't

good. Argitori System was a good idea, it was big with no habitable planets but lots of Spacer settlements, lots of rocks and dust and lots of places to hide. On the other hand, lots of rocks and dust made these speeds fatal, and if they couldn't slow down soon before they got into the thick stuff, they wouldn't need rescuing.

"Engineering, status!"

"We're on it! Rerouting now... give us a moment!"

A minute crawled by, agonisingly slow. Erik examined Argitori on uplink to reacquaint himself. Thirteen planets, four gas giants in the middle, some rocky-but-nasty inner worlds circling an amazing trinary star system of two class-A monsters at the centre circled by a smaller class-M further out. The gas giants had about a hundred moons between them, and those held a busy population of about sixteen million settlers. Debogande Inc had interests here, Erik recalled a large refinery operation and a lot of precious metals, plus a half share on a large colony, but couldn't recall which.

"Power up, the jump lines are back!"

"Stand by, dumping now!"

Pulse out, then back in again, less violent than acceleration but violent enough... nav now showed velocity closer to two percent light, and if they were where nav thought they were, time for perhaps some minutes' coasting.

"Shahaim this is the LC," said Erik, trying to inject some strength into his dry voice. "Are we clear to move about? I want to come up." Because he couldn't see everything from down here that she could see up there.

"LC, my plan is to shut down and run silent, I don't see any hostiles ahead of us, nothing could have beat us through jump." Because nothing went faster in jump than *Phoenix*, except another ship the same class, and there were precious few of them. *"Free to move about."*

Erik unbuckled, floated up in zero-G, then pulled himself over the chairback to go check on Lisbeth. She was out, eyes closed and facemask firm — he checked her pulse and it was fast but steady. He unbuckled her, but then Thakur was floating in with sure, steady grasps of her hands.

"LC you get to the bridge," she said. "I'll take Lisbeth to Medbay and an acceleration sling." And when he didn't move immediately, "Go now!" But not unkindly, edging him aside to check the unconscious girl's vitals and mask attachment.

Erik hauled himself away with difficulty, away from the bridge to where Dale and others already had the dorsal hatch open and tight. "Someone shut down the shuttle," he told them, "she's still on standby." And pulled himself through the hatch into a blast of freezing air from the umbilical tube.

Then past berthing crew at the grapples, and tight space between bulkheads, secured with netting and acceleration slings where marines could ride out manoeuvres while waiting to board a shuttle. He overhanded up the corridor, past zero-G equipment bays and outfitting where a lot of marines' gear was secured, then finally made the core hatch. The umbilical lines were humming, and he grabbed a passing handle and made sure to tuck his hands in as it yanked him up the core tube. The space was narrow and always claustrophobic, but it was the only way to move between the gravitational quarters and the non-G midships when the crew cylinder was engaged. Some designs used elevator cars, but on a ship with as many crew as *Phoenix*, no one had time to sit around waiting for cars to arrive.

He passed delta bulkhead, then got off at gamma-b, main-quarter, over-handed fast down the ladder until rotational gravity began to shove him into a wall, then headfirst, and he flipped over and slid down feet first with increasing speed down several levels, jumping to a new ladder each time. Finally he hit floor and ran into a corridor, heart-in-mouth the way you always were when moving about in combat — a hard thrust here would turn a ten meter corridor into a lethal drop, head first. Most crew injuries in combat were impact-related, self-inflicted by manoeuvre, and some huge number of spacers had died over the ages by simply being out of a chair or acceleration sling when bad news appeared on scan.

Up A-main corridor and straight into the bridge, a wide, narrow rectangle with rows of seating posts out on either side, and the Captain's chair in the middle.

"Commander on the bridge!" someone yelled, and then Shahaim was pulling herself from the chair, and holding the helmet for him to grab and pull on. It settled with an automatic correction of straps, then a sudden blaze of 3D visual that showed him everything he'd been missing down in the shuttle — position, trajectory, rows of blinking status lights and highlight bars. He strapped himself in, as Shahaim helped, and grasped the twin joysticks to feel the familiar interplay of interlocking controls.

"LC has command," he announced.

"You have command," Shahaim acknowledged, and retreated to a secondary post.

"Status by post," he requested, in that huge rush of relief just to finally be here. This seat he both loved and dreaded more than anything else in his life.

Reports came in, and it wasn't great. They *had* been hit getting away from Homeworld, it wasn't clear who but countermeasures had engaged and *Phoenix* had returned fire. Crew was undamaged, so the hit had been elsewhere, and by the looks of things had made a mess of the jump lines. Main thrust was overheating too, they'd nearly blown the core pushing so hard to get away — one of those things Erik was glad in hindsight he hadn't known. That gave engineering some ideas of where the damage was, but *Phoenix* wasn't cooperating in giving them a better idea.

"Well we can't keep running if we can't jump, and we can't jump again with that damage," Erik said with certainty. "And if we have to thrust again at full max, we might just blow the mains anyway. Priority is we have to fix the damage. On a jump that distance, we're a good thirty hours ahead of anyone coming in behind us, and no one in this system suspects any trouble yet. Unless anyone has a better suggestion, we'll hide in the outer system and run dark while we try to fix it."

"Argitori's a damn busy system," Second Lieutenant Geish said from Scan. "We'll have to manoeuvre a bit to make position, plus everyone just saw that entry now, or will do in a few hours. That'll narrow our band of possible hiding places. With this much insystem traffic, good bet someone spots us no matter how dark we run."

"Agreed," said Erik. "But it'll take them time, and we have to hope we can fix the damage by then."

"No chance we can get help from the local Spacers?" Second Lieutenant Karle wondered from Arms. "Plenty of repair facilities here."

"Not once Fleet comes howling in in thirty hours demanding our heads," said Erik. Though perhaps they shouldn't write off all possibilities in that direction. "Scan, I want passive monitoring of all insystem traffic. Look for Debogande-affiliated vessels." Silence on the bridge as they all considered that. "No idea if it'll help at all, but worth keeping in mind."

After a final velocity-dump, Erik stayed in the chair for the next two hours before handing off to Lieutenant Shahaim and heading back to medical. Crew he passed in the corridors looked at him warily, save a few friends who gave him real smiles or other looks of approval. He still wore his dress uniform, for one thing. Dress uniforms on a combat ship were usually a no-no — no one liked others 'putting on airs'. Least of all those with last names like his.

In medical he found Spacer Carlton from second-shift engineering, whose sling had snapped in the push for several broken bones and concussion. Erik made a point of talking to him before seeing his sister, and Carlton managed a smile, drugged up on painkillers and not feeling much. Doc Suelo said he'd be off for two weeks and on light duty for two more.

On the next bunk was Lisbeth in her civvie jeans and blouse, mask and cuff-sensors on her arm. She was belted in, in case they moved again suddenly, and the entire opposite wall was sliding rails so the medbay would pivot to vertical-G in the event of hard thrust. The mattress was formless-gel, to support head and limbs under heavy-G, and all the life support and other equipment was worked seamlessly into the walls.   Fleet crew visiting downworld after a long tour often freaked out at all the loose objects and clutter.   Erik knew a guy who had been severely injured by a stray toothbrush.   In space, and in Fleet most of all, everything was racked and stowed.

"She's fine," said Corpsman Rashni, one of *Phoenix*'s five. 'Doc' Suelo ran med bay, technically he was Corpsman Master Petty Officer, but in Fleet tradition for a ship's senior medico, 'Doc' was simpler.   "Her bloodwork's a little down, so I hooked her up.   Just need to monitor her stress levels for another thirty minutes to be sure, then she can go."

"Thanks Rash," said Erik, and sat on the neighbouring bunk. "Lis, how you feeling?"

"I'm okay.   Can I take this mask off?"   Rashni shrugged assent and left on other business.   Lisbeth took it off, careful of the cuff on her arm, and the intravenous needle with it.   She looked exhausted, dark rings under her eyes.   "I'm sorry.   I don't want to be any trouble.   I just... I don't remember anything after that first push.   How many Gs was that?"

"We maxed at 10.5, averaged at 10.1 in that first phase." Erik smiled, and took her hand.   "You lasted nine minutes conscious.   That's better than a lot of folks did here, their first time."

"It's just so hard," Lisbeth said weakly.   "I don't know how you do it."

"Well honestly it doesn't happen *that* often.   But you do get used to it.   Or your augments do, they need to get worn in, like a new pair of shoes."

"If it happens again, I might just take a shot and sleep through it if that's okay."

Erik patted her hand.   "Lis, I'm going to get you off." Lisbeth frowned.   "We're in Argitori System, there's lots of Debogande traffic here.   I'll get you onto one of those ships and..."

"How?   You can't spare a shuttle, you lost one at Homeworld, and there was another still on the ground."

"AT-7 is not a military shuttle Lis, we can afford to spare it..."

"No you can't, *Phoenix* is supposed to have four shuttles, now you've got three. Losing one to drop me off is stupid, you can't even deploy all of Major Thakur's marines with three, let alone with two. And a civilian shuttle might come in handy if you're on the run, what if you get to some other system and need to sneak your way in to some facility or planet? A civilian shuttle can do that, a military one's got no chance."

"Then I'll find another way," Erik said firmly. "Lisbeth, you can't stay here. Fleet's going to try and kill us, do you understand that? Some of them will doubt HQ's story, but most won't. HQ will be panicking now — *Phoenix* wasn't supposed to get away, they didn't imagine this could happen, and having a flagship running through settled space spreading bad news about Fleet HQ is beyond a nightmare for them. You being aboard might have stopped them killing the shuttle where everyone can see it, but it's not going to stop them trying to kill *Phoenix* where no one can."

"Erik," Lisbeth said quietly. "What are you going to do?"

"I'm going to get you off the ship. And that's final."

Lisbeth's eyes blazed with temper. "For god's sake, would you stop making this about me? What about *you?* What about your ship, what about all your crew? And what about all of our family? This is so much bigger than me being stuck on this ship Erik, this is some of the most important people in all human space trying to remove their biggest competitors by force!" She pointed outward, endangering the plugs in her arm. "You think I'll be that much safer out there? You think you could arrange private transport back to Homeworld that could get me there alive? Or out of captivity by people who've shown they'll stop at *nothing* to get their way?"

"Then we'll direct-signal some passing insystem freighter and transfer you to them…"

"Erik you're trying to hide! What a risk to take, for just one person!" Erik ground his teeth in frustration. Lisbeth clasped his hand with her other hand. "Don't just talk about me. What are you going to *do*?"

They gathered in the Captain's quarters, just off the bridge. From here, the Captain could get to the command chair in ten seconds if he wasn't otherwise occupied. Sometimes even ten seconds wasn't enough. The room fit eight, though it was a tight squeeze, like everything on a warship. Erik sat on the folding workdesk, a wall display giving visual feed of Argitori overlaid with status basics — vector-off-system-plane, solar relative velocity, alert status. Alert status now was orange, one below red, which was combat.

The room was filled with people who would normally have answered to Captain Pantillo. Now more than ever, it didn't seem real that Pantillo was gone. Erik ran third-shift, a glorified fill-in, someone to warm the seat and keep things ticking over until something bad happened, when the Captain would retake the seat. In meetings like this one, Erik typically sat to one side and took mental notes, keeping track of ways to be useful in supporting the people who ran the ship. Now *he* ran the ship, and all of these veterans, some of whom had been running these posts, or other posts like it for thirty years or more, were all looking at him.

"We're in the elliptical plane," said Lieutenant Shahaim. "After the last burn we're off projected entry by point three nine, and it'll grow bigger the longer we drift."

"What are the odds someone saw that burn?" asked Second Lieutenant Geish.

Shahaim shook her head. "Inside the plane the system's pretty thick, they'd have to be real close to see it. So long as we don't pull a major burn, or use major weapons — or jump, naturally — we should stay hidden."

Lieutenant Shahaim was first-shift Helm. Helm's job was to plot course tracks for the pilot — the Captain — to fly, and to be the co-pilot and watch all those things the pilot could not. With no command staff available, Helm was next in line to fly the ship, as Shahaim had done. Second Lieutenant Geish usually sat second-shift Scan, but had now been promoted to first. Normally that post was filled by Lieutenant Kwok, but Kwok hadn't come up to Fajar

Station. Both Shahaim and Geish were in their sixties, and had been doing this a very long time.

"What are the odds of hitting something?" Erik asked.

Everyone looked at Lieutenant Kaspowitz. "For the next forty hours, pretty low," said Kaspowitz, first-shift Nav. He was too tall for spaceships, really, and always looked hunched in small spaces. "After that, we get into the middle-belts, there's a lot of dust, lots of rocks and ice. Quite a few mining bases. We're not passing too close, but not everything's on the charts. Lots of privateers in systems like this, you never know whose scan range we run into."

"In which case we'll need to move," said Erik. "Rooke?"

"We're looking," said Second Lieutenant Rooke. "We're running drones, it's definitely in the five-panel, which means it clipped the mains and took a couple of feeds... core armour soaked most of it but there's shrapnel damage. Fiddling around in there is hard, especially while we're underway." Rooke was second-shift engineering chief, again filling in for Lieutenant Chau, who hadn't returned. Rooke was young, younger even than Erik, a tech-genius with IQ off the charts whose real passion was astrophysics, but with the war on had decided to channel his skills to the human cause. No one doubted he had the skills to be head engineer, but experience and temperament were another question.

"The five panel is the real problem," Rooke continued, glancing distractedly at the slate in his hands. "The jump lines are severed, clean through. There's a two meter section just gone, no conductivity at all. That's why we came out of jump sideways, the field was just... out of alignment."

"Can you fix it?" Erik asked.

"We can patch it," said Rooke with a wince. "But it'll take... hell, I don't know. Could take a week. But a complete fix needs docking and repair, proper facilities."

"And how safe would a patch be? If we need to jump again?"

Rooke shrugged. "Should hold for one jump. Might hold for two, if we're lucky. Three, no chance." With a questioning gaze. 'Where are we going, LC? How far do we need to jump?' And a whole, huge bunch of other questions all wrapped up in that. When will I see my family again? If ever?

Erik took a deep breath. He couldn't put it off any longer. "Okay," he said. "You'll want to know why you're here."

"I told them why we're here," said Major Thakur. She stood against a wall in more comfortable marine fatigues, jacket and sidearm. "I told them everything."

Erik nodded. And tried to put himself in their shoes. "Well then. Rather than me talking, I'm sure you'll have questions. Fire away."

"What did you see?" said Geish. Broad-faced and troubled. "When you saw the Captain? I mean... how did they kill him?" Thakur hadn't seen that bit, Erik recalled, and he'd not had time to tell her.

"When I went to visit him," he said. "They asked for me, you recall. Captain Sudip arranged it, or we thought he had." Thakur nodded calmly. "I went through security, I had my dress uniform on, but couldn't take a sidearm through the scanners. They took it, and... an escort took me to the Captain's room. I thought he was sleeping. By the time I realised he wasn't, I was already inside. It was a single shot to the back of the head, and I looked in my pocket and found a... well, it looked like a pen, but it smelled like a gunshot. They must have slipped it in my pocket as I went in. And I got bloody fingerprints all over it when I pulled it out, of course." Bitterly. He couldn't escape the feeling that somehow, this had been his fault. But who could have seen it coming? Who would have believed such a thing?

"Did he suffer?" Kaspowitz asked quietly. Kaspo had been a favourite of the Captain's. A great friend, to the extent that captains were allowed to have friends among lower ranks... which everyone else was, when one was captain. Kaspo loved books too, and was funny and irreverent given the chance. Of all the first-shift bridge crew, Kaspo had always been warmest to Erik, and given his relationship with the Captain, Erik had no doubt they'd talked about him often. Between captain and senior bridge officer, that was to be expected and encouraged.

"It looked point blank," said Erik. "From the wound, I doubt he suffered. But he may have seen it coming, I don't know." Thakur frowned at him, as though guessing there was more. "There was a data chip in his front pocket. I thought if he'd seen it coming, he might have left something."

"Where is it?" asked Thakur.

"I swallowed it. I didn't see any other way to keep it, I was searched after they burst in. Nearly twenty-four hours ago now. When I get it back, we'll read it and see if it's anything."

"Can we afford to wait that long?" Rooke asked pointedly.

"We'll get it back from the plumbing filters," Erik said drily. "I'm sure we've plenty of ways to keep busy before we stoop to those depths." Another time, some might have smiled. Now, none did.

"LC," said Geish, still looking troubled. "If... I mean, how can you be sure HQ killed him? I mean..."

"Because no one else had access," Thakur cut him off. Her voice was unusually hard. "Because of the obvious effort to set up the LC with the murder weapon. Because of Fleet Admiral Anjo's attempt to bribe the LC previously. Because they're the only ones with anything close to means, motive and opportunity, and they've been orchestrating this whole thing from the beginning. What more do you need?"

"There's still so much we don't know," Geish objected. "The Captain had a lot of political friends, and there's no telling who else might have wanted him dead."

"Like who?" said Thakur.

"Well, like the LC's friends. All these big business interests, who the hell knows what..."

"You shut that down right there," said Thakur, with a dead-level stare and a pointed finger. That was serious. Geish closed his mouth, but his eyes were defiant. "You don't want to believe HQ did it, fine. You cast any aspersions on this man or his family, you're crossing a line with me." Pointing at Erik. "The LC pulled himself inside out trying to help the Captain, his family pulled a lot of strings to help, and his *civilian* sister in Medbay put her ass personally on the line to help us get out where a lot of decorated uniforms would not. None of us would have made it up here alive if not for her. Your difficulty accepting facts is not the LC's problem. You push it far enough, it'll become *my* problem."

Silence in the room. Discipline among spacer ranks on a ship was not typically the marine company's responsibility. The situation was unprecedented, and Major Thakur laid it out so clearly that even the blind could follow — in the uncertainties of command and legitimate authority that had descended, *she* was the enforcer of discipline, and the guarantor of the lines of command that every ship needed to function. Her reputation alone was such to make that work without further threats. Hopefully.

"I'm sorry we're here," said Erik. "I feel like I should have known, or done something more. But I can't imagine what that might have been. I understand no one wants to be here. I forgive those of us who've already chosen not to be. To the rest of you who'd like to leave, I'll do my best to accommodate that safely, sometime soon. But given what HQ have shown they're willing to do to anyone who rocks their boat, I can't guarantee that you won't be safer staying here, even with half of Fleet out trying to kill us."

Silence as they considered that too. Second Lieutenant Geish clearly didn't like it.

"I'm going to try and find out what's going on. We have a few clues. In time we may find more. My great uncle Thani Gialidis told me that he thinks this has something to do with our alien allies, and if anyone's in a position to know, he is. Maybe the Captain found out something in that direction he wasn't supposed to. In the meantime, we can safely presume that each of us on this ship has now been marked for death by humanity's senior soldiers, either on *Phoenix* or off it. To stop that from happening, we'll all have to do our jobs as well as we've ever done them. That's what I ask of you now."

They all left, save for Thakur, who stayed until the door was shut. "That was well done," said Erik. "I know it wasn't for me personally, and I don't take it that way.   But to guarantee discipline… it was well done."

"No," said Thakur. "You can take it a little personally if you want." With a very faint smile. Erik blinked. "And don't worry about Lisbeth with the crew. She can share my quarters, I've plenty of room and she's entertaining company."

"I'd… thank you. That would be perfect. She does worship you, you know." Edgily.

Thakur shrugged. "She's young. In her world, women aren't like me. She seeks to test her own possibilities. Naturally she's intrigued, yet she's not the only one who learns." Erik nodded slowly. "A few things you'll need to know now that you're acting-captain. Firstly, I hear things you don't. Spacer crew won't talk in front of me, but they talk in front of my marines, and my marines tell me things because ratting on spacers doesn't count. For this reason, the captains who know most about their crew's scuttlebutt are those captains with the best relationship with their marine commanders."

"I did know that," Erik acknowledged. It was still a little confronting to hear it confirmed so baldly.

"So," said Thakur, "this relationship works best on first names, when we're alone. I'm Trace." She smiled and held out her hand. "Pleased to meet you properly, Erik." Erik took her hand. The sheer nervelessness of the woman confounded him. Given what she'd just done, a matter of hours ago, in ship time at least. "Now, something's still bothering you. Out with it."

Erik gave up on wondering how to put it, and drew himself up. Trace liked straight-shooting, he could do that. "You, going in shooting."

Trace nodded slowly. "What about it?"

"I'm still not sure it was necessary. I don't quite recall deciding to get into a shooting fight with my own commanders. Becoming a rebel. It seems you made that decision for me."

"I did," Trace agreed. "It needed to be done."

"Why?"

Trace considered him with narrowed eyes. "You're truly asking?"

"And my sister. You knew she worshipped you. You knew she'd do what you asked. She nearly got herself killed because of it, and may yet die because of it." The strength of his fury surprised him, buried until he gave voice to it. That she'd interfere so bluntly in those things he valued most, and put his sister's life in danger, and all without consulting him. He'd thought they were coming to respect each other, and this felt like betrayal.

She frowned. "What about me makes you surprised by this? Did you think I was the 'good guy'? The peaceful Buddhist meditating on a rock? What about my record and reputation gave you such an idea?"

"It's manipulative."

"And blowing someone's head off isn't?"

"You had no right to put her in danger like that."

"Well perhaps I'm not as smart as you, but I can't think of any other way we could have gotten out of there alive."

"That's not the point!"

"It's *entirely* the point. It's the only point. Secondly, perhaps you'd better ask yourself exactly what you're angry at. Lisbeth is your sister, she'd do anything to help you just as you'd do anything for her, and I gave her the option of doing so. She's a woman of legal age and she makes her own fate. You don't come into it."

"You should have told me. She's my sister, and you should have told me."

Trace gave him a look like he was a puzzle she was working on. Not an especially fascinating puzzle, but one she'd occasionally play with on her spare time. "Sure, maybe. But I was pretty sure you'd say no. And then we'd be screwed."

"So you went behind my back?"

"Absolutely. In that situation, with both the Captain and Huang still in play, you were only third-in-command, and on matters not directly related to ship command, I ranked you. I was considering the prospect of ground combat, should HQ make a move like they did, and ground combat is my speciality. I'm better at it than you are, and in hindsight I think the outcome shows it."

"And do I still have to worry about you going behind my back now?"

"You can worry all you like," Trace said coolly. "The question is, what are you going to do about it?"

"Major," Erik said firmly. "We're not contemplating ground combat here. I won't tolerate senior officers under my command going off half-cocked on their own initiative. Are we clear?"

Trace smiled. "Won't tolerate," she repeated. "That's good. I like the sound of that." She put a finger in his chest. "The thing is, rich boy, you've got to mean it. You're in charge now. I'll back you one hundred percent if you're truly in charge. But being in charge means doing everything necessary to ensure the survival of your crew, and the accomplishment of your goal. Right now your goal is to find out who killed the Captain and why.

"That means making difficult choices, and putting people you care about in danger. If those decisions get too difficult for you, even when there's no other call to make, then tell me now and we'll put Shahaim in charge. You're twice the pilot she is, but she can at least make a call — made a tough one coming here as she did."

"And if you don't like my calls? You're just going to go behind my back again?"

"Not if you *make* the call," Trace said firmly. "On Homeworld, you didn't make one."

"You don't know that, you didn't ask me!"

"I guessed. And I guessed correctly. Didn't I?" With a hard, meaningful look. She put the finger back in his chest. "Two things the Captain taught me — always plan ahead, and always assume the worst. It shouldn't *be* up to me to do that, yet on Homeworld it was. You don't want me going around you again? Don't need me to."

CHAPTER 9

Erik sipped coffee in the command chair, and watched the screens. The 'Captain's' chair, only that didn't sound right. Trace had called him 'acting-Captain', but she was forcing it. Erik didn't think she meant it any more than the others did.

Lisbeth appeared beside the chair, also clasping some coffee. She didn't make a face as she sipped, Erik noted. *Phoenix* coffee was far below the quality of what she was used to. "Where are we?" she asked, peering at the command screens.

A few of the officers up and down the bridge aisle glanced at her. Rows of faces in their chairs, pale in the wash of display light, amidst the humming of ventilation and the ever-present rumble and thump of the cylinder rotation. Most were only strapped in loosely, not expecting immediate trouble.

Erik looked at his sister. Her hair was pinned up and tied at the back... too long for crew, but acceptable for a spacefaring civvie. She wore a plain spacer jumpsuit with pockets and webbing straps. Life support pouch, medical kit, harness hooks. Standard spacer gear. Regs said anyone not wearing it would be confined to quarters.

"If you're going to stand there," Erik told her, "then take hold." Lisbeth blinked at him. "That's what we call it — 'take hold'. It means brace, grab something, never stand unsecured." Lisbeth took a hold of a display mount. "Good." He pointed at a screen, uplinked and zoomed to show her their location. Lots of tumbling rocks and ice, entire fields of them, spanning millions-by-millions of kilometres. Some blue markers nestled in amongst them, with datalinks attached.

"The blue dots are settlements?" Lisbeth asked.

Erik nodded. "Mining colonies. These are the official ones. The green are ones we've picked up chatter from, sensors mark their position. They're not registered."

"Illegal?"

"Maybe a few, but most are just privateers. Illegal's always been a relative thing for Spacers."

Another reason why Spacer and Worlder systems of government didn't get along. Worlders had all these rules and regulations. Spacers did as they pleased, and there were no health and safety inspectors out here. They signed private contracts with private entities, and if they didn't like the conditions or the pay, they left. Governments who interfered were voted out. In some of the rougher places, busybody do-gooders who stuck their nose into private affairs went missing, permanently.

And then there were the taxes. Outside of Fleet Tax, Spacers barely knew what the word meant. 'Debt' they understood, but barely tolerated. Worlders racked up enormous debts paying for things that weren't absolutely necessary. Spacers lived in closed eco-system loops where a mismatch between inputs and outputs meant death. They managed their money the same way, and gave their elected reps just enough to keep the lights on. Worlders thought Spacers spartan and miserly, and didn't understand that out here, such traits were not choice or character, but survival. If Spacers had to live under Worlder politics, wasting their money on luxuries and making their businesses unprofitable through taxation, they'd rebel, perhaps violently. Given the strategic high ground that all Spacers lived in, by virtue of what they were, that was a fight they'd always win.

"They can't see us?" Lisbeth asked, nodding to the dots on the screen.

"They'll know something jumped into system further out," said Erik. "But it happens a lot, and there's so much junk in this system, it won't bother them that they can't see it."

"Aren't big trans-lighters supposed to run transponders?"

"Sure. But not all do." A shove from the attitude jets knocked them briefly sideways, and Lisbeth gasped and grabbed her support. "And that is why we take hold."

"What was that?" Her eyes were wide. "Was that a rock?"

Erik nodded. "The autos dodge them. It'll happen a lot more, we're getting into the thick stuff now. But it's good cover."

He indicated a small gold dot on the screen before his chair. "See that? Insystem freighter, this one looks like a bulk hauler. Container cargo, so consumables, people-freight. It's about three minutes light from us, heading insystem. Might take it a week to get there, they don't rush when there's this many rocks."

"How close do they have to get to see us?"

"A freighter like that, maybe ten seconds light. Their sensors aren't great. The military grade stuff, like what will be chasing us shortly... maybe a minute light, if we stay quiet."

"Light will take half a day to cross this system," Lisbeth murmured.

"Sure, but if they have enough ships, their odds get real good."

"Don't we have to shut down more systems to run silent?" Lisbeth indicated all the glowing screens across the bridge. "Doesn't it give us away?"

Erik smiled. "Space is big, Lis. And we're well shielded. If they're close enough to sense this, they're close enough to see us, so it won't matter. We'll only give ourselves away if we jump, thrust above one-G, fire or squawk. There's not even much light out this far, and we're painted black, so good luck seeing us visually. We're pretty stealthy too, so active scan's unlikely."

"Lots of other things out there that *we* can't see," added Kaspowitz from the neighbouring Nav post to the left. "Because we only see them when they do something similar. Our scanners are far better than most, but most freighters only boost up engines enough to coast. If they're not talking, or they're not within about one minute light, no chance we'll see them. Ten seconds light or less, in the thick stuff."

"Lis," said Erik. "Lieutenant Kaspowitz. That's the Navigation post."

"Hi," said Lisbeth, more subdued than usual when she met interesting new people. She stepped and shook his hand briefly. Kaspowitz smiled — an odd look on an odd-looking guy, narrow face, big nose, but friendly.

"And down that end, there's Second-LT Geish on Scan, Jiri on Scan Two and Shilu on Coms.   Over here on the right is my second, Suli Shahaim on Helm, Karle on Arms, Harris on Arms Two. Operations and Engineering are down back."

"Don't some ships have Engineering on the bridge?"   With her degree, Engineering was the post Lisbeth would know most about.

"Yeah, well some ships are small enough for that, but *Phoenix* is so big, you can't put the Engineering Chief so far from his engines.   He's down back where he's needed."

"Second Lieutenant Rooke, right?   I read about him."

"Yep.   Crazy smart guy."

"He only got two points better than me at college," Lisbeth said mildly.

"Is that right?" said Kaspowitz.   Down the aisle, a few faces smiled.

"Yeah," said Erik, "except he was fourteen at the time."

"Still counts!" Lisbeth retorted with humour.   "He's fixing the engines?"

Erik touched an icon and the vision flipped.   "Look here." The screen showed infra-red.   A drone image, of *Phoenix*'s hull, somewhere by the engines.   Through the outer plating was drilled a large, nasty hole.   "The drone's mated to our controls so it'll stay with us as long as we don't jump or thrust hard."

"Looks bad," said Lisbeth with a shiver.   "Can Rooke fix it?"

"He says probably he can patch it.   But it'll need dock to get it done properly."

"Debogande facilities in this system," Lisbeth suggested. Again faces about the bridge glanced her way.   And Erik's.   "The big processor in the fifth planet system is all DE.   And the insystem shipyards in the second belt.   I checked the map."

"We're about to be crawling with Fleet," said Erik, chewing a nail.   She was right though — it was tempting to think about. "Those will be the first places they'll look."

"Maybe if we need parts though?" Kaspowitz suggested. "Could contact a sub-lighter, get them to bring something? Or ditch it on a near track?"

Erik thought for a moment. If they risked it, it could be his chance to get Lisbeth off the ship. "Depends how much company we get. And how bad Rooke needs the spares..." Jump alarm flashed, right on cue.

"Jump contact," Geish announced, and everyone paid very close attention to their screens. "Bearing 174 astern by inclination five. Signature suggests a warship."

"Someone followed us," said Kaspowitz. "Question now is how many."

"He came from Homeworld?" Lisbeth asked quietly. Erik said nothing, eyes fixed on the screens, not wanting to tell his sister to shut up in front of everyone.

"She's coming fast," Geish continued. "Could be a combat jump, stand by." Because if it wasn't a combat jump, she'd dump velocity immediately. Thankfully Lisbeth didn't ask any more questions. "She's at five minutes light, offset angle, she'll miss us by plenty. Still no dump." Another jump alarm. "New jump contact, bearing... 174 by five, same as the first mark. Still no dump."

"She's gunning," Shahaim muttered, staring at her screen. "She's got all safeties off, wouldn't want to be a twitchy sub-lighter in her path..."

"New jump contact!" Geish cut her off. "Same as before, 174 by five. I'm getting an offset spread, could be a combat formation..."

"New jump contact!" shouted Jiri on Scan Two. "173 by five... new contact, new contact!" As another two arrived in quick succession.

"More and more," added Geish, his jaw tight. They proliferated across scan like raindrops on a lake, ripples overlapping and spreading. Seven, eight, ten, thirteen...

"Son of a bitch," someone murmured. For a moment there was deathly silence, but for the hum and thump of white noise. "Looks like a fucking invasion fleet."

"All of this for us?" Lisbeth whispered.

"Scan," said Erik, with as much calm as he could muster, "track and mark all incoming. When they can't see us, some of them may try to blank signature and run dead."

"That's gonna be hard," Geish said grimly. Across the screens, new contacts continued to proliferate. Thirty. Thirty three. Thirty nine.

"Fuck me," someone muttered.

"No transponders," said Kaspowitz. "They don't want us to know who they are."

"Yeah," said Erik, forcing a casual drawl to cover the cold dread in his stomach. "Yeah, well, that figures." Lots of old friends in this bunch, for sure. Ships they'd been in combat with. Ships whose capabilities, and whose captains, they knew intimately. Some with good friends aboard, some with ex-lovers. No present lovers or family, Erik hoped… he'd have to check manifests. Damn risk otherwise, on both sides. Suddenly he was glad they weren't broadcasting transponders, for fear of what some of his own crew might do, rather than fight friends.

"LC," said Second Lieutenant Karle, at Arms. "They're not seriously going to try and kill us, are they?" Karle was young. His post made him responsible for shooting back, if it came to that. He'd already done that, Erik recalled — the docked ship at Fajar Station. *Tabitha,* that had been — an armed merchant, unfamiliar to most. No one knew if there'd been anyone aboard when Karle had blown it away.

"Be nice to try and talk to one of them direct," Kaspowitz suggested, looking at Erik.

"Direct laser-com, sure," said Erik. "Only we don't know who's who. Or if any of them are even vaguely sympathetic. And even if we do get a captain who is, he'll have to worry about crew." Like I do now. The implication hung unsaid, like a sword over his neck. "Tell you what I'd like right now, is a nice, large rock.

Something to snuggle up against, block our signature. With this many ships in, we're not going to last long just staying quiet. Not long enough to fix that damn hole, anyway."

"Jiri, you get on it," said Geish. "I'll track our friends."

Trace took a break from reviewing unit status when her quarters uplink told her Lisbeth had arrived. She entered her room to find the girl carrying the little bag she'd brought on the shuttle, standing between the double bunk, folding wall table and wall closet, and looking a little lost.

"You can have the right closet space here," said Trace, opening the door and showing her. "You pull out the racks like this, then lay your clothes flat and use the covers to hold them in, so they don't fly around in manoeuvres or when we cut G. The head's just up the corridor on the left, it's unisex but the boys are polite. Or if they aren't, they'll hear from me about it."

Lisbeth peered, looking dazed. That little shoulder bag was all she had in the world. Now she had to share this small compartment with another woman, and couldn't even get a private bathroom. Given how huge her accustomed bedrooms surely were, to say nothing of kitchens, dining rooms and gardens, it must have been a shock.

"Are you okay?" Trace asked with concern.

"I'm... I'm pretty tired." Lisbeth managed a weak smile. "That's all." It was well after midnight, Shiwon-time, Trace recalled... if you counted jump as instantaneous. Physiologically it wasn't, the body aged at least a day, or more like a week if you didn't keep fit and prepared. In real time, the longest jumps *Phoenix* did took days. Sometimes you felt it immediately, other times you got a jolt that kept you awake for ages.

"Well we're running shifts again," said Trace, with a glance at ship-time on uplink vision. "You know how that works? The bridge has three shifts, the rest of the ship has two. Normally the Captain's on 0600 to 1400, that's first shift. Then second-shift is

1400 to 2200, then third-shift. Given all the people we're missing, I think Erik will cut that to two shifts and put all his best crew on first-shift, so you're not going to see him much.

"It's 1510 now so try not to sleep too long — I sleep through third-shift so we'll do better if we match schedules. But you can come back here any time you like if you need some alone-time — I'm only ever here to sleep or change. You can use a slate to access ship library, you can watch primary-scan if you want, or track status, or else there's a big selection of entertainment if you want to relax. Just remember, always pull the net across when you sleep, you've seen these?"

"I've seen them on a vid," said Lisbeth, as Trace demonstrated how the net pulled across the bed, and secured to the bed rim by steel latches.

"Good, so the release is here." Pointing to the button. "Emergency life support is the bottom of the main closet, the yellow and black stripes. And most important..." she reached the space between wall table and closet, where a canvas wrapping stood from ceiling to floor. Hit the release and the canvas seals ripped as a couple of acceleration slings hummed into the room on steel runners in floor and ceiling. "These will deploy automatically if bridge sounds the 'take hold' — big alarm, flashing lights and announcements, you can't miss it. When you hear that alarm, get in the sling. Don't do anything else, just get in like you've been shown, and brace. Do *not* stay in bed — even with the net across, the rear thrust will just put you through the wall, you're lying perpendicular to thrust and you'll slide off. If you need any help, use personal coms, but again, if we're under thrust, no one can actually move to help you. Any questions?"

Lisbeth shook her head. The girl looked like she could use a hug. Trace was unaccustomed to dealing with civvies in such close quarters, and thought that might actually work. She put her arms around the girl, who did the same back, and just held her for a while.

"Your brother's mad at me for getting you involved," Trace said as she let her go.

"Well you can't really blame him for being protective," said Lisbeth. "We Debogande women are really asking for it. He came out here to serve, and we stayed at home. Of course he's protective — that's what he's been doing out here all these years. Protecting us with his life."

Trace smiled at her. It was more maturity and perspective than she'd expected. And she reprimanded herself for repeatedly underestimating the girl. "That's true enough. But he was protecting a lot more than just you. Whether that was foremost in his mind or not."

Thrust correction hit them, unannounced, and suddenly gravity cut in half as the correction pushed the ship 'down', then sideways as cylinder rotation took them around. Lisbeth flailed for balance with a squeal, and Trace caught her in a two-armed embrace and fell them both sideways into the closet until it passed.

"Lots of rocks out here," she explained, pushing them back upright. "Just remember to never stand unsecured." And she noticed the girl was in tears. "Lisbeth?"

"Oh god." Lisbeth wiped her eyes furiously. "How stupid. It's just... I don't like this. Not being able to trust gravity. And that 10-G push to jump was just... I don't know if I can do this, I just feel so claustrophobic!"

"It's a hard thing to get used to," Trace said diplomatically. "But your brain will adjust in time. You have to trust that it will."

"How did you get used to it?" Lisbeth asked desperately. "Is there some kind of... I don't know..."

"Some kind of trick? No. I adjusted because I became Kulina Vidyarthi at age eight. I've trained for battle ever since. I've a head for heights because at age ten they made us do the santipurna arohanako — it means 'peaceful ascent'. It's basic ropes and limited safety harness up several thousand meters in the Rejara Phirta Range on Sugauli, all weathers, day and night. The difficulty of adjusting to spacetravel is the brain facing something unexpected. By the time I got to space, I didn't have many of those left."

"Weren't you scared?" Lisbeth whispered.

"On the climb, the fearful ones are the most likely to fall. You learn to control it, or you die. Or you survive but fail and are disgraced, which is worse."

"I don't think I could have done that."

"You've never tried. Therefore you lack self-knowledge. That is why you're scared. The only way to gain it is to try. Perhaps you'll fail, but at least then you'll know."

"It's a little late for me to do the peaceful ascent and become Kulina," Lisbeth said shakily.

"But it is not too late to gain self-knowledge on this," said Trace. She hit the door. "Here, on this ship. Start today."

Leaving her quarters, Trace walked the back-quarter galley and got herself a half-decent sandwich from the selection window where the chefs would leave them when prepared. She ate it while strolling through Assembly, where rooms and corridors gave way to open steel gantry racks and stacks of armour suits and weapons, all tightly locked and secured in case of manoeuvres. Marines did maintenance on their armour, polished visors and cleaned weapons, often in singlets as the heat from all the running powercells caused Assembly to run ten degrees C hotter than the rest of the ship.

Phoenix's marine company had five platoons, forty-four in each, plus Trace's own Command Squad for two hundred and twenty eight total. Officers and non-coms took her presence passing through as invitation to report, which it was, though in reality she was always on call and only common courtesy kept her from being interrupted all-shifts. All of what they told her was minor — a few mending injuries or illnesses, inventory updates, the usual routine. Mostly, she knew, they just wanted to touch base, and see her look them in the eyes and know they weren't completely screwed.

There was a lot of disbelief, and a lot of grief, barely covered. Most marines maintained some distance from most spacers, but the Captain had been different. Any who had served aboard this ship for long enough had come to learn that the stories about him were not just stories — they *saw* it, saw the rapid calculation, the unexpected manoeuvre, the sheer genius that saved friendly lives and took unfriendly ones. When you rode in a steel shell entrusting your next breath to the nerve and skill of a single man, you came to appreciate that man's skill when, after so many missions, you were still breathing, and so many others were not.

And the Captain had always come down here, strolled these echoing, rattling, steamy parts of back-quarter where most spacers rarely trod, and talked with the marines like they mattered to him as much as his spacer crew. And they'd seen him emotional at their funerals, and proud at their ceremonies, and they'd come to love him as a second father — or for some less blessed, as marines often were, a first father. And now he was gone, in disputed circumstances, and many of them just wanted to know what the hell had happened, and who was to blame, and why.

Trace vouched for Erik's version of events, and that was enough for nearly all of them. The responsibility somehow felt more daunting than usual. She wondered as she strolled, talked and ate, how that was possible. Her usual responsibility was life and death, commanding these men and women whom she loved into battles knowing that some, and perhaps many, would die or be horribly wounded. It didn't seem reasonable that *any* responsibility could weigh more heavily than that. Yet somehow, this one did, like a gravitational mass from which no amount of thrust could provide escape.

She supposed it was one thing when the karma all flowed the one way. All of these marines would still have been in battle if she were elsewhere, during the war. Their precarious fates had not been her doing, and in time she'd come to accept that her judgement in command would usually get somewhat fewer of them killed than most other commanders could manage. But this was something else. All the Fleet's other marines were looking forward to a long period with no fighting. Perhaps even a permanent period, in this short-scale human view of things. But not *Phoenix*. These marines still hung in the balance, pushing upstream into the onrushing flow of karma heading the other way. And that was her responsibility in a way that their fates in the war itself had never been.

After Assembly she went to the gym and punched a bag until her fists hurt. She did that until Kaspowitz arrived, ducking the overhead, then leaning on her bag as she hit it.

"Your left's a bit low," he advised her.

"What was that?" said Trace, continuing to strike between weaves.

"Your left, it's…"

"What? My what?" Thud thud. "Stop mumbling." Kaspowitz grinned. They were old friends — she'd been on *Phoenix* about a third of her life, yet that was only half of Kaspo's time. He was an odd guy with no discernible ambition and an irreverent sense of humour, and from her first arrival here as a green Lieutenant, she'd preferred his company, of all spacers, to anyone but the Captain's. Kaspo didn't need, didn't stress, didn't bitch and didn't covet. What he did, exceptionally well and with very little bullshit, was his job. "You know, if you'd occasionally do a bit of exercise, I might listen to you."

"I tried it once," Kaspowitz admitted, leaning hard on the bag as she jolted him. "Did irreparable damage to my self-esteem. Doctor said it was too dangerous for a man of my sensitivity."

"You know," Trace panted. "It's almost as though some of us…" thudthudthud, "… think we're fighting a war. While others…" thudthud "…are just here to laugh at the universe."

"You know, you're far too smart to be a marine. That thing you do with your mouth." He clicked his fingers. "Sentences, that's it." Trace grinned, and kept punching. "We're fighting a war, Trace. *We're*."

His eyes were suddenly serious. Trace stopped punching, and wiped her face. She leaned on the bag opposite him. There were others in the gym, punching bags, lifting weights, running on treadmills. But despite the noise, someone might overhear. "Captain didn't tell me any specifics," she said quietly by Kaspowitz's shoulder. "But he said the Worlder-Spacer Congress divide would blow up and kill more people than the Triumvirate War if we weren't careful. And that he'd said so openly, to anyone in High Command who'd listen, and a bunch who wouldn't. I know he was thinking of a run for politics when the war ended. And I know that scared a lot of people, given his status."

Kaspowitz nodded slowly. "So this doesn't surprise you?"

Trace looked up at him, nose to nose. She didn't allow herself much physical intimacy with men on *Phoenix*, having found it got in the way of just about everything. But in all these years Kaspo had shown no interest in her that way, outside of the odd playful remark. As she'd overheard one spacer putting it when he didn't know she was there, you could only get so turned on by cold steel. "I think they were hoping he'd get killed in the last few years. But you know the Captain — they were never going to get that lucky."

"We sure got all the tough assignments," Kaspowitz said darkly. "You tell the LC this?"

Trace made a face. "Not in so many words. I don't want him to just take my word for it. Some people look up to me too much, stop using their own brains. If we need anything from him right now, we need him to use his brain."

Kaspowitz considered her for a long moment. "You trust him?"

"I think he's as straight as a bulkhead. Which from me is a compliment. So yeah, if he says he didn't do it, I trust him implicitly."

Kaspowitz rolled his eyes a little. "Yeah... but that's not all I meant. Do you *trust* him? I mean, all our lives, in his hands?"

"You're bridge crew, I'm not. Do *you* trust him?"

"Heck of a pilot. First class. Smart as hell, qualified, brave, principled, ticks all the boxes. I dunno. Something's missing."

Trace nodded slowly. "Self belief. And that might be our fault." With raised eyebrows at him, meaningfully.

Kaspowitz thought about it. "Yeah. Yeah maybe. We didn't give the kid the easiest run."

"And he said, that Fleet Admiral Anjo said, that the Captain picked him personally."

Kaspowitz blinked. "Seriously? You believe that?"

"The LC or Anjo?"

"Either."

"Captain was still alive when Anjo said it, LC could have asked the Captain himself, proven Anjo a liar. Anjo was trying to butter him up, offering him a big job, get him with the program. Too dangerous for Anjo to lie then. And you know the LC, he lies about as infrequently as I do. If he says Anjo said it, Anjo said it."

"You think the Captain saw this coming?" Kaspowitz's eyes were wide in a manner rare for an old spacer who'd seen everything. "Picked the LC as some kind of cover? Get the Debogandes involved on purpose?"

"Captain would never put the ship in danger by picking someone not qualified," Trace said with certainty. "I think he got lucky that Family Debogande produced someone that good, and couldn't resist the opportunity. *Don't* suggest it to the LC. Kid struggles for confidence as it is." 'Kid', she realised as she said it. He was three years older than her. Yet still it seemed like the right thing to say.

"Yeah," Kaspowitz said heavily. "Next question, you think we have any friends out here?"

"Sure. Friends enough for a captain to refuse a direct order to fire? Doubt it."

"End a lot of careers, wouldn't it?"

"What do you think?"

"I think," said Kaspowitz, "that they'd never fire on Captain Pantillo. But he's dead, they're saying the LC killed him, and lots of spacers never cut the LC an even break because of his family. There'll be a lot who are confused and skeptical, but disobeying a direct order to fire on a ship commanded by the guy who HQ say killed Captain Pantillo?"

"Honest answer," Trace requested. "I vouch for the LC. Would that sway anyone?"

"Marines, sure. Fleet captains, a little, but not enough to stop them pressing the button."

"That's my reading," Trace agreed. "Besides, Kulina council will excommunicate me now. To a combat officer that's not just a disgrace, it's a death sentence."

"Oh hell," Kaspowitz muttered. "I'm sorry Trace."

Trace shrugged. "The Kulina shall want for nothing," she said with a faint smile. "And shall regret nothing. What kind of hypocrite would I be if I started caring now?"

Kaspowitz smiled at her. Put a hand in her sweaty hair. "You hang in there kid. I wouldn't trade you for the whole fucking lot of them." He kissed her on the forehead, and left. Trace hung on the bag for a while longer, thinking. And feeling that there were so many people she'd die for on this ship, it made survival seem unlikely.

CHAPTER 10

Lisbeth woke to the sensation that she was falling. Because she *was* falling, or at least gravity was tossing her out toward the bed netting, and her heart hammered in panic as she grabbed at the net. And then lay there, staring at the bottom of Major Thakur's bunk above. She wrestled with the unfamiliar uplink network for a moment before finally finding the time. It was 1649, she'd been asleep barely an hour, and didn't feel very rested. It was hard to rest when your subconscious expected gravity to smack you into the ceiling at any moment. And the net wasn't much comfort, because gravity really *was* that changeable out here, just a side-effect phenomenon of distance plus velocity plus occasional shifts in trajectory.

She lay in her bunk trying to visualise what lay about her — the incredible distances, the speeds at which they were currently crossing them, tiny by what *Phoenix* was capable of with jump engines engaged but still astronomical enough. If Scan missed one of those rocks, she wondered, would they even feel the impact? Or would a strike at many tens of thousands of kilometres an hour destroy the ship so quickly that the nervous system would be incinerated before it had time to even register what had happened?

How many men and women had that happened to, out here, over the decades? How many had been there one moment, living, talking, reading, laughing. Then the next second, gone, without even an explanation or warning? If you were going to die, surely you deserved some kind of explanation of what killed you? Some realisation that you were actually dead? She imagined souls, frozen out here in some dark limbo of perpetual astonishment.

Gargh! She couldn't lie in bed and think about such things, she'd go insane. She managed an uplink to the room display, and the wall above the small table lit with several options. She picked Scan, and it showed the nearest planetary system in relation to them — another half-hour's light away, a massive gas giant with many moons and lots of insystem traffic. In between, lots and lots of rocks and ice… and that was just the tiny fraction Scan could actually see. Anything could be hidden in there. With a lot of the pursuing Fleet ships now scattering ahead and running silent, anything could be.

"Attention all hands, this is the LC." It was her brother's voice on the intercom. *"Attention all hands, this is the LC. Scan has spotted a nice big rock not too far off our path, it should make a decent hiding spot for us, it appears to have a good metallic signature, should confuse our signal, and isn't tumbling so we can get real close. To rendezvous with it we'll need to proceed with a one-G burn for the next two hours and seventeen minutes. We are currently at burn-minus-five minutes, I repeat, at burn-minus-five minutes. All hands prepare for a one-G burn. LC out."*

An alarm sounded, high and wavering up and down, like some mournful animal's howl, and the room lights began to flash in time. Lisbeth lay where she was, clutching her bednet with her heart thumping in rising panic. Her uplink visual flashed, an incoming call, and she opened it…

"Lis, it's me," said Erik in her inner ear. *"Where are you currently?"*

Before she could answer, another call overrode without her even inviting it… *"Hi Lisbeth,"* said Major Thakur. *"LC you're busy, you go do your job. I said I'd look out for Lisbeth and I will."*

A small pause. *"Okay Lis? Just listen to the Major, this is very basic, nothing to worry about."* His call disconnected.

"Lisbeth?" said Thakur.

"I'm here."

"Okay, all that this means is that the wall opposite the door is about to become the floor. Are you in bed?"

"Yes."

"So, first you disengage the bednet, then you sit on the bed with your back to the wall. Once you're out, put the bednet back on so the sheets don't go everywhere. That's it. You'll notice that all the thrust-ward walls on the ship have green lines where they join the ceiling." Lisbeth looked, and sure enough, a green stripe ran from wall to wall. She unhooked the bednet, fingers fumbling on

the locks, and let it wind across on its own power. *"That's so you know which way gravity will go when we burn. Always remember which wall has the green stripe — we call it the G-wall."*

As she scrambled to sit on the bed end, Lisbeth recalled a documentary she'd once watched where spacers had called it the 'K-wall', because it was the one that killed you. "Okay, I'm sitting with my back to the wall." And remembered to pull the bednet back across, and climbed on it to hook it in.

"Right, as soon as we thrust, the crew cylinder will stop rotating. You wait ten seconds, then the all-clear will sound, and you can move around. Obviously all the things that require cylinder rotation to work, won't. So the toilets, showers, etcetera. Everything else, well, you'll discover that spacers learn to improvise. Any questions?"

"No." Her heart was still pounding, but she felt a little better. "No, I'm fine. Thank you Major."

"If you need any help, hit your personal com call and someone close-by will come to you. See you soon."

It was slightly ridiculous to have one of the war's greatest heroes personally waiting on her, Lisbeth thought. She didn't think Major Thakur was the kind of person who'd respect the civilian notions of privilege that came with having a last name like Debogande. But then again, the Major was a marine, and however important, she didn't have nearly as much to do on a ship as a spacer did. Being a Debogande didn't make her unique on this ship — being a civilian did, and the marines would look out for any civilian the same way, Debogande or not. The fact that it was the Major looking out for her was probably due to the fact that she was the current ship commander's sister, and letting her mix with lower-ranked crew could be a violation of the command hierarchy. If the Debogande family had had no money or big name, she'd have been treated the same by virtue of Erik's rank.

At one minute the com started a ten second countdown. At ten seconds the count was for every second. Then a thunder that rumbled through the walls, floor and bed, and a shove from behind. Blankets slid upon the bed, and the groan and squeal of various things shifting weight about the room. It felt as though the room were being tipped upon its end, like some giant had come along, grabbed the nose-end of the ship and pointed it to the sky.

Now she was flat on her back. It was the oddest thing, but not quite as scary as she'd imagined. The wall, as Major Thakur had said, was now the floor, and she was lying on her back with her feet up in the air. The ship sounded different, the white noise of cylinder rotation that became so omnipresent that she'd gotten used to it, had now disappeared. In its place was a low, rumbling thunder, and the metallic rattle and squeal of separate parts vibrating against each other.

Lisbeth sat up carefully, and the speakers announced the all-clear. It took a while to convince her brain that this new orientation was not about to violently revert, dropping her face-forward on the once-floor that was now the wall. Her bunk bed was now vertical before her, sheets fallen in a heap within the bednet. Carefully she stood up. If thrust suddenly stopped, she reminded herself, she wouldn't fall — she'd be weightless. Even that previous 'normal' gravity had only been the function of the rotating crew cylinder. Without it, everything floated.

The wall screen above the table was now at her feet. And the table rim, she saw, had a thick edge that now doubled as a seat, as the twin chairs were of course bolted to the 'floor', now beside her. She sat on the table rim, and contemplated the door. It was far above her. How odd, the room had seemed tiny when that wall had been the wall. Now that it was the ceiling, the door looked like the mouth of a well she'd fallen into, and was now trapped at the bottom of. And yet the Major had said that once thrust had begun, she'd be free to move around. How the hell?

Then she noticed that the rim of the top bunk had rungs on it, like a ladder. She hadn't noticed that before, and if she had, wouldn't have guessed why. Now it was obvious. Sitting trapped in here, without even a bed to rest on, seemed like a horrid way to spend two hours and seventeen minutes. Besides, this wasn't quite as disorientating as she'd feared... and fear itself, she was becoming quite sick and tired of. Fear was debilitating, and she hated it — the thudding heart, the endless, breathless tension. She recalled what Major Thakur had said, that those who feared most often failed on the climb, or died. Fear was sometimes useful, but when the thing you feared was present in everything around you, and prevented you from dealing with your situation practically, it became a pointless distraction.

And what had the Major said? Gain self-knowledge? Start today? If she asked Erik for permission to wander, he'd say no, and she'd be stuck here. And she hated to bother the Major again with her weakling, civilian requests. She was a grown woman, she could go for a walk if she wished. And so she put her hands on the bunk ladder, and climbed.

Atop the bunk, she could reach the door quite easily. The door did not open immediately, and a beeping alarm sounded in the corridor outside. Then it opened, very slowly. When it stopped, Lisbeth grabbed the rim and walked her feet up to the end of the bunk. That got her shoulders out the door, and...

"Ware!" came a call as some legs passed her, and jumped the door she'd opened. That had been why the alarm in the corridor — the doors now became trapdoors into which people could fall. She heaved herself up quite easily, and scrambled over the edge.

The corridor looked different, floor on one side, ceiling on the other. She followed the spacer who'd passed, and saw her jumping the doors at her feet whether they were open or not. That seemed like a good idea, and Lisbeth copied. Most insystem freighters did not have this problem, of course, as they were designed so that 'aft' thrust was the floor, in a vertical stack. Without jump engines, they'd accelerate at 1-G toward their destination, then turn over at halfway and decelerate at 1-G all the way in. Jump engines made it possible to gain or lose enormous velocity instantly, and so most insystem travel for FTL ships was coasting without thrust, with gravity from cylinder rotation only.

The fear returned when she reached the first trunk corridor. It ran a good portion of the crew cylinder from fore to aft, and now as she approached the corner, the once-innocuous passage yawned at her feet with a sheer, endless drop. Traction lines she'd not seen before had appeared, and now ran up and down the shaft, one line heading up, the other down. Spacers rode it up and down, standing on the little footrests, clipped to the rope with their harness. The woman Lisbeth had been following took a little wand from a pocket and extended it to the length of her arm. Then she took her harness clip, unhitched it and mounted it on the extended wand. A fast clip to the upward rope, then it caught on the next empty handhold. The woman stepped off as her harness pulled tight, and swung to the rope, put her feet in, and rode it up.

That simple huh? Lisbeth watched in amazement as someone else got off at her level, and using the wand to clip the harness to another rope line that extended into the corridor from above — that must have also popped out automatically when the thrust kicked in, Lisbeth thought. She hadn't noticed it before. They didn't even stop the rope, just hooked, jumped and swung into the corridor mouth like some tree swinging primate.

Lisbeth didn't particularly want to do that, she was sure she'd miss her level or lose her nerve... or worse, jump without attaching properly, and fall. But she recalled more documentary footage of people getting off when these ropelines touched the bottom. Surely she could manage that?

She searched several pockets and found the wand-thing. Extended it, and found how it attached to the harness hook — she *was* an engineering graduate after all, she told herself firmly. And she knew how to rock climb and use safety harnesses, there were plenty of engineering tasks that required it. Then she waited until a clear foothold appeared on the down-rope, reached with her clip with hands that only shook a little... waited until the footrests passed and clipped just above them. The clip snapped immediately shut, and her triumph lasted a split second until the descending handholds caught the clip, and she realised her harness was about to yank her over the edge.

She managed not to scream, and jumped. And fell, yanked tight on the harness and swung into the rope, spinning around in dangling confusion, the rope hitting her face and burning her hand as she flailed at it. And grabbed, heart hammering, and scrambled to find the footrest with her feet… and got on.   She hung there, gazing about as the corridor walls rose past her…

"Ware!" called a voice from below, and the next person rising past her fended off as her feet nearly kicked him in the head.

"Sorry!   I'm sorry!"   But he was past and going up, and someone waiting on the next corridor down to get on was looking at her oddly.   She'd done it, she realised with elation.   Only now the corridor was doglegged forty-five degrees sideways, and the ropeline simply dragged at the corners — she saw someone coming up below having to walk up the wall to get around without banging the corner. Here on the outer side of the dogleg was a big elastic net sticking halfway out into the corridor.   To catch falling spacers, she realised.

She pushed around the outer edge, thankful the rope handholds were offset so that descending and ascending spacers wouldn't hit that corner at the same time, squeezed past another rising, then hit the next dogleg corner with her butt as the corridor straightened out again.   That corner was cushioned, and opposing it on the far wall was another big elastic net.   So any falling spacer who missed the first net would hit this corner, obviously, and bounce across to land in that net.   Theoretically.   She wondered how many who did so didn't survive it.   In a 10-G push, a five meter fall was like fifty meters at 1-G.   Even a two meter fall would probably crush you like an egg.   What was left after a tumble down this corridor at 10-G, she didn't want to think about.

Beyond, the corridor end was approaching.   Now *this* looked simple enough, and she unclipped her harness and simply stepped off as the rope passed its end pulley and went around.   There.   And looked up the vast height above with a real sense of accomplishment. Now, she thought.   Engineering.

Engineering HQ was built with its back to the rear cylinder bulkhead.   The main entrance door was now a hole in the floor with a rope ladder on one side, and a rope on the other.   "Ware!" someone called as she peered in, and she stepped quickly aside for a spacer in a hurry who sat on the doorframe, grabbed the rope, then slid down at speed.   The rope ladder was to come up, Lisbeth guessed.   Well, she'd done this before in PT classes.   She sat, legs over the edge, took the rope and told herself that this was nothing compared to what she'd just done.   Then slid off, and let gravity take her down with the rope on her jacket arm to save her the rope burn.

And looked around as her feet hit the bottom.   She was to one side of a bridge not unlike the main bridge, with various scan posts before wide screen arrays.   People still sat in those chairs, flat on their backs, and talked back and forth or on coms.   Here on the 'floor', people who wanted to talk to them stopped and looked up. Getting in and out of those chairs would take a boost, Lisbeth thought.   She peered up at one, and saw display screens showing engine schematics, jump line routes, and vid feeds from various drones probing the damage.   Those drones would now be burning at 1-G just to keep up.

The woman in the chair looked back at her, her head just a little above Lisbeth's own.   "Hey.   Lisbeth Debogande, right?"

Lisbeth nodded.   "I've got a masters in engineering from Getti College, graduated top of my class.   Specialised on a starship track, I was wondering if…"

"Hey Rooke?" the woman said into coms.   "You wanted another eye on those jumpline schematics?   I've got you one."   She pointed, for Lisbeth's benefit.   "That way."

Ducking under chairs and posts, Lisbeth found a young-looking black man sitting crosslegged before a portable display mount, with two others crouched alongside pointing and talking tersely.   One glanced up as Lisbeth approached.

"Um, hi… I'm Lisbeth Debogande, I've got a masters in engineering from…"

"We know," said the man who'd looked, and handed her a slate.   "This is set for jumpline schematics, the comp will feed you your area, you need to walk through the auxiliary powerloadings, they're haywire at the moment and we don't trust auto diagnostic when that happens.   Watch for spikes, report anomalies.   Got it?"

Lisbeth nodded rapidly, took the slate and looked for somewhere to sit.   "Just… anywhere?"

"Anywhere at all," the man said drily, and returned his attention to the young black man's screens, and their ongoing conversation. That man's nametag read Rooke, and his shoulder stripes were a Second Lieutenant's. He didn't even glance at her. Lisbeth found a seat against what used to be the floor, and got to work.

Erik lay back on the command chair, a boot stuck against a display support to keep the circulation going. Ahead and closing, Scan zoomed on the rock they were chasing. They had visual now — a dark blob against the bright starfield. They were approaching from darkside, so only a faint crescent was visible from Argitori's three distant suns. It did not tumble, as Geish had said. It was roughly ovoid, and a touch over a kilometre long, plenty big enough to hide Phoenix from half the sky.

"Well this is interesting," said Geish, cycling through several of his most advanced displays. "Several of the surface features look regular. Same shape and size. Scancomp says an eighty-three percent chance it's been hollowed."

Erik frowned. "We're a long way off the elliptic plane for a settlement."

"An insystem settlement, sure," cautioned Kaspowitz.

"But what are the odds?" Geish replied. "An FTL settlement here? Whose? And out of all the rocks in the system, we just happen to find this?"

Erik recalled something the Captain had told him once, in conversation over a drink during second-shift. "Second Lieutenant, did you find that rock off auto-search?"

"Standard auto-search," Geish confirmed.

"But scancomp memory plays a role in that," Erik pressed. "I mean there's millions of rocks out here, maybe thousands with suitable trajectories."

Geish frowned at him, rolling his head on the headrest to look. "You're saying scancomp found this rock for us?"

"Something the Captain told me." Erik chewed on a nail. "Ghosts in the system, if a ship's been around long enough. It finds things, long locked into memory, no telling how it got there."

"Yeah but we wipe excess data from comp every few years," Jiri added from Scan Two.

"Not on this warship we don't," said Kaspowitz. "LC's right. I've seen it. Navcomp finds weird little things like that all the time. Statistical anomalies. *Phoenix* may have latest tech, but her memory's old as the Ancients."

And the tech didn't come from us. No one said it, it was in the back of everyone's mind. All of Fleet's fundamental technologies had been given to them by the chah'nas. It wasn't the first time they'd done that — the first time had been to save humanity's ass against the krim. But the Triumvirate War had been more of a booster, a high-tech kick in the pants to keep the humans moving along at a suitable rate. And this time, the chah'nas were not humanity's only friend, as the alo had joined in as well — not so much in fighting, but certainly in weapons and industry. In the latter part of the war, they'd even begun granting humanity limited use of their coveted warship technology. Only a few had been built, hybrids of existing human and new alo technology, but those few had performed spectacularly. Perhaps the most prominent of those, was *Phoenix*.

"Looks dead," Geish added of the rock. "If it was active I'd be getting some heat signature, some echo off a reflective panel, some external structure. This one, nothing."

"LC," said Second Lieutenant Shilu from Coms, "I'm getting transponder traffic on that new arrival, 179-by-7 off trajectory."

"Yep," said Jiri after a moment. "Yep, I got that, that's chah'nas. Warship *Tek-to-thi.*"

"She was on Fajar Station with us," Erik recalled. "Kulik Class vessel, not our size but fast. Someone sent her after us."

"To watch, or to participate?" Shahaim wondered. "Sure is real noisy of her to show up in human business and broadcast like that."

"Chah'nas are a noisy people," Kaspowitz said drily.

Erik recalled the chah'nas ambassador at his mother's party. Recalled it nodding to him, and raising a glass in one of its four hands. Uncle Thani warning that this whole thing had the smell of aliens about it. Alien allies. This ship was making noise. It made him wonder what else was hiding out there, running faster than them to get ahead of their current position with no announcement at all.

"Scan," he said. "Keep your eyes peeled. That ship might be trying to get our attention. Let's make sure she doesn't have all of it."

"Aye LC," said Geish in a tone of agreement.

"Could push harder to make that rock?" Shahaim suggested.

"Any more than one-G and our tail lights up like Festival. This is as hard as we dare push without drawing attention. There's just too damn many of them out there."

He just hoped they made that damn rock before someone sprang them. With the jump lines shot, their next jump would be more likely fatal than any incoming ordinance.

No sooner had thrust been cut and G returned to normal than word came from the bridge for a boarding party to suit up. Forty minutes after that, and in the midst of armoured preparations in Assembly, Trace got a call from Erik himself asking to meet her at her quarters.

She jogged back and met him at the door just as he arrived, it being about equal time from Bridge and Assembly. She opened and gestured him in, and saw the bednets holding loose sheets bundled against the G-wall.

Erik turned on her with concern. "Where's Lisbeth?"

"She's been down in Engineering the last few hours. Helping Rooke with analysis."

Erik stared. "She went down during the *push?*" Trace waited calmly for him to realise she'd already answered that question. "And you let her?"

"I was busy. You were busy. She used her judgement. I talked to Warrant Officer Chau, she said Lisbeth's been sitting quietly, making herself useful."

Erik put his hands on his head and stared at a wall. "She went down the corridor?" Again Trace waited for him to realise that there was no other way to reach Engineering from here. And she'd already answered that question. "Good god Major…"

"Your sister is a very bright girl. She's going to be stuck with us for some time. I assure you, she will not like being stuck in a small room for all that time. She'll need to find her own way, and you're going to have to let her."

"Fucking Kulina. You know, not everyone's as tough as you…"

"Everyone *is* as tough as me," Trace said with certainty. "It's just that not everyone knows it. Now, you had something to show me?"

In frustration Erik pulled a chip reader from his pocket. "I got this back from maintenance just now from the plumbing filter."

"Your bowels work fast."

Erik hit a button, and uplinked a connection to the room display. Captain Pantillo's face appeared. Or rather, a blurry close up of the lower part of his unshaven jaw. But the voice was certainly his, rough, tired and very low. As though worried someone was listening.

"*Okay,*" he said. "*To whoever finds this. I'm pretty sure it might be you, Erik.*" A deep breath. "*And I don't think you're going to like how you find it.*"

Trace stared at the screen. And found herself tilting her head, as though somehow that change in perspective might reveal the rest of the Captain's face. He was talking into some kind of handheld device. Something simple that hadn't been confiscated from him, or that he'd rigged with a simple memory chip. A watch? Certainly he was in a cell, lying on the bed. Probably the same cell Erik had found him in.

"*I can't speak long. Just know that this whole thing runs very deep. I can't tell you what to do, because like what happens when the LC assumes command and I can't make the chair, you'll have to make your own decisions based on circumstances as you find them. Don't ask what I'd do. If you've found this, I'm no longer here. Follow your judgement. I'd never have asked for you to be in my crew if I didn't trust it."*

Trace glanced at Erik, and saw him struggling with emotion. Moisture in those brown eyes, dark brows knitted.

"I won't apologise for what I've dumped you in. On a personal level I am profoundly sorry. But as you'll find the deeper you dig, this is so much bigger than me, or you, or all of us together. We're all about the bigger picture. That's why we fought this war. I trust you can handle that bigger picture as you've handled it up till now.

"I can't tell you much specifically because I can't be sure who's going to find this chip. Revealing what I know might reveal my sources, who have to be protected. But know that this story begins where the last story ended, and humanity's fate is not nearly as much in our hands and arms as we'd thought. The more things change in this galaxy, the more they stay the same.

"Tell my family that I love them. My blood family, and my ship family. Trace, please protect them all. I know you will. And keep an eye out for that man we've discussed, you'll find him interesting, I promise. Gotta go." The camera view lifted briefly from his jaw to a closeup of his eyes. Familiar, slanted, wrinkled with experience the treatments typically hid. Smiling, she just knew, even though she could not see his whole face. Smiling at her. At them all.

The screen blanked. Trace blinked back tears. She could not trust herself to speak.

"A couple of things," said Erik, his voice tight. "First, who is 'that man you've discussed?'"

"Don't know," Trace lied. Speaking was difficult. "I'll have to think about it. We discussed a lot of people."

Erik nodded. "The other bit is after he talks about his sources. Clearly that's all code, he's trying to tell us something. Humanity's fate is not nearly as much in our hands and arms...

149

clearly he's not just talking about aliens, he's talking about chah'nas. Hands and arms, it's unnecessary to say both, the allusion is to many hands and arms."

Trace nodded, and wiped her eyes, trying to focus.

"The more things change in the galaxy, the more they stay the same... well the chah'nas are trying to restore their empire, we've always known that. But most of their fighting has been against sard and kaal — most of their old empire is what the tavalai held, and that's all with us. So I'm thinking someone's done a deal about that."

"There's been speculation before," Trace agreed with an effort. "But we're not just giving them their old territory back, any human leader who gives away what we paid such a price for would find his neck in a vice real quick."

"Exactly," said Erik. "So this is something new. As to what he meant by 'this story begins where the last story ends', I've no idea. I mean which story? There's so many stories."

"Yeah," Trace said slowly, thinking hard. "You've got me. That might be the key, though. It sounded almost like he was giving us directions." She nodded at the chip reader. "You should play that for the whole ship, when we've got a moment. Or let copies circulate. They deserve to see it. Learn what they're up to their necks in."

Erik's eyes widened a little, taking in her full meaning. "Let them see I didn't kill him?" he said drily. "Doesn't entirely prove that does it? Not for the totally conspiracy-minded."

"Couldn't hurt," Trace reasoned. "Now I've got a boarding party to lead, and you've got a ship to fly in proximity. Try not to crash into it."

CHAPTER 11

"That's definitely a docking port," said Geish, as *Phoenix*'s floodlights lit upon the rock's uneven side. An arm protruded, only a few meters, but inviting. Directly alongside it, a big circular indentation, covered by a steel door within. Big enough to fly a shuttle into, were it open. "And that looks like a cargo port beside it."

"We don't design it like that," said Shahaim, with awe. "That takes some massive structural work. Looks like they hollowed the whole thing, you could put a ship in that."

"Might still be one in there," Kaspowitz added. "Small one, anyhow."

"Engineering's too good for chah'nas," said Erik. "They're good at ships, but they never bother with rocks. This is tavalai work." Which during the Chah'nas Empire had been basically the same thing. Chah'nas had done the ruling, and the head-kicking when required, while the tavalai had done the administering, building and money-counting. The Empire's bureaucrats, they'd been called. Before the bureaucrats had gotten sick of their muscle and decided, with some success, they could do without them.

"Scancomp says Chah'nas Empire," Geish agreed, flipping through multiple spectrums. "No idea what it is, could be some kind of command and control. Do we have records of what Argitori was under the Empire?"

"Far reach of tavalai space," said Kaspowitz. He was something of a scholar, largely self-taught, on Spiral history. Long service on *Phoenix* had given him a lot of bunk-time spent reading. "There was mining, but the chah'nas were occupied with other species, had trouble keeping everything together further in. This could have been a watch post, or a mining scout, or both."

"Any records of anything else like it around here?" Erik asked.

Kaspowitz shook his head, flipping through screens. "Nope. There were sizeable mining and refinery operations on Qualek and

Iprosha, but those had support stations, all long gone, dismantled for parts in the fighting when the Empire came apart."

Erik chewed a nail. After the fall of the Chah'nas Empire, the First Free Age had begun under the primary guidance of the tavalai. That had lasted the best part of ten thousand years. During the latter few thousand of those, a new race called the krim had crawled from their sulphuric hell of a homeworld and gained access to space, thanks to generous loans of tavalai technology. Krim claimed their territory here, their homeworld only a few jumps from Argitori. The range of the Free Age had expanded, and this former fringe territory became the centre of krim space... along with what humans now called Homeworld. Beyond that again, was Earth, separated from the Free Age Range by krim space.

"Tavalai gave all this up to the krim," said Erik. "No chance at all this was a krim base?"

"Very unlikely no," said Geish with certainty. "Krim didn't like minor outposts, they went big with everything. And they redesigned everything they didn't like."

"Like Earth," Jiri muttered.

"Krim could have occupied it for a while," said Shahaim. "Especially when we were tearing them apart in this region. They didn't have the resources for anything other than fighting, something like this they would have just left alone."

"I agree," Erik said grimly. "I think Order Four applies. I'm calling it — Second Lieutenant Karle, if you see any sign of hostile activity, you have my command to fire on your initiative."

"Aye sir," said Karle, adjusting his toggles and running main fire protocols on all *Phoenix* weapon systems. Order Four was one of Fleet's oldest. Humanity was fairly sure they'd wiped out the krim, but the possibility of small surviving settlements remained. Even now, seven hundred years after the krim's demise, Fleet captains everywhere were under orders to watch for possible survivors in remote places like this, and continue the extermination. In all those seven hundred years there had been no official sightings of living krim, but always there were the rumours, through Fleet and merchanters, of things kept quiet. Given recent events, Erik could

152

easily imagine Fleet lying about such things, to maintain the happy illusion that the krim were all gone.

"They're going to be very old and very self-sufficient if they've been here seven hundred years," Kaspowitz suggested. "With all our insystem traffic, they won't have been moving around much."

"Krim have the emotional life of plankton," said Erik. "Patience is a strong suit." He flipped coms. "Major, I've commanded Order Four, be advised."

"*I'm so advised,*" came Trace's voice. "*I'll be quite happy if the little bastards are in there.*"

Erik raised eyebrows at Kaspowitz. It was a very un-Kulina thing for her to say. Though obviously she was playing to her marines, revving them up. "Sugauli was thick with krim," Kaspowitz reminded him. "Hell of a fight taking it off them, that's where the Kulina legend began. All Kulina are raised with those tales of the olden days. She probably *will* be happy if the little bastards are in there."

Trace was locked into the midships dorsal docking port, zero-G and hooked into wall handles in case they bounced. About her were Alpha Platoon, armoured and sealed like her, packed along the tight walls and ceilings like some heavily armed insect colony. Ahead of them, at the airlock mouth, was the DACU — the Docking Assault Clearance Unit, known by marines everywhere as 'Plugger' because it filled a docking tube like a plug, heavily armoured and returning fire if necessary.

"We think it's at least ten thousand years old," Trace told them. "Something this size is probably rotational, only the rotation stopped somewhere along the way. We might expect an outer gravitational rim, the inner core is probably fusion but we don't know what's still there. Keep an eye out for booby traps, if it's an old Chah'nas Empire facility we don't know under what circumstances it was abandoned or who moved in since. Order Four has been invoked."

That got a growl of approval from Lieutenant Dale, who commanded Alpha.

"Alpha and Charlie will enter with me, we'll split and take a half each. Echo will hold reserve here, Bravo and Delta on standby. Questions?" No reply. "Good. This might be an archaeological expedition, but *Phoenix* marines come prepared."

"*Saddest thing about krim being all dead is that we can't kill them anymore,*" Dale added. That got some loud, approving noises.

A crash of grapples. The dock operator indicated a seal, which was an aggressive operation some likened to forced sex. The inner airlock door closed on Plugger, which held itself steady with little bursts of compressed nitrogen thrust. The outer airlock opened onto a cold, yawning passage that Trace could see in inner visual as Plugger's feed came back to them.

A burst of gas and Plugger drifted into the passage. Temperature sensors showed it was nearly 110C below freezing. "*Too cold for life,*" someone remarked. "*Looks dead.*"

"Let's save that judgement until we're in," said Trace. "Anyone home would have seen us coming, they could have flushed the outer rim to freeze it, make it look deserted. Alpha Platoon, advance."

As Dale's marines unhooked from the surrounding walls and pushed forward, the inner airlock door opening once more, now that there was no immediate incoming fire. They formed a drifting formation behind Plugger's advancing bulk, little thrusts from their suit jets keeping them in position. Trace would have led in herself, but she knew her Lieutenants didn't like it when she put herself out front all the time.

When all of Alpha's troops were past her, she went herself. As *Phoenix* Company commander she had a command section of eight, led by First Sergeant 'Stitch' Willis, who'd been wounded fifteen times, retired twice, and found peacetime didn't agree with him. Willis was sometimes called her bodyguard, and took more pride in that than anything else he'd done in sixty-two on and off years of active service.   He took position at her side now, as mist fogged her visor as warm *Phoenix* humidity froze in contact with ten-thousand-year-old air.

"*Got reasonable air pressure,*" Dale remarked.   "*Some kind of life support's been working.*"

"*Composition reading says it's breathable.   Freeze your tonsils though.   Not much CO2, either the scrubbers are working or there's no one breathing here.*"

"*Docking entry ends ahead,*" Dale said tersely.   "*Keep it tight marines.*"

Plugger broke into open space, Dale and his formation close behind.   Trace heard someone catch breath at the size of the interior hold.   They were inside a cross-corridor that you really could have flown a shuttle in — a good fifty meters across and nearly perfectly circular.   Directly alongside this little docking passage, it opened into another huge circular passage, no doubt leading directly to the doors they'd seen from the outside.   All in pitch black, save for the multi-spectrum non-vis light that Plugger shone through the space, lighting it all up on their IR.

"*Phoenix*, you seeing this?" Trace asked in a low voice. "Alpha Platoon hold here, let Plugger take middle position."

"*Yes Major we're seeing it,*" came the LC's voice in her ear. "*Tavalai do good work.*"   Ten thousand years ago, Trace thought. Or far longer, as ten thousand only marked the fall of the Empire. But the Chah'nas Empire had been around for eight thousand years before that.   Eighteen thousand years ago, humans had been building with mud.

She recalled a memory, herself as a young girl, no more than ten and struggling through a period of poor meditative practice and general rebellion.   She wasn't entirely sure, she'd told one of her siksakas bluntly, that she wanted to be violently killed before the age of thirty, as the statistical likelihoods predicted.   'But oh my child,' the siksaka had told her.   'The wonders you will see first.'

Couldn't argue with that, Trace thought, gazing around.   And more amazing yet, she was thirty-two years old, and still here.

"Tell them if they do find any jumpline systems we can cannibalise, let me know," came Rooke's request from Engineering.

"Could he actually cannibalise a ten thousand year old chah'nas jump engine?" Shilu wondered.

"Yeah, that kid probably could," said Geish. Erik watched three screens — Rooke's repairs on the left, Trace's feed in the middle, and Geish's scan feed on the right. Trace's feed was the most fascinating, but his job wasn't to be fascinated, it was to watch for threats to *Phoenix*. But it was hard not to stare at the helmet-cam visuals of those huge, precisely hewn caverns in the rock. Trace's voice came through calm as she split her platoons, now a little fractured by static. Interference would get worse the further they went into that metallic rock.

"Those look like elevator shafts," said Kaspowitz with amazement. "Huge ones. What the hell were they keeping in this rock?"

"Clearly it used to spin if it needed elevators," Shahaim added. A spacer brought her some coffee, which she sipped. They were technically well into second-shift now, but when things got serious, first-shift always took charge if they could.

"That's a heck of a lot of air volume in there if it's all pressurised," came Rooke's voice over coms. *"Something's clearly been running. Hell of a technical job if life support's still running over ten thousand years. The better guess is that someone's either using it now, or has been back periodically to keep it running in case they needed it."*

"Thank you Second Lieutenant," said Erik. "You wouldn't be taking time away from repairs to watch the monitors, would you?"

"I can do both," came the defensive reply.

"Make sure you do."

"LC?" said Lieutenant Shilu from Coms. "I didn't want to say anything earlier, it didn't seem worth mentioning. But the last thirty minutes I've seen a proliferation of transponder activity

156

identifying itself as Debogande-related traffic." Erik frowned and peered at his scan feed more closely. Shilu's coms feed overlaid onto that image, showing which ships and bases were identifying themselves as what, if anything. "You see, usually the company name is last? After the ship name and registration? See how they've shifted to first?"

Shilu was right. Ito Industries — that was a regional group owned by Debogande Enterprises. Their primary operation here was a big industrial cluster in the lunar system of the fifth planet — a gas giant. Erik could count... five Ito Industries pushers at various velocities through this part of the system, and all had their corporate affiliation first, not last.

"That changed in the last half-hour?" Erik asked.

"Yes sir," said Shilu. "I figure we could try and laser-com one... this freighter here, *Abigail*. She'll be within one second light in eleven hours at her current course, assuming she holds heading."

"Some of Fleet are very good at spotting laser-com if they're close enough," Geish cautioned. "We certainly are. And with so many of them running dark, we don't know exactly where they are."

Erik gnawed a nail. "Tell me again when *Abigail* approaches closest. I'll have another look then."

Did he really want to involve local corporates in this? Certainly he could tell them his side of the story. The Debogande network was enormous through human space. It could spread the word, possibly provide them with help and even shelter if they could just lose this damned Fleet pursuit. But that word would be getting out anyway, from Homeworld — Fleet couldn't stop it, it would go where ever natural commerce took Debogande ships, which was everywhere. He *might* just be putting local civvies in harm's way for no good reason, and they might not thank him for it. Just because they drew their paycheques from Debogande Incorporated didn't suggest the kind of kill-or-die loyalty that existed on *Phoenix*. There were some diehard loyalists, and principled spacers who hated government interference in commerce, be it Fleet or otherwise. But there were just as many Fleet loyalists who'd squawk their location to the nearest Fleet warship.

He looked back to Trace's feed.   If they had to move in a hurry, it was going to be a hell of a rush to get all those marines back aboard in time.   But they couldn't be snuggled up close to a hollow and possibly inhabited rock without knowing what it was.   He glanced at the deployment timer — T-plus-7 minutes and counting. Come on Major, don't take too long.

Trace found the elevator platform at the end of the massive shaft in the rock.   It loomed ahead like the nose plate of a starship, a big circle of solid steel, fifty meters across.   It latched to the rock sides on big runners that ran down the walls, accompanied by powerlines and piping.

"*Wow,*" someone murmured, at the sheer size of it.

"*Keep it tight boys and girls,*" said Dale.   "*Close to the walls, you're a sitting duck in the middle of the shaft.*"

Alpha Platoon floated in a ringed deployment about the shaft, three squads of twelve in three sections of four, for thirty-six total. Add an eight-man heavy squad for forty-four per platoon... and Trace's Command Squad of eight including herself, and there were fifty-two of them, while Charlie Platoon's forty-four went up the other shaft.

"*There's the platform access,*" said Sergeant Manjhi, as tacnet lit up that space, filling in the architecture as they went.   It looked like the mouth of a hangar, dark and opening onto the elevator platform.   The suits generated enough of their own below-vis spectrum light to make everything bright enough, if ominously patchy.   But inside that hangar, all was dark.

Alpha's lead elements took position about the doorway with little bursts of thrust, while others drifted gently into far-range, touching feet down on the platform.   "*Looks clear,*" said one.

"*Proceed inside,*" said Dale.

"*Second Squad, proceeding inside,*" said Sergeant Hall. "*Watch the blindspots people, nice and easy.*"

Trace watched them go, hovering off a further wall and watching on tacnet as Charlie Platoon did similar up the other end. So far the asteroid layout was looking symmetrical. She'd come with Alpha instead of Charlie because she had to pick one, and to her usually reliable memory she'd gone with Charlie on another op more recently than she'd gone with Alpha. Tough headkickers or not, marines could get quite sensitive if they thought she was favouring one unit over another, and she had to be careful she wasn't. None of her units needed micro-managing, and at this point she could watch from the rear and only speak when needed.

Her point-men's visuals showed her the hangar layout while she was still outside — there were three branching corridors, all wide and flat-based, suggesting rotational gravity when the asteroid was spinning.

"First Squad take the left corridor," she told them. "Second and Third, take the right. Ignore the third corridor, it looks like a circumference route, it'll just take us across to Charlie Platoon. I want us moving down and away from *Phoenix*, and I want division into groups no smaller than squads. Lieutenant Jalawi, you hearing this?"

"Major you're a little broken, but I hear you want us moving away from Phoenix, divisions into groups no smaller than squads, affirm?"

"Affirmative Lieutenant, let's go." She caught every word of Charlie Platoon's commander, but the static was worse than she'd hoped. They deployed ahead, allowing her command squad to move in, small bursts of jet thrust into the hangar's cavernous mouth. Here was another huge chamber, with what might be control room windows overlooking. She could imagine shuttles here, anchored to the floor by gravity, serviced by... chah'nas workers, probably. Back in the Empire, tavalai had been doing the office work, not flying shuttles.

The branching corridors were also big, though nothing like the size of the elevator shafts behind. Huge piping filled them, running along like bundled straws. Ahead, armoured marines drifted into those gaping mouths like children playing in the hallways of giants.

Dale took First Squad right with Second Squad, Trace took her Command Squad left with Third Squad, while Heavy Squad split into two sections of four, one behind each. They progressed at what would have been a sprint had gravity been in effect, but at this scale felt like a very slow walk. Now the static really began to break things up, tacnet flickered and showed units a tentative orange rather than blue, and accompanying vis-feeds turned snowy. Air temperature remained a steady minus 110C, though laser-scan on the walls showed a warming trend. At the next forty-five degree junction she sent Third Squad ahead, and went right with Command Squad and the four-man Heavy section.

"Okay people," she told them, "we'll have as many as seven different groups spreading through this rock and our coms are snowy. Let's not shoot each other by mistake — if you see movement, query and identify." Because tacnet was telling her it could only be sure of where half of her guys were.

"*This middle pipe here's reading plus-50C,*" said Private Rolonde. "*Something's definitely on.*" Her voice was tense. Far-deployment in a hostile environment did that too — if someone lost environmentals out here, the air looked only marginally breathable and the temperature was positively deadly, and *Phoenix*'s warm corridors felt a long way away.

But this was more than that. They were in a search pattern because *Phoenix* required them to thoroughly search the asteroid, and quickly. But what *Phoenix* required was putting them at greater risk, by dividing their numbers, if something hostile was about. But there was no choice to it — the ship's safety came first, and with all the hostile shipping about, they didn't have time to examine the rock more slowly in strength. She could deploy another platoon, she thought... but that was against all established practice in these situations — carriers never deployed more than half their marines at a time if they could possibly help it, in anything short of a full scale strike. That way if something very bad happened, *Phoenix* would still have a reasonable complement left.

160

They flew past smaller side corridors, cut into rock but capped with steel bulkheads... and on the right, something slightly larger, but still far smaller than this current one.

"Check this," said Trace, and put an arm out for a blast of sleeve-thrust to slow her down. "Deploy right, all cover." They moved like a well-oiled unit, several in tight by the corners while Private Ugail tossed a handball into the corridor. It spun and adjusted its flight, feeding vision and scans back to them all, showing nothing. Save for some tubes in the wall further up that didn't look like more pipes. "Might be elevators, could lead to the core. Advance. Heavy Section, watch our tails."

The Heavies covered the entrance, their massive chain-guns and cannon no effort at all in zero-G. Until they had to fire them, that was. Sergeant Willis led them in, and the temperature began climbing to minus 90C.

"Radiant heat," said Willis. *"No convection in here, it won't travel much. I guess it's coming through the walls."* The tubes on the wall ahead were indeed elevators. They burrowed up into rock and disappeared.

"What's the bet those go to the core?" said Private Van.

Trace ran laser-scan on it... and got a vibration. She cut some static-filled conversations elsewhere through the rock, and listened just to the vibration. A ticking. Clatter clatter. Tick tick. Like someone rolling a tin can along a metal floor. Click clang. Very faint.

"What the fuck is that?" asked Rolonde, evidently listening to the same thing.

"What's what?"

"Laser-scan on the elevators, listen."

"I don't know of any auto-mechanism that makes a noise like that," said Trace, suddenly very aware of how isolated and walled in they were in this vast, alien place. Her heart thudded harder, and she took a deep breath to calm herself. On the climb, the fearful ones fell. "We're going to assume something's alive in there." She flipped to broadcast. "All units this is the Major, reassemble on my position, we've got a way to the core but we're only going in there in force..."

A roar of gunfire over coms, then explosions. Shouts and yells, garbled static and a screech of metal on metal. Trace wanted to yell at them to report position, tacnet showed little but orange and blank space, but she knew that more shouting would just add to clutter. They were marines, they'd get a clear com soon enough...

"Hacksaw!" someone was yelling above the noise. *"This is Alpha Two, hacksaw! Hacksaw!"* And even Trace's blood ran cold, because far worse than krim were hacksaws — AI drones, remnants of the Machine Age twenty-five-thousand-years gone, the bloodiest horror known to have befallen flesh-and-blood sentience in this part of the galaxy. Humans had only encountered their surviving warriors a handful of recorded times, though every now and then a ship would disappear in some remote region, and people would wonder.

"Form up!" Trace shouted. "All units rendezvous and regroup!" As Sergeant Willis yelled at Command Squad to make defensive formation. "Let's get away from this elevator now — Willis, heading 110, let's get to First Squad!"

They displaced, thrusters firing, jetting down the narrower corridor with terse instructions back and forth to watch formation... the elevator exploded just as the Heavies left it, showering them with shrapnel — something up above had put a bomb down the shaft as she'd feared.

"Third Squad, make my position! Make my position! We are headed 110, rendezvous with First Squad, Alpha Company rendezvous on First Squad!" Just hoping they could hear as the walls shot by, and tacnet showed a static mess of blue units and red, meaning hostile, but nothing that made sense...

"Clear that corner!" said Willis as they approached another big transit corridor ahead, and Rolonde and Terez fired airburst grenades to clear anything hiding around that corner... explosions then something else flashed...

"Cover!" And Trace hit jets and slammed herself back-first into the wall as fire came in, bounced and fired back amidst a hail of

outgoing fire. *"Seekers!"* Someone threw a handball and tacnet showed a flash of visual, something many-limbed and spider-like amidst smoke and fire, then vision vanished in a burst of thrusters.

"Advance!" said Trace and they went, the handball recovering enough to show several more spidery things jetting onto the walls in the opposite direction. Trace locked on an SR and fired it on tacnet, jetting forward as she saw it turn that sharp corner, then something blew in a flail of legs, and incoming fire shredded the exit ahead. "Wait!" Trace yelled over the shriek of disintegrating metal, grabbing a pipe to halt herself short. "Let 'em spend ammo! Load SRs!"

These units hadn't spotted the handball, so didn't know they were being watched. It suggested visual vulnerabilities, or processing ones.

"Fire!" More short-range missiles streaked from backracks, turned a sharp corner and... "Go!"... before they hit, a burst of thrust as they did, then into the vast open corridor as multiple strikes hit the walls. Trace fired right where one ought to be, auto-jets correcting for recoil to stop her tumbling as she skidded sideways and into the far wall — multiple strikes amid the smoke, she saw metal limbs coming apart, fragments flying.

Then the others of Command Squad were firing at the second as it jetted forward, losing limbs and weapons in a hail of heavy fire, but Trace was already looking around for others... and directly above was a hole in the ceiling. She put a grenade through it just as they came, blasting one into a tumbling collision, yelling "Above you!" and firing on full auto and rapid-cycle grenades.

Command Squad split in all directions, as amidst them came twisting debris, and several still active hacksaws — and for the first time she saw it, six-limbed, an armoured thorax, variable-articulated sensor head with multiple weapon mounts blazing fire. It slashed and spun in all directions at crazy speed, someone's suit went spinning, another spider came apart at close-range fire and shattered. An explosion sent it Trace's way and it hit the wall alongside, twice the size of an armoured marine, and she jetted backward to dodge a squealing saw-blade that sliced straight through the wall she'd been on.

She blasted it, and then the Heavies were firing from the corridor exit, and the last one still fighting came apart like paper in a hailstorm. Tacnet told her Ugail was dead, and she could see Sergeant Willis was too — his suit was in two pieces, that saw-blade had gone straight through him.

"Cover and reload!" she commanded, smacking in a new mag. "Blow those things' heads off, let's be sure! Injuries, report!"

"*Major, Sergeant Willis is...*"

"I know that, I said injuries dammit! Pay attention!" Elsewhere she could hear fighting ongoing. Echo Platoon would be deploying now from *Phoenix*, making Bravo and Delta the fighting reserve — she couldn't talk to them from here and so couldn't stop it if she'd wanted to.

"*Major I'm legged.*" That was Rolonde, voice tight. "*The suit's drugged it, don't feel much.*" More firing, as others finished off the twitching hacksaws.

"Private Arime, escort Private Rolonde back to *Phoenix*, don't stop for anything." It was a risk — if they met hacksaws on the way they were probably dead, two marines alone couldn't defend much, especially with one wounded. But Echo were on their way, and they'd meet backup soon... and she couldn't take wounded where she was going. "The rest of you, that hole in the ceiling is our way in. Hacksaw nests have queens — we attack the queen, the others will rush to defend her, we take pressure off our units. Let's go."

It was insane, of course — that little hole in the ceiling was tight and dark. But it led somewhere where the hacksaws were, and as Trace recalled reports on nests, the AIs were reluctant to use heavy firepower near their core. They built things in nests, mostly other AIs, self-replicating the only way machines could, by powered construction. Damage to that, in this isolated facility, could be difficult to fix, especially in this system where survival depended on not drawing attention to themselves. It gave attacking marines a slight chance, and forced the drones to get up real close to engage them.   It meant that she and her Command Squad would probably die, but at the benefit of saving, if it worked, nearly everybody else.

She jetted at hard thrust toward that dark, bullet-pitted hole, and not one of her squad hesitated to follow.   "Nine point nine!" Corporal Rael yelled on the way in.

"Nine point nine!" the others replied.   Ten billion souls in Sol System when the krim hit Earth.   Nine point nine billion dead. It had been humanity's battle cry for the past thousand years, and the hacksaws weren't the only ones who talked in numbers.

CHAPTER 12

"All hands," Erik told the ship, "be aware, emergency undock could occur at any time. I repeat, emergency undock could occur at any time." He flipped to marine channel. "Lieutenant Crozier?"

"Copy LC," came the Delta Platoon commander. She was the other senior marine still aboard besides Lieutenant Zhi of Echo Platoon, and next in the dock to leave or defend.

"Lieutenant I may have to break dock at any moment, prepare your troops."

"Copy LC."

"We're not going to get clear?" Geish asked in astonishment.

"Not yet," Erik said grimly, staring at the screens, ears straining to gain any sense of the chaos unfolding in the rock.

"Sir, I'm with Second Lieutenant Geish on this one," said Shahaim. "Those hacksaws can operate in vacuum just fine. They're sure to have other exits around the rock, and if they can get out, they can latch to our hull and cut straight through…"

"Second Lieutenant Karle," said Erik. "Do you have Armscomp dialled to near-defence?"

"Yes Captain. I mean yes LC." Very tense, with fingers and thumbs hovering over multiple handgrip buttons. Between him at Arms One, and Harris at Arms Two, they could handle near and far range threats simultaneously.

"Sir," Shahaim tried again, "they're so small and fast that at this range, and with the rock for cover, we're going to have blind spots and a few of them will get through…"

"We've got marines getting hurt in there," Erik said firmly. "They'll need medical attention immediately, if we have to evac them via the shuttles it'll take time, and the shuttles will be a lot more vulnerable to hacksaws than *Phoenix* is."

"Sir," Geish said angrily, "if any of those things get aboard…!"

"The Major has it under control," Erik shut him down.

"Sir this is a *hacksaw* nest! She could be dead!"

"The Major has it under control," Erik repeated coolly. And gave Geish a glare. "That will be all, Second Lieutenant."

"Aye sir." Geish looked grim.

"And watch those damn scans, hacksaws aren't the only thing we're worried about."

Trace put her Heavies on point and told them not to let the drones shoot first. They responded by blowing everything to hell on the way in and alternating the lead to let the others change mags and cool barrels. Corners that would otherwise be cleared with a visual inspection were instead air-burst grenaded, and several ambushing drones were blasted, or tried to attack once they realised their 'ambush' was blown and got shredded by chainguns instead.

The corridor wound through hard rock and confined engineering levels, a blur of steel gantries and support structures for systems Trace didn't recognise. But the hacksaws didn't appear to want them booby trapped, and there were a lot of electrical and other piping that Trace guessed were sensitive to high explosive.

The corridor ended with a hatch that Trace commanded blown, which the Heavies did with gusto. Trace threw a handball through the wreckage and saw... she wasn't sure what, a mass of systems that looked like nothing human-made. But there were no obvious threats, and tacnet was getting better at identifying hacksaws off handball sensors, so they burst through and took position...

And found themselves amidst a spidery tangle of steel beams, gantries, cables and pipes, all reworked and welded like some grotesquely beautiful piece of art. Or the inside of an insect's nest, on a thousand times the scale. Passages twisted away in all directions, never a straight line. In amongst it all were machines and machinery — zero-G formers, refiners, 3-D printers, all alive and blinking. Trace's HUD told her the air here was plus-31C — warm but not humid. This was where the heat was coming from, and the AIs must indeed have flushed the outer corridors to vacuum when they saw *Phoenix* coming, then let the life support air reflush to get such an abandoned, freezing look.

"Hold," Trace told her remaining unit, as they drifted to cover positions with effortless coordination. These had once been inner crew quarters and systems around the central reactor, she thought... but under however many centuries of hacksaw occupation, those old walls and divisions had been erased, and replaced with this. A colonised system, for the utility of the colonisers, who did not need gravity, or walls and doors. Air, they'd evidently kept, for the excellent insulator and heat-retainer it was.

A check of tacnet showed her no further fighting. She couldn't see everything, the feed remained as snowy as ever... but several other units she could see now advancing toward the core as she had, along similar routes. There should have been desperate resistance, now that she'd penetrated the inner sanctum, but there wasn't.

"Okay," she said carefully. "There's a chance that might be it. There might not have been that many of them, and maybe we've killed them all."

"*Or maybe they just don't want to shoot up their pretty nest now we're in it,*" Corporal Riskin countered between hard breaths.

"*Or they're waiting until we're deep inside then we get it from all sides,*" Terez added.

"That's possible too," Trace agreed. "The reactor should be up ahead. Probably they've rerouted the bridge controls to here as well. Let's progress slowly. You see anything moving that's not human, shoot it. Don't relax now, we're nearly there."

"*Oh no chance of that,*" murmured Van, staring wide-eyed at the nest. Every human instinct told a sane person to go the other way. But marines and sanity did not always agree.

They moved in slowly, weaving on jet bursts between the spidery mechanisms. They did not shoot to clear corners here — a lot of this environment looked as though it could do anything if damaged, including explode, catch fire or electrocute everyone within fifty meters. Machinery running lights cast ghostly shadows through the web of steel and cables, and drifting steam swirled in zero-G eddies.

"I got big power readings," said Riskin. *"Heading 290."*

Trace gave a thrust that way, rifle searching the shadows. Her hands wanted to shake, but knew better. On the climb, the shaking ones fell. It felt strange not to have Sergeant Willis here beside her, but she couldn't think about that now. Preferably not ever. Sometimes she wished she could just crawl into a cave, and meditate, and never come out. So many connections to the world made so many conduits for pain, like raw nerves to her soul. If she could remove them all, she would.

Ahead, her audio fed her the deep, pulsing throb of an alien mega-core. Ten-thousand-year-old-plus engineering, purring away to make power for these new guests. She could see it now, the great toroidal arc of some older fusion design, surrounded by a thick mass of rubberised electrical work, like a writhing nest of eels that fed around these spidery strands.

Here before the reactor, a cluster of control plates and a lot of relatively exposed wiring. Within the control plates, something unlike anything Trace had ever seen before. Unlike anything most humans had ever seen before. Its body was snakelike, articulated, effortlessly adrift in zero-G. It had various protruding arms, thin and articulated like a slender spider. Its head was circular, numerous sensors encircling a single, giant red eye. And its body, silver in the dim systems light, was rippling, like wind across a field of wheat.

"Major?" It was the LC's voice, faint and crackling. *"Major, where are you? I'm getting reports that the fighting has stopped, can you confirm?"*

"LC," Trace murmured, and transmitted visual feed. "Take a look at this." And to her marines, "Don't shoot. Yet."

She jetted past the last obstructions, and halted. The thing slowly writhed and turned within its control panels. The red eye lifted, as though to peer at them. Another ripple fled down its body, then back up just as fast. The effect was caused by thousands of tiny metal plates, Trace realised. Protruding from that long body like scales, and rippling in coordination to make this extraordinary effect. She'd never imagined AI might communicate like this. Creepy as hell, and chilling at this range... but oddly, mesmerisingly beautiful.

"*Hu-mans,*" it said. Or she thought it said. The voice modulators were odd, multi-toned and well-synthesised copies of human speech... and yet, somehow not. It was hard to pinpoint exactly where the sound was coming from. "*Hu-mans. Why did you kill the children?*"

Trace drew a deep breath. And heard, through the static, the LC swear in disbelief. "So. You speak English."

"*Why?*" Plaintively, almost aggressively. Ripples zoomed up and down, in great agitation.

"Your children were trying to kill us," Trace replied. "We are soldiers. UF Marines. Trying to kill us is a very bad idea."

"*Humans always aggressive,*" it said. The voice was changing even now, deeper, more melodious. As though perhaps this was its first encounter with humans, and it was learning from her speech what sounded right. "*Humans always kill the children. We must defend ourselves.*"

Trace gestured around. "Do you control all of this? Are you plugged into the entire asteroid system?"

"*We always control. The children would not have hurt you. You should have gone.*"

"We're hiding," Trace explained. "We needed this rock. Can you be unplugged?"

"*Why?*" Again plaintively. "*You have already killed the children. What more?*"

"We need this rock," Trace repeated. "Can you be unplugged?"

It writhed, back and forth within its panels. "*Major,*" came Erik's voice through the static. "*There were a number of sides in the AI wars. They split at least six ways. The truly hostile ones were nothing like this. We might be able to talk to it.*"

Trace switched channels briefly. "LC, that reactor can go critical if the controller wants it. We'll have time to get clear, but we'll lose the rock and draw every eye in the system onto our position." Back to external. "Can you be unplugged? We will not harm you if you unplug. Give the systems to us. We will be gone in time, and you can rebuild your children in peace." It was a lie. Hacksaw nests were always exterminated to the last circuit.

"*Children cannot be rebuilt,*" it said sadly. Yes, sadly. It certainly sounded sad. Trace refused to believe it. "*We have not the resources. The humans always kill the children. They will lie to the children too, to get them to unplug. The children do not want to die, we have still so much to do!*"

"*Major,*" Erik tried again. "*This isn't a warrior queen! It's something else... talk to it, you might get something!*"

"This rock is no use to us without control," Trace told the queen. "You must give us control, or you will die."

"*There is no purpose without the children,*" said the queen. The red eye glowed at her, unblinking and wise. For a moment, the ripples were still. "*The humans always kill the children. I am ready.*"

Trace shot it through the eye.

Erik did not want to go down to Assembly to greet the marines back aboard. The Captain had done so frequently, but it could be intense down there after casualties had been taken. There would be a lot of corpsmen treating wounded, a lot of life-and-death activity, and he did not want to be in the way. And he was not entirely sure that the marines would want him there anyway.

He had plenty to keep him occupied on the bridge, and went to Medbay when the chaos had settled down a bit. Medbay One was mostly full, fifteen out of twenty beds occupied. Medbay Two was also full — of bodies. A corpsman told him that the count was fourteen, but they weren't sure they'd recovered everyone yet. There were marines in there, some in tears, but keeping clear of corpsmen doing organ recovery — no one begrudged them that, even with the latest bio-synth aboard, sometimes the only thing that saved a wounded marine was one of his dead buddy's organs.

Erik returned to Medbay One and talked to a few of the less seriously wounded. One was Private Rolonde, one of the Major's Command Squad, her leg on ice, white-faced and stunned. It wasn't the leg that did it — First Sergeant Willis was dead, the guy who lead Command Squad and watched the Major's back while she was commanding the entire formation. Willis had been thought as indestructible as the Major. His marines couldn't believe he was gone, and Erik worried at the effect of this loss so soon on top of losing the Captain.

Trace arrived in the sweaty undershirt and light pants that marines wore under armour, and proceeded to talk to her people. Her touch was effortless as she clasped their hands, and spoke with quiet affection. She kissed several, put her hand in their hair, nothing like the cold-steel machine she was in combat. He could see how they looked at her, the relief at seeing her safe and here with them. The sense that despite everything, things would somehow work out, so long as the Major was here. Erik did not envy Trace her profession nor her lifestyle, but he envied the hell out of this. While he valued his many good friends on *Phoenix*, he doubted any loved him as much as this, nor needed his input as Trace's people needed her. And he was scared, to think of what would happen to them all if they lost her too.

She came to him before finishing her rounds, knowing that debrief came first. "What's the damage?" he asked her quietly as they stood by a wall as out of the way as they could get.

"Fifteen confirmed," said Trace. "One there wasn't enough left to bring back. Likely seventeen, there's two missing and not much hope. Twenty wounded." She indicated the adjoining emergency ward, where the most serious were in surgery or intensive care. "Five serious."

Erik took a deep breath. Thirty-seven, out of ninety-six who went onto the rock. It was seventeen percent of all *Phoenix* Company. Even Trace looked a little stunned, that hard, glassy-eyed expression of someone accustomed to control but finding it difficult.

Erik wanted to say that he was sorry, but that was redundant — sorry didn't help, and too much emotion only made everyone feel worse.

"You took the rock," he told her instead. "We've got a fighting chance of getting the ship repaired now. It was well done."

She nodded stonily. "Bravo and Delta are finishing the sweep, they'll do a full recon. I could send Echo too since they're relatively fresh, but..."

Erik shook his head. "I don't want more than two platoons in there at a time. We still might have to move suddenly, and we can't afford to risk more."

Trace nodded in agreement. "I'm going to have to rearrange a bit to fill in the gaps in Alpha and Charlie. With any luck we'll get maybe ten of these guys back in a week, the rest will take longer. Depends how much G we have to pull in the meantime."

"We should get a rest for a few rotations at least." He put a hand on her shoulder. "Don't worry about readiness. Just get your people healthy and make sure they get some rest. You included."

"I'd like to go back in and help supervise the recovery," said Trace. With anyone else, Erik might have been surprised. "I've got some ideas about those hacksaws, best to make sure Engineering don't miss anything."

"And of course the techno-nerds will need you to hold their hands and wipe their backsides," Erik added, attempting humour.

He was surprised and relieved when she managed a small smile. "They'll be okay. You're letting Lisbeth go over?"

Erik exhaled sharply. A joke, he realised. "Fuck, don't even say that. She'll want to, just you watch."

Trace smiled a bit more, and put a hand on his arm. "Sorry. We might get some tech out of it, at least." Which was completely illegal in any Spiral Age. But right now, no one cared. "Those things are just..." She gazed into nothing for a moment. Remembering. "Twenty five thousand years old. How is that even possible?"

"Could be much older, the Machine Age went for twenty thousand more before that. But they die of age too, or something like it... presumably they change their parts when they need to.

These ones might be relatively young, they were making new ones in there."

"We didn't find much mining equipment. Whatever they needed to make a fully functioning nest, they were short. If they'd been anywhere near full strength, we'd have been wiped out. They just fight like death itself."

"Hey, you too," said Erik.

Trace gazed at him for a moment. "You didn't want me to shoot the queen. Why not?"

Erik did not answer her immediately. He still was not happy about it, but this hardly seemed the time or the place for another of their arguments over command and jurisdiction. "The Captain taught me things too," he said finally. "Things I'll remember all my life. One of them is that not every problem can be solved with a bullet."

"You know what she could have done to the rock reactor," said Trace. "This one needed a bullet. Ship safety comes first."

"Trace... we're in a unique situation here. I mean, a hacksaw nest. What are the odds?"

"We're a warship, we don't do alien diplomacy."

Erik frowned. She seemed needlessly argumentative about it, when he hadn't wanted this fight at all. Was it troubling her? Did she want him to convince her of something she wasn't sure of herself? "Trace, that thing was smart. It was listening to you. Bullets are tools. Words are tools. You could have used either. But you chose the one you always choose."

"*I'm* a tool," she said flatly. "My life has a single purpose, and I've trained all my life to further my method of achieving it. I'm not some utility knife that can just activate a different blade — I have one blade, and it's sharp."

"And what is that single purpose again exactly?" Erik said with faint exasperation. "Service to Fleet? Who are now trying to kill us?"

Trace swallowed, and looked away. More unnerved than Erik had ever seen her. "Service to the human cause," she said quietly.

"Ah yes, the good old human cause again. The Kulina serve the human cause through the agency of Fleet, which can do no wrong. No individual interests, no matter how strong and right, can compete with the righteous necessity of Fleet. If you still believed that shit, Trace, your best course would be to sabotage our engines and blow us all to bits, and save Fleet the effort."

Trace stared at him. And had nothing to say.

Erik put the hand back on her shoulder. "If you died in that rock?" he said. "That would be a great loss to the operational integrity of this ship. But the far greater loss, to me, would be *you*. You're not just a tool, Major. You're my friend. All of these people here love you. And giant pain in my ass or not, I'd miss you."

Trace looked emotional. And astonished him by putting her head to his shoulder — not a hug, just a quick half-embrace that two friends might use in passing. Then she parted, with a whack on his arm, and returned to her wounded marines.

CHAPTER 13

At 0200 Erik was in bed and as far from sleep as ever. For one thing, his quarters were unfamiliar — these were the Captain's quarters, all personal items thankfully sent to storage by someone else so he didn't have to deal with that emotional burden. But he felt like a fraud lying here in this bed, like the servant in some wealthy house who tries on the owner's clothes when he's away on business. And he was certain others in the crew felt the same to see him here.

Crew rotations were a mess with all the holes in the ranks, though thankfully his junior officers were sorting that out without need of supervision. They simply lacked the bridge crew for three rotations, and so were down to two. That didn't matter so much now, as in these circumstances he was in the Captain's chair far more than a usual eight hour shift anyhow... but over the long haul it was going to become a drag. The main problem was they now lacked pilots. As acting-Captain, he was senior pilot. He toyed with the idea of making Shahaim second-shift commander, but dismissed it just as fast — he needed a good co-pilot, and she superb at that. As a senior-pilot, not so much, so she was more use where she was.

Lieutenant Draper had even better Academy scores than he did, but was green as grass. Lieutenant Prakesh had been second-shift Helm, but had been on PH-2 with Lieutenant Chia and Dean Chong when it was destroyed. That left another Academy whizz-kid, Second Lieutenant Dufresne, as Draper's Helm and co-pilot. Kaspowitz had said drily that given some encouragement, experience, and a good bedtime story before sleepytime, they'd do fine. Draper and Dufresne were just a few meters away in the bridge right now as he lay in bed, in effective command of *Phoenix* in one of the nastiest situations the ship had ever seen. That alone made the thought of sleep laughable. And he wondered, lying here in the Captain's bed, if Pantillo had thought similar thoughts about young Debogande in the Captain's chair. Worse, Dufresne was a known Fleet loyalist from a family of loyalists, and no one was completely certain she wouldn't just hit some fireworks to show everyone where they were.   Right now the situation was desperate enough that they had no choice but to hope that her instincts for self-preservation overrode her grander loyalties.

His buddy Remy Hale was over on the rock right now, heading Engineering's scouting efforts, accompanied by Bravo and Delta Platoons.   Unable to part with more than a handful of people for their scavenger hunt, Remy was rounding up marines and some off-shift spacers to sort through the hacksaw nest.   *Phoenix* had left Homeworld without the needed overhaul or resupply — Erik had listened as Rooke explained what they were missing, but about half of it had gone over his head.   Trace was over there too, of course, foregoing sleep in search of whatever it was she was searching for. Erik was unconvinced that it had to do with anything beyond her troubled state of mind.

He lay now with the slate on his thighs, watching various vid-feeds from the rock on one side, and nav-feed on the other. Rooke's ETA on repairs was now a vague sixty-plus hours.   Lisbeth was still down in Engineering, as far as he knew.   She had indeed volunteered to go to the rock — it only made sense, she'd argued, given she was non-essential and personnel were so short. Thankfully she'd only argued her case in Engineering, and even they'd turned her down.   No doubt not wishing to be blown out an airlock by the LC.

Nav-feed showed *Abigail*, now seven hours from her closest projected pass to their current position, on her way toward Maga, the Argitori fifth planet.   She'd be turning over soon to decelerate, approaching mid-point of her one-G thrust journey.   Still she was broadcasting Ito Industries ID in that unusual configuration, as were the rest of them.   Approaching seventeen-seconds-light on a different vector was *UFS Chester*, a very familiar First Fleet cruiser. Two-seconds-light beyond her, was *Fortitude*, another cruiser.

Chester was commanded by Captain Lubeck, an old friend of Pantillo's.   Erik had met him a few times on station call.   Would he be angry, blaming LC Debogande for his old friend's death?   Or would he be asking questions of why the *Phoenix*'s crew hadn't done in the rich-kid upstart themselves? Surely it must have dawned on many that something was odd with Fleet HQ's story. If LC Debogande had killed his Captain, then surely *Phoenix*'s crew would not be currently backing him, given how much more they'd loved the Captain than his supposed killer. There'd be a mutiny on *Phoenix*, or something else to stop them from ever getting this far in the first place.

But then there was Trace, who held the *Phoenix* crew in thrall with her legendary status. HQ could accuse her of being in on the murder, and point to the bloodbath in the holding cells as indication that she'd lost it. Her marines obeyed her unquestioningly, and once aboard *Phoenix*, spacer crew would find themselves with marine weapons in their face if ever they questioned the LC or the Major's command. There had been isolated cases before, of marines hijacking spacer vessels. Given the utter mismatch in close-quarters combat skills, that was a fight marines would always win.

But for that whole conspiracy theory to work, Erik thought further, HQ would have to convince everyone that Trace had gone nuts in the first place, and plotted with her LC to kill her Captain. Anyone who genuinely knew her would know that was silly. Of course, most of those who genuinely knew her were marines — ship captains might have met her in passing, but spacers and marines lived largely in different worlds. Possibly there were a lot of ship captains out in Argitori system right now, hunting for them, who were personally prepared to believe evil things of Major Thakur... but those of them with marines aboard would likely be hearing it from their marine commanders. Had the situation been reversed, and *Phoenix* were out there hunting some other ship who was in *Phoenix*'s current situation, Trace would have been chewing the Captain's ear off if she thought the accused marine commander incapable of what was being described.

So which of the ships out there had marine complements? *Phoenix* was a carrier, and carriers were made bigger than most specifically to hold a large complement of marines. Accommodation for two hundred plus extra troops plus equipment and transport was a heck of a lot of weight to pile onto a warship whose survival depended on speed and mobility. So designers had had no choice but to upscale every other system as well — bigger thrust engines to push the extra mass, bigger jump engines to move between stars, and bigger and more numerous weapons to protect the whole, expensive enterprise. Troop carriers were slow and vulnerable, but combat carriers were about the most deadly thing in space. They also cost about the same as five perfectly effective cruisers, and were blasted by some Admirals as overrated and a waste of resources.

The United Forces Fleet was actually seven fleets. Each fleet had three combat carriers, for twenty-one total. Erik didn't recognise any of those here, though it was possible others were on their way. He was also noticing a distinct lack of *Phoenix*'s most familiar support vessels. They varied, *Phoenix* did not have a 'support fleet' as such, though doctrine was that combat carriers would always operate with numerous support where possible, being too valuable to risk alone. But over the past four months' operations, a usual bunch had accumulated, and those crews and captains had come to know each other well.

He did not see any of those vessels here. Small wonder. Probably HQ was sending word to other fleets and forces within rapid response range, to find captains who knew nothing of Pantillo personally, and would believe whatever nonsense they were told. Most particularly they'd get those captains whose primary skill was to climb the greasy pole, and would not disobey an order to round up their grandmas were their next promotion contingent on doing so. Erik knew there were many. The Captain had bitched about very little, but when he did, those other sorts of captain were usually the subject.

Still, that presence of marines onboard ships looking for them was worth considering. He made a call to Second Lieutenant Abacha on second-shift Scan. "Hi Karli, it's the LC. Just a note, I'd like you to make a list of any ships out there with smaller marine complements. Trace it back to their jump signatures when they first arrived and make some guesses from who we know was at Homeworld."

"Aye LC," Abacha said warily. *"We can assume they won't send anyone friendly after us, right?"*

"Exactly," said Erik, thankful Abacha understood. "So see if you can get me a list of probables. The Captain had Worlder sympathies, we all know it. You don't have to do it yourself, but get someone or someones to go back over those captains who were at Homeworld, and match them against known political sympathies, if any. It might not be on record — ask around if it's not. I'd like to know exactly who's out there, and I just haven't been around long enough to know all this old gossip. The guys who knew were the Captain, and Commander Huang."

"Aye LC, I'll get on it. And LC... I don't know if you saw, but thirty minutes ago, that chah'nas ship manoeuvred."

"I saw it."

"It looked to me like a search grid move, something they're coordinating with someone else. I think she might not be alone." Another chah'nas ship nearby. Running dark.

"Interesting. Keep an eye on it."

"Aye LC."

Because of all the ships and captains searching for them, the ones with the least compulsion for mercy toward *Phoenix* were the chah'nas. Erik wondered drily how many more of them HQ would bring in to look for them.

Off the main hangar Trace had passed through in the marines' first armoured sweep of the rock, the Engineering crew had found corridors converging to make crew quarters and control rooms. Trace glided along them now in zero-G, her suit light illuminating wall panelling, doorways and light fittings, and trying to imagine it all as it had been, ten thousand years before.

The artwork astonished her. She paused before one such piece, gazing at abstract shapes carved into the rock wall, and wondered what it had meant to those who'd made it. There were circles and crescents that might have been planets, and some triangles, all run through with beams of what might have been multi-spectrum light.   In the design it seemed to refract into different beams, then pass through an eye, surrounded by... clouds?

It could only be tavalai, she thought, wishing the air were warm enough, and clean enough, to open her visor and take a closer, unfiltered look.   Only tavalai would take the time and effort to carve pictures into rock.   Chah'nas weren't much on art beyond the crudely symbolic, and krim hadn't been known to even comprehend the concept.   On Sugauli, there wasn't anything left of krim but some old mines and ruined settlements.   No artistic flourish to recall an entire species by.   But the krim hadn't appeared to care about that, so it seemed pointless that humans should care about it either.

"Big deal," said Private Van, arriving at her side to peer at the shapes.   *"A kid could do this."*   Trace sighed.   Krim weren't the only ones without artistic appreciation.

"You know T-Bone," she told him, "I did tell you to stay behind and sleep."

"You did," said Van.   *"What's your point?"*

"My point is that for a commanding officer, I seem to have very little say in who comes with me."   She waved him on, and the rest of Command Squad behind him.   None of them had listened when she'd told them to stay, but her reprimand held only affection.

Grand passages opened into stairs, and an open elevator in the middle of a circular walkway.   Trace peered through doorways, and found rooms stripped bare save fittings for water, electricity and others.   All the air was pumped in through great vents hidden behind wall grilles.   The machines didn't need air, but they preferred a higher temperature than the super-freeze their metal bodies would drop to in a vacuum this far from any sun.

Trace found Ensign Hale and two Engineering colleagues in a command room.   It was a big, circular space with a pronounced step-up to some large chairs on a platform overlooking the others. In the centre of the room, some artistic decoration in what would have been a central power column and ceiling support.   Further around the rim were the main workstations, smaller chairs facing onto blank frames where long ago, display screens would have been mounted.

Hale and another spacer drifted by one of the big command chairs, with cables fed into one of those empty sockets. Trace's uplink found a construct running in the room, and opened onto an engineering-geek conversation about data feeds and programming languages.

"Wow," said Corporal Riskin from Alpha Heavy Squad, who'd also come along with his chain gun. *"Those command chairs are bigger, right?"*

"Chah'nas," said Trace, turning off her suit light. The techs had portables set up, and she didn't want to blind anyone. "These lower work stations are for tavalai. The big boss chah'nas sit in the big chairs, and crack the whip on the tavalai down here."

"Poor bloody froggies, huh?" said Terez with dry sarcasm. *"Must have sucked for them."*

Yes, Trace thought, looking around. Yes, it must have. Tavalai were very far from slaves in the Empire, but they'd followed chah'nas rules. And by god did the chah'nas have rules. Strict caste segregation amongst their own kind, strict behavioural codes, strict everything. Chah'nas society was a maze, and when they'd been in charge, everyone else had been forced to appreciate their bizarre sense of order. Chah'nas weren't inherently cruel or parochial — so long as you played by their rules, you'd get a fair run. They'd discovered early that tavalai were better at bureaucracy and what they regarded as 'lower-level governance', than chah'nas were, and from then on, tavalai had been regarded as a separate caste within chah'nas society who specialised in precisely those lower-level functions. It had grown to entail quite a bit of power, and tavalai who remained satisfied with that had done quite well, and been treated 'fairly', as far as that went.

But tavalai were a creative, intellectual and argumentative bunch, and many of them were naturally inclined to squabble amongst themselves, and with their then-overseers. And the chah'nas would eventually get sick of it, and start handing out punishments, and tavalai would recall that ultimately it was the people with the bigger stick, and the greater utility in its use, that got to make the decisions. They'd learned that lesson well, over the millennia. Though perhaps not quite as well as humans had.

One of the voices in the construct, Trace realised, was Second Lieutenant Rooke's. "Hey Rooke," she told him. "You're not taking time away from fixing the ship to dabble in alien archaeology, are you?"

"I had a choice between this or sleep," came Rooke's voice. He was back in Engineering on *Phoenix*, watching all this on a VR setup. *"I chose this, it recharges me better than sleep."*

"Is it useful?" Trace asked dubiously, drifting across.

"Well they've got some amazing fabrication tech up in the nest," said Ensign Hale. She was Erik's friend from second-shift, which generally overlapped with bridge crew third-shift. With various absences, she was now second-in-charge of Engineering. Ensign was a low rank for that, but no one seemed too fussed — Engineering was one department everyone agreed was overflowing with talent. *"We think it was tavalai tech in the original base before the hacksaws arrived and took it. If we could find where a few more of those are, it would save us a lot of searching."*

"Lots of stuff we can't fabricate on Phoenix," Rooke explained. *"A rock this size, we might be able to make stuff we'd normally have to go to station dock for."*

"You're going to convert the rock into a factory to make parts to repair *Phoenix*?"

"A small factory, yeah. We're missing a whole chunk of jump line, it was a lucky shot, it's not something ships just carry. But we should be able to fabricate a new section, if we can get the raw materials and the right fabricators, plus a little more manpower."

"I can put some marines on it, if that would help."

"Do you have anyone with engineering experience?" Rooke said skeptically.

"How many degrees does it take to push buttons on a fabricator?" Trace retorted. "We operate heavy equipment all the

time, our suits for one thing.   Tell them what to do, they'll do it."
She glanced at Riskin.

Riskin nodded with a wary look around.   *"If it means getting the hell out of here, hell yeah."*

Trace floated to Ensign Hale's shoulder, to peer at a display of the data they were extracting from the cable port.   "Are you seriously getting data you can read?" she asked.

"Yeah."   Hale looked excited.   *"Incredible, huh?   It's an old tavalai coding routine.   Ten thousand years old and we can still read it."*

"I suppose there's not much living here to age everything," said Trace.   She ran a combat glove tip across a dash frame.   It collected a layer of fine particles.   "There's no humidity, and it's cold all the time."

"No microbes," Hale agreed.   *"We scanned it, there's nothing else alive here.   It's incredibly old, but it's in great condition."*   Trace prodded a seat cushion.   The synthetic surface compressed oddly, and did not spring back when her finger left it.   It was very old, certainly, but completely undisturbed.   She wondered if the crew who'd sat in these chairs could have imagined this — suited humans, a race unknown to tavalai and chah'nas at the time, prodding around in their quarters ten thousand years later.

"Actually it's very interesting," said Rooke, as though continuing some earlier conversation that Trace had rudely interrupted.   *"The human records from when we ran into krim for the first time showed a lot of them just didn't believe it.   Not the krim — the whole Spiral civilisation, fifty thousand years back to the Fathers.   They talked a lot about the impossibility of technological stasis — they thought fifty thousand years was far too long for civilisation to remain essentially the same out here."*

"Well it wasn't the same," Hale corrected.   *"The Fathers were the only ones in space that far back, everyone else came later."*

"Sure, but humanity at the time was going through the Acceleration — we see it everywhere with all species, all the low-hanging fruit being plucked, I mean we were just a few centuries out from horse and carts, and no electricity.   Just massive change,

across about five hundred to a thousand years, heavy industry, micro-circuits, bio-tech, and finally FTL, etc. So they thought technology always moved at that pace, they didn't realise how much it slowed down once you got out here, into large-scale FTL civilisation... I mean once you get into quantum computing there's only so much further you can push it. Same with everything. They thought spacefaring aliens ten thousand years ahead of them would be unrecognisable, would have evolved beyond physicality and mortality, become trans-human gods. A lot of the science-folk didn't like discovering that even the tavalai and alo were still far away from anything like that. Post-Acceleration, civilisation actually reverts to something more like what humans had for thousands of years pre-Acceleration — similar weapons, similar tools, similar lifestyles, relatively slow change."

Trace left them to their work and conversation. Marines did not chatter as they worked, but Engineering was filled with different kinds of people whose brains and culture worked in different ways. She did not begrudge them that, so long as they were effective, and *Phoenix*'s techs were certainly that.

Back in the hangar, she found Delta Platoon's second squad hauling large nets filled with hacksaw parts, heading back to *Phoenix*. Sergeant Lai gave them a halt when he saw Trace, marines jetting with difficulty to stop the nets of clanking, drifting parts getting away from them.

"And the techs say it's entirely safe to bring these back aboard?" Trace asked Lai, peering at the assorted junk through the netting. It looked like someone had dismembered some giant robot spiders. Mostly these were power units, CPUs and weapons, she saw. Some dull sensor eyes stared out at her accusingly.

"Techies insist it's not a horror movie," Lai said drily. *"They don't come back to life in the middle of second-shift and cut our throats while we're sleeping."*

"Better fucking hope not," someone muttered.

"And we can reverse engineer any of this?" Trace asked dubiously.

Lai made an exasperated gesture. *"Hey Major, the techs are still up in the core, screwing around in that nest. I'm just a marine."*

"Insects specialise, Spanky," said Trace, prodding some of the parts. "Don't be an insect." Sergeant Calvin 'Spanky' Lai snorted. No two bits of molded body casing were identical. The head casings were all different, alloy steel of great strength and low mass. Probably it had insulating and conducting properties too. There was no reason to make them all different unless the insides were different too. Did hacksaws build natural variation into their designs? "I wonder how old they are. All of these parts can be made locally with the fabricators, except for the CPUs. They'll have the knowledge to copy themselves, but without the fabricators that can actually print the circuits, it won't do them any good."

"Maybe they take the CPUs of dead hacksaws with them," Private Ijaz suggested. *"From where ever they came from. Maybe they've only got a limited number of fabricators and they have to keep recycling their dead."*

"Why can't they just make new fabricators?" someone wondered.

"This is crazy advanced stuff," said Trace. "Pocket fabricators won't do it, you need whole facilities. AI reproduction was never very efficient when they got this advanced. Big advantage for organic life — we don't have to spend half of our resources and labour just reproducing new ones."

"Sure, but we don't live forever, either."

"Neither do they, apparently," said Lai, looking at the broken parts. *"You know we're violating ten kinds of Fleet law on the AI restrictions by studying this? Usually we'd have to report it, hand it over, or if that was impossible, destroy it."*

"Yeah, well Fleet are already trying to kill us, so there's not much more they can threaten us with. And right now we need every edge — who knows what our techs will find useful in here."

"Major?" Trace looked about at the floating armour. On coms alone, it was often hard to tell who was speaking. *"Here, it's Melsh."*

"What is it Smat?"

Some repressed grins within faceplates. They loved that she knew all their nicknames, many of which were rude or silly. The lower ranks found it funny to hear those names on her lips. Ehud 'Smat' Melsh had earned his for being a 'Small Man Always Talking'. *"If we're recovering junk now? Does that mean we're not going to be making a station call for quite a while?"*

Silence amongst them, awaiting her answer. She looked around at them. "You've seen the Captain's last recording?" There were nods — within articulated combat helmets you could see that. "Captain made that right before the LC went to see him in holding. I was only marginally surprised LC found him dead — I've told you why before. I think Spacer Congress was shit scared of him running for office, I think they've got the armchair admirals' balls in a squeeze, or vice-versa, and they planned to have him framed. Ruin his political career, now the war's over. Only he wouldn't roll over, and the LC wouldn't, so they framed the LC with his murder to kill two birds with one stone."

"That sounds right to me too Major," said Lai. There was a hard note of challenge to his voice, as though daring any of Second Squad to disagree with him. *"You'd know better than us anyhow."*

"No," Trace said firmly. "No I wouldn't. Your opinions matter. You didn't just hand in your brains when you put on the uniform. I'm flattered that you respect my opinion, but don't just replace yours with mine. This whole thing, the wars, the fighting, the service — it only works if you truly believe what you're fighting for. So if you don't believe it, tell me. And if you don't feel this is your fight, and you'd like to get off the ship at some point, then I'll do my best to accommodate that ASAP, and the LC has said he will too. At the moment however, given what they did to PH-2 and to the Captain, I can't guarantee they won't just whack you the minute they reach you. Because otherwise yes," she looked back at Private Melsh, "we might not be making a station call for quite some time."

"Major?" ventured Private Carter. *"You're saying HQ will just murder us in cold blood? Their own marines?"*

187

"They've already done it," said Trace.   "Ask the guys on PH-2."

They said nothing more.   Most of them were unmarried with no children — most marines left that for when their tours ended. For some of them, that was a long time, but the human race was fertile either internally or externally for 150 years plus, so the window of opportunity was wide.   But even without families of their own, they still had other family and relatives to return to.   This situation was keeping them from all of that, and could quite likely get them killed, just when it was looking like they'd survived the war.   Yet despite her encouragement, none of them spoke.

Hell of a thing, Trace thought.   She loved the loyalty of these men and women, and for the most part shared it.   But at a time like this, she couldn't help but feel guilty for it, and wish that someone, anyone, would speak up, so that she didn't feel like such a tyrant.

"One more thing," she added.   "And I've told others to spread this around.   Keep an eye on the LC for me.   And his friends in bridge crew, and his sister.   Because amongst us marines, I can go to sleep certain that even if any of you disagreed with me, you'd never be a threat to me.   I can't be sure I'd say the same for the spacers.   That's all."

CHAPTER 14

Erik awoke at 0500 on the dot, after a few hours' sleep, and checked the scans. Positioning was not radically different from last he'd seen them, ships in similar places. *Abigail* was twenty hours out from closest approach. He checked Lisbeth, and her uplinks informed him she was asleep, and in Trace's quarters. Trace was still on the rock, with Bravo and Delta.

A new broadcast was coming through, from *UFS Warrior.* Coms had a recording, it was looped, playing endlessly. He opened it. *"This is the warship UFS Warrior, to all vessels. The UFS combat carrier Phoenix has been declared a renegade vessel, by UF Fleet command. Repeat, the UFS combat carrier Phoenix has been declared a renegade vessel by UF Fleet command. UFS Phoenix is currently in hiding somewhere in the Argitori System. Do not be alarmed, UF forces and allies are here to help find and neutralise this dangerous fugitive.*

"UFS Phoenix is under the command of Lieutenant Commander Erik Debogande, who is wanted for the premeditated murder of the Phoenix's Captain Marinol Pantillo, and upon further charges of treason against the human United Forces. We urge all Phoenix crew hearing this message, remove this man from authority immediately. These charges stand only against Lieutenant Commander Debogande — I repeat, only against Lieutenant Commander Debogande. Remove him, and all Phoenix crew shall be considered innocent of all standing charges. Fail to do so, and Phoenix crew will be considered as guilty as the many they are currently protecting.

"Accompanying this transmission is video footage of the Lieutenant Commander's violent breakout from holding cells in Shiwon, causing the deaths of ten military personnel."

The footage began. It was the Shiwon holding cells all right, covered with bodies and blood. The camera did not spare any sensitivities. It was all Trace's work, including the guard alongside Erik on his bed, head splattered across the wall alongside… and others. Numerous others. Dear god. Trace was no lone gun — like all modern soldiers, she was primarily a team operator whose real skill lay in group coordination and tactics under pressure. But even so, the gap between the average *Phoenix* marine, and these poor schmucks guarding the holding cells, was enormous. Many could have done damage like this. But Erik suspected only Trace could have gotten him out alive in the process. It was what separated her from most soldiers at any level — a laser-like focus on objectives. If she could have gotten him out without killing anyone, she'd have done that instead.

He called second-shift Coms. "Lassa, it's the LC. Why wasn't I woken when this transmission came through?"

"Didn't think it would change anything, LC. Draper said let you sleep." Erik snorted and cut connection. Probably right, sleep was more important. But still he'd have liked to know immediately.

He got up, popped a stim and threw on gym clothes. Outside his door, Private Carville scrambled to his feet from where he'd been sitting. Cocky kid from Lieutenant Dale's Second Squad, spiky hair, chewing gum. "Hey LC. Gonna pump some iron?"

Erik frowned. "Private, were you sleeping in the corridor?"

Carville grinned. "No sir. Just dozing, you know marines, could sleep in a closet. I feel like hitting the gym too sir, let's go."

Erik rolled his eyes and threw a glance back into the bridge as he left, Carville following. The bridge looked calmly busy, monitoring a dozen things at once. Draper's back, in the command chair. "You're watching my back?" he asked as they walked. "Did the Major order that?"

"No sir," Carville said cheerfully. "Just synchronising my location to yours. Nothin' to it."

"Glad we cleared that up," Erik said drily, sidestepping traffic in the main corridor.

"Sir, how about you try out the marines' gym today? We got some real cool kit in there."

"You've got exactly the same equipment as the spacers' gym," Erik replied.

"Yeah but we use it better."

190

Erik headed straight down the corridor, having no intention of heading around to back-quarter.   Trace was spooked if she thought someone was going to jump him.   And suffering from the usual marine prejudice about the reliability and loyalty of spacers. Still he got looks in the corridor, spacers looking at him sideways, with none of the casual calm they'd once used.   Erik took a deep breath and tried to think of other things.   It wasn't like he didn't have more important things to worry about than his personal popularity on ship.

The spacers' gym had far less people than usual for shift-minus-fifty.   Erik got on the treadmill, and figured that recent events had disrupted a lot of lives and schedules.   He didn't understand it himself, why people skipped gym when rattled.   Routines kept him sane, and this one most of all.

He ran hard, Carville on the machine alongside, then did presses, the heavy resistance arms on the weights machine straining — no free weights on a warship, everything had to stay in place in 10-Gs plus.   He did pretty well at it, which was partly inherited genes from his father, who was not a slim man, and partly the augments and micros that doubled the functional consequence of all exercise.   In a sweaty singlet and bare armed, he was one of the bigger guys in the gym, but knew better than to think it counted for much.   Carville was slimmer, yet could take him down in a gum-chewing heartbeat.   Trace was smaller again, and could break his neck without effort.   With augments, visible size counted for little — power came from speed, and when he and Carville took turns hitting the bag, Carville's hands seemed to blur, and Erik nearly had the air knocked from his lungs just leaning on the leather.   Marines were given an entirely different grade of physical augment, and trained endlessly for violence as spacers did not.

Kaspowitz came across from the treadmill, dripping sweat as Erik stretched down.   "Hey LT," said Erik.   He had to use rank, with Carville here.   "And the Major told me you never exercise."

"I never exercise where she can see me," Kaspowitz corrected, with a glance down at Carville stretching.   The Private grinned.   "It's humiliating."

"Know the feeling, LT," said Carville.

Kaspowitz looked at him a moment longer. Knowing very well what he was doing here, in the spacers' gym, a marine private exercising with the ship Commander. Probably everyone in the gym knew, but Erik was studiously not looking. He'd also know who ordered Carville here, especially given how well he knew Trace. Erik wondered just who was running this damn ship, anyway? Lately he was feeling as much a passenger as Lisbeth.

Kaspowitz sat down also to stretch, and Erik joined them on the floor. "We've all seen the Captain's last recording," said Kaspowitz, trying in vain to touch his toes. It was a long way to reach, for him. "I was thinking — 'this story begins where the last story ends.'"

Erik nodded. There'd been quite a bit of speculation about that, he'd overheard. It fit, given the Captain's love of books and stories.

"Have you heard of Operation Urchirimala?" Kaspowitz asked. Erik shook his head. "It's tavalai. They worship the old ruins of the Ancients... or maybe 'worship' isn't right, tavalai don't really do religion. But they love anything old, and the Ancients are the oldest. So ever since it's been looking like they'd lose the war, they've been scurrying around transcribing all the old symbols from all the Ancients' sites they've got, before the barbarian humans get them. That's Operation Urchirimala — it means something like 'Operation Recovery'... or close, my Togiri's a bit rusty.

"Anyway, it's a story. Tavalai love stories too, anything about their elders, the older the story the better. Now the chah'nas tell stories as well — they have the Po'to'kul scrolls, those things every warrior carries around with him. The longer it gets, the more phases of the warrior's life it covers, the more prestigious it becomes. There's lots of terms in the chah'nas languages for 'marking the scroll', like we say 'turning over a new leaf'. Each marks a new phase of life, and you know the chah'nas, always climbing their damn caste hierarchies."

Erik nodded, holding his toes without effort. "You talk about this stuff with the Captain?"

"Oh he knew *way* more than me.   He'd have been a great scholar, could have taught this stuff in university.   Anyhow, Merakis."

Erik frowned.   "Merakis?   The temple world?"   Everyone who'd been to school had at least heard of it.   It had been in tavalai space, recently captured by the UF.   Strategically it was unremarkable, and had no special interest to industry.   But it had been important to the Ancients, who'd built some of the most amazing old structures there in all the known galaxy.   And being so old, and so interesting, it had become important to the tavalai as well.

Kaspowitz nodded.   "Chah'nas never found it that important, but the tavalai did, and the chah'nas were interested in controlling the tavalai.   So they restricted tavalai access — you know the chah'nas, things are only as valuable as other people's desires make them. You want something, they'll take it away just to see how hard you'll push to get it back, everything's a contest to them.   So Merakis became a symbol of control, the unofficial seat of power.   Whoever had it, the legends say, controls the galaxy."

"Huh," said Carville.   "That might be *their* legend.   We don't give a shit."

"Don't be so sure," said Kaspowitz.   "We only just got it last month, when Kalida fell.   Big push, caught the last tavalai there by surprise.   And Fleet's said no one's allowed in since, everything's restricted.   Big rumours about secret Fleet missions there, but no one knows for sure."

"And the Captain talked about this?" Erik asked.   He had to force down the hurt feeling that the Captain hadn't talked about it with *him.*   Kaspowitz had known him far longer, and far better.

"Just that he found it very interesting," said Kaspowitz.   "He wondered what they were up to, and said he'd love to go.   It's the place where the stories of this galactic civilisation begin and end."

"He said *that?"*

"Well no.   But the tavalai caught there were involved in Operation Urchirimala.   All archeologists, artists, academics, that's the word.   No soldiers.   Recording stories, all the stuff they'd not had the guts to dig up for thousands of years because they hate disturbing old things."

Erik nodded slowly, switching legs. "Yeah. That's real interesting. I'll have to check the latest Fleet orders on Merakis. Thanks LT."

"No problem." Kaspowitz got up. "Don't be late."

"Oh, one more thing," said Erik as he recalled it. "The Captain said to the Major on the tape, something about 'that man we'd talked about'. You don't happen to know who that was?"

Kaspowitz shook his head. "No, a few of us were talking about that. But if he directed that straight at the Major, you can bet it was something he only discussed with her."

"Yeah. Thanks LT." Kaspowitz nodded, and left. Erik would have asked if he thought Trace was being honest when she said she didn't know who the Captain was talking about... but one did not question the honesty of officers in front of the troops they commanded.

A minute later Erik got up with Carville and followed. Erik had a private shower cubicle in the Captain's quarters — the only one that did on the whole ship — so he headed back to the bridge.

Just out of the gym, someone yelled to Carville, "Hey Benji! Got you that thing you wanted, right in here!"

"Oh hey, LC?" Carville scrambled up the side corridor. "Just one moment huh? Two seconds!"

He turned a corner. The door behind Erik opened, hands grabbed his throat and arms and dragged him backward before he could make a noise. Erik fought, got an arm free and caught a wrist — searing pain in his forearm as a knife cut him, and now the choke hold at his throat was tightening as he kicked and flailed in total darkness. He propelled his first attacker backward, they crashed into something, and he nearly lost control of the hand with the knife, surely headed for his throat if he did.

The second attacker hit him repeatedly in the midriff, trying to make him let go. Erik managed to get his teeth into the knife arm and bit as hard as he could, drawing a strangled yell. Fingers clawed at his face, and someone said harshly, "Give it! Give me the fucking knife!"   As the two men tried to transfer the blade in the dark, and make it fast.

Combat training reasserted, with desperate fear, and Erik stamped on a foot, missed, then snapped his head back trying to headbutt the man who had him.   The knife fell to the floor with a clatter, and Erik kneed the second man who bent for it, then kicked, then threw his first attacker back into a wall and swung, connecting with little.   A body hit him and he went down against something hard, tumbled and wrestled with the man who fell on top...

Then a flare of light as the door opened, followed by the loudest expletive he'd ever heard as Carville leaped on them and began pounding the knife-man to a pulp with repeated, bone-breaking impacts and cries of pain.   Erik had just acquired enough leverage on the man atop him when suddenly the weight was gone, Carville flung his attacker into a wall and began rearranging his internal organs.

"Benji!" Erik gasped.   "Private!   No, don't kill him!"   As Carville stopped punching.   "That's an order!"   As others blocked the light in the doorway, and yells of alarm went up the corridor, calls for a medic.

"But sir!" Carville snarled, with a handful of jumpsuit beneath a lolling, balaclava-covered head.   "I really, really want to!"

"Yeah me too," Erik panted, as someone else helped him to his feet.   "But I want to ask some questions first."

Erik sat in one of the spare quarters off main corridor, ceta-b section, and watched a monitor.   Behind him, Second Lieutenant Karle held his wrist so that his cut left forearm could stay vertical where Corpsman Rashni could staple it.   Rashni had wanted him to go to Medbay to do it, but Erik wasn't going to miss the interrogation for anything, let alone see it delayed to wait for him. And Medbay was full of marines far more badly hurt than him, and they deserved the peace of mind to not see their ship falling apart around them as their commander was sewn up after a mutinous attack.

In the adjoining room, Petty Officer Lawrence was slumped on one of the wall chairs.   Spacer Doraga was in Medbay with the seriously injured marines, with Doc Suelo cursing Private Carville for giving him another patient to care for.   Some were suggesting that Suelo should direct resources elsewhere.   The interrogator was Jokono, one of Lisbeth's four security guys.   Jokono had been a high level police inspector before joining the personal Debogande security team for a significant pay raise.   Interrogation, he'd said, was something of a speciality.   Kaspowitz and Shahaim were also here, first-shift having been delayed while second ran overtime.

Trace entered, sweaty in light under-armour shirt, and peered at the screen.   "I leave you guys for just a few hours," she said mildly.   Kaspowitz smiled.   Erik didn't.   Trace peered at his arm. "Oh nasty," she deadpanned.

"Up yours," Erik told her, eyes not leaving the screen.

"He said anything yet?"   Nodding at the screen.

"It's him, Doraga and Cho," Shahaim said grimly.   "Cho set up Carville, there was a bottle of pretty rare whisky he's been after for weeks.   Got his attention for five seconds, they grabbed the LC into a side room, would have knifed him.   But the LC's pretty strong, and they weren't that good."

"I've had a word with Benji," said Trace.

"Don't be too hard on him," said Kaspowitz.   "He's a good kid."

"He's a marine," said Trace.   "He fucked up, and he'll take his lumps like the rest of us, good kid or not.   What's the connection between these guys?"

"Just friends," said Shahaim.   "Haven't been on the ship too long, two years max."   She paused.   "One of their friends is Dufresne."

"Hmm."   Trace looked down at Erik, expecting a comment from him.   Erik said nothing, staring at the screen as Jokono pressed a line of questions, patient and repetitive.   "Are we going to haul in our second-shift co-pilot for questions?"

Again Erik said nothing, grimacing slightly as Rashni's staples stung. "Short of pilots as it is," Shahaim muttered. "I don't think we can. Can't have bad morale on the bridge."

"Can't have disloyal pricks sitting Helm either," said Karle. He and Dufresne didn't get along.

Trace squatted at Erik's side to get a better look at the screen from his angle. An uplink connection opened. Erik blinked on it. *"Hey,"* said Trace's voice in his ear. *"Look at me."* He did so. Her dark eyes were intense, with none of the business-as-usual previously in her voice. She stared hard. *"You start feeling sorry for yourself, and I will personally smack you black and blue. Do you hear me?"*

Erik felt a wave of hatred. He deserved better than this. He'd nearly been killed, and here was this blasted woman again, sticking in this knife of her own just when he was most vulnerable. Some supporting friend she was. He glared at her.

"Good," she said. *"Hate me, hate them, hate something. Just don't you dare curl up into a ball like a child. This whole ship is depending on you, so get your shit together."*

Lisbeth awoke to find her uplink gave her 0812. And came fully awake with a gasp — she was late! The main-ship and the bridge were both running two shifts now, and first-shift started at 0600! She'd set her uplink alarm herself, how could she have slept nearly three hours past it?

She detached the bed net and climbed from the lower bunk, still in her clothes as all spacers slept, never knowing when they'd need to move. Boots, where were her boots? The under-bunk locker, of course. She unlatched and pulled it out, finding boots alongside her little bag of toiletries that was all she had on this ship, besides her few clothes in the 'closet'.

When she had them laced, she stood... and saw for the first time that Major Thakur was here, on the top bunk, apparently asleep.

"Lisbeth?" Still her eyes were closed. She'd been over on the rock all 'night', she had to be exhausted.

"Um yes?" Should she call her 'Major'? That didn't seem right, she was a civilian. Calling everyone by their ranks was a military thing.

"Three of the crew tried to kill Erik a bit over two hours ago. We've caught them, your security man Jokono is helping with the interrogation."

Lisbeth stared at her, heart thudding in panic. The Major's eyes opened, half-lidded, head on the pillows. Watching her calmly. It was a test, Lisbeth realised past the fear. Everything was a test, with this woman, on this ship. The Major was here catching a nap, surely everything was being dealt with.

Lisbeth took a deep breath. "He's okay, right?"

"He has a cut on his forearm. He needed a few stitches. I think he's a bit shaken, but that's understandable." This from the woman who'd just led two platoons of marines through a hacksaw ambush, and personally shot their queen. And was now discussing the attempted assassination of her ship's last remaining commander as though she were listing groceries to be bought.

"So, what? Do we just expect the entire crew to rise up in mutiny now?" Lisbeth couldn't quite keep the tremble from her voice.

"My marines have all the guns," Thakur replied. And let that hang there, to be considered. Lisbeth nodded, doing that. And put a hand on the Major's bunk to steady herself, recalling that she shouldn't be standing unsecured anyway. Though they'd slowed down a lot to make this rock, and debris impacts were no longer such a threat.

"Yes," said Lisbeth. Took a deep breath. "Sure. Great. Because that's what it all comes down to, isn't it?" With some accusation. She wasn't sure who she was angry at. There was nothing the Major could do about it.

"Yes," said Thakur. "Sadly, in this galaxy, who has the most guns determines everything. Why didn't you tell me your security people were so good?"

Lisbeth blinked. "I don't recall you asking."

"My oversight. Jokono's exceptional."

"He was Chief of Investigations on two major trading stations. But you know, my family pays very good money, we recruit the best. I would have just brought my regular bodyguards to the shuttle, which means Carla and Vijay, but Jokono's chief of household security and insisted he come along with Hiro."

"Carla and Vijay are marines?"

"Ex-marines yes."

A faint smile from Thakur. "No such thing. I could use some replacements. If you could talk to them and see what they want to do, I'd appreciate it."

Lisbeth nodded slowly. "Carla's got a husband back on Homeworld, so… I dunno." Thakur nodded calmly. "Vijay's always up for a fight though. He's family, he's been with us for ages. And the last is Hiroshi. He was United Intelligence."

Thakur raised her eyebrows. "Which division?"

Lisbeth smiled faintly. "He doesn't say. And we don't ask. His skillset's a bit scary, so you can guess."

"I've made arrangements for all four of them to take two spare rooms just up this bulkhead ring. Spacer section, but fifteen seconds' sprint away. They were back near Engineering before."

Lisbeth nodded. "Good. That's… that's a good idea."

"You're going down to Engineering?" Lisbeth nodded again. "Good." Thakur closed her eyes again. "Tell Rooke to get his ass moving. I want to get away from this rock and out of this fucking system. And Lisbeth, when you head down to Engineering? Stay in back-quarter, on the marine side of the ship, okay?"

No sooner had Lisbeth left the Major's quarters and turned aft, she found Hiroshi at her side. "Oh hey Hiro," she said, pleased to see him. "I haven't seen you, what's been up?"

"That was our fault," Hiroshi Uno said grimly. He was not a tall man, barely taller than Lisbeth. Asian features, he said the name dated back to someplace from old Earth called 'Japan'… Lisbeth didn't know much about it, Homeworld wasn't the place for old Earth 'remnants', as such folks were sometimes called, who still clung to long-dead identities. "We kept asking after you, but they put us down the other end of the ship and told us to shut up and do what we were told. And we were a bit intimidated, and we didn't press it."

"You?" Lisbeth was astonished, and a bit amused. "Intimidated?"

"Well, maybe nothing intimidates the great and mighty Lisbeth..." Lisbeth snorted. "But the rest of us have grown up on tales of *Phoenix*. Jokono's run entire security divisions, but to him a *Phoenix* Lieutenant is god. Our mistake, this ship's a mess."

"Not on this side it isn't," said Lisbeth as they passed the mess, marines fresh from armour rotation carrying food back to quarters or elsewhere. One of the men gave her a little salute and a thumbs up in passing — a tough-looking guy with ripped muscle, tattoos and scars, but that only made her feel safer. Lisbeth smiled at him.

"Yeah, this is the side of the ship to be on," Hiro admitted. "*Phoenix* might be a letdown, but Major Thakur's just as advertised. You bunking with her... well, we figured we couldn't make you any safer."

"The Major said she needs replacements."

Hiro nodded. "Vijay yes, Carla maybe."

"That's what I told her."

"We're still technically employed by your mother. The contract fineprint says 'all contingencies', no matter how dangerous or crazy. It basically says we have to die for you if it comes to it."

Lisbeth blinked at him, sidestepping some traffic. "It's not put *exactly* like that, is it?"

"No, but it means the same. I'm in. I didn't take up this line of work to be safe and comfortable, and I knew what I was signing when I signed it."

"Well Hiro," said Lisbeth, "it seems to me that we're stepping very close to that state secrets stuff that you never talk about. Plots at the highest level of Fleet and Spacer Congress. Wouldn't know anything about that, would you?"

Hiro looked uncomfortable. "I'll think about it."

"Think hard. I know you swore an oath, but so did they, to protect and look out for their own people. They broke it first."

A bulkhead marked the beginning of Assembly, where the ship framework opened up, and walls and ceilings disappeared. They were replaced by gantries, armour racks, mobile cranes and acceleration nets. Marines climbed and swung, locking armour into vertical racks, operating armoury feeds, performing adjustments. The place smelled of grease, hot metal, sweat and faint, acrid smoke. Shouts echoed, equipment and chain-feeds rattled, and armour whined and crashed, while the deep bass thrum of ventilation fans tried to keep the stale air moving.

Lisbeth stared in amazement. Marines really did live in another world from spacers — she couldn't see a single non-marine present. And no techs either, as marines did all their own tech-work on suits and weapons. So much for the dumb-and-violent stereotype, Lisbeth had looked over the schematics on marine armour before and it wasn't simple stuff. But marines seemed to like being underestimated for their brains.

"When you want to move around the ship?" Hiro said to her. "Always come through back-quarter. And always make sure you tell one of us first."

"I'm not going to fit in real well if I have a bodyguard following me constantly."

"Well no," said Hiro. "What's your point?"

On the way into Engineering she saw an uplink feed showing that a lot of people were gathered in a deck 2 storage room. She climbed a ladder to get there, and found Ensign Hale amid vertical storage racks that slotted into floor and ceiling. Two others were helping her with sorting several large storage boxes of very alien bits and pieces. And Lisbeth took a sharp breath — these were hacksaw parts.

She came over and stared. Quite a few of the parts had bullet holes or shrapnel gashes, courtesy of *Phoenix* marines. Hale saw her. "Hey Lisbeth, wanna give us a hand? Processors in A and B racks, weapons in C and D, everything else in E and F."

"Um sure. Hey, is this safe? I mean...?"

"Will they come alive in second-shift and eat us? I sure hope not." Lisbeth liked Remy Hale — she was short, pretty and easy-going. And she was a good friend of Erik's, from when Erik had been third-shift commander. Erik had mentioned her to Lisbeth before, at various times, in his messages home. "We've scanned everything for residual power sources, removed everything latent. The thing with machines, they don't work without power."

"What about microwave, radiated and non-linear transmission?"

Hale smiled, hefting a large torso-part out of the box with a clank and rattle, and carrying it to the racks. "Those too, scanned and ruled out." She dumped the part into the storage net. "Face it kid, these things are dead."

Lisbeth pulled several dead steel limbs aside, and stared down on a big head-unit the size of her chest. A single dead sensor eye, multi-phase and obviously densely constructed of some advanced, photo-voltaic structure... all exposed thanks to the multiple bullet holes straight through the middle. Additional sensor add-ons around the lens. Oversized and far too vulnerable for a hacksaw drone. This was the queen that Major Thakur had shot.

"Incredible," she murmured. "This thing could have seen the Fathers. So old."

"Sure, unless it was made yesterday," said Remy. "No telling with hacksaws. Heard a story about a tech on *UFS Farsight*? Ten years back, he recycled some converters from dead hacksaws in an emergency, increased subsystems efficiency by a thousand percent until it melted. If we get desperate, might get useful."

Lisbeth stared down at the old, dead queen. And had to remind herself that it wasn't sad that this frightening, majestic creature had ended up here in a box of parts in a *Phoenix* storage room. This thing had killed seventeen marines, and had been the mortal enemy of all flesh-and-blood lifeforms for nearly fifty thousand years. Given the chance, its kind would rise up again and exterminate the lot of them, human, chah'nas, tavalai and all.

She repressed a shiver, and got to work.

CHAPTER 15

It was quiet on the bridge, save for operational chatter from Coms and Scan. Second Lieutenant Dufresne hadn't spoken or looked at anyone when Shahaim had relieved her. Former-inspector Jokono was now coordinating with Chief Petty Officer Taigo to see various steps taken to monitor Lawrence, Cho and Doraga's other friends as well. Two marine privates now stood on guard at the bridge entrance — no armour and only sidearms for now, they didn't need any more to keep loyalty-challenged spacers at bay, and anything heavier would look very bad. Erik thought it looked plenty bad already.

"Penalty for mutiny under Fleet law is death," Shilu said into a silence. "Penalty for attempted murder under any circumstances is death." Erik said nothing, watching the screens. "Just saying."

"Are we still under Fleet law?" Geish replied. He looked unhappy. It was his default look these days, heavy-set and solemn-eyed. "And who mutinied, us or them?"

"You shut that down, Second Lieutenant," said Kaspowitz. "They started this when they murdered the Captain."

"After which we," Geish retorted, "or Major Thakur more correctly, took it upon herself to decide that Fleet law no longer applied, the perpetrators would never be caught going through channels, and declared war on the entire human race, on the behalf of *all* of us..."

"I said shut it down!" said Kaspowitz.

"That's all right Kaspo," Erik intervened. "Let him speak." Pretending wasn't going to make it go away. Geish spoke for some significant number of *Phoenix* crew, and putting his fingers in his ears wouldn't make it better. Trace had said not to curl into a ball and hide.

"Fleet is the only system that works, out here." Geish gestured at his scan screens. At the vastness of Argitori System beyond. "It's the only thing that's held the human race together for a thousand years. Without it, we'd be the krim — extinct. I loved the Captain as much as anyone here, but... but we can't just tear it all up for one man."

"Firstly, you *didn't* love the Captain as much as anyone here," Kaspowitz said coldly. "You want plain talking, let's talk plainly." Geish glared. "Secondly, Fleet is a tool made for fighting wars. War's over. They're the only power in human space, and they don't want to lose it. We've all seen it. We all know the scrambling that's going on in Spacer Congress. We kid ourselves we're democratic — humanity hasn't had true democratic leadership at the centre for... what two centuries? We tried it for a bit during the five hundred year peace, but Fleet didn't like it..."

"Because the tavalai's goons kept attacking us!" Geish retorted. Erik had to think that he agreed with Geish on that. That was an odd feeling — agreeing with his enemy. It led to a sense of detachment. Which felt kind of good. Leaders were supposed to be detached, to view things objectively. "Yes Fleet runs the government, yes it's not a true democracy... so what? Let the *Worlders* run things? Divert ninety percent of Fleet's budget to more schools and hospitals on their comfortable planets? I like schools and hospitals as much as the next person, but they don't do you a shitload of good when we've all been killed because Fleet couldn't defend us!"

"I agree," said Erik. Everyone looked at him. And saw that Erik's eyes remained on the command chair screens, which took their own eyes back to their jobs, even as their ears strained for the LC's next words. "With both of you. Fleet's been our saviour. I'm proud to have been a part of that. I'm proud to still be a part of it. But saviours will become villains in time, given long enough.

"My parents always told me that Fleet would become a tyrant eventually, once the war ended, if we weren't all very careful. But they thought it could be stopped. They thought that brave and thoughtful men and women could work hard behind the scenes and stop it from happening, and stop this great legacy from being tarnished." He took a deep breath. "I never believed them. Which I guess proves that kids probably should listen to their parents more."

"Look all this politics is very interesting," Shahaim interrupted. "But it doesn't help our situation. Honest assessment, what percentage of the crew are against us?"

"Define 'us'," Kaspowitz said sourly, looking at Geish. Geish studied his screens.

"The Major's assessment is about a twenty percent sympathetic to Fleet," said Erik. No one questioned how she'd know — no bridge officer truly knew what the majority of the crew really thought. Bridge was a bubble, none of them really had time to mix with the regular crew, and lately least of all — not because they were elitists, but because they were just too busy. But the Major's marines roamed free, and the Major was certainly *not* in a bubble from her marines. "Remember all the unsympathetic ones from first-shift never turned up. So most of that twenty percent of trouble are second-shift, since they were already up here under Commander Huang and never had a choice."

"We could let them off," Jiri suggested. "Twenty percent of current crew is... what, sixty-five people? Seventy? Put them on a shuttle, let Fleet pick them up."

"Firstly," said Erik, "we're already a shuttle short and one of the three we've got is a civvie replacement. I don't want to lose another one." Because Lisbeth had been right about that, though it had taken a marine deployment for him to really see it. "Secondly, if we leave them, they'll give away our position. Thirdly, given how bad Fleet wants this all covered up, I think it's pretty likely they'd frag the shuttle like they did PH-2, erase all trace. This whole thing's just too embarrassing to them now."

"They'd never do that," Geish scoffed.

"You seriously haven't been paying attention, have you?" Kaspowitz accused him. "Did you even *see* what they did to PH-2?" Again Geish didn't reply.

"I think we're stuck with them for now," Erik finished. "With any luck we'll find some safer harbour in the future, and they can step out there, find their own way home."

"And we're sure there's no issue at all with the marines?" Karle asked.

"Very sure," said Erik. "They love Fleet too, but marines bond something fierce, and this lot bonded to the Major and the Captain. Fleet HQ killed the Captain, so you can guess what that means. Plus they live in each other's pockets and they suck at keeping secrets. If anyone was harbouring those kinds of sympathies, his buddies would have smelled it by now."

His com blinked, and he put it through. "*Hey LC,*" came Rooke's voice. "*I've got the fabricators set up on the rock, they're producing several grades better than what I can do on Phoenix. That should get us a workable replacement stretch for the section of jumpline we lost.*"

"How soon?"

"*Another ten hours to make it? Then ten more to fit it, maybe fifteen to test it...*"

"We might not get fifteen hours to test it. Better make sure it works first time."

"*Aye LC, but, well... um yeah, aye. I'll try.*" Techs hated being told they couldn't test it first. Erik understood why, but they had their operating requirements, while he had his. Ultimately his were more important.

"And Rooke? Good work getting it set up so fast."

"*Yeah, well it turns out marines can actually press buttons and run machines. Better hope they don't figure how to fly the ship or we'll all be out of a job.*"

"I've got something," Geish said tersely, staring at his screen. He fiddled some software. "Looks like a tight laser-com transmission on *Abigail.*" Erik had told Geish to watch the insystem runner *Abigail* in particular. "It's coming from *UFS Chester.*"

Erik put it up on screen. *Abigail* was close now, passing barely five seconds light nadir of their position. *Chester* was somewhere above that, and thank god *Phoenix* had found this rock or both would have seen them hours ago, silent running or not. They'd gotten lucky — the laser-com just happened to be passing near on this angle, they were nearly in line. And it showed Erik that he'd probably made the right call, not trying to use laser-com to contact

Abigail himself.   Someone with *Phoenix*'s level of scan technology could quite possibly have seen.

"Looks like Captain Lubeck wants to have a quiet word with *Abigail,*" said Shilu from Coms.

"Yeah," said Kaspowitz, eyes narrowed.   "But why?"

"You don't talk narrowband unless you don't want anyone else to hear," said Shahaim.   "When you're entering a hostile system in force you talk aloud, you let everyone hear your hails.   Looks like Lubeck doesn't want HQ to hear."

She glanced at Erik.   Erik chewed a nail.   It suggested Lubeck didn't buy HQ's bullshit, and wanted to ask around. *Abigail* was the closest Ito Industries vessel transmitting with those odd re-ordered transponders.   If Lubeck were making a hostile demand of *Abigail* he'd broadcast it so everyone could hear — it was the fastest way to inform fellow UF ships of the situation, and would serve as a warning to other Ito Industries vessels.

"Keep a very close eye on that," Erik told Geish and Jiri. "But let's not jump to conclusions.   There's a chance it means Lubeck doesn't buy it.   It might give us an opening if we have to run.   But let's not bet on it."

"Could try to talk to him?" Kaspowitz suggested.

Erik shook his head immediately.   Tempting as it was, he knew he couldn't do it.   "Silence is our only friend right now, we've no thrust and won't be ready to run for a full rotation at least.   We don't give that up unless we've got something a damn sight more solid than hope."

Trace stood locked into the top half of her armour, headset on and windmilling one arm after another to try and get the shoulder calibrations right.   The synchronisation had been off since the fight, too much power pushing against not enough feedback, and all marines learned that with these systems there was nothing to do but tinker, adjust, and tinker again.

"So what do you think?" she asked Carla and Vijay, Lisbeth's two marine bodyguards as they gazed around at the familiar echoing racket of Assembly. Marines edged past in the narrow space before ascending armour racks, and someone yelled warning while walking an adjoining aisle with a clump of heavy metal footsteps.

"Familiar," said Carla. She was a big woman, with short hair and a physique that screamed augmentation, a tattoo from *Thunderbird* scored across one thick bicep. *Thunderbird* was a Third Fleet combat carrier with a reputation nearly as formidable as *Phoenix*'s. She'd only made full-corporal after fifteen years, but anyone who'd survived three terms with an honourable discharge would get respect from any marine anywhere.

"Cool," agreed Vijay. He was even bigger, had done eight years and risen to Staff Sergeant on *Dragonfire* before losing an arm in combat. That arm was cybernetic now, but there'd been complications, two years off for medical reasons, during which he'd received an offer of employment from the Debogande group. Fleet did not begrudge anyone leaving after a two-year wound, and he'd been a privateer for seven years now, but still felt something incomplete.

"Thing is," said Jokono, "we're still employed by the Debogande family. The contract is actually with the family too — signed to Alice Debogande herself. Not to any of the companies. Inner security protect the family primarily."

It made sense, Trace thought. The family and the companies were not always the same thing. Jokono was brown, lean and calm, somewhere in excess of one hundred years old with all the experience that gave.

"We breach that contract," Vijay added, "we could get sued or go to prison."

"So don't breach the contract," said Trace, swinging an arm as servos whined and hummed. "Protect Lisbeth. Protect Erik too. Right now, that means defending this ship."

"Agreed," said Jokono. "But Erik and Lisbeth are under threat from within the ship. It seems unwise to focus our attentions outside, while the threat to our employers is within."

"And do you really want marines who are working as temps?" Carla added dubiously. Trace knew exactly what she meant. Serving meant the commitment of just about everything. If you served, in marine forces, you had to mean it. "We're here to look out for Lisbeth, and for Debogande family interests. That might not seem as noble as what you guys do, but the family's been great to us. And in my opinion they're almost as important a force in human space as Fleet is."

"No, I can see that logic," Trace said calmly. Surprising them a little. "Fleet are protectors. Industrials like Debogande Inc are what we protect. They're the civilisation, we're just the shield."

"Right," said Carla. "And for me, protecting them means as much to me as protecting *Phoenix* means to you."

"And I dunno about all the companies," Vijay added, "but the family itself are good people. We had a guy get killed in a random attack a few years back, some nutjob had a go at Katerina. You wouldn't believe how they looked after his family, put his kids through college, got his widow an allowance and then a job when she was ready to work again. Good people."

"From my experience of Debogandes on this ship," Trace replied, "that doesn't surprise me either. But if we get out of this system alive, we're going to be on the run. There's going to be some investigation to be done, some serious digging around, and probably some politics as well — things that overly specialised Fleet soldiers probably aren't that great at. So what I'm saying is that we could use some help, from non-typical operatives. And I'm also saying that the safety of the broader Debogande family, not just the ones on this ship, will rest upon the successful outcome of this entire fucked up situation.

"This will need a resolution for any of them to be safe. And being here on this ship gives you all an opportunity to be a part of that resolution in a way that you couldn't if you were back running family security on Homeworld. They can find other people to replace your immediate functions back on Homeworld, but having you here represents a strategic opportunity for the whole Debogande family. If you help us."

They thought about that.   "Hey Major!" yelled Staff Sergeant Spitzer from a level below, through the steel gantries. "Got the readiness inventory up, looks like we're gonna be down another four suits!"

"Yep!" she replied.   "Be down in five!"

"You do realise as well," Jokono added, "that this whole command structure on *Phoenix* is a great legal pickle?   I'm not a lawyer and I've certainly never been a JAG, but I've got a pretty good idea about Fleet law.   Your authority to execute people for mutiny and treason comes from Fleet Command, but you're currently in rebellion against Fleet Command.   If they could return to Fleet HQ, Lawrence, Cho and Doraga would get medals."

"I'm well aware of that," said Trace, loosening the feedback tension on the elbow cuff with her uplinks.

"Do you have any ideas how to address the problem?"

Trace shook her head.   "There is no addressing it.   There never was.   Command authority's a game, Jokono.   At ship level, at Fleet level, at the highest level of human government.   Those people are in charge because there's a general consensus beneath them that they are in charge.   That's it."

Jokono frowned.   "But without legal authority…"

"There's no such thing," Trace said firmly.   "The legal authority you're talking about exists because people think it exists. It's data on a chip, it's a piece of paper, it's an idea in people's heads. My marines on this ship also have an idea in their heads, and it's that their loyalty to me and each other now drastically outweighs their loyalty to Fleet since Fleet tried to screw us.   Whose idea of legal authority is superior?"

"You're saying you're going to just make your own laws?"

"We all do.   Humans always have."

"And for the past thousand years," Jokono said meaningfully, "the Kulina have put aside all such selfish temptations to make their own laws and meet their own desires in order to serve the broader human cause."

"They have," Trace said shortly.   "I still serve the human cause, Jokono.   I'm no longer sure that Fleet does."

At the end of first-shift, Erik found Lisbeth in machine shop one, seated at a bench amidst automated repair assemblies and fast-moving techs. Robot arms blurred in motion, repairing damaged circuits and pumps, or fast-molding new parts, while techs dashed between, assembling and examining what came into their hands. Rooke had people outside in suits now, working with the drones to patch and repair in preparation for replacing the damaged portions of jump line. Ten hours, he insisted. Rooke had never run a repair job this big on his own — usually he was second-in-charge under Lieutenant Chau. Chau had rarely missed a deadline by so much as an hour. Time would tell, literally, if Rooke could do the same.

Lisbeth talked with her security guy, Hiro, running bits of odd-looking junk under a high-intensity scanner. Erik put a closed coffee mug on the bench beside her, sipping his own, and she glanced in astonishment. And hugged him hard.

"I'm so glad you're okay," she whispered, barely heard beneath the machinery commotion.

"Me too. Sorry I couldn't call in before now, I was…"

"Don't be silly, you've a ship to run." Lisbeth resumed her seat, as Erik nodded to Hiro, who nodded back. He didn't know family security well, given how rarely he'd been home the past few years. But his parents played a large hand in selecting them personally, so there was no questioning the quality.

"So you're helping out?" Erik asked, glancing around. None of the other techs even glanced their way, being far too busy. Remy Hale didn't think there'd be any security problem in Engineering, but he was glad Hiro was here all the same.

"Sure, when there's something for me to do," said Lisbeth. "But I'm not much on operating these machines, and these guys move faster without me. Mostly I've been running diagnostic in preparation, but they're actually cutting and shifting stuff in the engines now, so diagnostic time's over." She indicated the parts she was running through the scanner. "These are hacksaw components, CPU portions mostly. It's just incredible stuff."

She indicated the eye-pieces. Erik peered. The little fragment in the scanner didn't look much to the naked eye, but through the eyepieces it exploded in complexity.

"That looks almost like crystal," said Erik. "Barely looks mechanical at all."

"The database can't place it," said Lisbeth, eyes shining with enthusiasm. That surprised Erik. With all that had happened, he didn't think she'd find much room for positive emotion. *He* was still rattled, and having trouble finding happy thoughts. "We're supposed to be loaded with data from previous hacksaw encounters, but the database says it doesn't recognise any of this. Erik, I think this is an entirely new genus of technology. I don't even know where to start."

"Wait... a *genus* of technology?" That was a biological term.

Lisbeth nodded fast. "Genus, yes. The AI race evolved in a range of different directions — different technologies, different evolutions. They were actually victims of their own evolution, technology changes its fundamentals far faster than biological evolution changes us. Different groups of AIs isolated from each other by vast distances became over thousands of years almost unrecognisable to each other, that's when they started having all their wars."

"Right." Erik nodded, sipping his coffee. Trying to remember his deep Spiral history. This, he was finding, was the hardest part of being in command — keeping track of everything. As third-in-command, most stuff had ultimately been someone else's responsibility. Now it was all up to him, and he felt like a juggler keeping multiple grenades in the air while people were shooting at him. Add chronic lack of sleep, and a sizeable dose of personal fear, and he wondered how the Captain had ever managed. "There were five different phases of history, each one involving multiple factions."

"Well the latest research suggests there could have been more like twenty different phases, it depends how you measure them. There's some old kaal texts that suggest that some of those divergent groups didn't join the civil wars, they just disappeared. Erik, I think this might have been one of them." Ah, Erik thought. That was why she was excited. At any other time, he'd have been excited himself. "That would explain why they're in such a populous system as this one but never bothered anyone. They were just trying to be left alone."

"Sure." He blinked, and ran a hand over his hair. "Well no one's going to look to mine a rock out this far, when there's far more lucrative lunar systems around those gas giants, and the inner asteroid belts. Anything out here's just a lot of fuel and trouble, I guess they knew they were safe enough if they kept quiet. Can you learn anything useful from this?"

"I don't know," she said dubiously. "I'd love to work on the software parameters though, see if it can figure out how it all works. If it gets enough data it might..." and she repressed a laugh. "Oh wow I just thought, what a subject for a doctorate! I'd really kick some academic ass." And looked at him in almost apologetic mirth, inviting him to join the joke. Because it was a ridiculous thought, given everything else.

Erik smiled and gave her shoulder a squeeze. "Yeah, you would. So how do you like bunking with Trace?"

"The Major? I barely see her actually, but she's been great. It's all a bit surreal."

"Tell me about it."

CHAPTER 16

Erik was awoken at 0316 by Lieutenant Draper. *"LC? We've got a situation here."* Erik rubbed his eyes, blinking away some unpleasant dream and extending the scan beside his bed on its extension arm.

"I'm here. Report."

"Chah'nas warship Tek-to-thi just pulsed jump engines on direct intercept course with Abigail. They are at four-point-two-five seconds light, we estimate interception in thirteen minutes realtime." Which was close enough that if *Phoenix* weren't snuggled up to this rock, *Tek-to-thi* would likely spot them whether they ran dark or not. *"There has been no coms announcement, Tek-to-thi continues to broadcast full chah'nas signature. Also, the warship UFS Chester has pulsed jump engines on a departure heading, twenty-two minutes ago. I didn't think it significant enough to wake you, there's ongoing activity among all visible support vessels."*

Erik released the connection, propping himself on the tethered pillow and fighting the bednet for space. "Dammit, that fucking laser-com was spotted. Someone told *Chester* to leave and now *Abigail*'s under suspicion." He stared at the screen for a long moment, the dots and plotted trajectories. A chah'nas warship was going to intercept a human insystem vessel in human space? In front of a fleet of other human warships? *Tek-to-thi* was closest, it was true, but the sheer gall of it shocked him. Could whoever was in charge of this circus find no one else willing to do it? Or was there some other reason specific to chah'nas and *Tek-to-thi*?

He flipped channels. "Second Lieutenant Rooke, what's our ETA on repairs?"

"Uh, good news LC, we're running three hours ahead of schedule. Always under-promise and over-deliver, huh? Be done in two hours max." Well no you damn fool, Erik thought — when delivering repair ETAs to the commander you gave him facts and nothing else. But he couldn't complain now — it was good work, if it was true.

"Bridge, this is the LC. Second-shift is relieved, first-shift will be taking over, sound the change-over." The alarm sounded on his uplink. Erik killed it, removed the net, rolled from bed and hoped to hell someone brought him coffee, and soon.

The chair was six strides away from his door, and Draper was already unbuckling latches to move the displays enough to get out. "Commander on the bridge!" someone said loudly, and Draper followed with, "Commander has the chair!"

"I have the chair," Erik echoed, quickly taking the vacated seat, and Draper helped him buckle in. "Status please."

"Alpha and Charlie Platoons are on the rock," said Draper. "Along with another twenty from Engineering. Rooke's got thirteen in suits along with the drones, they're fixing the jumplines now, been at it solid since second-shift began. And word from the Doc, one of our marine criticals passed away. Private Len, Alpha Platoon."

"Dammit," said Erik. He couldn't recall exchanging so much as a word with Len, but that hardly mattered. He'd been *Phoenix*, and one of Trace's, and they all hurt. "On ahead, Private Len."

"On ahead," the bridge echoed. The rest of first-shift were arriving, as second-shift vacated their chairs, not quite as intricate a procedure for them as the command-chair but close.

"Thank you Lieutenant," said Erik, staring at scan-feed. *Tek-to-thi* was closing fast, no sign of deviation. One didn't make moves like that in any territory if one didn't mean it. There wasn't a damn thing *Abigail* could do about it — she had four-Gs thrust in her, maybe five. *Tek-to-thi* had jump engines that could gain the velocity in seconds that *Abigail* could make in days. "That will be all. Get some food and make it soon, we might be leaving in a hurry."

"Sir," said Draper, and left. Probably he wasn't happy at being relieved. Erik had never been, when he'd been constantly pulled from the chair just as things got interesting. But that was junior bridge-crew's lot on a warship, just minding the chair until the adults arrived.

"You see this fucking shit?" Kaspowitz growled as he arrived at Nav. "You don't intercept human sub-lighters in human space. Someone should blow this guy a new asshole." Which was harsh language, coming from the brainy Kaspowitz, but summed up what most Spacers felt on the matter.

Erik switched channels. "Operations?"

"*Aye LC?*"

"Get me a shuttle on standby ASAP. I want someone out there for our techs in case we need them back aboard in a rush." It was always faster to put them on a shuttle and grapple it than wait for slow techies in suits to climb back aboard themselves.

"*Aye LC, one shuttle on standby for EVA recovery. We'll be on in three minutes.*"

Erik switched again. "Lieutenant Dale, do you copy?"

A pause, then a static-crackly reply. "*Copy LC, this is Lieutenant Dale.*"

"Lieutenant we've got a situation evolving out here, I want to you begin the return of all non-essential personnel to *Phoenix*. Further, I want all preparations for immediate withdrawal of *all* personnel to *Phoenix*, ASAP."

"*I copy that LC, immediate return of non-essentials and immediate preparation for total return.*"

"Copy Lieutenant." And to the bridge, "Helm, ship status change to orange, if you please."

"Status change to orange, aye LC," said Shahaim, doing that. It would pull everyone out of bed, and make all preparations for combat. The adrenaline charge across the bridge was palpable. Erik thought it vastly preferable to the previous feeling of helpless dread. Rooke had better be right with that ETA…

"We gonna go get him LC?" Kaspowitz asked.

"We can't stop that interception," said Erik. "And we can't play our hand too early, our tail's still in pieces. Someone else might stop that four-armed bastard from taking our ship, and then we'll have revealed ourself for nothing. But if he boards *Abigail* it'll take time. We can get him when he peels off."

Karle glanced across from his full weapons systems check in progress.   "Sir, we can't decompress that ship if she's taken prisoners, we'll likely kill them getting them off."

"He won't be taking prisoners," Erik replied, gnawing his thumbnail.   "Letting him board a human ship in full view of a busy system is one thing — letting him take human prisoners could cause proper mutiny among other Fleet vessels."   Some of whom were surely doubting their orders even now. *No one* allowed alien vessels to boss about native shipping, anywhere in the Spiral.   If a human vessel did this to a chah'nas vessel in chah'nas space, allies or not, the crew would be skinned alive.   Sovereign species space was *sovereign*, and that rule had been true in all sentient-governed space for as far back as anyone had records.

"Be nice to interrogate one of their crew though, like they're about to interrogate *Abigail*," Shahaim muttered.   "Find out who the hell gave them permission."

"Exactly," said Erik.   "Kulik class warship Mr Karle.   Get armscomp primed for it now, if we hit her we'll hit her tail then board her.   *Phoenix* has him out-gunned and out-powered, and he doesn't know we're here.   This is as good an ambush spot as we'll ever get."

"Sir," Geish said warily from Scan, "we're currently surrounded by warships trying to find and kill us... if we commit to a boarding ourselves we'll be an even bigger sitting duck than that chah'nas is now..."

"He'll take off when he sees us," Erik said confidently.   He should have been frightened, he'd never commanded *Phoenix* into anything as hot and complicated as the pursuit and boarding of an unwilling warship.   But he'd always been very good at this in sims, and seeing their relative positions, he knew the odds didn't get better than this.   "That'll give us velocity to keep clear of pursuers for long enough.   And Mr Geish, record all of this please, I want everyone to see what our grand Fleet is letting this alien fuck do to our sub-lighters."

"Aye LC, already doing that."

"Lieutenant Kaspowitz," Erik added. "Plot me a course to Merakis, if you please."

"Already got one LC," Kaspowitz said cheerfully, calling it up to display. "We can two-jump it with a course change at Rikishikti."

"That'll be a heck of a thing with our new weld-marks still fresh on our tail," Shahaim muttered, looking at that.

"Yes it will," Erik agreed. "I have faith in Mr Rooke." Another flip. "Major Thakur, you up yet?"

"That's cute," she replied. *"What's up?"*

"I have a job opportunity for you. Chah'nas warship, Kulik class. Likely combat boarding at velocity, hostile entry and several prisoners for questioning, senior officers if possible. You interested?"

"Sounds like fun. I'll do my recon now, get back to you in five with a more detailed plan. But for now, just know that I'd like an entry somewhere near the nose, with those main access corridors that gives me a straight shot to main crew and bridge, on a Kulik that's not too much space to cover in... oh, say three minutes flat."

From anyone else it would be a crazy boast. Erik knew Trace Thakur didn't make crazy boasts. "Three minutes it is from the nose, their dorsal layout may not give me much choice but I'll try."

"LC, incoming transmission," Shilu announced from Coms. "It's from *Abigail*."

"All United Forces, this is Ito Industries sub-light freighter Abigail! All United Forces, this is Ito Industries sub-light freighter Abigail! We are subject to hostile approach from alien warship, repeat, subject to hostile approach from alien warship! Please ward off, we are unarmed, repeat, we are unarmed, we are a human commercial vessel on peaceful commercial business..."

The woman on com sounded pretty scared, watching that trans-light monster doplering in on her. Probably she couldn't believe her own Fleet were going to let this happen... but why would a chah'nas warship be charging them if they weren't sure they could get away with it? It had to be because *Chester* had talked to them, attempting privacy, but been spotted.   Now Fleet would be wondering if *Abigail* knew something, with its Debogande-owned ID transponder, but couldn't do it themselves because Fleet hitting unarmed human merchants would make them enemies in Spacer Congress.   Let the alien do it.   Let the chah'nas do Fleet's dirty work.   Were chah'nas command and Fleet command working together on this?   To screw over everyone else?

"LC, this is Dale."   The Lieutenant's voice cut off his train of thought before it could fully form.   *"ETA on return of non-essential personnel, minus ten minutes.   Others can be back in sixteen once you give the order."*

Erik thought about it, gazing at the screens.   "That's too long Lieutenant," he decided.   "Start pulling them back, cut off whatever they're up to that takes them further out than ten minutes."

"Aye LC."

"We're not going to be moving for another hour and fifty anyway," Kaspowitz questioned, meaning Rooke's repair ETA.

"I got a bad feeling," said Erik.   "That chah'nas bastard had friends, I'm sure of it.   This could be a trap to lure us out."

"And we're still going to bite?" Geish asked skeptically.

"That's a human ship, and if the chah'nas wants information he'll have to board and question," Erik said grimly.   "Gives us the perfect excuse to do the same to them.   I want to know what he knows, if we have to twist it out of one of them in *Phoenix* confinement."

"Now we're talking," Kaspowitz agreed.

"Incoming Fleet transmission," said Shilu, and put it up without asking.

"...approaching chah'nas warship is merely questioning the insystem freighter Abigail on Fleet authority," the voice was saying. *"No prisoners will be taken, I repeat, no prisoners will be taken. Authority is given for logistical considerations, and the chah'nas vessel has given assurances that all Abigail crew will be treated with the proper courtesy."*

"Someone's upset," Shahaim growled.   "I bet a bunch of them don't like it, command has to make that transmission to shut them up."

"This is just strange," Kaspowitz said grimly.   "Since when do chah'nas get this liberty in human space? Something's changed."

"Whole bunch of people out here tiptoeing along the edge of mutiny," Erik agreed.   "It's not just us.   Damn right something's changed."

They waited.   *Tek-to-thi* dumped velocity and merged with *Abigail*'s position.   The frantic com broadcast stopped.   No Fleet vessels moved to assist.   The bridge crew were brought coffee and a sandwich as they waited.   One of Engineering's warrant officers wanted some extra time to collect a useful fabricator from the rock. Erik turned him down, as the others came aboard.   PH-1 hovered off stern from the repair job, ready to haul the suited techs inside if they had to move, and Trace told him that she, three of her Command Squad, and Second Squad from Echo Platoon, were in position in the mid-ships combat dock.

Then they waited.   Erik tried to stop his racing thoughts, and keep his heart rate under control.   Waiting was the worst thing ever. A marine had told him once that when Trace was a young Lieutenant, and higher ranks had access to her suit's vitals, they'd once found that while waiting for a big assault, her heart rate was actually slower than her usual low level.   Erik wondered what it was doing now, and thought probably the same — almost comatose.   She meditated, of course, like all Kulina.   Apparently it worked, though he had no idea how.   He only knew he'd give anything to be able to just turn it off, like flipping a switch, as she seemed to do.

Five minutes short of Rooke's ETA, *Tek-to-thi* began to move.   "I'm reading a one-G thrust," Geish announced.   "Nothing big, he's just cruising."

"If he leaves," Shahaim said urgently...

"He won't pulse so close to another ship," said Erik, mouth dry. Another channel. "Rooke! How long?"

"Two minutes LC!"

"Two minutes on the clock?" No reply. "Rooke dammit, two minutes on the clock, call it!"

"Aye LC, two minutes on the clock! Mark from now!" The timer started.

"Two minutes on the clock!" Shahaim announced.

"Helm, condition red. All hands battle stations."

"Aye condition red, all hands battle stations!"

The alarm sounded. Erik gripped the controls more firmly, and adjusted the arm braces as they pressed to his elbows. The seat actuators shifted and kicked, like an old warhorse waking up, smelling battle ahead. He opened more uplinks, and found ship systems opening across his inner vision, doubling against the screens — his own personal Head Up Display on his irises.

"LC, is it worth it?" Shahaim asked.

"We're strategically blind out here," said Erik. That, he hated most of all. "We don't know what the hell is going on, but my Uncle Thani says whatever happened to the Captain was tied up with our alien allies, and now we've got chah'nas violating all established rules in our pursuit. Someone gave him permission to do this, and come after us, and I want to know who and why."

Operations showed him everyone still off-ship now pouring back aboard through mid-ships, behind the rotation cylinder. They wouldn't have time to get back to gravity, and would have to ride the next bit with the engine techs down back. Flight systems showed green, attitude control, main engines, nav, weapons, scan, com... he tried to stop his hands shaking on the controls, one false twitch and he'd hit the attitude jets and blast the techs outside tumbling into deep space. Those guys had to be sweating bullets, knowing that one false move from them or their LC could see them left behind or worse...

"Still pushing one-G, no change!" said Geish.

"Get ready in case we surprise someone," Erik told him. "Could be someone running dark real close."

"We're done!" yelled Rooke. *"Everyone clear, get clear now!"* Erik saw the drone feed, suited figures hitting full thrust away from *Phoenix*, into the open cargo door of the waiting shuttle.

He gave it another five seconds, then hit undock and kicked them away from the rock with an attitude blast that knocked them sideways, such were the unpredictabilities of course-correction in a rotating cylinder. "PH-1," he announced, "departure at one-G, make it fast."

"*Copy LC,*" came Lieutenant Hausler, the shuttle pilot. *"We'll be following."*

Erik hit thrust and kicked them back in their seats. He needed space between him and the rock before he pulsed. Fifteen seconds later and PH-1 was chasing them, and Erik lifted thrust to 2-G as the shuttle roared at 4, reeling them in. Shuttle feed showed him a brief 5-G, ETA ten seconds, then Hausler cut power and let their velocities equalise just as he crashed the shuttle into the midships grapples and locked tight. Hell of a move, it reminded him of just how good you had to be to get a spot on *Phoenix* in the first place, and his confidence surged.

"*PH-1 is onboard!*"

"*Phoenix* is leaving, jumpline startup all systems green," said Erik, watching the powerup. If Rooke's repairs were off by a fraction and something blew now, they were finished.

"All green, all good!" Shahaim called.

"Target locked!" Kaspowitz confirmed.

"Let's get that fucker," said Erik, and hit the pulse...

...and everything stretched...

...and stretched...

And snapped back to reality, and they were racing, like a stone from a slingshot. Erik hit mains hard, and pushed them at 7-G... only four seconds until the chah'nas saw him, four seconds more for him to see their move... not fast enough, and he hit the pulse again...

...and emerged truly flying, Nav projecting all kinds of alarming rocks and obstacles that now dopplered and were a struggle to see at this velocity...

"Contact!" Geish shouted. "One mark at 288 by 30 nadir! He's seen us, he's coming about to pursue!" That was a silent runner, one of those they hadn't seen, and thank god it hadn't been any closer when they'd run…

"Arms!" said Erik. "A shot past the target's side! Do not fire at anyone else unless fired upon!" A thump as *Phoenix* fired, reaction-powered rounds that would keep accelerating at 30-Gs for another few minutes, a necessity with FTL warfare where the danger of overtaking your own ordinance was very real.

"He's running!" Geish called. "He's running hard! Heading nadir, 10G thrust!" And here was where the trap worked — *Phoenix* had been outer-system of *Tek-to-thi,* meaning the chah'nas couldn't run directly away from *Phoenix*, or he'd be heading straight into the star. To jump away, he had to head nadir or zenith — and starships didn't turn corners easily, jump engines could gain or lose you instant velocity, but course correction took time. "He's pulsing!"

"He's only three degrees off our course!" Kaspowitz announced. "He can't jump like that, he'll pass gravitational inversion…"

"Incoming fire!" called Jiri. "He's shooting at us!"

"Arms," Erik replied, "let him have it." More thuds, and the rapid whine-and-rattle of reloads.

"Defensive is outgoing," Harris announced as *Phoenix*'s defensive fire pumped rounds into the path of the chah'nas' incoming.

"Course correction!" Erik swung them full sideways and hit the full 10-Gs as everything thundered and shook. He could barely move the hand controls at these Gs, but with uplinks and finger buttons it didn't matter. Their course shifted a fraction of a degree, then another. Something blew up in their path in a mass of blurred static, then flashing past — incoming ordinance hitting *Phoenix*'s defensive fire and detonating. No way the chah'nas had enough defensive weaponry to do the same to what *Phoenix* was pumping in his direction…

"*He's pulsing again!*" Geish announced on uplinks, unable to use his voice in this thrust. "*He's dodging our fire!*"

That was a mistake. *Tek-to-thi* shot away from them once more, giving Erik an opportunity to straighten out briefly and... *"Arms! Target all to dorsal, we're gonna come out right on top of him!"*

All weapons swung that way, and Erik hit the pulse even harder than the chah'nas... and tore after him, closing with deadly speed as Arms put down a spread of preemptive defence... then dumped velocity right on top of him, spinning to put him in the dorsal arc as all weapons fired...

Multiple flashes on scan, fireballs from which *Tek-to-thi* emerged pinwheeling like a thrown stick, shedding pieces as it went. "Got him!" Karle announced between fear and excitement. "Got him hard, he's spinning!"

"Disable!" Erik shouted. "Proximity disable! Get his guns!" More thuds as *Phoenix*'s close range cannon opened up on the spinning vessel... they were real close now, full visual, no more than a few kilometres and Armscomp could calculate that like shelling peas. More flashes across the ship's nose and flanks, then a big flash as proximity warheads from a missile battery shredded the chah'nas's dorsal emplacements.

Erik swung them in a full arc around the target, giving Arms a good look, to be sure they'd got everything. "Good, now straighten him out for me!"

"LC, we have vessels responding to our lightwave," Geish warned. "Another few minutes and they'll be all over us."

Arms fired again, proximity detonations against the target's hull that slowed the spin. One blew a large part of the aft section off, and the spin slowed to a near stop, deprived of mass.

"That'll do, we are inbound... Major Thakur! Twenty seconds!"

"Twenty seconds, copy."

Erik timed his run nose first, braked hard with retros and called, "Impact forward!" Combat carriers were designed for it, and they crashed forward with a heavy thud, stopping the spin entirely. Then a simple kick forward, roll to align the combat dock amidships and fix the big grapples to the enemy's nose...

Trace's ride on the combat dock ended when the charges engaged — shaped explosives affixing to the enemy's nose with a boom! that rattled everyone inside their armour.

"Secure those main passages!" she said tersely as grapples clanged and crashed outside. "Move fast and stop for nothing. We want officers, not crew, kill anything with red shoulders, disable anything with blue." Not that they'd likely encounter much opposition, the chah'nas crew hadn't been given much time to don pressure suits. But then, chah'nas often erred on the side of violence, and they may have suited up in advance of the intercept, in anticipation of human trouble. Could this whole thing have been a trick to lure *Phoenix* into this engagement?

Dock irised open and she kicked off her berth and jetted in past torn debris and hull armour. She found a corridor, hit the wall and pushed off hard — with cylinder rotation gone the warship was zero-G and now zero-atmosphere. She powered up the corridor, simply scraping and bouncing off when her course drifted. Caught a corner hard and came about into the main corridor — chah'nas warships made human warships look like pleasurecraft, everything was dark steel and the glare of a few surviving lights.

Movement ahead as a chah'nas emerged from a doorway, helmeted and suited with weapon in hands — she shot it and jetted past, then grenaded the corridor end as another took aim from cover. On coms she heard more shooting and terse calls, and she caught a doorway short of the corridor end to halt herself, then Arime came past and they covered both ways at once. Arime shot something, and Trace jetted to the doorway the Kulik Class schematics said would be 'extra-crew', and checked the door sensor. It showed emergency yellow — the chah'nas colour for 'good', or what humans would use for 'green', meaning the far side of the door was pressurised.

Trace indicated to Arime, stuck a magnetic mine on it and pulled herself aside for cover. It was a shaped charge, so little shrapnel and in a vacuum explosives had no shockwave. This one blew a hole through the lock mechanism. Arime hauled the door open with powered-armour strength, a rush of escaping air, then Trace put a handball through the gap... saw several chah'nas crew thrashing and fighting for breath. And one, well covered in a six-limbed pressure suit, struggling to get his weapon to bear on the door. Trace tossed a flash-bang and went in fast after it, launched off the wall at the suited chah'nas and tackled him spinning into the wall. Behind her, Arime shot the two suffocating crew, more threat-neutralisation than mercy, as Trace clubbed the suited chah'nas repeatedly hard in the midriff to incapacitate without greatly damaging the suit. With powered-armour strength it was easy to twist two arms behind him, cuff them, then throw him at Arime.

"Get him out!" she said — the suit had no officer's markings, unsurprising from an emergency suit, but if you found three crew in an emergency decompression, and then chah'nas or human you could usually bet the only pressure suit went to the officer.

She guarded Arime's rear out the door with the prisoner, and nearly shot the next six-limbed, suited figure to erupt from a neighbouring door... but this suit was merely propelled by explosive decompression from the room. Its limbs were limp, but a glance in the bowl helmet showed it occupied... but the face was not chah'nas. Trace glimpsed fur, big, folded ears and sharp teeth... and desperate, wild eyes looking at her, shouting something Trace couldn't hear with no coms or atmosphere between them. A kuhsi, who was safe in a pressurised room, but had now busted out and apparently desperate for rescue...

Trace grabbed the suit, hit suit thrust and powered after Arime, calls on coms as all her marines retreated, tacnet showed them all accounted and moving fast. Trace hauled the half-empty pressure suit bouncing around a corner, rifle aimed behind in case some remaining chah'nas crewman was stupid enough to show himself, but none were.

And then they were back at the shattered entry hole that carved through decks melted like butter, and the glare of *Phoenix* spotlights that her visor blackened to keep dim amidst the cluster of armoured bodies.   Then a fast rush inside, the iris sealing behind as grapples crashed and thrust powered them away once more... and then acceleration slings amid the cold steel walls, throwing the prisoners and rescues in and finding some for themselves because *Phoenix* was about to move...

"This is the Major," Trace said as she hit her own sling and sealed herself in.   A fast glance around showed others doing the same, like insects in cocoons all up the combat dock.   "All aboard and sealed, go go go."

Erik did not need to be told twice, cut the grapples and blasted them clear.   Mains punched them back into their seats, as he loaded Kaspowitz's Nav settings and saw the solution track ahead of him.   They were still moving fast, and scan showed ships racing after them, ships pulsing, ships at considerable portions of light though apparently refraining from fire least they hit the chah'nas ship.   But they couldn't change trajectory in the way Kaspowitz's course required at this speed, so he dumped velocity hard and let the crippled alien ship go shooting off ahead — with any luck any other chah'nas in system would chase it down to rescue its remaining crew rather than chase *Phoenix*.

Another hard dump, then he swung the ship sideways and powered into an 11-G thrust.   *"Three minutes!"* he told them all on uplinks, blinking to stop his vision becoming a giant blur, fighting hard for air.   *"Arms, auto-fire, lay down cover!"*   He couldn't hear or feel the thump of outgoing fire, the rocking and roaring vibration of the mains drowned it out.   Course changing made them slow, while around them intercepting ships were gaining at an alarming rate.

"We're going to get incoming before we've finished the course change!" Geish warned.

"Can't help it.   Arms, full defensive!"

"Aye LC!"   There was nothing for it but to hope that Arms would intercept anything that would hit them before it did.

Engineering gave him an overheat warning on the mains, but it was the jumplines that bothered him, not the well tested and relatively undamaged main engines.

At two minutes, incoming arrived, continually accelerating rounds detonating on proximity fuse, thirty klicks, five klicks, two klicks, a bright flash as defensive intercepted one a klick short. Too many and too close... Erik re-primed the mains, abruptly cut thrust to the collective gasp of everyone on the bridge, waited for the reactor to re-boot, then slammed it on again. And suddenly all the rounds were detonating ahead, where *Phoenix* would have been, as Nav scrambled to recalculate based on that last move. Then the rounds were detonating behind as enemy Armscomps over-adjusted.

"That cruiser at red-three is gonna get real close to our mark!" said Karle, toggling fire and threat assessment as Erik held the roll to keep the guns in line. Red-three marked the third-closest enemy threat, but the fastest closing... Erik didn't want to hit anyone, just defend their escape, but if they left him no choice, *Phoenix* weaponry was more than a match for anything chasing them.

"Arms, lock red-three with everything and fire!"

"Aye LC, he's still too far out..."

"I know just hit him!"

Karle did that... and Erik felt a disorientation as dizziness hit him, then a jolt as uplink augments hit him with a stim jolt to keep him blacking out. Mark arrived, and Erik rolled without cutting thrust, and let Nav line them up for first pulse... wham! as something blew just to one side, intercepted or near-miss he couldn't tell, then a flash as something hit red-three, and he pulsed hard...

...and came out racing, suddenly far too fast for incoming ordinance, but the jumplines had a red light, flashing on the perimeter of his overcrowded vision. Any other time he would have bailed out, but there was simply no choice, and grav readings dropped below critical as velocity piled up, and suddenly all the lines on the jump Nav were matching.

He hit pulse, and Argitori system stretched in white sound and noise...

CHAPTER 17

And arrived, somewhere else, and a long, long way away from Argitori. That red light was still flashing, and speeds were about thirty percent too high, but that was normal for crazy combat jumps... only this was Rikishikti, which had retained its old krim name by virtue of being too insignificant for anyone to be bothered changing it.

Nav details crossed his eyes, blinking more easily in the lack of thrust but blurred as always from hyperspace time-dilation. It was the physiological equivalent of not sleeping for three days, and staring at a screen for most of them. Rikishikti, small red dwarf, a big, hot gas giant in a close orbit that was slowly melting it, a few rocky outer worlds and some very old, tumbling bits of ice. A dull and boring system frequented by no one, but providing enough mass to pull a speeding ship out of hyperspace.

Nav finally got its bearings and gave him a position — forty percent further down the gravity slope than they were supposed to be. But the dwarf's mass was low enough that it wouldn't mess them up particularly.

"Engineering, this is the LC. Rooke, I've got a red light on the jumplines, give me a yes or no on the next jump." He dumped velocity while he waited for Kaspowitz to recalc the jump. The warning light remained unchanged, the dump hadn't broken anything else. It could just be a bad sensor.

"Nothing here," said Geish. "Navigation buoy says seven transits in the last week, that's it."

"Don't believe those fucking things," said Kaspowitz. "They lie. LC, give me another few minutes to recalc."

"That's okay, we've got time." The nice thing about being in one of the Fleet's most powerful ships was that they always arrived well before anyone else. "All posts report."

"Arms green LC."

"Coms green LC."

"Scan green."

"Nav needs a drink LC." Erik fought back a smile, sipping water from the seat pouch. He couldn't quite believe they were still alive. Surely something had fucked up somewhere.

"Engineering is green LC. Still checking that jumpline but it's just that one light, nothing else, could be nothing. Mains are fine, I'm not getting any readings of damage."

"Operations is green LC. PH-1 is locked and secure, both other shuttles are secure, all Engineering crew accounted for." Well thank god for that. Now for the one he was dreading.

"Major Thakur? You guys okay down there?"

"We're good LC. Zero casualties, one chah'nas prisoner, two rescued kuhsi prisoners. I thought it was just one, but turns out there was a kid squashed into the suit as well. We had two chah'nas prisoners, but one went for a gun just now and... well, now there's one."

Erik couldn't quite believe his ears. "Outstanding Major. Just outstanding, you've excelled yourself. My appreciation to you all."

"And ours to you. Incredible bit of flying, the Captain couldn't have done better."

"Amen," Kaspowitz echoed as he worked, and some others echoed it again. Erik still didn't believe it, he could think of at least five things in that last passage he could have done better or faster. And it was one thing to say you were as good as Captain Pantillo, quite another to actually know what that meant, as he did.

"She took two minutes fifty-six on the dot," said Jiri with a half-grin of disbelief. "And didn't lose a man. That's ridiculous."

"That's 'cause we're *Phoenix*," Shahaim said loudly. "And don't let these fuckers forget it."

"LC," came Kaspowitz. "Nav is locked in, got you a course."

"Good." He flipped coms to shipwide. *"Phoenix*, this is the LC. Two jumps to go, just hold tight. Let's see if we can do this in one go."

"*LC this is Rooke. I think we're okay. Closer interrogation reveals nothing, I think it's just the light… it's the mag oscillation sensor, but I think it might just be reading disruption from mains.*"

"Green it is. Two dumps and a course correction, stand by." First and second dump passed without any further protest from the light. Erik held them at a 5-G burn for twelve minutes, seeing no reason to push it harder in this deserted system without immediate navigation hazards, then burned at 8-G for another ten to improve position and starting velocity upon the gravity slope, considering their deep entry.

And then when everyone down to the implacable Major Thakur herself was surely cursing him and muttering that he should just jump already, he hit two pulses in succession, watched the lines match, and once more flung them out into the void…

…and back in. Everything was shaking, and he just knew something wasn't right. The red light had made several friends, and the escape lines kept trying to rejoin and fling them back out into hyperspace, despite the great mass racing up at them in the stellar distance. Sounds and vision came at him oddly, as though doplering, colours shifting into realms where they did not belong. Were they actually out of hyperspace? You weren't supposed to be able to experience hyperspace, the human brain was structurally incapable of processing what it found there, and the sensors the scientists took across the gulf in research ships never recorded much more than static…

Erik tried to flex a hand on the left axis control, tried to find the jumpline toggle. That reach of his hand seemed to take a lifetime, fingers flexing out into the infinite distance…

…and back in fully with a crash of reality, alarms blaring, attitude reading a sideways slide and everyone shouting at once. "Dumping!" he shouted, recharging the lines to do that, and watched with helpless dread as the indicators barely moved, then slowly crawled as the power flowed. Come on, come on…

"That's not good!" Shahaim yelled from his side, watching the same thing he was. "That's not good at all!" If they couldn't charge, they couldn't slow down. If they couldn't slow down they'd cross this entire system in a few days and fling into deep space where no one travelled sub-light, and no one would find them, and they'd all die a very slow death from starvation or suffocation, depending on how long they could keep the ship running...

"Engineering!" Erik called. "Get me a charge!"

"*I'm on it!*" A pause. "*Try it now!*"

The lines moved, and finally a full charge. Erik hit the pulse, and everything blurred out of phase once more... then snapped back hard. This time the charge came quickly, and he hit it again. And found them at a much more sensible velocity. Heading was a little off — they were nadir on the new star, heading 'beneath' it, out of the plane of planets and moons which they'd be astronomically unlikely to hit, and the associated debris which was much more likely.

"Nav?" he called.

"Looks good to me LC," said Kaspowitz, relief plain in his voice. "Good job."

"Helm?"

"Systems look good. We can coast here, take a look at whatever went wrong."

"Okay everyone, this is the LC, looks like only two jumps this time. We'll have to do the third jump later. All posts call in."

They did, and all were unchanged save for a very anxious Second Lieutenant Rooke in Engineering. When everything was finally cleared, Erik gave them freedom to move around, and called Draper up to command.

He almost fell when getting from the chair, whether from nerves or the accumulated stiffness of two jumps straight. He braced himself with effort, and found the two marine guards ready by his quarters, having used the paired acceleration slings in there to avoid abandoning their post. They accompanied him around to back-quarter, along the central marine corridor and into Assembly, in time to catch Trace and some of her marines sliding down the access ladders from the core transit that everyone had to use to move from midships to the crew cylinder while rotation was operational.

There were plenty of other marines about, some armoured for simple protection as marines often would when riding a jump run, many checking the rows and rows of stacked armour and weapons as was procedure after every big move. The unarmoured others gathered also, and there were shouts and yells as the returning marines pulled off their helmets and handed off weapons.

"PHOENIX! PHOENIX! PHOENIX MARINES! ECHO PLATOON, FUCK YEAH!" They yelled louder when they saw Erik, moving aside for him. None touching him, just shouting, not wildly, but with purpose. "LC! HELL YEAH LC!"

Trace gave him a wry smile as he approached, sweaty with wet hair stuck to her forehead. She held out her hand, and he smacked it hard, and clasped, and ruffled her wet hair. "Best fucking marine commander in the Fleet," he said loudly, and they roared.

"Best fucking carrier pilot in the Fleet," she retorted, and they roared again.

"LC! LC! LC!" And Erik found himself smiling, and covered in goosebumps. Never mind that they'd all almost died in that last reentry, and might have broke the damn jumpline again. This was something he'd never truly believed he'd get, from these people. And never truly realised how badly he'd wanted until now.

Trace yanked his head down to speak in his ear above the noise. "And if you tell me differently, I'll kick your ass."

Erik laughed.

Trace's first priority after every planned Op was debrief — you didn't get good at this stuff by chance. It took endless practice and review, but right now ship life was getting in the way.

She arrived at Medbay Three, newly opened with One and Two now full of wounded or dead, warning screens active above the door to say the pivot had been active, and as spacers liked to say with dry humour, objects in the room may not remain as you'd left them. Doc Suelo came to her as she arrived — a darker 'African' shade than her, faintly grey and vastly experienced. *Phoenix* was his fourth warship, and in between he'd run vast Fleet station hospitals, big city hospitals, and in his younger days, frontier medical wards on outposts no one had heard of. He'd come back to active duty, he liked to say, because some young punk of a captain had suggested that he might be getting too old for it, and he'd re-signed to spite him.

"I'm sorry Major," he said. "But she's becoming a problem, and if I can't venture into my own ward, I'll have to tranq her."

"Not like I have anything else to do," Trace said mildly. It was not her habit to complain, but as command staff on a warship, her most precious commodity was time. Long experience had taught her to defend that commodity forcefully when necessary, in the sure knowledge that others would take it from her if she did not.

"You're the one who rescued her," Suelo reasoned. "She might remember that. I don't want to tranq her with her kid there, if we get off on the wrong foot we'll have to lock her up for the duration, and I know from experience that kuhsi hate confined spaces. I wouldn't have asked if I didn't think it was important."

Time-short or not, if there was anyone on the ship who could get a favour from her, it was Suelo. "Good job getting all our criticals through the push," she said. "I was certain we'd lose another one or two." In heavy-G manoeuvres, the badly wounded often died. There was no helping it, and ship commanders had it drummed into them in the academy to ignore the possibility, least they get *everyone* killed.

"I was certain too," Suelo said sombrely. "The LC was down here just now talking to a few of those conscious, looking real relieved. You know, that boy's starting to grow on me."

"We'll start a fanclub," said Trace, and reached for the door.

"You're going in like that?" Trace held up her forearm guards and gloves, borrowed from a light-armour suit. Suelo nodded warily. "Just be careful. She hasn't cut anyone yet, but those blades will open you ear-to-ear if they catch you right."

Trace nodded, hit the door and went in. Within was a broad medbay, runners down one wall where the pivot would tilt the whole room in heavy-G. Bunks were built into broad frames running through the walls. On the furthest one, the rescued kuhsi sat with her cub. She wasn't hooked up to lifesupport or even an IV. A flask of water sat on the bed table, and a sandwich that had been opened, and the meat picked out of it. Didn't med-staff know that kuhsi didn't eat vegetables? Probably not bread either.

She sat on the bed now, watching Trace approach, knees up, teeth bared in a snarl. Big ears back, eyes wide with fear and threat. She'd been much more sedate coming aboard — the suit had had a leak, evidently she'd had to get into it in a hurry, and pull her kid in too. Mild decompression had meant she'd been barely conscious when crew had pulled them both from the suit. Now consciousness had fully returned, and she was scared insensible. In the bunk beside her lay the little boy, one big ear protruding up from the pillow. Beneath a neighbouring bunk, Trace spied the remains of another sandwich, sent flying there with its tray, probably when a corpsman had tried to offer it to her.

Trace climbed onto the neighbouring bunk and sat there. The kuhsi stared at her, faintly trembling with tension. She had tawny fur, brown fading to pale, dark at the tufts of the ears. A powerful jaw, short whiskers, and long, blade-like nails protruding from her three middle fingers. A lot of females had those removed, she'd heard, voluntarily or otherwise. These were short, but looked effective enough. They made slice-marks in the gel-mattress even now. But pretty though she looked to human eyes, she did not look especially healthy. A cut marred both lips, and her ears were notched, one bent unnaturally. An eyelid drooped, partly swollen. And her jumpsuit and jacket were filthy and torn. Some dark patches looked like they might be blood. Old injuries, Trace saw.

"Do you recognise me?" Trace asked. Indicating her own face. "I saved you. In the chah'nas ship." The eyes widened immediately at that word. The ears dropped. Not a big fan of chah'nas, it seemed. "Chah'nas did this to you?"

A hiss, sharp teeth bared. Then a flash of forward movement, claws unsheathed and flashing for her face… Trace blocked with her forearm guards and remained otherwise unmoved. The kuhsi retreated fast to her bunk, crouched and trembling. It hadn't been a serious move, no bodyweight committed, she hadn't fooled Trace for a moment. Just an attempted scare.

A hissing, punctuated growl and cough — language, more frightened than frightening, and a gesture to the door with that many-clawed hand. That was clear enough, she wanted humans gone. Given this was a human ship, that was going to be a problem.

"*Phoenix* database," Trace said to empty air. "Access translator, authorisation Major Trace Thakur. Identify kuhsi language, recently spoken." She waited. And waited. Usually it was much faster than this, *Phoenix* had all of Fleet's files, and those files were extensive, particularly of 'friendly' species.

Trace held the kuhsi's gaze, unblinking. That wasn't easy, those golden eyes were most inhuman and intense. But there was an advantage in letting it know who was in charge. Now to let it know that she was not only in charge, but not a threat. That would be a real trick, in this mood. One of its sharp incisors was missing, she noted. It was beginning to look like someone had been very mean to this frightened alien. Her gaze shifted to the cub. Unmoving, perhaps sleeping. He hadn't flinched at that latest noise.

"*Hello Major,*" said *Phoenix* database in a cool female voice. "*I'm afraid the database could not identify the language spoken. I will continue to analyse further.*"

"Is the language kuhsi?" Trace wondered. This one could have been in space for a long time, out among the other aliens. Possibly it spoke alien tongues, just not English.

"*The database can confirm with ninety-nine percent certainty that the language just spoken is a kuhsi language. I will attempt to place it within the kuhsi language family, in the event that the precise language cannot be ascertained.*"

Trace took a deep breath, looking calmly at the kuhsi. "So. Our database doesn't know where you're from. Given that our database has something like five hundred known kuhsi languages, that means you're from somewhere small and remote. Someplace without a modern economy yet. Given that you're a female out here in space, where no females are supposed to be, I'll guess further that you were kidnapped, or maybe a sex slave..." she glanced again at the little cub. "Probably trafficked by your own people. Which might explain the kid. He'd be about... seven? Our years or yours. Which means you might have been out here a while."

She flipped channels on the uplink. "Doc? This one's a real mess. I don't know if this is just kuhsi psychology, I think there's a chance if a human had been through what this one had, she'd be about as insensible."

"*Well, just... do what you can, Major.*"

"Your little boy doesn't look well," Trace told the terrified alien. "You're scared for him, but you're going to hurt him worse if you don't let us treat him. I'm sure you know what a medical bay looks like." She uplinked to the wall display, and flipped it to the security cameras on Medbay One. The kuhsi looked, wary of some kind of trick. There were *Phoenix* marines, her marines, in bunks identical to these. Hooked to machines, wounds treated. Trace pointed to them. Pointed to the beds around. And pointed to the little boy. His clothes looked even more filthy than hers.

The kuhsi bared her teeth in an answering snarl. Trace sighed. "Okay. You don't want us here. That's fine." She rummaged in a pocket, calmly pulled the little tranq gun she'd got from storage, and shot the kuhsi in the chest. With a scream the kuhsi launched at her throat. Trace caught her wrists without effort, and simply held her like that — fast as lightning she might be, but she was neither healthy nor strong, and Trace simply waited for the drugs to take effect, and kept the kuhsi's teeth from her neck in the meantime.

When finally asleep, Trace placed her carefully on the next bunk, and rolled her gently to one side, arranging limbs most comfortably then prying the mouth open to check she wasn't about to swallow her tongue. Damn sharp teeth in there, and sure enough, the left incisor missing. Only the socket remained, and this girl was far too young for that to happen naturally.

Trace had the cuff on her arm and breather on her face by the time Doc Suelo got in the room — all the vitals looked fine, or the machine told her they were, having automatically figured it was treating a kuhsi and having all the medical parameters preprogrammed.

"Major, what the hell?" Suelo exclaimed as he strode over. "I told you I didn't want her tranqed!"

"In my experience Doc, people get me involved when they've arrived at an obvious solution they know has to be taken, but can't do it themselves. That kid's not in great shape, we're wasting time."

She strode around the bunk and crouched by the little boy. He had his mother's colour, but was even skinnier. She put the cuff and breather on him, and the machine started giving her feedback... a fast heartbeat, low blood pressure, general poor health. She took his hand and pressed the fingers, making the claws flex out a little... they'd been cut, he had barely more nails than she did.

"Someone's declawed him," she said. "Do they grow back?"

"Yes," said Suelo, rigging the female up to an IV. "It's not fast though." The claws were a marvel of bio-engineering — there were only vestigial nails left on little finger and thumb, but the middle three were huge, the length of half a human hand when extended. Retracted, they segmented in unison with finger joints, giving kuhsi middle fingers a clicky, awkward coordination. Extended, they locked together, and were obscenely sharp.

"Poor little guy," Trace murmured, stroking the cub's head. Such improbably big ears. Kuhsi's biggest problem with spacetravel, surely, was helmets. How did they stuff their huge ears into them? His mother's had barely fit within that oversized chah'nas helmet. "If she's one of their trafficking victims, this little guy might be the product of rape. If she's not talking, might be an idea to run genetics in the meantime, just to be sure he's her's. Know what we're dealing with."

"So how does she end up on a chah'nas warship?" Suelo asked, coming over to check on the cub.

Trace shook her head. "We'll have to ask when she's more sensible. Get good restraints, and when she's conscious, show her *everything* before you administer it to the boy. Don't let her out, just show her that you're caring for her boy. And might be an idea to only let women touch either of them. Given where she's been, and how kuhsi males can be..."

"Yes," Suelo agreed. "Yes, that's probably wise. Thank you Major, you can go now." Drily. "Your soothing feminine touch is no longer needed."

Trace paused by the unconscious female's bed on the way out. "Oh and feed them some fucking *meat* too... which idiot gave them sandwiches?"

"Let's just say alien physiology wasn't high on the corpsman qualification exam."

Gazing down at the sleeping kuhsi, Trace concluded that someone's neck needed to be broken. Possibly many necks. The galaxy at present was serving up an unending supply of them.

The chah'nas crewman barely fit in his chair. *Phoenix* did not have a brig, as such, just excess crew quarters that could be used as such in a pinch. That meant wall-bolted chairs between bunks, all human sized, and barely accommodating a 7-foot-plus frame, wide shoulders and elongated shoulder-blades accommodating that formidable extra pair of arms. The lower pair were cuffed behind his back, the upper pair on the tabletop.

Erik stood by the opposite bunk, not wishing to have to look up at the big reptileoid. Jokono stood at his side, and watched. Private Carlson stood by the door, armed despite the prisoner's restraints, just in case. Chah'nas weren't just big, they were strong, and this one looked as though he'd been working out. Chah'nas soldiers were augmented too, like humans.

"Greetings *ally*," this one said, in contemptuous deadpan. A chah'nas mouth didn't look particularly well-suited to human speech, with big lower tusks and underbite, but like humans they were omnivores, and had nimble vocals. This one spoke in a deep, bass growl, four eyes fixed unerringly on Erik about wide, inverted nose. "This is not much thanks for the species that saved your species from extinction."

"You attacked a human vessel in human space," said Erik. "That's an act of war against any species, it's about the only thing all species of the Spiral agree upon. Why do it?"

"I am a lowly crewman," the chah'nas said. "I don't know these things."

"My marines caught you near the bridge. Three chah'nas but only one spacesuit. You got the spacesuit."

The chah'nas's nostrils flared. "So what?"

"Among chah'nas, the suit would always go to the higher rank."

"I am marginally higher ranked. A common crewman nonetheless."

"What's your name?" Jokono asked calmly.

"Kel-ko-tal." Barely taking his eyes off Erik. Eye contact was a sign of respect… but 'respect' among chah'nas did not mean what it did among humans. Chah'nas always tried to best those they respected. "I am of Ko-sheel caste, warrior third-grade, by way of Ama-shaal caste, warrior fourth-grade. Not that that means anything to you." Contemptuously.

"You're right," said Erik. "It doesn't mean a damn thing. Your ship proved no challenge for mine, both my ship and my marines are without a scratch or a casualty."

A glare from Kel-ko-tal, and finally a lowering of the eyes. If you could get dominance over a chah'nas early in conversation, you took it. "We were ambushed," he muttered. "It was not a fair fight."

"And what would a lower-ranked crewman know of the tactical situation?" Jokono asked. "Even human lower-ranked crew rarely know what happens on the bridge, yet you describe events like you were there." Kel-ko-tal growled, perhaps realising he'd been outplayed.

"Civilised peoples have rules," the alien muttered.

"We do," said Erik. "Rules like not attacking other species' ships in their own space. Once you do that, it's war, and there are no rules in war."

"We are not at war! We are supposed to be allies. Human and chah'nas, we were victorious together, and now you dishonour that effort with your treachery."

"You say *Phoenix* took an unfair advantage against you — what do you call it when an FTL warship intercepts an unarmed sub-light freighter?"

"We call it following orders."

"Orders from whom? From chah'nas command? Or from human command?"

Kel-ko-tal gave him a look with four eyes narrowed. "Why should either surprise you? You know what you did. Murderer of your own Captain. Ambition without rules is like a cancer. We see this condition among chah'nas too, and we exterminate it where ever we find it."

"Captain Pantillo was the greatest captain in the human fleet," said Jokono. "He was loved above all others by his crew. Do you think the current crew would rally behind the man who killed him if they believed that tale?" With a nod to the marine standing at the door.

Kel-ko-tal glanced. "I know that this one is the son of wealthy and powerful people," he said, looking back at Erik. "Humans value wealth more than chah'nas. Such corruption is unsurprising."

"Then you know nothing of humans," said Jokono.

"Who ordered you to attack *Abigail*?" Erik pressed.

"No one. She was talking to your other ship, the *Chester.* It was suspicious. We investigated. Your command had given us leave to do so upon entering Argitori System. No specific command was given to board *Abigail.*"

"*Which* command?" Erik demanded. "What level would stoop so low to give permissions to the likes of you?"

"The highest level!" Kel-to-tal said defiantly. "The *only* level of human command that deals with us *aliens.*"

Erik and Jokono looked at each other.   It was a hell of an admission.   The prisoner was talking about the Big Three — Fleet Admirals Anjo and Ishmael, and Supreme Commander Chankow. Given that Anjo was the only one on Homeworld when *Tek-to-thi* had been there, it could well have come from him.   Fleet Admiral Anjo had given a chah'nas warship permission to do as it pleased, with unarmed human commercial vessels, in a human system?   That admission alone would see Anjo's head roll, if it reached the right ears.   But Fleet Admiral Anjo was not a man known for career suicide.   This permission of his had led to a chah'nas vessel intercepting a human vessel in full view of a very busy human system, so it wasn't exactly inconspicuous.   How had Anjo thought he could get away with it... unless there was something else going on that would exonerate him?

Jokono caught Erik's eye and nodded slightly — good, that meant.   Jokono was a former police investigator.   He thought in terms of constructing a case, bit by bit.   But who would prosecute it, Erik wondered?   One renegade warship?   They'd need friends, elsewhere in human space.   If they found a way to survive out here, on the run from their own Fleet, this was still going to get awfully difficult and complicated.   And very dangerous for other people too — if they could find any allies elsewhere willing to help them play this game against Fleet High Command.

"The kuhsi prisoner and her son," said Erik.   "Where did you get her from?"

"The furry thing and her little beast? I forget."

"Is your memory defective?   No wonder you have achieved so little with your life."   Again the four narrow-eyed glare.   "Tell me or I will dispose of this defective thing."

"Fleet regulations will not allow the killing of prisoners," Kel-ko-tal said defiantly.   "And human officers always follow their silly little rules."

Erik's smile was genuine.   "My own Fleet want to kill me. You think I care about their rules?   Their rules said chah'nas can attack unarmed humans in human space.   Fuck their rules, and fuck you if you won't cooperate." He glanced back at Private Carlson, hefting her weapon with menace.

Kel-ko-tal thought about it. It was always difficult to tell what went on behind that fearsome face. But Erik knew that for all their bravado, chah'nas did fear, just like humans, and had nearly as much difficulty reading human faces as vice-versa. There were few suicidal species in the Spiral, even the krim had been said to fear death, if only in the abstract sense that the species needed to live on to exterminate others. And Erik recalled the AI queen, before Trace had shot her. 'I am ready', she'd said. Had she feared, before the end? If not, why had she needed to be 'ready'?

Kel-ko-tal shrugged. "The furry thing was acquired at Tellus. It is of no importance."

Jokono leaned forward. "Then why was she on a Kulik Class warship?"

"A toy," the chah'nas smirked.

"You're lying," said Jokono. "Sexual perversion among chah'nas is rare. Interspecies perversion even rarer." He was right, thought Erik. Chah'nas could be brutal, but were rarely cruel. They liked the sport of a contest, and torture, including rape, was no contest if the victim could not fight back. "What are you hiding? Who is she?"

Kel-ko-tal said nothing. It was dangerous to think that humans were smarter or better at things than certain aliens, and yet chah'nas had a reputation among humans of lacking subtlety. And humans, chah'nas complained, were conniving and tricky. By chah'nas standards, perhaps that was true.

"Where was *Tek-to-thi* headed after Homeworld?" Erik pressed. "Our records show you were docked at Fajar Station, arriving from chah'nas space. You are a Kulik Class, chah'nas Fourth Fleet, First Squadron. It makes no sense that you were sent to chase after us, with all the human warships doing the job... unless you were heading in our direction already. Where were you going? Heuron? That's where all the big commanders are right now."

Kel-ko-tal made a show of looking bored. And with no intention of answering further questions. Jokono gave Erik a look that suggested they'd get little more from the chah'nas from here on. Erik nodded, got to his feet and left Jokono to the ongoing job. Jokono was tireless, finally given something on this crazy ship he could do well. He would be hours yet.

CHAPTER 18

"Rooke says the damage isn't so bad," Erik said. "It's just a minor system, he's fixing it now." He didn't mention that that minor system had nearly gotten them all killed. Saying so was redundant — out here every minor system malfunction could get you killed, and they all knew it.

Erik, Trace, Kaspowitz and Shahaim were in the Captain's quarters, taking the opportunity to down a meal. Visitors on warships sometimes wondered why everyone always ate in their quarters or at their post — the answer was of course that there was simply no room for a galley. Only a kitchen, from where hungry crew could pick up a meal and take it elsewhere.

"I think you're right," said Kaspowitz, eating his favourite stir fry from a plastic bowl. *Phoenix* kitchen wasn't much on variety. "I checked the records — *Tek-to-thi* was just recently promoted to command group in chah'nas Fourth Fleet."

"Yeah, I thought it was odd I hadn't heard much about it before," said Shahaim. Suli Shahaim was encyclopaedic about ships and captains. She was the latest of four generations of starship pilots, and had been given a head full of names and history from the tales her grandparents told her as a girl. "A new promotion from main fleet would do it."

"You mean you can't list all the ships in chah'nas main fleet?" Erik teased.

"No, not even me." With a faint smile. "Who's her Captain?"

"Can never remember chah'nas names," Kaspowitz admitted. "Big dude though. Much competitive chah'nas fury."

"Shit," said Shahaim. "Think we killed him?" A silence as they thought about that for a moment.

"On the other hand," Kaspowitz said, "who gives a fuck?"

Shahaim rolled her eyes a little. "It wasn't a moral statement. Of course he was asking for it. It's just getting… big."

Everyone knew what she meant. Previously their own Fleet HQ wanted to kill them. Now chah'nas fleet, and probably most of the chah'nas race, wanted to kill them also. Finding out exactly why had better provide some reasonable possibilities for survival, Erik thought grimly. Possibilities other than eternal exile or piracy.

"We can get to Merakis on our next jump," said Erik. "If that was the place the Captain was talking about, the place where all the stories begin and end, maybe we'll find some answers there." He gazed at the wall screen. It was simple visual, angled up at Rozdenya system from their lower nadir plane. A great disk of bright dust, a protostar in formation with the rest of its system. The child-star was just now undergoing ignition, as gravitational mass accumulated more and more gasses, and compression made them burn with such force the hydrogen nuclei fused, an endless, roiling mass of thermo-nuclear explosions.

In his years away from home, he'd occasionally had time to stop and gaze in awe at the universe, and wonder if the rest of it was as unsettled as this little, violent sector of the galaxy that humans called the Milky Way. Life was rare, and sentient life rarer still, but the current ratio appeared to be one sentient, intelligent spacefaring species per ten million stars. There were a hundred billion stars in this galaxy alone. That made approximately a thousand spacefaring species in the galaxy. So far they'd found twenty-six of them. Surely, hopefully, there were other corners of the galaxy where species mingled who got along with each other far better than this bunch did.

"So how do we do this?" Shahaim said quietly. "I mean, what's the end game?"

Erik exhaled hard. "I don't know. I've no idea how to answer the question without more information. I'm hoping we'll find more information on Merakis. Some clue that the Captain left us."

"I'm just..." Shahaim wiped dark curls from her forehead, in obvious distress. She was in her seventies, from a Spacer family that had business ties to Debogande industries, among others. Like many women, she'd done her service in several parts — an early stint as a young officer in the merchant navy, then time off for kids, then a return, once the kids were grown, upon realising that this part of her life, the service part, was the only thing that could replace the void of purpose left by her children's departure into adulthood. One of those kids was now a warship pilot herself, Erik knew. "There has to be some kind of future here. Some kind of purpose. Because even those in the crew who support you now, aren't going to support you if they can't see that this is all in service of something worthwhile, you know?"

"You don't think finding out why the Captain was killed is worthwhile?" Erik said edgily.

"Wait," said Trace, holding up a hand. "Suli, you said 'support you'. That's not right. This isn't about supporting Erik. This isn't just about him. This is about us. About *Phoenix*, and what the Captain made us."

"You're right," Shahaim said tiredly. "You're right, I misspoke. I mean, it's not the danger, we've all faced danger. We knew we could get killed in the war, but the war meant something. Something grand about the future of humanity. So what's *this* for? *Phoenix* means the world to me, but with all respect to you all, *Phoenix* is just a means to an end. Trace, you of all people know what I mean — the Kulina pledged their lives to the human cause. The Kulina themselves are not important — only the human cause is important. Without that cause, the Kulina are nothing, right?"

Trace thought about that. And did not have anything immediate to say.

"It's the loneliness," said Kaspowitz. Everyone looked at him. "Isn't it? I mean, we were out in situations like this in the war, lots of aliens trying to kill us, but we knew we weren't alone. Now we don't know that. And Suli's right, if we're just doing this alone for the greater glory of ourselves... well I'm not sure I see the point."

"So what?" said Trace, with a hard edge to her voice. "Do we give up because it's hard?"

"No I'm not saying that," Kaspowitz began.

"We're not alone," Erik interrupted. "Captain Lubeck was talking to *Abigail*. He'll have been instructed not to. He'll have been instructed to watch for any Debogande-friendly vessels communicating with us, or helping to hide us in any way. He talked to *Abigail* instead. I'm not even sure he didn't mean to get caught. He had to know he could be spotted, the risks were pretty big in a system crowded with that many high-tech sensor systems. I think Lubeck was making a statement, one way or the other, that he didn't like what was going on. Actually finding anything out from *Abigail* was probably secondary — I mean, what could any insystem sub-lighter really know?

"Let's face it, Fleet's whole case against us is plain suspicious. It doesn't make any sense that I would kill the Captain, the Captain was known to be friendly to at least some of my mother's politics, and thus my family's politics. My only possible motivation to kill him could have been my family's scheming things behind the scenes to upset any future move into politics from him… but anyone who knows that situation knows that the only people frightened by the idea of the Captain going into politics were Fleet.

"The more people talk about it, the more they won't buy it. Add to that, Trace is on my side, and Kulina are known to be incorruptible. Suspicion will grow. We need to tap into that suspicion, get some people on our side, and bring the people who planned this to justice. I'd guess there aren't very many of them, it's just a few very powerful folks at the very top of the command structure. Fleet Admiral Anjo for one."

"You're missing one big thing," Kaspowitz replied sombrely. "You're assuming that senior Fleet officers who hear our side of the story, and believe it, will automatically side with us. We all know this is about Worlders wanting more power. Most of Fleet's senior officer corp are diehard Spacers. Hell, I'm a diehard Spacer. Before all of this, I'd have said we need greater Worlder say in human politics like a hole in the head. I reckon that's a strong majority position on this ship even now."

He glanced at Shahaim. She nodded reluctantly. Trace said nothing. She'd grown up on a planet, and so had been a Worlder by birth... which of course became null when she'd gained her Fleet commission, as all Fleet, officers or enlisted, gained automatic Spacer citizenship. But either way, no one had ever thought to ask Trace if she even voted. Kulina just didn't get involved in that sort of thing, their cause was so much larger.

"So I'm guessing," Kaspowitz continued, "that a lot of senior Fleet officers will figure out that we're innocent, and that HQ murdered the Captain, and framed our LC, and all of that. But they won't do anything about it. Very reluctantly, but given the larger stakes, what's one ship?"

"Sure," Erik said darkly. "And what's a man's honour, come to that?"

"We did no dishonourable things in the war?" Kaspowitz replied. "If the cause is big enough, people will justify dishonour. Most Fleet officers don't want Worlders to have more power. The Captain was a strange fish in that respect, and from most captains' perspective, he's put us on the wrong side of that fight whether we like it or not. It's the purpose of ships like *Phoenix* to die for the cause of human security. I reckon a lot of them will justify that it doesn't matter if we die fighting the tavalai, or die fighting Fleet itself in Fleet's effort to keep incompetent fools from running humanity's wars. And you know... if the Worlders were running things? If we had genuine democracy? We'd all be fucked — and we all know it. Those fools would have us bankrupt within a generation, and then we'd get exterminated all over again because we wouldn't have enough money to keep Fleet operating."

Erik couldn't argue with that. He'd heard the same over and over from his parents, his elder sisters, and everyone in the family whose entire business was business, and the handling of money. Worlders lived surrounded by plenty, and without the pressing awareness of finite resources that Spacers lived with, just wanted to spend. Those from the Spacer culture of frugality just wouldn't tolerate it. And with the financial troubles many worlds had already created for themselves, the popular clamour to rescind the Fleet Tax on those struggling worlds had grown, to rolling eyes from Spacers who retorted that Fleet was the only reason those worlds were settled by humans in the first place, and they should have thought of those responsibilities before spending billions on credit they didn't actually have.

"Captain said it would start a war," Trace said quietly. Everyone looked at her. She didn't talk about her conversations with the Captain often. "He said there were plans afoot, among the Worlders, to get power. One way or the other. I wasn't interested at first, I told him that my cause was to help win humanity's wars against aliens. Domestic squabbles weren't my concern. He asked me to consider what I'd actually have won for humanity if we won the foreign war only to be destroyed by the domestic one. I didn't have an answer."

"Did he say what plans?" Erik asked.

Trace shook her head. "He wouldn't. He kept secrets. But he had friends among Worlders who told him things, he admitted as much. Powerful friends. He said the war was brewing, that it might take thirty years to get started, or it could start the very day the foreign war ended. It turns out, it was the latter. And its first shot was fired at him."

She looked upset, holding it in with that stony-faced control. Erik leaned forward. "Trace. It wasn't your fault."

"You remember just after the parade?" she said to him. "He ordered Lieutenant Dale to accompany you to see your parents. He knew the threat even then. I still doubted. I should have insisted on his own security."

"And what could you have done?" Erik retorted. "Trace, he was court-martialed and put in solitary. You had reason to go in shooting with me, because the penalty for murder is death, and it was obvious Fleet were killing us off one at a time. But when the Captain was court-martialed he wasn't about to be charged with a capital offence, you had every reason to believe you could get him out by following procedure."

"I should have pushed him to remain offworld."

"He would have ignored you."

"I could have convinced him, I know it."

"You don't know it," Erik said gently. "You wish it. Listen, you're having an attack of emotional subjectivity. Probably it's quite alien to you, but the rest of us know it all too well. You loved him, and it clouds your recollection. The objective truth is that the Captain knew the risks, and purposely kept the rest of us in the dark to try and keep us safe. Or safer. He took the burden upon himself, as he always did. It was a very Kulina thing to do, probably the reason he and you always got along so well."

"That sounds right," Kaspowitz murmured. "Fleet *could* have arranged for us to mysteriously disappear in that last fight. All of us. Ships have accidents all the time, friendlies hit friendlies by mistake. He kept us out of it. He never seemed surprised that they charged him."

Trace blinked hard, and gazed at the beautiful elliptic disk of star and planets in formation on the screen. "When I was a child, I attained the highest level of moksha in my meditation. I was praised on it, and held as an example to the other Kulina students. It helped me to overcome my fears and frailties. I was fastest on the climbs, and best at weapons. If ever I was troubled, or I found difficulty, I would meditate on it, and practise, and the solutions would come to me.

"But for the past few years, my meditation has suffered. The Captain spoke often of the growing corruption in Fleet HQ. He warned me never to repeat what he told me, or it could harm my career, and my safety. He said that Fleet was a tool to be held in the hand, and it needed a calm and wise mind to wield it. But if the hand came to rule the mind, then all the good that Fleet has done these past centuries could be destroyed. By our own hand.

"I meditate on it, and no solution comes. As Kulina, service to the Fleet, and service to the human cause, are one and the same. Only now I find that the one is coming to war with the other. For Kulina, this feels as though the right hand is attacking the left. These past years I've meditated more than ever before, but the old peace of my childhood is gone. I do not know that I shall ever find it again."

"Trace," Erik said gently.   "That man the Captain spoke of. The one you'd talked about. Have you thought who that might be?"

"I've a few possibilities," she said.   And returned her attention to her food. "I'll tell you if I come up with anyone."   Erik realised that he *was* getting to know her better.   It was the first time she'd said anything that he was certain was a lie.

After several hours of watching repairs in the vain hope that someone would find a use for her, Lisbeth finally gave up and went to the galley.   Ten minutes of pestering one of the three chefs got him to whip up a marinade sauce with yoghurt, fruit juice and spices, then quick fried his best meat slices in it.   Then she went to Medbay Three with Carla, and almost managed to do it without any wrong turns.   *Phoenix*, she was learning, wasn't so hard on the directionless — getting lost just meant you wound up back where you started.

Medbay Three had marines in it now, she'd heard someone in Engineering talking about how Medbay One was crammed with living and Two with dead, while Three was just the kuhsi and her kid.   Well no wonder she'd been scared, Lisbeth thought, looking around at the marines in the bunks.   When this place was empty it looked like some scary science lab, the kind of place an alien prisoner might get dissected.   Now it looked like a medical bay, and alien guests could see they weren't about to be subjected to anything the humans didn't do to themselves.

The kuhsi were up left, the mother and cub on separate bunks side by side.   Alongside the cub, a female marine sat on the bench seat that protruded from the wall, and held a cup for the little boy as he sipped with a straw.   His head was propped on pillows, and his mother was watching anxiously.   Her wrists were locked to the bed frame, Lisbeth saw, and a heavy belt fastened her waist to the bed.

"Get back in bed Private," said a Corpsman as she hurried past.

"Hey shove it Corpsman," the marine replied without hostility, holding the cup. She had one leg in a heavy brace with various cords leading out of it, as did the cuff on her arm. She looked up as Lisbeth and Carla arrived. "Lisbeth, hey." Lisbeth blinked. When did every marine on the ship suddenly get on first name basis with her? "I'm Private Rolonde, Jess Rolonde. I'm in Command Squad. Was in."

"With the Major," Lisbeth said as she realised. She'd have shaken her hand, but Rolonde's hands were busy. "Nice to meet you. And this is Carla."

"Hi Jess," said Carla, with that easy familiarity of one marine to another. "Real sorry about your Sarge. I knew a couple like him when I was in service, sounds like a hell of a guy."

"Yeah," Rolonde said reluctantly, looking back at the drinking cub. As though not trusting herself to speak about it, with anyone. She stroked the little boy's head. "Yeah."

Command Squad's infamous First Sergeant had been killed against the hacksaws, Lisbeth recalled. She wanted to add her condolences, but it just didn't feel right, from a civilian. Who was she to speak of such things, among these hardened warriors? What possible comfort could a pampered rich girl give?

The mother kuhsi was looking at them with those beautiful golden eyes. Anxious, but not terrified. Apparently she'd calmed down a lot. Kuhsi sometimes had terrible nerves, Lisbeth knew. With hunter reflexes came a wild fight-or-flight reflex that was often difficult to control.

"Here," she said, and took the top off the container she carried. She walked to the mother, with what she hoped was a comforting smile, and held the container for her to smell. "It's sho'gharch, one of my kuhsi friends from college ate it all the time. Smells good, yes?"

She put it on the round, soft-edged side bench, took out a piece of meat and tore it in half. Put one half in her mouth and chewed. It was a little simple by human standards, but tasted good enough. She offered the other piece to the mother. She accepted, cautiously opening her mouth. And chewed when Lisbeth gave it to her.   Lisbeth pointed to the rest of the meat, and back to the little boy, with eyebrows raised in question.

"Yes?" she said, nodding.   It wasn't a common kuhsi gesture.   The mother swallowed.   Then copied the nod, awkward and exaggerated.   Lisbeth smiled broadly, and gave the meat to Rolonde.   "Here, you feed him.   It has to be from that side, I can't sit between him and his mum or she can't see.   Just let her see what you're doing."

Rolonde put the drink bottle into the bed frame holder, and tore up bits of meat to feed the boy.   He was looking quite calm, Lisbeth was impressed to see.   Occasionally he'd throw a glance at his mother, but without great concern.   He seemed to have better instincts than her about who was friendly.   And barely even looked when Lisbeth sat on the end of his bed.   The first human instinct when looking at kuhsi was 'animal'... until you saw those eyes look your way, and saw the calculation there, and the dexterity of the fingers.

"Would you look at those big ears!" Lisbeth marvelled. "Isn't he gorgeous?"

"You had kuhsi friends in college?" Rolonde asked, appearing as intrigued as Lisbeth.   She was a lean, strong woman with dark-blonde hair and blue eyes.   Not as big as Carla, but Lisbeth knew that with augments the physical size counted for little — Major Thakur was proof of that.

"Yes I did.   They were on an exchange program from Choghoth, we studied at my university.   They were top students, really smart, spoke excellent English.   Well, as excellent as any kuhsi can speak a human tongue, their mouths won't make some of our sounds, and our throats can't handle their coughs and clicks."

"Hard to use your lips and tongue like we do when you've got those sharp teeth," Carla reasoned.   The mother only had one of those big front teeth, Lisbeth noted.   She had some little gel plasters on visible cuts, so she'd allowed a corpsman to treat her.   What the hell had happened to them both?

"Only boys though, right?" said Rolonde, holding some meat for the mother to see, before feeding the boy.   He ate hungrily, and seemed to enjoy it, using his own fingers now with unrestrained hands. "Careful, you'll get messy fingers kid."

"Yes, only boys leave Choghoth," Lisbeth agreed. "Girls stay home. Two of my kuhsi friends thought that was pretty awful too, but they weren't optimistic about it changing. And then some other kuhsi... well, I didn't make friends with them. They were assholes to girls."

"Choghoth," said the mother. The humans stared. Her pronunciation was very different, with a richness deep in the throat, and a mid-word click, that humans couldn't do without spraying the room with phlegm. "Choghoth, home."

"A-hah!" said Lisbeth with delight. "You *do* speak some English. I bet you were just scared before — you know I heard kuhsi get insensible sometimes when they're scared, forget everything they've learned."

"Humans too," said Carla.

"Careful, it's just one word," said Rolonde. She smiled at the boy. "Hey buddy, I bet *you* speak some English, kids always learn faster. What is your name?" He seemed more interested in eating. "I'm Jess." She pointed to herself. "Lisbeth. Carla." At the others. And she pointed the finger at the boy.

"Skah," said the boy around a mouthful.

"Skah?"

"Oh perfect!" Lisbeth exclaimed. "Skah! That's so cute."

"And her name?" Rolonde pointed at the mother.

"Nah-ny."

"Nah-ny?"

"Mommy," Lisbeth translated with a grin. "He can't pronounce 'm'." And remembered you weren't supposed to grin around kuhsi, they only did that when they were about to bite your head off. "And does mommy have a name? Skah, mommy name?"

"Tif," the boy conceded. "Nah-ny nane Tif. Nore prease."

"Can't pronounce 'l' either," said Lisbeth as Rolonde gave him some more. "He won't like my name. But so polite!" And she looked at the mother. "Hello Tif."

Tif rattled her wrist restraints in reply, with meaning. Rolonde held Skah's hand for a moment to indicate the finger claws, then mimed striking, and mimed her own throat being cut, both hands to her neck and gaping. Lisbeth thought it all a bit graphic, but Rolonde made it comic, and Tif put her head back on the pillow with a look that might have been exasperation. So she knew why there were restraints.

"Tif?" said Lisbeth. "*Phoenix* database, please translate to Gharkhan... *Phoenix*? Will it do that?"

"*Phoenix* database," Rolonde interrupted. "Translator program, Private Jessica Rolonde. Translate to adult kuhsi subject, in Gharkhan."

"I mean she has to speak some Gharkhan whatever her native tongue, doesn't she?" Lisbeth reasoned. "Tif? Tif please understand, we'd love to take off those restraints. But human skin is not as tough as kuhsi skin, you can hurt us with those claws and the ship regulations say we have to keep the restraints on if we think you might hurt us."

A bedside speaker coughed, rumbled and clicked through a series of kuhsi vowels in Tif's ear. Tif gazed at them.

"Tif, this is a warship," Lisbeth tried again. "You understand? These people are soldiers. If you threaten them, they can hurt you very bad. They don't want to hurt you, and they don't want to hurt Skah. So please don't threaten them, yes?"

Tif muttered something. "*Human ally,*" said the wallspeaker in a disembodied female voice. And added, "*Translation additional; subject kuhsi adult female is speaking Gharkhan, but has a very strong foreign accent. Unable to precisely identify. High possibility from Heshog Highlands.*"

"Tif, are you from Heshog?" Lisbeth pressed. Hearing her speak was not especially fascinating, Lisbeth had spent four years at college with at least a few kuhsi around. Some of them never shut up. "Heshog Highlands?"

Another awkward nod from Tif. She said something. "*Near,*" said the wall speaker. She'd said more words than that. Lisbeth wondered how much the translator was actually getting.

"And yes," Rolonde added.   "Humans are allies to kuhsi. You're safe here."

"*Ally like chah'nas.*"   Her gold-eyed gaze was full of accusation.

"Tif, what did they do to you?" Lisbeth asked.   No reply from the kuhsi.   "They hurt you and were holding you prisoner, I understand that.   But we attacked them and rescued you.   We're not their friends."

Tif thought about it.   Looked about the Medbay.   A number of other marines were listening, having little better to do, lying in a hospital ward.   "*I was pilot.*"

Lisbeth and Rolonde looked at each other.   Rolonde looked very skeptical.   It didn't seem likely.   "You were a pilot?" Lisbeth repeated.   "What did you pilot?"

"*Shuttle.   Student.   From Highlands.*"   Again the translator was skipping a whole bunch of words.   Lisbeth frowned, trying to focus on that and not the sounds from Tif's mouth.   "*Academy. Trained as pilot.   Job with Lord.   Top of class.   Big job.*"

"So, wait… you were a… a scholarship student?   From a poor region in the Heshog Highlands?"   Tif waited for the speaker to translate that.   And nodded vaguely.   Good enough.   "You trained in an academy?   Which academy?   I didn't know any academies on Choghoth trained women."

Tif spoke two words, but the speaker only gave one.   "*Lord.*" The other word must be his name then.

"Lord… Kharghep?"

"*Lord Kharghesh.*"   This time the translator got the whole thing.   Now why did that name seem familiar?

"I heard about him," said Rolonde.   Lisbeth was surprised, then chided herself for it.   Why shouldn't a marine private know things about kuhsi current affairs?   Many marine privates knew a lot more about the universe than over-educated upper class girls, having travelled so much more of it.   "He was a moderniser.   Wanted to change the old kuhsi ways, lots of resistance from conservatives. He died just recently.   An accident, I think."

"No accident," said Tif.   Morose, her ears down.   Little Skah stopped eating and looked at her, ears also down.   Clearly distressed also, because his mother was.   *"Murder."*   Silence in Medbay.   Lisbeth looked at Rolonde.   Rolonde looked as surprised as anyone.   *"I saw.   I Lord Kharghesh mistress.   Lord Khargesh make kuhsi woman free.   Many mistress, many good woman."*

It wasn't as suspicious as it sounded.   Kuhsi had clans, and big lords had many mistresses.   Kuhsi didn't do marriage, nor monogamy in any human sense, though a mistress to a big lord had better not sleep around if she knew what was good for her.   It meant only high rank males got to procreate, which made the lower ranked rebellious.   A very big lord could have as many mistresses as he wanted.   Supposedly a *reformist* big lord could attract thousands, of their own accord, if it got them an education and jobs, things too often denied to kuhsi women.   Maybe hundreds of thousands.   Choghoth was not a small planet — four billion kuhsi, going on five.   Half of what Earth had been, before the krim killed it, and at a similar technological level.   And now that kuhsi had FTL, their territory was expanding.

"Old kuhsi not want new kuhsi world.   Free woman bad.   Kill Lord Kharghesh.   I saw.   Put me on chah'nas ship, with Skah."

"Why Tif?   Why put you on a chah'nas ship?"

Tif stared at her, very direct.   *"Kuhsi human ally.   Human tell kuhsi, let woman free.   Reform this.   Reform that.   Old kuhsi not want change.   Chah'nas meet big kuhsi.   I saw.   Tell big kuhsi, old kuhsi — you not change.   Chah'nas not like change.   Old kuhsi not like change.   Make new ally — chah'nas, kuhsi.   No more human, maybe."*

Wow, thought Lisbeth.   "But why take your kid?" Rolonde asked.   One comforting hand on the boy's shoulder.   "Why take Skah?"

"Skah son, Lord Khargesh," Tif said sadly.   Looking at her little boy, head back on the pillows.   It compressed one of her long ears, folding it.   *"Lord Khargesh big kuhsi.   Big lands.   Skah..."*   The translator didn't get the last word.

"Skah what?" Rolonde wondered.

"Heir," Lisbeth breathed. "Skah is Lord Khargesh's heir."

"So why give him to the chah'nas?" Erik wondered, sitting in the command chair. All first-shift was at post around him, plus Lisbeth by Shahaim's chair, and Trace by Kaspowitz's. Rooke's latest repair job counted down on a screen — just a few hours, he assured them.

Lisbeth shrugged. "She wasn't clear. I don't think it's wise to push her further. She's told us quite a lot, I think she'll tell us more as she trusts us more. It's not like we have any political allegiances left." A silence, as that comment fell to the deck like a lead balloon. 'Oh', Lisbeth mouthed silently, realising how that sounded.

"I think they were headed for Heuron," said Kaspowitz, eyeing his nav-display, measuring the jump trajectories. "It's all in line, we know that's where Fleet High Command is now. Supreme Commander Chankow's there, a bunch of chah'nas top command. Lord Khargesh runs a big territory, that's nearly two hundred million kuhsi."

Which on one of those old homeworld planets was enormous, Erik knew. Humans had lost that a thousand years ago, lost the emotional connection with old roots in the land, old political systems and cultures. Countries, they'd been called on Earth. A lot of them had been racially and ethnically homogenous, which was similar to today, but back then there had been so many *different* homogeneities. Different countries, with different peoples praying to different gods and speaking different languages. They hadn't often got along, with plenty of wars resulting. Humans today often forgot that point — aliens hadn't started the violence. Before aliens had come along, humans had been busily killing each other. These days at least, that was rare.

But it wasn't rare amongst kuhsi. They didn't have countries, but they had an interwoven mesh of clans, bloodlines and traditional territories, spiced up by lots of old racial and cultural differences.   It was a lot more stable than it had been, thanks to modern technology making warfare far too costly to be a frequent event between big powers.   Lord Khargesh had run the eighth biggest clan... a hugely powerful man. Erik's brief scan of *Phoenix* database revealed more details, big reforms to gender roles being one of them.   He seemed more an economic rationalist than a moralist, he said it was economically inefficient for women not to work the higher skilled jobs they were qualified for.   He'd had a lot of support, but a lot of enemies too.   Obviously he had, if what Tif said was correct, and he'd been murdered.

"It's strange," said Erik, chewing a nail.   "My father likes to complain about humans being so inflexible, but it turns out we're incredibly flexible next to nearly every other alien species. Chah'nas still run their caste system like some antique model, technology doesn't change it.   I mean we started giving women power in modern society far before the kuhsi did... and if they hadn't met us, fair bet they wouldn't even be considering it now."

"You know," said Trace, "if you keep chewing those nails, you're going to lose a finger."   Lisbeth giggled.   Erik considered making a face at her, but thought it wasn't proper for a warship commander.   "Old guard kuhsi don't think humans are a great influence.   They think they might be better off with chah'nas as best friends."

"That'll be tough without contiguous territories," Shahaim added.

Trace shrugged.   "In the old feudal days of Earth, rival lords would keep the children and heirs of neighbouring territories hostage.   To control who inherited those lands, and to make them behave.   Maybe giving Skah to the chah'nas does the same thing. Chah'nas controls who inherits Lord Khargesh's lands, or at least have a big say.   If that's where the reformers are, that'll give them a big say in how vocal those reformers are.   Maybe."

Erik made to chew his nails again, and stopped with an accusing look at Trace.   She looked serene.   "Kaspo, how soon could we reach Heuron?"

"Um..." Kaspowitz did some fast calculations. "From Merakis? Another three jumps. Big ones, maybe fifteen days realtime."

"And we could beat everyone there? From Homeworld?"

Kaspowitz looked cautious. "Sure. What are you thinking?"

"Get there before everyone else does. This whole shit with the Captain was a local job. Doesn't seem likely Supreme Commander Chankow was in on the specifics. We show up there, no one knows we're renegades yet. We cruise in, pretend everything's normal, ask some questions."

"What if Chankow *was* in on it?" Shahaim countered. "He didn't need to be in on the specifics, it could have been just a general instruction or plan."

Erik shrugged. "There's that."

"How would we explain being in Heuron when we're supposed to be at Homeworld?" Kaspowitz added. "Hell of a course change."

"And there's that," said Erik. "We're smart folk. We'll think of something."

"Can you lie?" Trace asked. "You don't strike me as the dishonest type."

"Are you kidding?" Lisbeth laughed. "He can lie like a senator."

"Can *you* lie?" Erik asked Trace. "Or does that break some kind of karmic rule?"

"I shot numerous innocent people dead to get you out of detention after pretending to be on their side," Trace said calmly. "What do you think?"

Silence on the bridge. Lisbeth turned a little pale. Erik just considered Trace, narrow-eyed. She was a bit of a landmine sometimes, just blowing up with hard truths at unexpected moments. Erik thought it was becoming a little predictable. Her innocent expression seemed to protest his look's accusation that he was onto her.

"Seems a hell of a coincidence that the *Tek-to-thi* was on its way to Heuron carrying the heir to Lord Kharghesh's empire," Erik mused.   "But now that I think about it, it's probably not a coincidence at all.   If *Tek-to-thi* was in kuhsi space, it needed an excuse to come through human space.   Homeworld celebrations did that, and now there's big command meetings at Heuron.   If they want to hand Skah off to chah'nas command in person, that's the excuse to do it.   Us going renegade at Argitori just gave them an excuse to leave Homeworld earlier.   Only their commander over-reached, got over-excited in the hunt as chah'nas will, got too close to *Phoenix*... which can be fatal.   Tif's just damn lucky her ship got boarded, and by marines as good as ours.

"It just confirms that the chah'nas are up to things, politically. The kuhsi are *our* allies, human allies, but now the chah'nas are playing games and trying to win them over.   It means hitting *Tek-to-thi* was worth it, because Tif and our chah'nas prisoner just confirm we're on the right track.   The chah'nas alliance is the key in this, and whatever the hell they're up to trying to get their old empire back.

"Which leads us to Merakis, the spiritual centre of that old empire.   If we're going to drop in on Heuron unexpected, we'll need all the information we can get first.   The Captain pointed us at Merakis, where all the Spiral's stories begin and end.   First things first."

CHAPTER 19

Erik blinked hard at the screens as they resolved before him. Merakis, dead ahead. Nav seemed certain they were right in the slot, and for a pleasant change there were no red lights flashing on the Engineering screen. All posts reported green, and for the first time in a while, this jump arrival did not seem particularly terrifying.

Merakis was an odd system, and one of the few in settled space where the entire system was known by the name of its most famous world to avoid confusion. The system was centred by a pleasant F-class star, but had a paired red-dwarf binary in deep orbit — three stars total with the two little dwarves doing a twirling dance about the rest. Merakis was the third and largest of five major moons about a huge gas giant in the star's habitable zone. The giant had kept Merakis in steady orbit despite several billion years of interference from that deep-orbiting binary, a property that led to two thirds of the settled worlds in the known galaxy being technically catagorised as moons.

Merakis itself was barely habitable, with thin atmosphere and mild gravity, though it had been alive once with a benign and undramatic ecosystem. But for reasons unknown to anyone, it had found the favour of the Ancients, a fact that had in turn made it a magnet for every spacefaring species to rise to prominence in this part of the Spiral.

"I'm getting chatter," said Shilu, tuning through the multiple spectrums that *Phoenix* could receive. In a three star and two gas giant system like this, there was a lot of clutter from multiple radiation sources, squealing up and down the frequencies. "Nothing human."

"Fix on those beacons," Geish added. "All where they should be."

"We're right in the slot," Kaspowitz confirmed, as the incoming feeds from Scan and Coms gave him the data he required to conclude that. "Zero-point-six hours out at this velocity."

That made this a combat jump. Zero-point-six hours would scare the crap out of anyone at Merakis. Which was precisely the point, as this was the tactical equivalent of high ground. They were forty degrees above system-elliptical, matching trajectories with Merakis's orbit in a way that suggested Kaspowitz had nailed the entry window. But recently conquered systems were usually jumpy, and had defensive pickets placed out along the known and likely entry angles to prevent incoming sweeps exactly like this one.

"Nothing on near scan," Geish said tersely. "Looks undefended."

"Might not have responded yet," Erik replied. Hands off the control grips for now, there was no point at this velocity, and the autos kept them steady. If someone was lying dark, they could fire up at any moment. "Anything from the beacons?"

"Nothing," said Shilu. "They're not talking." Which meant they had no idea who'd been in or out of this system in the past days and weeks.

"Told you not to trust those things," Kaspowitz growled.

"Got planet chatter now," Shilu added. "Orbital, I think. Chah'nas, five immediate sources. No make that ten. Ten plus. All in combat encryption, I'm running it now."

"Could be a squadron," Shahaim suggested, watching the Engineering systems in case anything had broken loose again. "Looks like a squadron."

"What the hell are they doing here?" Karle wondered. "We conquered this system, this is human space."

Except that Erik had been suspicious about that since Kaspowitz had first mentioned Merakis to him. He'd checked Fleet orders on Merakis, something he'd had no cause to do until then, and found a ban on movements. That wasn't uncommon, Fleet had all kinds of reasons it didn't want its own ships travelling to particular systems, some better than others. But for Merakis it didn't make much sense. Merakis had arguably greater civilian value than military. It wasn't a great industrial system, though there was industry here in various worlds and moon-systems... all ex-tavalai, of course.

And then there'd be the academics and scientists clamouring to come here, all now indefinitely delayed. This place had great spiritual value to the tavalai, and by all accounts they'd been quite upset to lose it. Thus the Operation Urchirimala Kaspowitz had mentioned, to gather and store all the scientific and cultural data they could gather before humans came in and ruined it. This was a symbolic prize for Fleet, if nothing else, and possibly even a bargaining chip with the tavalai, in the ongoing surrender negotiations. Possibly tavalai could be allowed continued access, under supervision. Erik thought that a fair concession to the rule-respecting tavalai, who were unlikely to abuse the privilege, if it got humanity a better deal on the shape of colonial rule to come.

But instead of finding the place crawling with human vessels, it seemed now empty of either military or civilian human ships. Instead, there was a squadron of chah'nas military vessels in close orbit about Merakis, apparently unconcerned of any threat. What the hell was Fleet doing, allowing this? Chah'nas hadn't captured this system, most tavalai space wasn't anywhere near current chah'nas space, and Merakis in particular was not.

"This was the spiritual centre of the galaxy for chah'nas too," Kaspowitz reminded them. "If only because they knew everyone else valued it. It became their prize. I'd guess they've returned to claim it."

"Not in our fucking space they haven't," Erik said firmly. "Shilu, new IFF broadcast. Identify us as a tavalai warship, combat carrier Ibranakala Class."

"Aye LC!" Shilu replied as the shock of that rippled up the bridge, little looks and glances amongst the crew. "Tavalai warship, Ibranakala Class, IFF upcoming."

"Hell yeah," said Kaspowitz. "Watch 'em scatter."

"What if they don't run?" Geish cautioned.

"They'll run," said Erik. "On our current angle of attack they don't have a choice."

"If they don't move soon," Karle added, "we'll get about half of them."

"I can see that," Erik acknowledged as Armscomp displayed on his screens. The chah'nas were at the bottom of Merakis's gravity well, while *Phoenix* came hard and fast from outside. Any ordinance they fired now would accelerate at massive Gs under its own power, self-correcting all the way at targets that carried little V and would have to struggle long and hard out of that well. Armscomp projections showed incoming ordinance adjusting for trajectory shifts far faster than chah'nas vessels could make them, and being so close to planetary mass, they couldn't pulse to gain V.

"Oh man," said Shahaim, looking at that same display. "They're so fucked."

"They're so fucking stupid," Kaspowitz retorted. "Tavalai surrender was just weeks ago, they think they're that safe here?"

"Arms, lock all weapons," said Erik.

"Aye, locking all weapons," said Karle, fingers dancing on panels, then stick control grips. Preparing to end the lives of several thousand close human allies.

"Sir," Geish growled, "if we fire under tavalai IFF we could restart the war. If we fire under Fleet IFF we could kill the Triumvirate Alliance."

"Fleet's problem when they murdered the Captain," Erik said coldly. "Not mine. Mr Karle, proximity bursts on all ordinance, I don't want any strikes."

"Aye LC, proximity bursts all weapons. Done. Permission to fire?"

"Permission to fire."

Karle hit the triggers and *Phoenix* thumped and clanked with rapid outgoing cannon.

"Lightwave arriving in ten seconds," Kaspowitz advised. "They'll be seeing us shortly." And as long for light to travel back, and let them see what the chah'nas were doing in reply. They were sure to fire back, but their ordinance would be climbing the gravity well, and with full freedom of manoeuvre, *Phoenix* would be very hard to hit. Crippled by their lack of jump pulse, plus gravity burden, the chah'nas would not be.

266

"There's Eve," said Geish, locking long range scan onto something specific and orbiting Merakis at the higher end of low orbit. "She's got company, two docked. Looks otherwise fine, no sign of damage."

Which was just as well, because Eve was an archaeological treasure. Humans called it an O'Neil cylinder, but the Fathers had built it forty five thousand years before Gerard O'Neil was born. That made it the oldest structure of its size in the known galaxy. The Fathers had been nearly as fascinated by Merakis as the tavalai were today, and unable or unwilling to live on its surface, they'd built this huge, rotating cylinder nearby.

"Just be sure you don't hit *that*," Kaspowitz said to Karle. "Or else the whole galaxy will want to kill us."

Return-light arrived. Ten seconds later, the first chah'nas ships slammed on full burn. "Whoa," said Geish. "Full burn on one, three... seven marks. They're going."

"Bet that broke a few bones," Shahaim muttered. Probably it had done far worse than that — ten seconds was no time to get everyone secure before a full burn. Some chah'nas crewmen had just died down there, for sure.

"Scan," said Erik, "any idea what they were doing down there? What do their positions look like?"

"I think ground parties for sure," said Geish, staring hard at the projected chah'nas trajectories. "It looks like... well the northern settlement is fixed here, point A, latitude 58..." and that point glowed red on Erik's screen as Geish highlighted it. "And that's where these first three had sequential orbit... it's hard to tell precisely, but sure. I think they've left some people behind down there."

Erik called up a Merakis surface map. It was hard for spaceships to launch ground-parties because to launch shuttles to the surface, you had to hold low orbit. And low orbits moved, passing right around the planet, making communication and eventually rendezvous with the ground party upon return difficult. Geo-stationary orbit solved the communication problem, but geo-stationary was a long way up, and took a long, vulnerable age for shuttles to move back and forth from.

These chah'nas ships were a mixed pattern of geo-stationary and low orbit, which looked like they were covering planetary deployment... in three years of war on *Phoenix*, Erik had seen similar patterns covering entire planetary invasions, maintained by hundreds of ships, not just this rough dozen.

Erik flipped channels. "Major, you reading this?"

"*I see it. Looks like the chah'nas left some people behind, you want us to go down and clean it up?*"

"It's a possibility." He didn't like the idea of deploying his marines down a gravity well. He'd asked so much of them lately, and if *Phoenix* got bounced by an incoming sweep, Trace and her guys would be as stuck as the chah'nas were. "Let's assess the situation when we're closer."

"I think you might have a job to do in orbit first," Geish interrupted, fixing a close scan on Eve. "One of those two docked ships has gone, but the other one's still there. Looks like we might have caught one."

Four hours later, *Phoenix* was closing into proximity orbit behind Eve, and the chah'nas ship was still there. Erik could see clearly on screen that it was an armed merchanter — large holds, conservative engines and basic weapons. It had no shuttle racks, and beyond the crew cylinder rotation, was unmoving, and unresponsive to hails.

Its hold space made it nearly as large a vessel as *Phoenix*, but Eve dwarfed it to insignificance. Nestled against the hub docking end of the giant cylinder, the chah'nas vessel looked like a pilot fish beside a whale, an insignificant speck. Holding off at two cautious kilometres, *Phoenix* looked barely larger. Behind the busy chatter, there was an awed hush on the bridge. None of them had been to Merakis before, nor seen Eve up close. Erik had seen it before in photos, videos and simulations, but in real life, to come here in command of one of humanity's mightiest starships, and to find oneself so utterly overwhelmed, was a unique experience.

"*LC,*" said Jokono from the makeshift 'brig'. "*Our chah'nas prisoner claims he has no idea why his fleet is all over Merakis. He makes the astute observation that they must have had permission from someone very high up in human command.*"

"Very astute," Erik agreed. "Thank you Jokono."

"Polar drone confirming all clear on farside," said Geish. They'd let that one go on the approach, and it was now doing a wide polar orbit about Merakis to show them any approaches on the planetary farside... on that orbit, it should have minimum obstruction. *Phoenix*, on the other hand, was now so close to the planet, it could only see half the sky. Like generations of warship captains before him, Erik hated it.

"They all jumped," Shahaim reminded him, as though reading his thoughts. "Even if they short-jumped, we'll still have a few days before they reappear. The only reason anyone's doing a combat jump to Merakis is if they know something's wrong, and the only people who know something's wrong are those chah'nas we just scared off, and us. Or maybe the Fleet ships chasing us, but they don't know we came here, and even if they guessed, they'd be days behind us."

"Unless they get another combat carrier on the chase," Erik murmured. He began gnawing his nail again... only to remember Trace's reprimand, and cursed her silently. And fought back a smile, because it was kind of funny.

"There wasn't any combat carrier in Argitori when we left but us," said Kaspowitz. "If there's one coming, it'll still have a long chase to catch up. We *should* be okay down here for two days at least."

'Should' was a hell of a bet with the ship's safety, and over six hundred lives. Anyone who did arrive at combat V as *Phoenix* just had, would not be detonating warheads short on proximity fuses. But then, Erik reminded himself, the Captain had sent them here. They thought. Or Kaspowitz had guessed, rather... only that was unfair on Kaspowitz. He may have had the idea, but Erik was in

269

command, that meant all choice and responsibility was his. This was what they talked about in the Academy when they spoke of the burden of command. Anyone on the ship could have a dumb idea that got everyone killed, but that dumb idea was ultimately the fault of the officer who chose to implement it.

But was there any choice? What would Trace say about doing nasty things about which there was no real choice, only anxious discomfort? She'd say shut up and get on with it. Another faint smile, and he flipped channels.

"Major, this one's on you, however you want to play it."

"*Copy LC, we will reconnoiter in force. Echo and Bravo platoons on the nearside, we appear to have multiple secondary docking ports outside of the current inclination of that ship's weapons. Though if you'd do us the favour of blowing him away if he so much as twitches, we'd all appreciate it.*"

"Major, I am pleased to inform you that we have every weapon available trained on the chah'nas vessel, with all active targeting engaged, just to let him know it. If one of those guns moves, he'll die before it can fire."

"*That's what I like to hear. Departure in thirty seconds.*"

"Thirty seconds, LC copies. Good hunting Major, and stay safe." Which were two bits of oddly contradictory advice, but Erik was confident she'd know what he meant. They'd lost too many people lately. This time, he meant, let's bring everyone back.

"I wish to hell she didn't lead every damn away mission," Kaspowitz read Erik's mind. "Even she needs a break sometime."

"Problem is," Erik replied, "as good as all her Lieutenants are, when the shit hits the fan, she's better than all of them. And they all know it."

"*Here we go,*" said Lieutenant Hausler from up front, and PH-1 broke *Phoenix*'s grapples with a crash. Then a shove of the mains, a brief burst, then back to weightless. Trace sat locked into one of her rowed seats in main hold, watching scan scrawling across her visor. She'd done assaults on O'Neil cylinders before, but had never imagined she'd be doing one on Eve.

PH-1's maximum capacity was sixty armoured marines in a tight squeeze. Today she held fifty-two — Trace's Command Squad of eight, plus Echo Platoon's forty-four. The irreplaceable First Sergeant Willis had been replaced by Sergeant Kono from Delta Platoon Third Squad, who now received an on-the-spot promotion to Staffie. So now Lieutenant Crozier was unhappy that her Third Squad was without its leader, plus Trace had replacements for Ugail and Rolonde, the second of whom would be temporary. She'd have gone with just five in Command Squad, but none of her Lieutenants would hear of it, not even Crozier.

Again it didn't feel right not to have Willis here. She glanced around within her helmet visor, saw the visored faces of her marines all about her. Echo was lately casualty free, and eager for action. There was always survivor guilt when some other platoon got hammered, while yours was stuck in the rear. Some sense that the survivors from the engaged platoons were looking at you with accusation — 'where the hell were you?' In reality there was nothing of the sort, Alpha and Charlie had just happened to be at the centre of the hacksaw attack by pure chance, and Echo had been fulfilling the strategically vital role of reserve, while defending *Phoenix* at dock. Every marine in Alpha and Charlie knew that. But every marine in Echo Platoon felt it nonetheless. A commander had to bear it in mind, and guard that they didn't do anything reckless to make amends.

"PH-4," said Trace, watching their position as the two shuttles drew up to Eve's colossal side. "Hold off and keep those chah'nas gun turrets in view. We'll do this one at a time."

"*PH-4 copies.*" Combat shuttles had armament enough to make a serious mess of anything at this range, warships included. Now PH-1 continued to the dock, while her sister hung back, training every bristling missile on the chah'nas vessel alongside. Chah'nas didn't write their ship names on the hull, and this one was playing possum. *Phoenix* database suggested it could have been any one of a hundred chah'nas ships of the class. The databases updated themselves automatically upon arrival in every new system, querying and exchanging data with all friendly vessels. But the Spiral was large, the chah'nas fleet was large, and a lot of its ships went unseen by humans for long periods, sometimes indefinite.

Ahead, the shuttle's forward scan showed a minor dock beside the huge starship docks, all unmoving against the cylinder's rotating bulk. This entire endplate was counter-rotating, to hold it steady for docking ships. No way had that mechanism remained functioning for fifty thousand years — the tavalai had occupied this system for the past ten thousand years, had lived on Eve, fixed her, operated her, revered her. No doubt most of them had only just left, ten thousand years of constant habitation coming to an end. They'd thought they were surrendering to the humans. Trace wondered if the tavalai who'd remained here to welcome the conquerors had yet had that chance. Or if these chah'nas vessels had been the first of the victorious Triumvirate to arrive.

The tavalai wouldn't have liked that. Tavalai had overthrown the last Chah'nas Empire precisely because they'd grown sick and tired of their former masters. Chah'nas had never forgiven them for it. The Captain had always said, in quiet tones when only officers he absolutely trusted were around to hear it, that most of the reason the tavalai continued to fight so hard, was to avoid returning to the bad old days of subjugation under the chah'nas. He'd even gone so far as to suggest that in some ways, the chah'nas part of the alliance was a liability — chah'nas were often strategically unwise bordering on incompetent, and had the certain effect of motivating the tavalai to fight to the death. But the chah'nas alliance was the rock upon which human security had rested since the destruction of Earth. It was no propaganda to suggest that chah'nas were the entire reason humanity still existed — it was simple historical fact. Even now Trace felt uncomfortable with what they'd done to *Tek-to-thi*, and at the chah'nas prisoner held in the *Phoenix* 'brig'… no question *Tek-to-thi* had been asking for it by all the established rules of behaviour, but even so. 'Ally', the prisoner had said. That was something a lot of humans, and a lot of chah'nas, felt in their bones.

And this current situation, whatever the chah'nas's obvious wrongdoings here and in Argitori, was… uncomfortable.

Dock was an internal bay, rectangular and enfolding PH-1 in a total embrace. Grapples crashed, then a thud as the dorsal hatch engaged. Then a seal. "Go," said Trace, and her people closest to the hatch lifted restraints and floated in an orderly, heavily armed cluster to ready positions. Inside the inner hatch, plugger junior, a smaller version of the big *Phoenix* Docking Assault Clearance Unit, came to life and was thrust into the airlock like a big, heavily armed ice hockey puck.

"*Echo Platoon, standing by,*" came Lieutenant Zhi's voice.

"Copy Echo," Trace said calmly. "Go hard."

Outer airlock opened and Echo cleared the space with professional speed, unhooking in turn and filing patiently to the dorsal hatch, hands on the walls, overheads and each other to keep everyone together. No shooting came, and finally Trace unhooked, and fell in behind Staff Sergeant Kono as Command Squad followed the last of Echo Platoon out of the shuttle. Suit sensors showed abruptly plunging temperature, then recovering slowly.

The zero-G corridors were pressurised but no one was trusting the air. Echo Platoon moved fast through tight corners, Squads quickly capturing the docking bridge, which gained them a view of PH-1 quickly departing to make way for PH-4 with Bravo Platoon aboard. They wanted the dock of the chah'nas ship, but had to secure Eve's end-cap first, jetting along corridors leading to cargo storage, leading in turn to personnel access to the huge, mechanised systems that fed the neighbouring starship docks with fuel, air and cargo. Lieutenant Zhi took First Squad into those mechanisms while Trace headed with the rest toward main habitat, through multiple airlock controls, everything spotless and modern with that familiar tavalai touch — abstract artworks on the walls, much potted greenery with leafy fronds that sprawled across entire corridors, and suit sensors reading an extra half-atmosphere pressure and humidity thick enough to drink.

And finally they arrived at an observation lounge, with huge, wide windows looking up Eve's entire fifteen kilometre length, like looking up a great, green tube. It circled slowly, five kilometres wide and slowly revolving about the stationary central spine, with five wide spoke arms protruding from a central collar at regular intervals. That was how you got down to the rotating surface — out along the spine, then down elevators in the arms. To one side of her position, Trace could see the near-seamless join where the stationary end-cap met the rotating cylinder, and what should have been several billion tonnes of friction floated smoothly on magnetic rails that ensured no actual contact at all. Reactors powered it all, and the spine conducted it through the cylinder. Trace was sure most if not all of the subsystems were recent replacements, surely anything fifty thousand years old wasn't going to be working in any shape or form, even if the tech had been good. But the old shell, with all its incredible scale, had been here longer than humanity had been farming.

With Echo holding all the end-cap strategic points, Trace sent Bravo to go and get the chah'nas ship at dock. Even as she did it, tacnet was identifying scattered gunfire across the vast expanse of the cylinder. Third Squad up at the spine got some people out an access hatch into clear air, and they could hear the gunfire, mostly near, up this end of the cylinder. Then came the reports, sightings of chah'nas in the ancient streets below, with guns.

"*What the hell are they shooting at?*" muttered Sergeant Kunoz of Second Squad.

"*Tavalai,*" said Lance Corporal Raif. "*My guess.*"

Fair guess, thought Trace. Eve was clearly deserted save for whatever remnants of tavalai remained. Operation Urchirimala, Kaspowitz had said. Scientists, academics. Not soldiers — when the tavalai mounted a defensive operation it was obvious. And if they were, there'd be a lot of chah'nas dying down there. Tavalai were not equal to chah'nas one-on-one, but combat was rarely that, and tavalai were smart and disciplined. For all the chah'nas's martial boasts, they rarely broke better than even against tavalai. UF marines had a better record, and *Phoenix* marines better still.

Trace flipped channels. "LC, you getting this?"

"I see it Major. Looks like this ship of chah'nas was left behind to finish a job."

"It's looking like the ship itself is empty. What are your orders?" A few days ago she'd have pretty much decided her next course of action alone, and dared him to stop her. But this was different. He was different. What she saw here had no obvious cause, and no obvious solution. Here, it seemed entirely possible that Erik Debogande might have a better idea what to do than her.

"We signed a peace treaty with the tavalai," came Erik's voice in her ear. *"I'm pretty sure it didn't involve their civilians getting slaughtered. We let this continue, we are in violation of our oath as Fleet officers."*

"Right now our job is to defend *Phoenix*," Trace replied. Near one of the close support arms, tacnet identified a burst of heavy gunfire, multiple sources. It lasted five seconds, then stopped, as though by command. It wasn't a firefight, this was far too orderly. All of the gunfire seemed to be from one side.

"Major, we came here to find out why the Captain was murdered. The Captain's clues appear to point us here. I think this is what he wanted us to see."

Trace looked sideways at Staff Sergeant Kono. His return look was wary, and she could read it like a book — Kono didn't want to get into some nasty firefight to save a bunch of tavalai. They'd all lost so many friends to the tavalai over the years. Chah'nas shooting up tavalai civilians was bad and sad, but it happened. The chah'nas alliance was important, tavalai weren't. If you wanted to emerge from the war with your sanity intact, you ignored it and moved on.

"LC, if we go down there in strength, we're likely to end up in a big-ass firefight. I can't guarantee what happens from there."

"Well it's your call Major. I can't tell you how to do it. But chah'nas actions here aren't in the script that any of us were sold. Fleet HQ's running a different script, and my bet is that different script is the reason the Captain was killed. We have to find out what's going on. How you do that, I'll leave up to you."

It wasn't a cop out. It was what captains always did — give general orders, and leave it to the marine commander to figure out how to implement them. She was the grunt, ground combat operations were her speciality, not his, and if he'd started giving her tactical directions, she was well entitled to ignore him.

"Major," came Lieutenant Alomaim's voice. *"I'm at the chah'nas ship's dock. No sign of activity, no guards, nothing. The dock's not even active, it's not taking on fuel or air. Given the activity we see in the cylinder, my guess is they've left the ship empty to carry on their business down there."*

Erik was right, Trace realised. They'd come here to find out what the hell was going on with the chah'nas in particular. This was information. Like it or not, they were going to have to go down there. And the only way to go anywhere, with bullets flying, was in force.

"Okay, we're not just going to wander into a firefight as dumbfuck peacekeepers. If we go in, we go in to enforce situational dominance, as far as we can spread it. So I'm requesting that *Phoenix* back us up for situational dominance on Eve."

"You won't be able to enforce that very far with a few platoons in this monster."

"I don't care what happens elsewhere on Eve, I just need to control what happens near *me*. I'm going to try and carve out a safe zone around one of those support arms, stop everyone from shooting and try and get some sense from them. So I'll want some translation assistance for a loudspeaker announcement, and maybe some technical assistance too for the speakers if we don't have that expertise. Coms and Engineering could help see if we can talk to anyone directly, but given the chah'nas haven't replied to hails, I'll bet they know we're human and are ignoring us."

"Coms and Engineering are listening in, I'll get them on it."

"Good. Next I will need Delta to get in here and take that chah'nas ship, we can't have the risk it'll do something. Alpha and Charlie will remain as backup."

"Phoenix is so notified."

Eve's central spine was a huge structure of steel girders in interlocking triangles. They formed a tube through which rail cars ran, but *Phoenix* marines ignored the cars and jetted in formation up the enormous shafts between the girders. The spine was two-and-a-half kilometres from the habitation rim, and suit sensors here read the air a little less dense, like regular altitude on a planet, and centrifugal force pushed denser air outward to the habitation rim. Between the flashing girders, Trace could see great avenue layouts, wide roads and flat, wide buildings in oddly geometrical patterns.

The Fathers had lived here in their millions... or at least, Eve had that much capacity. Little historical record of actual settlement remained, as the Fathers were the only previous, known intelligent species to have met total extinction at the hands of another. The hacksaws had finished them, in a vastly earlier incarnation, destroying their own creators in order to take their place atop the galactic food chain. But the AIs had never had any interest in Merakis. Trace wasn't aware if humans even knew what had driven the Fathers from this place — hacksaw attack, or something else entirely.

Nearly a kilometre out along the spine, the shaft met five equally enormous support pylons, spreading out across the habitation tube like a colossal pentagram. Here her externals picked up the fizz of generators powering the magnetic rims, huge circular collars to support the frictionless rotation of those support arms about the spine. Sleek rail cars blocked the shaft ahead, and Trace's marines jetted to brake and slow themselves. They picked their way between girders, then out to the spinning rims, avoiding the capture nets and hand rails about the railcars that civilians would use in more peaceful times to enter and exit those cars.

Trace didn't particularly like descending by elevator, it made them easy targets for anyone on the ground with weapons heavy enough to penetrate the hard carbon. But jetting out to the gravitational rim independently was impossible without a hard collision — armour suits had enough thrust to push in zero-G but

277

nowhere near enough to lift off from one-G. She put Echo First and Second Squads on two different elevator arms, then took two later cars for Third, Heavy and Command Squads. Gravity slowly increased as they zoomed down the arm, the ancient habitation rim approaching fast, then arriving in a rush as the doors circled open and they all rushed out and down the steps of the biggest engineering support collar Trace had ever seen.

Echo First Squad already had position about the open space. It was paved, surrounded by trees and gardens like any pleasant, public space in a civilised, planetary city. Only now, looking up, the horizon bent all the way around overhead, and it was the central spine that appeared to rotate, not the rim. 'The things you will see first,', Trace recalled her Siksaka's words. The O'Neil cylinders she'd been in before had been nothing like this big. The oldest had been a meagre two hundred years. What an infant species we are, she thought.

"Major, we've got a patch on those speakers," said Lieutenant Alomaim with Bravo First Squad in the spine overhead, as Trace took a knee at a building corner for cover. *"We're trying frequencies but everything's jammed except for UF frequencies. It's like they've left them open for us."* Trace caught the note of hope in his voice. We might not have to shoot at chah'nas on the ground, that meant. *Tek-to-thi* was one thing, because *Tek-to-thi* had been abusing humans. This would be something else.

"Give me translation on coms." A light blinked as her suit did that. "All residents of this facility, this is United Forces Ship *Phoenix*, human fleet." That last for aliens who knew them by that name rather than the first one. "*Phoenix* marines are establishing a safe zone around the base of the fourth support arm, section O. I repeat, marines are establishing a safe zone around the base of the fourth support arm, section O. All individuals seeking safety must proceed there. *Phoenix* marines will not allow any individuals to be harmed within the safe zone.

"Should any individual seek to harm another individual within the safe zone, *Phoenix* marines shall fire on them, irrespective of species. I repeat, individuals harming other individuals within the safe zone will be fired upon.   *Phoenix* claims command authority over this facility in the interim, and all individuals shall accept this authority or face consequences. Message ends."

"*Got it,*" said Alomaim.   "*We'll put it out in Togiri and Gaida, and hope the translators don't ask them for directions to the nearest massage bar.*"   It was a *Phoenix* in-joke, having happened once in a distant sector of chah'nas space with an obscure dialect.

On tacnet, Trace could see Delta Platoon, having arrived by the Debogande civilian shuttle, flown by Lieutenant Dufresne of second-shift bridge crew, as they were now short of shuttle pilots. They were moving rapidly through the end-cap toward the chah'nas ship's dock.   She was quite sure Lieutenant Crozier could take a single chah'nas warship without supervision, occupied or otherwise. If there was going to be resistance, a fight on the docks would tell the story.

"All squads," she said, noting their positions on tacnet display. "Let's clear the zone. You have permission to fire only if you are fired upon, or if you see someone else being fired upon.   I do not care if that someone else is chah'nas or tavalai, a safe zone is safe, and we shall enforce it."

She could have come in here and wandered around in peacekeeper mode.   She knew a few commanders who would have done that, and was damn glad she'd never had to serve under any of them.   Marines existed to enforce situational dominance, and were poorly suited to any other role.   The best way to stop people dying was to stop people shooting.   And the best way to stop people shooting was to shoot them.

They fanned out, down adjoining roads between trees and low, wide buildings.   Trace moved behind Sergeant Ong and Third Squad for a street, then took a left to spread the line further, and take them looping around the support arm.   Four of Echo's Heavy Squad came with Command Squad, usual procedure in this formation to keep Command's numbers at a dozen.   Buildings here had much less glass than in human cities.   Humans needed windows and light, but these, while not unattractive, seemed almost to resemble brick or stone paving.   Like the dwellings found in a desert town, she thought — lots of ceramic and mud for insulation.

"*So were the Fathers dry desert critters or not?*" Private Terez wondered at low volume as they moved at a steady walk along the street.   It did not look made for vehicular traffic, but rather for pedestrians, with no markings nor sign of traffic coordination. Trace wondered if that was by original design, or what the tavalai had done to it since.

"*Sure feels like Serena where I grew up,*" said Arime. "*Everything's brown, save the trees.*"

"*The Fathers were from a hot, heavy world,*" said the newly promoted Staff Sergeant Kono.   "*Short build, big arms, inefficient body temp regulation.   Now watch your spacing and admire the architecture later.*"

"*Major?*"   It was Sergeant Kunoz, Second Squad.   "*We got bodies.   Tavalai, five of them, on the street.   Looks like they were running away, all recent.*"

Trace took that position off tacnet — just two blocks away. "Copy Sergeant.   Civilian or military?"

"*All civvies.   No weapons in evidence, though those might have been moved.*"   A visual came through, Sergeant Kunoz's perspective.   Circling two bodies, tanned green and brown, squat and clearly tavalai.   Short sleeved jerkins, loose pants, nothing military.   Blood stains like they'd skidded and rolled... shot while running, as Kunoz said.   "*Evidence of automatic gunfire on the trees and walls.   Very recent.*"

"Lieutenant Alomaim, you see anything?"   Lieutenant Alomaim's viewpoint was providing tacnet with additional data, some movement two blocks from here, and more elsewhere, where *Phoenix* forces weren't.

"*Laser acoustic registers some muffled gunfire,*" said Alomaim.   "*I think they're possibly indoors.   Or underground, this place would have a transit system, right?*"

"Yes, yes it would," Trace confirmed.   Command Squad reached another diagonal intersection, and along the left-hand road were taller buildings, perhaps apartments.   Beneath them, two bodies lay on the road.   "We have two more bodies here. Investigating."

Command Squad needed no instruction, Kono waving his troops left and right, walking crouched with rifles ready, sensors on full for any movement.   Neither of the tavalai appeared to have been shot.   But they lay a crumpled, broken mess all the same, one of them with an arm badly broken beneath the body.

"Thrown out of the building, looks like," said Private Van, scanning the high windows above.   Trace crouched to look more closely, with total confidence that she was well covered.   Tavalai had long, flat heads, with big, double-lidded eyes spread wide and slightly bulging.   Their mouths were huge, throats bulbous, like the frogs they were sometimes derided as.   But their bodies were strong, native to a heavier gravity than humans, and half again the air pressure.   With combat augmentation, their soldiers were not quite as fast as humans, but comfortably more powerful.

This one's eyes were gaping, mouth open in frozen horror. Trace wondered if in all her life, she'd seen more dead tavalai than live ones.   Dead, she decided.   These two had clearly been thrown from a height.   Their thick limbs lacked the size and muscular definition of soldiers, and their clothes were utilitarian, with many pockets.   She reached, and fished a computing device from one pocket.   On it hung a metal symbol, like jewellery.

"Watch!" said Corporal Rael abruptly, rifle tracking a running figure up the street end.   Trace stayed on a knee, but did not bother to aim, watching instead.   The runner was tavalai, also civilian, unarmed and frantic.   It sprinted at them in a powerful, loping gait that looked so different from what Trace was accustomed to seeing in tavalai battle armour.

"Hold your fire," Trace said calmly, knowing there was little need.   Tavalai did not play dirty tricks with bomb-rigged civilians. A chah'nas appeared behind the running tavalai, in light battle armour.   "Target!"   The chah'nas had two weapons in four hands, indistinct at this range.   "If he shoots, take him down!"

Instead, the chah'nas strolled from the street, raising a launcher as he went.   As soon as he was out of sight, a loud pop!

sounded, and the marines hit the deck and rolled for cover without a word spoken. But the grenade hit short, and blew the running tavalai straight into a roadside tree.

"Go get him!" Trace instructed, and Corporal Rael took off up the road with his section, while Kono, Terez and Van moved with Trace to the tavalai. This tavalai was also dead, an arm nearly missing, horrid wounds from the shrapnel blast.

"*Major,*" said Lieutenant Alomaim from high above, "*we just saw what looked like a chah'nas use a grenade on a running tavalai...*"

"Yeah I saw that too," said Trace. Alomaim was the least experienced of her five Platoon Commanders, and not everyone caught everything first time on tacnet. "He was at pains not to shoot at us, only the tavalai."

"*I guess they figured our tavalai IFF was bullshit when we were still hours out,*" Staff Sergeant Kono growled. "*Once they knew we were human, they got out and went to work. These guys don't know what happened to Captain Pantillo.*"

"*Major, he's out of sight,*" came Corporal Rael up the end of the street. "*Shall we pursue?*"

"No, hold that crossroad and wait for us. We'll..."

"*Major. Look right.*" Trace looked, back where they'd come. A doorway onto the street was open, and a tavalai head peered out, fearfully. Looking at them. Things must be desperate for a tavalai to look at a human with such desperate hope. But then, she recalled the Captain saying that the tavalai's great enemies in the Triumvirate were not humans but chah'nas...

"Weapons down," said Trace, and jogged that way. Kono and his two came also, hurrying to take up position about the street opposite. Trace confronted the tavalai. Its leg was bloody, wrapped with a rough, makeshift binding. It retreated back into the passage, limping and grimacing, not wanting to be anywhere near the road. Trace followed, weapon out to one side, unthreatening. "Hogi dagalama?" she demanded of it. "Hogi dagala, doli ma?" 'What happens here?', that was, in her utilitarian Togiri. All marine officers knew a little by official requirement, and learned a lot more on the job.

The tavalai slumped back against the passage wall, and shook its head. "Chah'nas kill us," it said… a deeper voice, Trace thought. In tavalai as in humans, that meant male. The vocals were a deep and multi-toned vibration, with a bubbling on sharp consonants that made understanding hard. "Chah'nas come two cycles, two days yes? Days? Two days, and they come here and they made us all line up… we are just scientists!" Frantic fear. Horror and grief, at what he'd seen. One didn't think the tavalai face could convey such things, so different it was from anything familiar and human. But it could. "Where were you humans? We were told, command tell us, they surrendered to humans! To humans only, we were expecting humans, and then the chah'nas came and they kill us all!"

Trace looked at Staff Sergeant Kono, guarding the doorway. Within his armoured visor, his eyes were grim. The alien asked good questions.

"How many of you?" Trace asked.

"There were five hundred and twenty of us on this facility. All scientists… we were collecting our final data. I… I am Chisdhorahmradaem, I am a linguist with the Narigalda Institute of Historical Studies, I… I was instructed to be here to give humans a tour of the facility." Those wide-set, amphibious eyes swivelled far forward to focus on her, seeking understanding. The wide mouth trembled. "If… if we are to lose this place, we can at least leave it in good hands and some human scientists I know are very good and respect the old things as we do, but… but instead we get that!" Pointing with stubby fingers, out at chah'nas, at death and slaughter. "Why did you do this to us? Have the Tavalim not suffered enough?"

Trace swallowed hard. "Listen, Chis. I am not here under orders from human command. Understand?" Incomprehension. "We are *UFS Phoenix*, and we are renegade from human command. Do you understand this word? Renegade?"

A fast blink with the inner, translucent eyelids, but not the outer. "I… yes I think so. They chase you?"

"They killed our Captain." Possibly it was more than she should say, but at this point she didn't see the value of deception. "I think our Captain saw this coming, he knew that human Fleet would betray you. Who amongst your people is highest ranked? Who can help shed light on this?"

"No no no!" Chis protested. "You will just save the senior people! You have to save all of us! Please, you must!"

"How many are left?" Trace retorted.

The tavalai began to shake. "There must be some," he said through tears. Humans and tavalai had that in common too. "There must be some left. Please."

Trace stared at the grief-stricken alien. This was not right. Whatever purpose the chah'nas had here, this was evil, and should by all rights be stopped. But her cause was not the tavalai cause, it was the human cause. The human cause had demanded that she kill many, many tavalai, tavalai much unlike this one in that they were soldiers, but those soldiers would have families just as her soldiers did, and those families no doubt felt grief just as this one did. Did feeling sympathy for a tavalai make her a hypocrite? On so many occasions, she'd *been* the chah'nas, as they were behaving right now. Not massacring civilians, but cutting vast swathes through tavalai soldiery, which had in turn, on occasion, opened tavalai civilians up to direct assault, and the horrors of collateral damage.

"Major, got a chah'nas out here. Different guy that shot our tavalai." It was Corporal Rael, up on the next intersection. *"Posture unthreatening, looks like he wants to talk."*

Trace left quickly, almost relieved to have that excuse. "Guard the tavalai," she said, and Kono left two behind before coming with her as she strode up the road.

"Could be an ambush," he warned, as much for his people's benefit as to warn her. *"Stay alert."*

At the intersection, Trace found there was indeed a big chah'nas, covered by Corporal Rael, whose other three marines covered the surrounding roads. Trace took position by a tree and beckoned the chah'nas over. The big four-armed warrior seemed to smirk, and came. He had light battle armour, nothing powered, but decorated with spiral patterns on the shoulders and chest. His rifle was on his back, a big pistol on one thigh, and other weapons in webbing about his person.

Not karko-tan, the elite warrior class. Those were like chah'nas marines — the elite combatants, always in advanced armour. That ship at dock was not a carrier, just a dokik-class cruiser. Chah'nas did not distinguish between spacers and marines like humans did — all their spacers fought too. Trace admired that about them — they specialised less than humans, and always looked to climb the ladder from one role to another. Some of their greatest warriors and captains had begun as cleaners and errand boys.

"*Phoenix*," it said, in clear English. Trace thought this one might be female... with chah'nas it was rarely obvious. "Why are you here?"

"You seem surprised," said Trace, looking up at it, shoulder to the tree. The chah'nas seemed pleased to see her cowering in cover while it stood exposed. Trace was unbothered. Soldiers who liked to proudly display their bravery by standing without cover usually ended up proudly dead. Professionals didn't give a damn how non-professionals felt. "Why? This is a human system by conquest."

"We have permission to be here."

"Given by whom?"

The chah'nas's four eyes narrowed. "You entered the system with a tavalai IFF. Our squadron had no choice given their position but to run or be destroyed. You may have just restarted the war, they think tavalai attacked them in violation of the surrender. Why have you done this reckless thing?"

"Speaking of violating the terms of surrender," said Trace. "You are killing unarmed tavalai civilians. This is a human system, they are under human protection. You will cease, or you will be destroyed."

The chah'nas considered her for a moment from that great height. "You are acting without orders," it concluded. No stupid alien this one, Trace thought. "What have you done?"

"We are *UFS Phoenix*," said Trace. "You know us. We outnumber you. We outgun you. You will tell us who gave you permission to be here, and what your purpose is."

"I will not," said the chah'nas. "You can shoot me if you wish, but I do not believe you will. Humans and chah'nas have won this great victory together. We together conquered this place, and restored it to its rightful ownership after ten thousand years of improper occupation. You will not squander this."

"Tavalai in this zone are under human protection," said Trace. "Harm them, and you will die."

The chah'nas smiled. "Frog lover. The weakness of humans is also known to us." It waved two hands dismissively — the diagonally opposing hands. Those were linked, in the chah'nas brain, and could not easily operate independently. "Do what you will. I will do what I must."

The chah'nas swaggered away.

"*Major?*" came Lieutenant Zhi's voice. "*You'd better come and take a look at this.*"

She went with Kono and two others, down a diagonal, past some high, ornate columns of what looked like a public building, then to a new intersection. First Squad were there, guarding the intersection. Trace could not see their faces, combat visors still in place, but something looked wrong. Body posture suggested as much, several leaning on things, or sitting, balanced against their rifle butts.

Lieutenant Zhi came up to her, and Trace looked at him in concern. "*Major.*" His voice in her ear sounded strained. "*Down there. Mass transit system, no trains, guess the tavalai didn't want to spoil the history of the place.*"

"What's down…"

"*Don't ask. Just look.*" Her soldiers never spoke to her like that. Not unless something was badly wrong. Trace took a deep breath, and signalled Staff Sergeant Kono.

There was a stairway leading down from the road, into a deep tunnel. Trace activated IR and kept descending in the dark. At platform level, she found two more marines — Khan and Lopez, tacnet identified them. Neither said anything.

Trace walked to the long platforms, where once long, long ago, passengers had awaited trains to take them elsewhere. Probably they'd have used magnetic rails, Trace thought, as that technology seemed a constant on this cylinder. She peered off the platform edge as she went, to see if the tavalai had put any kind of working system here at all to reuse this tunnel for its ancient purpose...

...and saw bodies. A carpet of bodies. Dozens of them, limbs entangled, all charred and blackened. Melted together, like some grotesque artwork of straining hands and twisted legs. An arm raised to protect a face, another covering his comrade as though to shield him from the flames... or had it been 'her'? Lovers, friends. Civilians.

Trace walked the platform rim, counting until she reached a hundred. The bodies were separated in places, where tavalai had tried to run. She knew why her soldiers, who were toughened by so many bad experiences, reacted so strongly. This was fire, flamethrowers used perhaps to save bullets, perhaps not to fill the historic site with holes. Perhaps to make it personal. Bullets could be fast, but flames without armour were slow agony. And she could see it playing out as she walked the platform, could see where screaming civilians had run and fallen, an isolated, charred corpse here, huddled on the ground as though trying to dig through concrete with bare fingers to safety. Others over there, set aflame while running. A great cluster here, where running, tripping tavalai had fallen atop each other, and been scorched to a single, melted ball of bone and flesh.

"LC," she said quietly, aware that *Phoenix* was tapped into her helmet cam. "Are you seeing this?"

"*I'm seeing it,*" came the subdued reply. Behind him, Trace heard someone on the bridge utter an oath. "*Major, we've got our first visual scans of the surface. Several of the primary settled sites have been razed. It looks like they were doing the same thing down on Merakis itself.*"

"LC?" It was Kaspowitz's voice.

"Go Kaspo."

"I think they were sent here to tear a hole in the tavalai's cultural memory. These are scientists and academics, they'll be some of the tavalai's best. They were expecting humans, they were going to show us around, beg us to look after it, and collect as much data as they could from the stuff they hadn't dared to look at before now. These are the people who write the story of tavalai history. And the chah'nas decided to wipe them out."

"And Fleet High Command decided to let them." There was cold fury in Erik's voice. *"Dear god. Major, make sure this is all recorded. I think there's a few trillion humans who need to see this."*

Trace reached the platform edge, and jumped down. She lifted her visor, and gasped a lungful of thick, humid air. The smell of charred flesh almost made her gag. But it didn't seem right to hide from it behind her mask and breather. This was what horror looked and smelled like. The horror that her own commanders had arranged, in concert with the chah'nas. She wondered whose idea it had been originally. Merakis was important to tavalai, so they all arranged to slaughter those tavalai best positioned to perpetuate that importance.

What would such people do next? Decide to do the same to human historians who failed to write of Fleet with the proper reverence? Do the same to Worlders who demanded more power? This was an effort to control ideas. These charred remains had once been the people who arranged the tavalai museums, who displayed the artefacts. Tavalai valued such things more than humans, who had lost so much of their history, and forgotten so much more in their endless march of wars and vengeance.

Trace could not bring herself to believe that it had all been a mistake. Humanity had survived from the edge of extinction, and fought back to the point where the prosperous future of humankind now appeared assured. Tavalai behaviour toward humanity prior to the Triumvirate War had been appalling. These were not one-eyed twists of history, they were objective facts that even some tavalai had admitted — the Captain had shown her those articles, and the Captain was as even-handed and wise a person as she'd ever known.

But the tavalai were not the krim. They were not even their primary allies, the sard or the kaal. For much of the Spiral's history, the Captain had also assured her, the tavalai had been a force for good. She'd never liked to fight them, had never taken pleasure in her kills, only a grim satisfaction from the job that had to be done. It had been her great hope that now, with the war over, perhaps humans and tavalai could begin a new conversation, free of posturing and defiance. This was certainly not what she'd envisioned. This was evil. And this evil was perpetuated by those to whom she had unconditionally sworn her life.

"Major?" Staff Sergeant Kono stood at the platform edge and looked at her with concern. Trace stood, clipped down her faceplate, and jumped back to the platform.

Lieutenant Zhi cut in. *"Major, we've got another two chah'nas up here. They want to talk to you, they're challenging our authority here."*

"Be there in a moment," said Trace, striding up the platform with Kono and the rest of Command Squad falling in behind and beside. She jogged quickly up the stairs, and found that indeed, another pair of chah'nas much like the first were confronting Lieutenant Zhi, weapons not to hand but looming aggressively. Pushy species, all of them. A little was never enough.

"You are Major Thakur?" one of them demanded as she strode to them.

"I am," she replied.

"I have a message from our commander," that one said. "He says that..."

"Shut up," said Trace. "That mess down there. Did you do that?"

The chah'nas smirked. "Good work with froggies, yes? Fire makes them crackle."

Trace pulled her pistol, and with rifle and pistol together shot both chah'nas simultaneously. They were dead before they hit the ground. "I changed my mind," she told her stunned marines. "All chah'nas on Eve will surrender or die. We'll make the announcement. Let's go."

CHAPTER 20

Medbay Three was getting a little crazy when Erik visited — in addition to various wounded marines and two kuhsi, there were now two very unwounded marines with rifles guarding five wounded tavalai. A couple of Medbay One's marines had recovered enough to go back to their quarters, but still the total number of occupied beds increased. Erik wondered how long that would continue.

Corpsmen had already attended to all the tavalai, patching gunshot wounds, performing minor surgeries to reattach tissue and insert micro-bios into the right spots to accelerate healing. Erik passed the two kuhsi, and noted the mother was sitting on her bed unrestrained, the cub on her lap, eating while scanning a slate and warily watching the bay's new arrivals. Both were looking much healthier — the boy especially. He looked up at Erik with bright, curious eyes as he passed.

Erik headed for the tavalai in the far corner, with the bandaged leg, and white hospital pyjamas that looked faintly ridiculous on that broad, squat, green-brown body. That one was engaged in muttered, distressed conversation with his neighbour, whose arm and side were wrapped. Both looked at him as he approached.

"Are you Chis?" he asked.

"I am." With a nervous glance at the armed marine nearby. "Why are there soldiers here? We are wounded civilians."

"It's been a long time since we've had tavalai on the ship," said Erik. "Please understand. We've been at war for a long time."

"I assure you, none of us were much good at fighting even when fit." He blinked repeatedly, the double eyelids flickering. Tavalai found human air very thin and very dry. No doubt his eyes were drying uncomfortably. "How goes the fight?"

"Little change from your last report." Erik could have taken the wall-mounted bench seat, but did not want to sit so close. He sat on the end of the bunk instead, by the tavalai's big feet. "Twenty-seven unharmed survivors, all under marine protection on Eve.

Three more critically hurt, our medical people are working on them now. You'll get their names as soon as we have them."

Chis looked at the neighbouring tavalai and spoke a stream of staccato, vibrating sounds. Just like kuhsi-tongues, Togiri sounded much different from tavalai mouths. Chah'nas tongues, oddly, were easiest for humans.

"Phoenix database," said Erik. "Translator programme, authorisation Lieutenant Commander Erik Debogande. Translate this conversation to Togiri, to all tavalai in this room."

"*Understood.*"

"Thank you," said Chis, cautiously. "You... why did you bring us here? There are medical bays on Eve?"

"We may need to move quickly. Wounded are hard to move, and we can't dock with Eve with the facility still unsecured. And we cannot spare medical personnel from the ship, they're needed here."

"And the twenty-seven on Eve?"

"There is a starship pilot amongst them, and several who could qualify as crew. The running plan is to let them take the abandoned chah'nas vessel. We'll give you assistance should you need it, then you jump to Kolatin, which is currently unoccupied and entirely tavalai. You tell them what happened."

"Twenty-seven." Chis seemed dazed, staring at nothing with those big, bulbous eyes. "There is no hope of more?"

"If there are, they're hiding and we cannot find them. But so far we've counted more than five hundred bodies. You said you numbered five hundred and fifty two. So the odds don't look good." He paused. "I'm sorry."

No marines had been hurt. They'd taken the chah'nas by surprise, and these chah'nas, judging by Trace's skeptical report, weren't particularly great warriors. After the first couple of exchanges, most had run, and with marines holding the spine high overhead, any chah'nas in the streets was in grave danger from snipers.

Reports from the captured ship indicated it had mechanical problems — nothing that a rotation of work couldn't solve, Rooke insisted, but enough to keep it from jumping. The techs over there now said it looked like chah'nas had been working to fix it when *Phoenix* had arrived. Unable to leave with their comrades, this ship had volunteered to stay, and carry out the dirty work, and sacrifice itself if necessary. When they'd found out the incoming ship was human and not tavalai, they'd probably concluded that sacrifice wouldn't be necessary. What human warship would possibly stop them from killing tavalai?

"Chis?" The tavalai did not respond, just stared blankly. It was shock, Erik thought. And grief. Erik glanced at the armed marine standing nearby. The marine looked unmoved. They'd had a different war, Erik knew, fighting tavalai face to face. For some spacers at least, it was less personal.

"Um kid? Maybe don't... um..." It was Private Rolonde, Trace's marine from Command Squad. Erik looked, and found the little kuhsi boy wandering over, his drinking bottle in hand. He passed Erik, quite fearless, and stopped by the tavalai. And offered his bottle, drinking straw and all. "I'm sorry sir," said Rolonde, "I'm not sure what that is. Fruit juice, I think."

Chis looked at the boy curiously. "His name's Skah," said Erik. "His mother over there is Tif. They're a long way from home."

"Why thank you Skah," said Chis, and sniffed at the bottle with those big, slitted nostrils. He sipped, uncaring that the straw had been in another species' mouth. Skah let him have the bottle, and Chis patted him gently on the head with stubby fingers. "Very kind of you. Your mother has taught you good manners."

Skah walked back to his mother, who sat on her bed and watched. Straight backed with ears pricked and chin up. Pride, Erik thought, as Skah climbed back to the bed beside her. Erik nodded to her, then looked back to Chis, who sipped from the bottle.

"You have all manner of species aboard this vessel," said Chis. It might have been dry humour. Erik had never talked to a tavalai for long enough before to recognise it. Certainly Chis's fluency and pronunciation was extraordinary — a linguist, Trace had said. Most tavalai soldiers knew only a few words of English. "I am surprised. I've never seen a kuhsi face to face. The galaxy is so large, yet we have somehow managed to carve it into portions, and hold each jealously from each other's grasp."

"For how long have you spoken English?" Erik asked.

"Over seventy-three of my standard years... that is... one hundred and sixteen of yours. We live regularly past three hundred of your years, I am one hundred and eighty. Learning English was a late life's decision for me. I thought perhaps it could be my contribution to ending the war."

"To know your enemy?"

"Yes." Chis sipped the juice, appearing to enjoy it. "You humans are the most terrifying development in the Spiral for the past thousand years. Imagine my surprise to be rescued by one."

"Tavalai should know terrifying," Erik replied. "You armed the krim."

"Yes," Chis agreed. "Yes we did. And you destroyed them. One of only two successful genocides in Spiral history. One was carried out by what you call the hacksaws. The other was by you." Erik glanced again at the armed marine. Private Shaw, it was, from Alpha Third Squad. One of Lieutenant Dale's, and looking itchy on the trigger to hear that assessment from the species who'd been killing his friends for the past hundred and sixty years.

"Do tavalai today still feel sorry for the krim?" Erik asked.

Chis looked surprised. "Sorry? Of course. We're at war, Lieutenant Commander. Or we were. So many of us have died. Naturally we'd prefer it was humans dying. You would not have wished the krim on us as well?"

Erik had heard this of the tavalai too. Argumentative. Blunt. Difficult. 'Even with your gun in his face,' he recalled the Captain saying once, 'a tavalai will still complain about your bad breath.' They had some enormous balls, no one disputed it.

Chis made a gesture. "But this is the war talking. We have all been talking the war for far too long. The truth is that tavalai make bad rulers. Perhaps the chah'nas were right about that. That was the way in the Empire — them ruling, us managing. We are excellent managers, you know."

"So I hear," Erik said drily.

"We question, we analyse. We enjoy detail. Chah'nas tired of it. 'Give it to the tavalai,' they'd say, it's in all their old records. 'Let the tavalai deal with it.' chah'nas are impatient with tavalai arguments. And tavalai decided, upon disposing of the chah'nas, that we weren't going to run the Spiral that way. We would not make impulsive decisions. We would not simply crush what got in our way.

"And so we found a species, on the edge of our territory… and that edge was the Spiral's edge, in those days. No other species between us, and uncharted space." With a glance at the two kuhsi, watching and listening with the translator set to Garkhan. "A vicious species. A hunter species, evolving into space on the back of a series of genocidal internal wars and arms races. No apparent capacity for compassion. A highly evolved race of killers, on the verge of galactic expansion.

"The chah'nas would have crushed them. Chah'nas have the ability to look a fact in the face. Tavalai do not. We questioned and argued. We supposed that krim too had a right to the galaxy that spawned them, and we should not discriminate. We thought that with the right guidance, we could help them to achieve a better path. A more peaceful path. We did not know of the yet-further system, the star Sol and the planet Earth. We granted krim that as their natural space without knowing about humans, until it was too late. And then our embarrassment was mortifying."

His bulbous eyes swivelled to Erik's face, searching. "We are the 'good' species, you see. The smart species. The compassionate ones. We could not admit that we'd made such a mistake. We tried to help in the war that followed, tried to make peace, but of course humans did not want peace with krim anymore than one can want peace with a lethal germ. You fought us *and* the krim, and many of us despaired because in truth, we understood. Yet we could not join you to fight the krim as we should have, because that would mean admitting our mistake, and besides, violent enforcement meant the kind of galaxy the chah'nas had run, and we had sworn never to indulge in again. And so we left, and… well.

The krim took our withdrawal for a licence to do anything. And they did the most horrid thing imaginable.

"And now the krim are all dead, and humans have joined forces with those who despise us most of all, these six-limbed monsters of our past whom we'd thought we'd vanquished for good. You are our nemesis, you know. Humans. You are our guilt and our hubris, and we know it every time we look at you, the thought that 'we made this, we made all of this happen with our failure to lead, we got one species annihilated and nearly the second, who now despise us for our failures and blame us for the death of their homeworld'. There are tavalai legends of great spirits brought to life as vengeance for failings of character. You are that, to us. The great monsters of our dark past, come to punish us for our sins."

"If you knew it was all a mistake," Erik said quietly, "why did tavalai not say so? Why not apologise and try to make peace?"

"Because it is easier to get milk from a stone than to get a tavalai to apologise," Chis said tiredly. He seemed a little light-headed from the drugs, Erik thought. Certainly it loosened his tongue... although he'd heard that many tavalai needed no drugs for that. "Someone says it's our fault, and someone else says wait, it's not that simple, and then someone else has another angle entirely... and by the end of the discussion we have a dozen opinions and a dozen new reasons to do nothing. We are stubborn, Lieutenant Commander." A ripple of the broad lips. "Perhaps you've heard that before. Would it have worked? Apologising?"

Erik thought about it. "I don't know," he said honestly. "The Triumvirate War was about actions not hurt feelings. Tavalai were screwing us bigtime, not allowing us our fair place in the seats of power, and letting your bullyboy friends the sard and kaal shoot us up any time they decided they didn't like where one of our colonies was placed."

"That was spiteful," Chis agreed. "We felt resentment at you, for making us feel so bad about ourselves. It is stupid, I know, but I cannot explain it any other way. And you scared us with your incredible military prowess... truly, it has stunned the galaxy, you do not look like such a martial species yet even your mentors the chah'nas dare not trifle with you. And the chah'nas saved you, and the chah'nas are always our nightmare returning, and we feared you would do to us, in vengeance, what the krim had done to you. It was fear and spite and stupidity.

"But the Triumvirate War was not truly about that. Perhaps it was about that for *you*. But in the broader scheme of things, the Triumvirate War is simply a plot by the alo and the chah'nas to use humanity's fighting prowess to restore the Chah'nas Empire and relegate the tavalai to lower-power status. You think the Spiral was bad under the tavalai? Wait a few years. What is coming will be infinitely worse. Most tavalai will tell you some version of what I just have, and how we regret what happened to humanity, and blame ourselves in large part for it. But very few of us will apologise for the Triumvirate War. I don't. We were right to fight it, and even in defeat, I think it was the right war to lose."

"Down on Merakis," said Erik. "There are chah'nas shuttles. Troops left behind when we scared their ships away. They've done damage, but *Phoenix* records of this world are incomplete. I'd like you to tell me what they've destroyed."

Chis closed his eyes. "I don't think I could bear it," he said quietly. "Tell me the coordinates."

"East 110, by North 044."

The tavalai's chest rose and fell with a deep, painful sigh. Chis was strong, Erik noted. And he was just a non-combatant civilian, presumably with no or few physical augmentations. It was enough to warrant the posting of armed marines to this medbay, even for these traumatised, wounded souls.

"That is the temple of the tenth caste," Chis said quietly. In the neighbouring bed, Chis's tavalai companion began to cry softly as the translator converted those words. "It has stood for nearly fourteen thousand years."

"I've been neglecting my studies on tavalai history," said Erik. "Remind me."

"Not just tavalai history," said Chis. "Chah'nas built the temple. Chah'nas have nine castes. For a long time chah'nas-tavalai relations were poor — both of us suffered under the hacksaws. The AI Age ravaged both peoples, but the chah'nas had the worst of it, because the chah'nas fought back. Tavalai made attempts at fighting, but when they met with disaster, we compromised and found some uses for ourselves, amongst the AI.

"When the AI were finally destroyed by the Parren Alliance, the parren adopted chah'nas as their right-hand assistants, and viewed tavalai as cowards. But when the chah'nas needed help overthrowing the parren, who were far less well-suited to rule than the chah'nas, they turned to us. And we became their managers, during the chah'nas empire, and chah'nas began to accept that we were better at many things than them.

"It is the tragedy of the chah'nas. They are linear thinkers. For all their brutishness, they are fair-minded and always give competitors their due. Tavalai earned their respect in management, and so managers and bureaucrats we became. The chah'nas called us their 'tenth caste'. They meant it as a compliment. Chah'nas have trouble finding a place for anything outside of their language and social structures, so they carved out a special place for tavalai. They even built the temple, here on Merakis, which they knew we valued, to become a part of the Spiral Progression."

Erik knew of the Spiral Progression. It was what Merakis was famous for — a succession of temples and monuments, built by each successive ruling race. Together, those monuments told the history of the Spiral, from the Ancients to the Fathers, skipping the hacksaws (who had no interest in monuments) to the parren, then the chah'nas, then the tavalai. And now, perhaps, back to chah'nas again. Was this why Fleet had allowed the chah'nas back first? To erase this mark on Merakis's surface that offended them, and perhaps to build a new one?

"But the tenth caste became our prison," Chis continued. "Chah'nas move up and down their castes at will. Tavalai were granted a caste of one, and chah'nas could not move into it, yet tavalai could not move out. We had no say in command, no say in laws, or little. We squabbled over matters of governance, over various small wars and disagreements. Chah'nas called us 'troublesome'. No doubt they were right.

"All the minor species chafing under the chah'nas came to us to indulge their troubles.   And we listened, because tavalai will always listen to anyone with a story to tell, and a trouble to share. There is an old joke the chah'nas used to say; they said that among friends, a trouble shared is a trouble halved... but that among tavalai, a trouble shared is a trouble multiplied, retold, translated into five hundred tongues and turned into opera.   Chah'nas found out our plotting with other species and threatened, and relations soured to the point that uprising and war were inevitable. We stabbed them in the back, brought their Empire down, and they've never forgiven us. We keep the Temple of the Tenth Caste in pristine condition, as we do all our history, to remind us." He took a deep breath, and blinked back tears. "And now it is gone."

PH-1 thundered and rocked through a light reentry, turbulence fading as speed reduced. Nav feed showed their position closing on Teras Tihl, ETA ten minutes.   There were five major archaeological sites on Merakis, but Teras Tihl was the centre, the one that everyone in the galaxy knew.   Trace reacquired the visual feed as communications with *Phoenix* reestablished... that wouldn't last long, low orbit would take *Phoenix* out of coms range soon, one reason Erik hated her being down here.

Lieutenant Dale wasn't happy either, giving her a grim look behind his raised visor, restraint bars securing him opposite amidst a row of Alpha Platoon marines.   Trace ignored him, visor down, observing the orbital feed.   PH-1's own feed replaced it as Lieutenant Hausler got a better view.   From forty thousand meters the surface of Merakis looked barren, red-brown like a desert. Deep colours swirled, like liquids mixing, only nothing liquid had fallen on that surface for a hundred million years. Once, long ago, before a massive meteor strike had removed most of the atmosphere, there had been sparse life. Now, the only things living were visitors.

Upon the top of a plateau, many kilometres wide above the surface, small, flat structures made a pattern.   They spread wide enough to make a town, but without the clutter. PH-1 dipped into a steep bank, spiralling about the settlements as it descended.

"Scan reads clean," came the co-pilot's voice. *"Nothing else airborne."* The drone they'd sent down first showed nothing nearby, and Merakis surface was devoid of hiding places. The chah'nas who had been here were long gone over the horizon. They could return, but they'd give plenty of warning with the drone aloft.

One of the buildings below was smothered in smoke, drifting across the others in the faint breeze. As they dropped closer, Trace zoomed enough to get a clear look at whatever it had been. A central, circular foundation beneath smouldering rubble. Separate wings, also destroyed. In what might have once been a courtyard, temporary dwellings, metal and modern, torn and scattered across the landscape like the remains of a shuttle crash. Scientific settlements, where visitors might stay while research was done. Trace did not think the tavalai would normally despoil the site with a settlement even a few days permanent... but they'd been in a hurry.

"There's another one," said the co-pilot, Ensign Yun. *"Over by the Father's Pinnacle."* Trace looked. Sure enough, by the base of the pinnacle, more strewn wreckage. The pinnacle itself had been invisible from higher altitudes, the same colour as the red-brown ground, tall and thin. It did not look as though there would be anywhere near it to hide. Further about the monument ring, the Cho'ar'as, primary work of the Chah'nas Empire. Huge, monolithic walls of stone, casting several shadows in the mixed light of local 'night'.

"Are there internal spaces in the Cho'ar'as?" Trace asked. It seemed surreal to be speaking of it in an operation. These were the great symbols of childhood textbooks, deep in tavalai space. When Trace was a child, Merakis had been far away from any human territory. Now, here they were... only somehow, the chah'nas had gotten here first.

A longer pause... clearly the pilots did not know. Nor did her marines. *"Major, there are a few internals in the Cho'ar'as,"* Kaspowitz confirmed from up on the *Phoenix* bridge. *"Better check them to be sure."*

"Copy Lieutenant." Looking at the mess chah'nas fire had made of tavalai temporary settlements, she didn't hold much hope.

PH-1 came down before the Temple of the Tenth Caste with a roar of thrusters. Trace dismounted with Command Squad, Third Squad and a Heavy Squad, while PH-1 lifted once more to fly Lieutenant Dale and the rest over to the Pinnacle. They spread, and walked in the light gravity amidst the scattered wreckage, sections of once-pressurised habitat shining dull silver amidst structural honeycomb and civilian internals. Bits of furniture, parts of bathroom fittings. Tavalai bodies. A few wore environmentals, but all were dead. There were chah'nas footprints on the sand, and a few of the bodies had extra holes in them, delivered at close range.

Trace left her marines to the search for survivors and clues, and surveyed the wreckage of the temple. It had had great domes, she knew. The circular foundations visible from the air had suggested as much. All was gone now, just great piles of collapsed masonry. Away from the ruins, the great Tiras Plateau stretched as flat as the surface of some great boardgame. Only the surreal outline of other monuments broke the featureless expanse. Above, looming huge on the horizon, was Gorah — huge and red-brown like Merakis, in partial crescent from the system's primary sun. The great bulk of the gas giant fell across those rings, casting them to invisible shadow.

Beyond, and above, several more visible moons. The largest was Shek, larger again than Merakis. They too were in crescent, and the light from them fell silver upon the sands. And far, far more distant still, the dull red glow of the system's outer-binary stars, circling a common centre every three days, which in turn orbited the primary star every eighty-five years. It was night upon the Tiras Plateau, yet the sky was alive with light, red-brown from Gorah, silver from the neighbouring moons, and red from the far-off binary dwarfs. A magical display of orbital mechanics, the turning gears that ran the universe, beautiful, majestic and cold. This was a world that had never known darkness, just an endless play of colour and shadow upon the rock and sands.

Sand crunched as Private Arime came to her side. *"Hell of a thing,"* he murmured on proximity channel, looking at the ruins.

Trace nodded slowly, gazing about. "Fourteen thousand years ago," she said. "Chah'nas built this thing. I finally get to see it, and I'm a single day late."

"It's like a bad marriage breakup," said Arime. *"Chah'nas and tavalai. This place was like a monument to love. Only the tavalai betrayed them, kicked the chah'nas out but kept the house and the jewellery. And now the chah'nas came back to destroy it in a jealous rage."*

"And we let them," said Trace.

Arime looked at her. *"Major, are you okay?"* Trace glanced at him in surprise. *"I don't mean to... it's just... well. You've been stewing."*

Trace smiled. Irfan Arime was just a private, and she was a major, but he'd been Command Squad for five years, and few knew her better.

"I have been stewing," she admitted. "I miss Stitch. And I miss Fly, and all of them." She looked back to the smoking ruins. "I miss knowing what I'm for."

"We're for Phoenix," said Arime, with certainty. *"That's what I'm for."*

"I'm Kulina," said Trace. "I'm for humanity. Five hundred billion souls, and all the trillions still to come. And in a place like this, I look about, and I wonder if even that isn't too narrow a viewpoint." She gazed across the monument-dotted horizon. "All these species. All these souls. The karma goes everywhere. We Kulina try to separate out the fates of humans from all these other fates. But this war is over now, and I'm no longer sure we can."

Arime smiled. *"That's too deep for me Major. I'm just a grunt."*

She hated it when they said that. "No you're not. No one is." She put a hand on his armoured shoulder, and trudged toward the ruins.

The search for survivors was pointless. On tacnet, Trace watched as Lieutenant Dale led several squads into the small exterior doors in the massive, smooth stone walls of the Cho'ar'as. Even on vid screen it looked incredible, walls three hundred meters tall, sheer and smooth rock, cast with red and silver light in the Merakis night. Low gravity made it easier, but still it was hard to imagine how such walls had been put in place. Monuments on Merakis could take decades to build, even with modern technology. But once standing, they stood for tens of thousands of years. Usually.

"Major," came Lieutenant Hausler's voice from above, where PH-1 was maintaining a steady covering orbit. *"It looks like some kind of vehicle has crashed over by the Ancients' Meridian. It's only small, looks like it might be a low gravity runner of some sort. You want me to come down and give someone a lift over?"*

"No," said Trace. "You keep your orbit, I'll go over myself."

She called the rest of Command Squad and they set off at a jog. The Ancients' Meridian was only a kilometre away. It was the reason all these other monuments were here, the one that had started the whole Spiral Progression on this world. Trace felt almost guilty for her eagerness to head this way, and ran easily in the low-G, as suit comp readjusted armour tension for more give in the joints.

Closer, and the low arcs of stone resolved more clearly. Three semi-circular bands, or arches, in ascending angles above the horizon. Meridians, of a sort. From a distance, they looked almost disappointingly simple.

Nearby they reached the vehicle that Hausler had seen — it was indeed a low gravity sled, powered aloft only by retros and flyable only on low-G worlds. It had been shot down, and several more tavalai lay in the wreck, dead beneath the arcs of stone they'd most likely dedicated their lives to study.

Trace left her marines to the examination, and walked beneath the great arcs. Upon the ground beneath them, several perfectly circular mounds. The tallest was central, directly beneath the stone arcs' midpoint, like someone had buried a perfect sphere in the sand. At outer-lying points, where planets might circle a sun, smaller spheres emerged. Looking up, Trace could see how the moons and rings around Merakis followed these great, arcing lines across the sky. It was an observatory of sorts, a model frame from within which to view the great, complicated expanse of the Merakis system. At different times of the day or night, she recalled reading in her children's textbook at school, shadows from those worlds would fall at significant points among or upon these spheres. Times could be told, and certain mathematical formulas would repeat with endless precision.

But more than that, some scientists said — the Ancients' Meridian modelled much of the near Spiral. Some of those formulas at play in the movement of shadows on the sand described exact distances of light between major systems where further Ancients' monuments had also been found. Other formulas described relative motion of those systems, the kind of coordinates that starship navigators knew by heart. Kaspowitz was going to be so jealous, she thought, looking about in awe.

The whole thing was more than three million years old. What had happened to the race that built it, and other monuments like it across the Spiral, no one knew. Their homeworld remained unknown, and no working settlement, nor sign of actual civilisation, had ever been found. There were countless theories, but no one even knew what the Ancients had looked like. The Fathers had paid great tribute to them, this race that had made even them look like infants. Others had sent out great searches, or studied their monuments for more navigational clues to the direction of homeworlds or settlements. Some suggested they were visitors from other galaxies, brought to this one by wormhole portal technology known to no one else. Others had thought them beings from other dimensions, or dimensions yet to come. Others still had worshipped them as gods. Trace thought that last explanation might be as good as any, in the absence of better knowledge.

With no weather to speak of, the stone of the central sphere remained utterly smooth and hard. Trace climbed up it — to get a better command view, she told herself, although the truth was probably different. From atop the sphere, she could see in all directions. The arc of surrounding monuments, the symbols of Spiral history. The orbiting worlds, the great rings, and her marines amongst them, playing out the latest, great and terrible chapter in this story.

Suddenly there were tears in her eyes, and the tightness in her throat made it hard to breathe. Personal hubris or not, this felt very much like the centre of all things. For one who had given her life to karma, and to the belief that personal choices could make significant alterations to the flow of fates, it was overwhelming. So many lives she'd seen lost, so many friends gone, and so many lives she'd taken. And now she found herself here, questioning everything that she'd ever been taught, and everything that she'd thought she knew.

A man had sent her on this path — the wisest man she'd known. She should not doubt all of her people's teachings on the instruction of just one man. And yet if the flow of karma had taught her anything, it was that no force was more powerful in the shapings of fate than the force between two people. This *was* her people's teaching. So how was it that she was the only one to have followed it here?

She knelt upon the top of the sphere, for a lotus position was impossible in armour. But the armour took the weight of her legs, and made it comfortable enough for someone who had spent as much of her life in armour as she had. She breathed deep, but did not close her eyes, attempting wide-eyed meditation so as not to close herself off to this amazing and enlightening view. On the sandy ground about the sphere, her marines gazed up at her in wonder and concern.

CHAPTER 21

Erik woke to Lieutenant Draper's voice in his ear, telling him that PH-1 was back. The time read 0402, and he dragged himself from bed, opened the narrow closet and pulled his jacket from the press rack. Rumpled leather, *Phoenix* patch on one arm, First Fleet on the other. Still it was far shinier than the Captain's had been, or than the one Kaspowitz wore now. In Fleet, an officer might be regarded well by the number of medals he presented on parade, but his true experience was indicated by how scuffed and faded his ops jacket looked.

He took the time to run the electric over his jaw — there was only ten hours growth there, but the one thing they'd taught him in the Academy that he already knew from his father was that a man only got as much respect as he gave himself. On watch outside his quarters this time was Private Lewell, and together they took a left straight off the bridge and around to back-quarter, then down the main corridor to Assembly.

There was the crashing and clumping of arriving armour, marines shouting, Charlie Platoon on duty to help the returning Alpha stack and rack in minimum time. Erik waited on lower deck, whacking Alpha marines on the shoulder as they passed, giving thumbs up, exuding as much general encouragement as he could. They seemed pleased enough to see him, but knew that he wasn't here for them, and passed word up to the Major that the LC was waiting for her.

She slid down a ladder railing nearby and swaggered to him with the aching legs of someone too long in armour, sweaty and exhausted beyond bothering to hide it. "No survivors," she told him what he already knew from her report. "No encounters, the chah'nas shuttles are scattered. We could hunt them, but they've got weapons too and we've no real advantage down there. We documented everything…" she shrugged. "It's all we can do."

Erik considered her for a moment. Something was wrong, beyond the exhaustion. Normally she met his gaze with hard steel.

Now she barely looked, distracted and avoiding eye contact. "I want to get out of here," he told her. "I'm sorry to do it now, you need sleep, but for what I've got in mind I'm going to need your help."

"You want to go to Heuron?" she said, walking and beckoning him after her. And to a marine in passing, "Fluffy, you're looking after that shoulder yes?"

"Course Major."

"Because I will put you on scrubs for a week if you keep skipping doctor's advice, you hear?"

Private Sarah 'Fluffy' Andrews grinned as she retreated. "Sure you will Major." The only time her marines ever doubted her word was when she threatened them with punishment for anything less than deadly serious.

"Remind me again how she got called 'Fluffy'?" Erik tried to memorise them, but it was hard enough with *Phoenix* spacer crew, let alone the marines.

"Barracked on Shantara, on a live fire exercise she managed to put a practice-round between the eyes of one of those cute little... what are they called? Big ears, fluffy things..."

"Oh right, yeah, I know them. Too many damn fluffy animals in this galaxy."

"Afterward she'd find little stuffed ones in her locker with a noose around their necks." Marines and their sense of humour. And in passing to another, "Hey Porky, nice job down there."

"Major, get some sleep," Corporal 'Porky' Barnes said in reply.

"Yeah good luck with that," said Erik, and Barnes rolled his eyes.

"Just lemme get some chow," Trace complained, turning off to the galley. "Hey Beatle, I saw that new tattoo, it's terrible."

Ahead of her, Private Lars 'Beatle' Tuo laughed. "Hey kiss my ass Major."

"Yeah make me," she retorted with a glare and a whack on his shoulder in passing. Erik had no idea how she did it. Most people would just collapse into a shower and bed, possibly get some lower rank to bring them a meal in quarters so they didn't have to deal with anything else.   But Trace staggered through corridors chatting to all her people, and joined the end of the meal queue like everyone else.

"Now Beatle," said Erik.   "Isn't he the guy who had an insect crawl up his ass on an exercise?"

"Yeah, they're on New Dakota, they like to burrow."   She leaned on the wall at the queue, and saw Erik fighting a smile. "He's lucky.   If it had laid eggs, they'd have called him 'Hive'. What did they nearly call you, LT?"

The man ahead of her turned, and Erik blinked, realising it was Lieutenant Dale.   Erik was tired from a few hours' sleep, but Trace was worse and she'd known who it was.   "They called me *Lieutenant*," Dale corrected her.   "LC.   Haven't seen you for a bit."

"Different life in first-shift," said Erik.   He'd found Dale intimidating, once.   Now he realised he didn't.   Dale seemed to regard him differently, too.   "Doc Suelo says you'll get Yalen and Malik back in a few days, they're healing well."

Dale nodded.   "They're already helping in Assembly, they look good."   Dale could have said something about Erik's last bit of flying, the *Tek-to-thi* intercept and escape in Argitori that was now legend among the marines, and among some of the spacers.   But he wouldn't, because it wasn't a marine lieutenant's place to comment on a commander's flying any more than it was Erik's place to offer opinions on ground combat ops.   The turf would be respected, or the natural order of things would fall apart.   But he didn't need to say anything — Erik could see in his eyes what had changed.   "Hey people!" Dale bellowed up the line.   "The Major and the LC are in the queue!   Someone get them their chow!"   And in a quieter voice, "What are you having?"

Outside Trace's quarters they found Shahaim and Kaspowitz already waiting, not about to enter without Trace's permission. Trace entered first, startling Lisbeth who was sleeping in the lower bunk.   "Oh, are you having a meeting?"   Blinking in the sudden light.   "I'm sorry, I'll go elsewhere, just give me a minute…"

"No you stay," said Erik. "Big family interests moving into Heuron, you know more about what the family's up to these days than me."

Lisbeth blinked in confusion, searching bleary-eyed for her jacket, wearing only a light, Phoenix-issue undershirt. "We're going to Heuron?"

Erik handed her the jacket from beneath the bed netting, and sat beside her. "Yes we are. Do you know why?"

Lisbeth pulled on pants, while Kaspowitz chivalrously looked elsewhere. Trace crawled into the far end of Lisbeth's bunk and put her back to the wall, opening a stir fry container on her lap. "Well, I mean it's a Fleet hub," said Lisbeth, frowning. Trace offered her a sip of juice, which she accepted. "I mean we've had it for nearly thirty years, it's far enough back from tavalai space to be safe but close enough to mount attacks from. And it's close to sard space, and pretty close to alo too... and I just happen to know we've got a shitload of investment going on there. Shipworks and repair yards especially, perfect place for it with so much of Fleet there all the time. But we can't go there, I mean, we'll be spotted and..." And her eyes widened as she realised. "Oh no we won't! *Phoenix* jumps so much faster than anyone else! They won't know what happened yet!"

"We're still two real-time weeks away," Kaspowitz confirmed, taking one of the wall seats while Shahaim took the other. "The fastest ship at Homeworld was *Dragonfly*, and even if they somehow got telepathic and guessed where we were going, they'd be two and a half weeks out, tops."

"Plus we've just demonstrated what happens when you try and string seven or eight jumps together back to back," Shahaim added. "Things break."

"Right," said Erik, cracking his own container, curried meat and veg. Chef had even slipped him a fresh papadam. He broke it and gave half to Trace. "But not too far off course are Carany, Nowa Polska and Chekov to name just three. Any of those could have had shanti-class carriers, or jupiter-class cruisers, any of which aren't *that* much slower than us. And we've been delayed and off-course ourselves. Worst case scenario, if one of them got contacted by someone from Homeworld, then went straight to Heuron, how much gap would we have?"

"I ran it," Kaspowitz confirmed. "Worst case, two days."

"Well that's not enough," said Shahaim in alarm. "We go there pretending everything's okay and not alarming everyone, we have to coast in from middle-beacon. That's a two day run in that system. If we're going to pull anything when we're there, that'll take a day or two at least, surely?"

Erik nodded. "We'll have to chance it. Hope they're not that fast, hope there isn't a ship sent to Heuron immediately. I mean they'd have to get lucky. Running a shanti-class halfway across human space without proper orders would take some balls."

"What *are* you planning to do in Heuron?" Lisbeth asked warily. Everyone looked at Erik. All with trepidation, save for Trace, who ate impassively, and sipped the juice Lisbeth held for her.

"Well I'm pretty sure Supreme Commander Chankow is there," said Erik, as offhandedly as he could manage. "Could ask him a few questions."

"You think he'll tell you?" Lisbeth asked.

"Depends how I ask him," said Erik.

Shahaim looked pale. Even Kaspowitz swallowed. "Oh fuck," said Shahaim. "You want to kidnap Supreme Commander Chankow."

"Kidnap might be a bit strong," said Erik. "Strongarm, threaten and blackmail are all on the cards."

"Erik, we don't know if he even did anything!" Shahaim protested further. "He's been on Heuron or at least well away from Homeworld! What happened to us was a rush job, a spur of the moment thing, probably cooked up by Fleet Admiral Anjo, and it all went wrong. The Supreme Commander probably had nothing to do with it!"

"He might not have given Anjo direct instructions," Erik said firmly. "But he'd have established a general understanding. No one, not even Fleet Admiral Anjo, has the greatest warship captain of the war assassinated unless he's absolutely certain that *his* ultimate commander will back him." He glanced at Trace. "What do you think? Is it doable?"

"Sure," said Trace around a mouthful. "But, few problems. First, *Phoenix* isn't supposed to be anywhere near Heuron, we're supposed to be at Homeworld. Got some explaining to do when we get there. Second, the Captain's not supposed to be dead. We can't just dress someone up as him cause they're not that dumb and we're not that lucky. Got some explaining to do for that as well... and for Commander Huang, who should logically be in command if the Captain's not." Erik grimaced. "Why fly *Phoenix* across human space without its Captain or Commander? Why's the LC in charge, why are we damaged, etc? What the hell happened to us that could explain all that?

"Fourth, we can't let crew have liberty on station dock. They deserve it, but... no offence guys, but we can't trust all the spacer crew. They'll rat to someone and then we're screwed. Got to jam internal coms too, standard secrecy provisions... not hard to do, but more explaining. Fifth, how do we get you," looking at Erik, "to see the Supreme Commander? Or even close? And how do we pull off an escape? Because in actual fact, Erik, I don't think it should be you at all. You're *Phoenix* commander now, acting-captain really, and we don't have another person aboard who can do that as well as you."

With a half-apologetic look at Shahaim. She didn't protest.

"Well then good luck getting close to Chankow without me," Erik told her. "Because if our Captain and Commander are somehow missing, then the Lieutenant Commander is *certainly* answerable for that, and that'll be the only context in which anyone from this ship will see the Supreme Commander outside of an interrogation in the brig."

"Well then we should snatch him at home," said Trace. "Or some other way, because if we get the information we're after, we're going to have to go running across human space once more to spread the word, and that's going to take the best starship jockey we've got."

"Trace, the security in Hoffen Station is ridiculous," Erik insisted. "You're not starting another firefight in the middle of a high security zone, I won't allow it."

"And since when was it your job to tell me how to conduct combat operations?" Trace stared at him. Lisbeth leaned quietly back against the wall between them, to take herself out of the line of fire.

"When did you become so damn eager to kill senior Fleet commanders?" Erik replied.

"When they betrayed all the men and women who'd served under them," Trace said coldly. "When they made it so that all the guys I've lost, that we've all lost, died for some fucking stinking lie."

Silence from the others. Erik held her gaze completely. "They didn't die for a lie," he told her. "They died to secure humanity's place in the Spiral. They did that. They didn't die for Fleet Admiral Anjo, or Supreme Commander Chankow. We make our own causes, Trace. And so does High Command, unfortunately."

This time it was Trace who looked away first. Back down to her food, to continue eating. "There are still tavalai at Heuron," she said. "Speaking of people who might help us."

"You know," Shahaim said edgily, "I'm not sure I went through all that war against the tavalai just so I could join them now."

"Me neither," said Erik. "But if that's what it takes."

"And... then, what do we do with this information?" Lisbeth asked. "Say you find there's some kind of conspiracy. I mean, clearly there *is* some kind of conspiracy, right? Who do you tell?"

"Everyone," said Trace. "We're *not* in this alone. We're one ship for now, but once people learn what's happened, I mean if we get *proof?* We might even be the majority."

Erik nodded. "It's not our problem, Lis. It's Fleet HQ's, when they decided to murder the Captain."

"I'm not talking about whose responsibility it is," Lisbeth said anxiously. "I mean this isn't really about fairness, is it? You all agreed to go and risk your lives in a war while most of us sat safely at home and applauded from a distance. No one military is in the fairness business. You're in the protection business. What if you find information that would start a civil war if it got out?"

Silence for a moment.

Trace swallowed her food, and washed it down with some juice. "I don't know what kind of civil war it would be. Worlders versus Spacers. Pretty hard to win a war from the bottom of a gravity well, against people at the top of one."

"Not everyone in space is a Spacer," said Lisbeth. "Debogande Inc employs thousands of them. Well, millions, actually. Half of all Spacer manpower has Worlder origins, if not actual citizenship."

"She's right," Erik conceded. "You're one yourself, Trace. And I would be one, if my family didn't have Spacer citizenship for life."

"Fleet don't count," said Trace, unconvinced. "Most of Fleet aren't political beyond the war. About half of my marines are Worlders like me, but the whole Spacer/Worlder thing just doesn't interest them."

"You think it might start interesting them?" Lisbeth replied. "If it was revealed that Fleet's leaders are plotting to crush any attempts at Worlder political activism? Like, I don't know, say if the Worlders were recruiting Captain Pantillo to their cause? Imagine a Spacer as popular as him, known to Spacers everywhere, elected to Spacer Congress? What if he was given senior leadership... and quite likely he would have been. He could have made an argument for increased Worlder Congress powers that could have brought lots of Spacer Congress with him."

Erik gazed at her, reconsidering the notion that maybe *he* was the Debogande most suited to politics. "Lis, did you talk about this much with Mother or Father?" She looked suddenly evasive. "What did they say?"

"Well you know Mother. She doesn't like to talk politics at home. Dad's the talker, but he says that's only because he doesn't know anything."

"Still more than most people," said Erik. "What did he say?"

Lisbeth sighed. "He said there was talk in Congress that the Family were employing too many Worlders. Spacer Congress of course. And taking lots of Worlder investment. Which he said is nuts, it's only about... oh, twenty-seven percent of total investment? Worlders put their money in Worlder things, mostly. But sure, we've been recruiting heavily with Worlders because they're ninety percent of the human population and that's where the talent is. And we pay well for good talent, and it's a way to get a leg up on those companies that won't do it..." She shrugged. "It's good business, that's all."

"I hear lots of stories about how Worlders don't adjust to Spacer life," Shahaim added. "High attrition rate, you spend thousands training them but they don't last more than a few years. Go back home to sunlight and beaches."

"Well yes it's a problem," Lisbeth agreed. "But we've been working on this fancy psych-program to predict those who won't make the transition. And Cora's been helping set up a model for new internships, we're taking lots of graduates in their mid-study break, find them work for six months, see who likes it and who doesn't."

"I wonder if anyone's done any studies on where those peoples' loyalties lie after five or ten years," Erik murmured. Toying with his food. "I mean during the war, anyone living in space is patriotic for Spacer Congress and Fleet because they know tavalai or sard could hit them anytime. And so much of the economy is Fleet-based, so all their jobs kind of depend on it. But now there's peace... I wonder how the Spacer Congress support base would hold up if Spacer industries kept employing Worlders? Who more and more kept their old loyalties?"

"Exactly," Lisbeth agreed. "What if they've looked at those trends and reckoned that in twenty or thirty years, Spacer Congress won't have the numbers to keep Worlder Congress from an equal, democratic say? Parity between Congresses?"

"Over Fleet's dead body," Kaspowitz muttered. "That's what they said in the Academy the whole time I was there. Humanity's killer demographics — we let Worlders take control, we wipe ourselves out."

Erik's uplink blinked, and he held a finger to his ear — the universal signal to let others know he was uplinked. "This is the LC?"

"Sir... we've got an issue down in ceta-b. You'd better come and see."

"What is it?"

"Our chah'nas prisoner sir. He's dead."

Erik stood in the doorway of the chah'nas's quarters, arms folded, and stared in disbelief at the mess. The prisoner was on the floor beside the bunk, arms sprawled. There wasn't a lot left of his head, and both the bunk and the wall behind were splattered with blood and brain.

Erik turned and looked at Sergeant Ong, Echo's Third Squad leader, who'd been stuck with this duty. "Sergeant. How the *fuck*?"

Ong looked unhappy. "I'm sorry sir, we..."

"You think I want a fucking apology? How does an apology help me?" Ong looked more unhappy. Trace leaned on the outside of the doorway, offering her Sergeant no assistance. "How? The fuck?"

"The tavalai sir. Chis. Said he needed a walk."

"He's been shot in the leg."

"Crutches sir. It's not too bad, the Corpsman let him go with Private Cowell as escort. He must have learned we had a chah'nas aboard, he... he caught Private Cowell unawares outside this room. Got his gun, hit the door, shot the prisoner. He's strong sir. Probably military training, not just a scientist."

"Sergeant, you've been fighting tavalai for what? Twelve years?" He glanced at Trace.

"Thirteen," she said.

"You know they're strong.   You know most of their civvies in hostile territory have at least basic military training, some of them advanced.   You also know they'll lie about it when asked.   None of this occurred to you?"

"No excuses sir," said Ong.   "Private Cowell was not properly warned to take suitable precautions, it's my fault.   I take full responsibility."

"You're damn right," said Erik.   "And maybe my fault too for forgetting that *Phoenix* marines are great at killing stuff and shit at guarding it.   Go, get.   The Major will deal with you later."

He left.   Erik gave Trace a brief glance in case he'd overdone it.   Her unconcern told him he hadn't.   She peered in the doorway.   "Aggressive little linguist, isn't he?"

Erik swore, strode to the neighbouring quarters and opened the door.   There seated on the bunk was Chis, wounded leg out before him.   A marine stood opposite, rifled pointed at the tavalai's chest.

"Why?" Erik demanded of the tavalai.

Chis blinked at him, slow and remorseless.   "Why do you think?"

Erik pointed at the room next door.   "He didn't do anything to you.   He's from a ship called the *Tek-to-thi*.   We captured him in a completely separate operation in Argitori System.   Nothing to do with what happened to you and your friends here."

"If you say so," said Chis.   "Will I be punished?"

"Do you care?"

"Not especially," the tavalai said coldly.

CHAPTER 22

Heuron was an M-class star, sedate and golden yellow. To humans it was remarkable, because it reminded them of the home they'd lost a thousand years before. A similar sized sun, four rocky inner planets, then some big gas giants in the middle orbits. For Fleet, the giants were where the action was, big lunar systems with lots of mining and settlements.

But fifteen thousand years before, the fourth and last of the rocky inner worlds had been settled by the tavalai. It was pretty and green, but tavalai were picky, and found the atmosphere too thin, and the gravity too low. Many tavalai born on Apilai, as they called it, migrated to more exciting worlds in the tavalai heartland, and Apilai's population never rose above a hundred million. Having won the system from the tavalai in battle thirty-two years earlier, humans had already doubled that, identifying the system as strategic, and moving huge transports with infrastructure spending and incentives for settlers. Humans found Apilai nearly perfect, and the Colonial Administration, which answered to both Spacer and Worlder Congresses, happily reported that in another twenty years with reproduction incentives and birthing tanks, Apilai population would hit the full half-billion.

Fleet were not entirely thrilled, because large Worlder populations forced Fleet to play a more defensive role, and increased Worlder political clout in that strategic system. But evacuating a hundred million tavalai who did not want to leave was not an option either, and nor was allowing those tavalai to remain the majority population on Apilai. Further, Heuron was such a strategic system that Fleet were going to be here in large numbers anyway, in which case the big Apilai population did not force any particular strategic realignment. And limited though Spacer-Worlder financial transactions were, a big Worlder economy in Heuron did add clout to system finances, and depth to local industry and talent production.

What made Heuron so vital to Fleet was its location — squarely on the far quarter flank of where human and tavalai space intersected, and close to where sard space began. Alo space, too, was a mere two jumps 'above', relative to its position upon the galactic plane, and for reasons known mostly to them, alo found it agreeable to put a permanent presence on Heuron such as they rarely put in any non-alo space. Thus Heuron had become a command-and-control centre for coordination between the triumvirate allies, despite being somewhat distant from chah'nas space. It had been a mustering point for many Fleet invasions and thrusts of the last thirty years, and remained a key hub in the merchant network, both military and civilian. For total human starship traffic, it was second only to Homeworld.

"Berthing list," Shilu announced as they came through, following the final, course-correcting velocity dump to match their path to that of Heuron V's.

"Copy, I got that," said Shahaim, glancing over the list while Erik listened with one ear to Rooke's ongoing conversation over jumpline integrity in Engineering. Heuron V was a monster system, seven starship-capable stations, hundreds of colonies, many of them former-tavalai but not all. The biggest was Hoffen, a 400+ berth behemoth in Lagrange between Tepanai, Heuron V's largest moon, and Heuron V itself. "Nav buoy says Hoffen has eighty-six free berths about the gravity rim, and two free at the hub."

"Com, query them," said Erik. "Request one of those two hub berths. Say minor battle damage."

"Com copies, requesting one of the hub berths," said Shilu. Shahaim gave him an anxious look. Docking at the gravity rim, a combat carrier's rotation cylinder was of course locked in place. This put three quarters of the crew cylinder out of action, particularly the marines back-quarter, which would be effectively upside down in dock. Usually this worked fine, since marines in hostile environments wanted to be out on the dock anyway, and marines in non-hostile environments wanted to hit the bars and other entertainments. Docked at the zero-G hub, *Phoenix* could keep the crew cylinder rotating, and keep back-quarter in full operations.

Stations knew this, and combat carriers under any kind of suspicion (meaning alien) were frequently denied a hub berth for that reason. *Phoenix* arriving in Heuron was suspicious in itself. Now requesting a hub-berth was more-so. But they had no choice, because for what was planned, marines were not optional.

"Lots of ships outbound," said Geish, cycling through the new marks that Scan was throwing onto his screen. "I'm reading... seventeen outbound, nine of them warships, looks like a whole bunch of different headings. All of those nine are on priority departure, they're breaking regular lanes, moving real fast."

"So where are they going?" Shahaim wondered.

"Station feed says we've had another... thirty plus departures in the last day," Jiri added. "That's an awful lot of people leaving all close together."

"Sir," said Shilu, "I'm getting a lot of chatter off that buoy. It's not on the official channels, the... the merchant channels are just crowded. I think the freighters have been loading stuff onto it."

"Have a listen and give me a summary," said Erik, not wanting to wade through a bunch of civilian messages. Any number of things could grab the attention of freighter captains so that they'd want to leave messages for other captains — price fluctuations, company collapses, legal actions. Something else had caught his eye. "Berth 117. *Diamond*. That's Homeworld VIP transport."

Kaspowitz gave him a quick stare. "Ali's here. So that's where he went."

"Maybe not just Chairman Ali," said Erik, starting to bite his nail, then remembering Trace's admonishment. "Maybe Chairman Joseph too." The two most powerful members of Spacer Congress. Erik's Uncle Thani was the third, and everyone had wondered where they were, during the Homeworld parades. "Damn strange that number one and two in Spacer Congress weren't present for the parades. It's not like they didn't have advance notice, and it's not like politicians to miss great photo-ops."

"Almost like they were using the parades as a distraction," Kaspowitz added.

"Exactly."

"Sir," said Shilu. "The... all the traffic on the buoy is just one thing. Fleet's passed an ordinance, and Chairman Ali signed it."

"I'm sorry to sound dumb," said Shahaim, "but what's an ordinance?"

"Emergency legislation," said Erik. "It bypasses the usual Congress vote in an emergency, just needs the head of Fleet and Spacer Congress to sign it. What's it say?"

"Um..." Shilu was still listening with one ear. "It seems they're putting a fifteen percent limit on Worlder ownership of Spacer assets. Also, um... limitations on Worlder citizenship, they're saying any Worlder working for a Spacer institution for more than two years has to give up Worlder citizenship for Spacer."

"Oh good god," said Erik. And stared blankly at his screens. Had it all been for this? Was this the start of whatever the Captain had been fighting to prevent?

"I'm not sure I understand," Shahaim said cautiously. "Fifteen percent... is that a lot?"

"Debogande Enterprises is about twenty-seven percent owned by Worlder interests," said Erik. "To cut it by twelve percent... well. That's about four times Fleet's annual budget."

"Fuck," said Shahaim, wide-eyed.

"Yes," Erik agreed. "They're trying to cut the Worlders out of space entirely. Cut off their influence, cut off their citizens getting jobs in space, turn them all into Spacers after two years, can't vote in Worlder elections any more, can't get Worlder benefits... hope most of them won't bother coming up here in the first place if there's no long term prospect in it."

"Gives Spacer authorities legal power over Worlder citizens," Kaspowitz said grimly. "Can't touch them if they've Worlder IDs. With Spacer IDs they can slap on travel restrictions, detain, question, blackball, the works. On security issues, Fleet can fuck around with Spacer civilian rights all they like, we've seen it before. Worlder civvies, not so much."

"I'm..." Shilu fiddled with some incoming feeds, adjusting reception. "I'm getting some TV from Apilai. News feeds it looks like." He blinked, then stared back at Erik. "There's riots. A Spacer admin building's on fire."

Erik gritted his teeth. "And all this while everyone's been marching up and down in parades on Homeworld. What a farce."

"Always said marching was overrated," said Kaspowitz. "Scan, check mark ID thirty-one, I think that's two ships instead of one. Looks like an intercept in progress."

"Hold on," said Geish, double checking. "Um... yeah, good catch Nav. I have no transponders on either at this moment, but it looks like a sub-lighter and an FTL, probably a warship."

"Could be another one of your family's LC," Shahaim remarked.

"Yeah, mommy's not gonna be happy," Erik muttered. "Get me a roster of all registered sub-lighters insystem, how many are we talking?"

"Hang on," said Jiri. As Scan Two, he took all the secondary Scan functions Geish was too busy to manage. The most up-to-date roster on all insystem traffic would come from the stations. "I got it, Hoffen Station feed says eight hundred and ninety registered sub-lighters, eight hundred and nine of them currently operational, the rest in repair and overhaul. If you're interested, I've got... sixty-two registered to Debogande-related industries." He raised an eyebrow. "Sounds a bit low?"

"Dammit," Erik muttered, and opened some new com links. "Hello Lisbeth? Lisbeth, I'm going to patch you, Jokono and Hiro into the bridge feed, please tell them to stand by."

"*Sure yes, hold on.*" A pause as she did that. Some questioning looks around the bridge — it was irregular to let anyone from regular crew listen in on bridge chatter, let alone civilians. "*Erik we're all here, go ahead.*"

"Guys, Chairman Ali and Chairman Joseph are both here, presumably Supreme Commander Chankow is too. That's the top leadership of Fleet and Spacer Congress both. They've passed an Ordinance restricting Worlder ownership of Spacer assets to fifteen percent, and said Worlder citizens can't work for Spacer entities for more than two years without taking out Spacer citizenship and losing Worlder rights. All hell's breaking loose, we've got ships running to all corners presumably to either spread the news, or to enforce it, and it looks like we've got Fleet interceptions of civilian sub-lighters taking place." Even as he spoke, Geish flashed another two impending interceptions up on his screen.

"Well Erik, look, that's..." Lisbeth took a breath, sounding flustered either from the situation, or from actually being asked to give advice to the commander of a combat carrier in a serious situation. *"They can't do that outside of martial law, I'm pretty sure. I mean I did some law on the side with my degree, and Mother's taught me a whole lot more that affects the family. This sounds dangerously close to a coup, they need Worlder Congressional approval before doing anything that might affect Worlder business interests, and fifteen percent would be... well that's economic vandalism, lots of people are going to be hurt by this. Working class even worse than us rich folk, it'll be the station hands and techs who get laid off first, you watch. That's a big chunk of Spacer business finance, Spacer business isn't anywhere near as self-sufficient as these Fleet chauvinists like to think, we all take Worlder money and fifteen percent just isn't going to cut it!"*

Erik couldn't help but feel a little pride. For a concise analysis on zero-notice, to bridge-crew who might not be as business-savvy as the heiress to such a massive fortune, it wasn't bad at all. "Well Worlder reaction isn't good, there's some rioting on Apilai and Fleet are intercepting some civilian ships, probably they're keeping tabs on those they think might be trouble. Which suggests there's some kind of organised Worlder politics here that could fight back... and we've all heard of Heuron Dawn, but I hadn't thought it was that widespread. Hiro and Jokono, can you guys add anything?"

"LC it's Jokono. Heuron Dawn is on the domestic security watchlist. In a martial law situation, that would give Fleet the authority to crack down pretty hard. Detention without trial for up to a month without legal representation, for one thing."

"Hiro, you used to work for Intel. Any idea how big Heuron Dawn is?"

"Well they're not actually an organised political party," came Hiro's voice. *"It's more of an unofficial thing, they keep their*

membership secret but the estimate is that about a third of Apilai's local congress are members. There's even talk they have some local tavalai support, but I think that's mostly a Spacer smear campaign. Intel consensus was that they're not a militant group yet, but had the potential to become one if things got serious. I think this situation meets that definition."

"In which scenario," Jokono added, *"the local Spacer security agencies would have orders to crack down on anyone with known Dawn ties. Private companies mostly, employment agencies, anyone in Spacer jurisdiction employing Worlders or Worlder sympathisers."*

"Yeah, and suddenly that two year Worlder employment restriction starts to make sense," said Erik. "They don't want Worlder patriots like Heuron Dawn building a base of support in Spacer jurisdiction. Thanks guys, I'd like all three of you to stay patched into Coms and listen to the chatter, see if you can help us figure out the situation."

"Of course Erik, we're on it," said Lisbeth.

"Helm," said Erik as he cut the com, "this looks like an opportunity to me. Under normal circumstances we'd have to stick to traffic guidelines, but this looks like a security situation. Fleet are intercepting local vessels, we've no idea if any of them are threatening to Fleet, we're incoming with battle damage into a blind situation and we're on a two minute light delay from station which will make a detailed assessment of the situation difficult."

"I agree," said Shahaim. "There's a good security argument to boost V and go in fast. We could cut out a whole thirty hours of approach, buy ourselves some more time."

"Plus they're going to be busy," Kaspowitz added. "We were betting on questions and suspicion, but with all this going on, they might barely notice."

"Oh they'll notice," said Erik. "But either way we can't waste the chance. Nav, lay us a course for mid-system boost at middle-V, let's try to get to Hoffen Station as quickly as possible. Scan, stand by to switch transponder to orange alert."

"Aye LC."

Hoffen Station gave them a hub berth, and *Phoenix* dumped velocity close enough to leave them a mere five hours of low-V coasting to station.

The plan had been to claim they'd been intercepted one jump short of Homeworld by an unidentified assailant, who'd put the hole in their side and damaged their jumplines. This ambush could only have been carried out, they'd insist, by someone who'd known their route in advance, which suggested a leak, and thus a traitor of some kind at a very high level. Supreme Commander Chankow would have to be informed as soon as possible, and no one else was trustworthy, so they'd changed course and headed for Heuron... only to have their jumplines fail, and spot a rock that appeared settled and thus a useful place to do some self-repair, only to find it occupied by a hacksaw nest.

The genius of this particular tall tale, Erik thought, was that the least likely part of it — the encounter with the hacksaw nest — was actually true, and could be proved by the hacksaw parts they had in storage. He was hoping that that fact alone would at least buy them enough credibility to get the rest of their story accepted. The necessity to tell Supreme Commander Chankow of the traitor personally was also going to give him a face-to-face meeting... in which he'd do something to get some information from him. Exactly what, he hadn't decided yet.

But closing in on Hoffen Station, no one from HQ had even asked to talk to Captain Pantillo, and Lieutenant Shilu's brief operations report had gone unremarked upon. Unauthorised station traffic was blank, no civilian or other networks broadcasting, so they had no idea what the situation was on station. Erik guessed it was very busy, and simply no one had the time. He had Shilu put in a request to brief Supreme Commander Chankow, and it too went unanswered. What the hell was going on in there?

"Well that's annoying," said Trace, peering at the extra camera rig the techs had put above the command chair's screens.

"You get the whole system set up and you don't even get to use it." The command chair's coms had a camera function, so the ship captain could be seen by whomever he was talking to. With superior officers, their use was compulsory. The engineering techs who'd installed the extra cameras insisted the software was simple enough — it would convert the feed of Erik's face in realtime to look and sound like Captain Pantillo. The special effects weren't hard for processors the size of *Phoenix*'s, and Erik was sure he knew the Captain's mannerisms well enough to do a reasonable job — it was used from time to time to fool enemy ships and commanders they had reason to talk to, on the off-chance any of them believed what they saw. But so far no superior officer had called, and as commander on station, he was going to have to leave the ship as soon as they'd docked. That would leave Lieutenant Shahaim in the chair, and Erik wasn't as sure of her acting ability.

"What does it mean?" asked Lieutenant Draper, who stood at the back of the bridge with Lieutenant Dufresne. With the LC off the ship, it was important that their two second-shift pilots knew the score first hand. "Why haven't they called?"

"Several possibilities," said Erik, watching the approaching bulk of Hoffen Station, slowly rotating, its rim filled with an endless, circling row of starships. "First, they're on to us, and I'll be arrested as soon as I leave the ship. In that case, Lieutenant Shahaim will be in command, and you are instructed to break dock immediately and run."

"Yeah, that's what you think," said Trace, with a glance at Shahaim. Shahaim nodded knowingly.

Erik looked back and forth. "You guys do actually know who's the ranking officer here?"

"Sure," Trace reasoned. "But as soon as you're arrested, you're out of the picture. And I think Lieutenant Shahaim and I are in agreement that the ship's survival requires you in the chair." Shahaim did not disagree with the younger woman. "Besides which, if you get arrested, I'll get arrested, because I'm coming with you. And good luck keeping my Lieutenants on *Phoenix* if that happens.

"My alternative plan is that we go out armed and in force. It's a messy station, we don't know the security situation, and station's not talking to us. We'll assume a hostile dock and deter them from arresting us in the first place."

Erik took a deep breath. A week ago he would have been angry, being contradicted by his partner in command (and in crime) in front of everyone. But it wasn't a bad plan, and everyone's consent that he was irreplaceable was flattering. "Sure," he said. "You're the ground combat specialist, let's do that. Second option is they're just too busy. I don't buy that, there's plenty of lower ranking officers on Hoffen, or in one of these other Fleet vessels, who could query us. Something else is going on.

"I personally favour a third option — this is politically complicated, and they're very unhappy to see *Phoenix* here at this moment. They think Captain Pantillo is still alive, they're wondering why the hell he's here, and they don't want to deal with him right now. Probably they think he's up to something, so they'll be very suspicious. I'd guess they don't want to talk to him right now for fear that he'll discern something about *them*. You know how good he was at reading faces.

"So everyone's pretending to be too busy to speak to us right now… only they're not entirely pretending, they probably *are* very busy. I've been in contact with Mitchell Klinger, CEO of Debogande Enterprises, Heuron Division. He's agreed to see me and offered me secure quarters… he's not a friend of the family but he's known to be a very good manager, we should be able to get a good view of what's going on from him. I think we can trust him but as the Major says, if we've enough guns along it shouldn't matter either way.

"Major, what will we need?"

"Command Squad would seem logical," said Trace. "Light armour only— full kit would seem overdoing it. I'd like you in light kit as well LC." Erik nodded — that was her prerogative to request. "We'll put a platoon on the dock until we learn better, if we learn better. One complication — our hub berth is directly alongside an alo vessel. Shtikt-class warship, so advanced even we won't want to mess with it.   Alo don't do marines, but they might not like us on their dock all the same, we'll have to tread carefully."

"They can lodge a complaint," said Erik.   "It's a human station, I don't really care what they think."

Trace nodded.   "Everything else, we can wing it.   Our story is that Captain Pantillo and Commander Huang were exposed to a toxin as a sabotage from within, as a part of the traitorous leak that got us ambushed, and are currently in medical and unable to be exposed to others.   It's actually not far from the truth with our internal crew troubles, and will match our actual security posture. Our platoon on dock won't allow anyone in, and we'll both be in the hospitality of Debogande Enterprises, so anyone calling on available command staff should call on us there.   If they want to see Captain Pantillo personally, we tell them they should have called on the way in.   And if anyone does call, Lieutenant Shahaim can… what was Lisbeth's expression?   Lie like a Senator?"

"Lie like a Congresswoman," Shahaim confirmed.   "I've got kids, I learned the art."

"A last thing," Trace added, "I'd recommend we prepare some of those hacksaw carcasses for transfer to station, Hoffen have some advanced labs, but mostly we need to maintain our story.   If the tale we're telling had actually happened to us, we'd be giving them bits of hacksaws for study.   And that might distract them from the rest of it."

"Yes," Erik agreed.   "Lieutenant Shahaim, please give the order to prepare some of our hacksaw material for relocation, and contact station labs to let them know it's coming."

Lisbeth had helped store and study the hacksaw remains, so when the order passed through Engineering to get some out of storage after they'd docked, she left Jokono and Hiro to their com feed and went down to storage with Carla and Vijay.

"We should get out there," Vijay insisted as Lisbeth followed Carla down the back-quarter corridor.   Both bodyguards were armed with the personal weapons they'd brought aboard, *Phoenix* marines seeing no point in removing them. "Or someone should. They'll be watching all *Phoenix* personnel on station, but they don't know us. If we can sneak on, we could move around and talk to some people, learn what's going on."

"Sure," said Carla, eyeing the passing foot traffic. "Let's let the LC talk to our company guy here, then we'll have some idea what to do next."

They climbed the next level up to storage and found Ensign Remy Hale already directing several spacers about the storage racks. "Lisbeth, good!" she said. "I was thinking we'd take the third and fourth torsos, they've got no technology we haven't got replicated in the others, and they've got some cool bullet holes that make our story look good."

"Um, sure," said Lisbeth, going over to help with the racks while Vijay and Carla took position at the door. "Just, I think the third torso had some really interesting heat diffusion that looked very different from the others? That's the amazing thing, they're all unique and..."

"Fuck!" yelled one of the spacers, scrambling back from an open rack. Everyone spun.

"Geri!" Hale demanded. "What is it?"

"It fucking moved!" Spacer Townsend said, backing away, her eyes wide. "I saw it!"

Lisbeth crouched to look at the segmented torso, suspended in netting within the sliding frame. Was it her imagination, or could she hear a faint whirring sound? The torso segment twitched, and the whole netting leaped as Lisbeth bit back a scream, and others shouted alarm.

"Get back!" Vijay shouted, putting himself between Lisbeth and the open rack, pistol levelled. "Get the hell back, all of you!"

"No wait!" Lisbeth shouted above the commotion. "It's... don't shoot it again, it's dead!"

"I don't care," said Carla, hauling Lisbeth to her feet and pulling her to the door while Vijay covered. "We're out of here."

"No! No wait, it's not... Remy, tell them it's not..." Remy Hale gave the two bodyguards a fast nod and wave, telling them to go while talking rapidly into her com. "Dammit guys, let me go!"

Erik stood in the storage room, Trace at his side. Rooke was there, mobile scanner in hand, turning slowly about as the readings changed. Remy was there too, and Lisbeth, still fuming at having been dragged away by her armpits. Three more marines were also present, fully armed. Trace would have brought more, only there wasn't enough room for them plus the techs and command staff.

One of the big wall racks had been extended, and a segmented hacksaw torso hung in the nets, periodically twitching. Several of the steel limbs in the vertical press racks also made an occasional rattle. Creepy didn't begin to describe it.

"So much for them not coming alive and murdering us in our sleep," muttered one of the marines.

"I *told* you," Lisbeth said with exasperation. "They're all disconnected, they can't hurt anyone, they've no means to move and all their weapons have no ammunition anyway."

"Sure fine," Trace said coolly, keeping one shoulder ahead of Lisbeth, her rifle levelled as she looked slowly around. "No one get any closer."

"No... look." Second Lieutenant Rooke stared only at his device. "It's... it's definitely coming from the alo ship. It's docked right alongside, we're, like, right inside its primary field, the hacksaws are just echoing that field..."

"A field of *what?*" Erik asked.

"It's... it's just a very modulated form of gamma, it's at harmless low levels but it's... it's present in every alo ship we have on record. The ones they operate, anyway — *Phoenix* doesn't have it, there's something different about the powerplants on the tech they give to us, and the tech they use themselves."

"You mean they're not *doing* anything?" Hale wondered.

"No, that's just it," Rooke insisted. "They're not doing anything different. They've just got engines on standby, basic systems running. Nothing special."

"Only no one's ever brought a dead hacksaw this close to an alo ship before?" Lisbeth asked, wide-eyed.

Rooke lowered his device and looked at her, as though properly seeing her for the first time. "Yes." He grimaced, as though realising the enormity of that. "Yeah. Shit." And put a hand to his head.

"So wait," Trace said in a low voice. "What does that mean? Alo use hacksaw technology? Or hacksaws use alo technology?"

"We don't know," said Rooke. "No one knows the alo. We're not allowed into their territory, they don't permit study, they don't talk, they've flat out killed any ship that goes anywhere it's not supposed to be in their space, ally or not. They're a mystery, we just know that they've been allies with the chah'nas for a few thousand years and they've got the most advanced ships and technology in the Spiral. And *Phoenix* is based on their tech, which is why it's so much faster than anything else we've got... save for a few others *also* based on alo tech."

"Unbelievable," Erik murmured. "Would have been nice to ask that queen a few questions while it was still alive and talking." Trace said nothing. "Only thing we know is there's no record of the alo being in space before or during the Age of the AIs. Is there *any* record of a connection between alo and AIs?"

"Well sure," said Trace. "I bet someone knows. Up in Fleet High Command. Another thing we can ask them, when we get their ear."

CHAPTER 23

At hub dock both the midships airlock and the bow airlock could be used, but Erik did not like to have too many entrances to guard from outside intrusion.

"We good?" Erik asked the waiting marines of Command Squad by the combat airlock, beside where Plugger's scarred, armed face was securely stowed.

"Wait," said Trace as he floated past them, and grabbed his belt to slow him. She then checked his webbing, his velcro pocket covers, his pistol, ammo and others, like a mother checking her child's uniform on the first day of school. A few weeks ago Erik would have found it annoying. Now he only sighed, and rolled his eyes to the amusement of the waiting marines. Trace finally finished, and gave him a whack on the backside for effect. "All good, let's go. *Behind* me, if you please." Staff Sergeant Kono operated the inner airlock door, and they filed in. The airlock was just barely big enough for nine of them, in light, un-powered armour and weapons. "What's that smell?"

"Aftershave," said Erik. "You might try it."

"Aftershave?" Trace asked with amusement. She pushed interactive glasses over her eyes, like sunglasses only with sophisticated targeting functions inbuilt.

"It's a well known fact that female marines don't shave," said Kono. "They shed."

Trace actually grinned as several of her marines sniggered, and the inner door closed behind them, everyone pulling on the loose airlock straps to keep themselves clustered tight as zero-G contact tried to push them apart. With Private Rolonde in Medbay, Trace was the only woman in Command Squad. It was impossible to know what if anything she made of the whole 'woman in command of men' thing, it was just one more of those topics no one had the balls to quiz her on. Now that he thought of it, Erik couldn't remember her ever making any kind of deal about gender one way or the other. Save for the whack on the backside just now, but he'd seen her do that to young female marines too, just an adult-to-junior way to say 'stay alert' with a smile.

The outer airlock opened, and cold air rushed in, lights bright in the short access tube. The marines caught the hand lines provided and pulled, effortlessly aligning into formation, Kono and two others ahead, Trace and Erik in the middle, then Corporal Rael with three more behind.

Arrivals was a big tube that ran personnel transport capsules, a big one rushing past even as they entered, full of spacers from some ship further up the hub dock. Beyond, through windows making gaps in the tube, a view into the enormous hub. It was like a giant tunnel in space, protruding from the hub of the rotating space station like an extended axle from an old-fashioned cart wheel. Inside the tunnel wall was a thicket of sub-light ships and shuttles, clustered about like bats to the roof of a cave. They flittered this way and that, seeking or leaving dock, shuttles heading downworld, freighters heading to nearby bases, moons, stations or refinery facilities, maintenance tugs performing visual inspection of the many hundreds of docking ports and access tubes. The whole inner hub was lit with a thousand floodlights, many blinking a warning red or yellow.

The big starships docked about the outside of the 'tunnel' walls, in far fewer berths. Starships usually preferred to dock at the rim, where the huge gantries that held them in place at one-G rotation could also serve as maintenance, and the station's huge cargo chutes and fuel hoses could see even a combat carrier like Phoenix refuelled and restocked in a matter of hours. Out here on the hub dock, the cargo and refuelling facilities were designed for smaller sub-lighters, and would take far longer. But if a ship was damaged, exposing it to prolonged one-G rotation was unwise, and repairs went far faster in zero-G where large replaceable parts could simply be floated to and from the ship.

"Lieutenant Commander Debogande!" Erik looked as he cleared the access tube, and found a dark woman holding to a railing beside the transport tube. About her were another four marines, in light kit as were *Phoenix*'s. "Captain Ritish, *UFS Mercury.*" She was secured, he was not, and she ranked him. Erik followed etiquette and floated to her, grabbing the railing to stop. Then a salute, him first, her answering. Ritish then offered her hand. "Sorry to surprise you, but command's kind of busy, as you might imagine. Didn't want anything discussed over coms, so they told me to come up here and see you in person."

Erik's heart thumped unpleasantly, but he kept his expression cool and professional. This was a different kind of threat to enemy fire. Surreal, given what he and *Phoenix* had just done, and Captain Ritish had no idea about. She'd find out soon enough, and would probably try to kill him and everyone on his ship when she did... but for now, he had to just pretend nothing had happened. Thankfully, you didn't rise to command staff in Fleet without learning to blow smoke up superior officers' asses from time to time.

"Captain, good to see you. And you'll know Major Thakur, of course."

"Major," said Ritish, with a nod of respect. Erik knew Ritish by reputation only — a relatively new captain, competent as all carrier captains were competent, but operating in an entirely different sector of the war to *Phoenix*. Heuron was one of those systems where many sectors came together. "You've come out prepared, I see?" With a glance across Command Squad.

"Well given no one would give us a direct briefing on the situation," Erik explained. "And given what we see on the newsfeeds. Thought it best to be prepared."

"Hell of a thing you guys being here," said Ritish, with casual intrigue. "An ambush, an assassination attempt on the Captain from within your own crew, then hacksaws?"

Erik shook his head in shared disbelief. "The war was supposed to be over, right? Craziest thing I've seen in three years at this post... actually we're preparing to bring some of the hacksaw parts we salvaged down to analysis on station if you'd like to see them? Just amazing things, we're packing them for transport now."

With a suggestive glance at the tube control panel by Ritish's hand. She took the hint and hit the call button. "I might just do that," she said with genuine fascination. "Casualties?"

Erik handed off to Trace. "Eighteen," she said. "And twenty wounded. We had them outnumbered or it would have been far worse."

"Man that sucks," said the marine sergeant with Ritish. "And just after the damn war had finished too."

"My condolences," Ritish agreed. "Damn shame. But clearing a hacksaw nest with only eighteen losses… your reputation stands confirmed, Major Thakur."

Trace nodded without comment. The tube rumbled and vibrated as a transport car approached — a big, oval capsule. Its doors matched the tube doors, then opened with a hiss of equalising air. They filed in, and found the capsule empty — the Captain's security clearance, Erik guessed, which allowed her to call a car exclusively for them. They took hold to rails and straps as the doors closed behind, and the car began a smooth acceleration.

"And your Captain's health, how is he?" Ritish pressed.

"He's okay," said Erik. "But our doc thinks the toxin may still be active so he's quarantined for now, and Commander Huang too. It was in the food, someone brought it to them in a meeting in the Captain's quarters. We've arrested the guy, he's been interrogated."

"And?"

"Nothing yet. Very resilient. But that's a part of the trouble — clearly this is a plot of some kind, against *Phoenix* and against the Captain. The Captain insisted we should come here directly, and that Supreme Commander Chankow should be informed. Of course we had no idea that Chairmen Ali and Joseph would be here as well, but while they are, they should probably hear it too."

Sporadic gaps in the tube offered flashing glimpses of the inner hub docks as they passed — freighters clamped to grapples, workers in exo-suits working on engines, cargo offloading into parallel chutes. Another car flashed by, heading the other way, filled with crew or station workers. Then a station stop, more crew awaiting a lift and probably annoyed that this car would not stop for them.

"So what's the situation here?" Erik asked.

"Damn mess," said Ritish.   She was quite pretty, Erik thought — tall, long-faced with pronounced cheek bones.   Age was always hard to guess these days, but if pressed Erik thought somewhere between eighty and a hundred.   It was a more typical age for a captain, and made him insecure of his own age and rank every time he thought of it.   Most carrier LCs were at least fifty. "We're rounding people up now."

"Rounding up?"

Ritish made a face.   "You'll see.   Lots of station workers with Worlder IDs suddenly got to go.   Just no time to do a full investigation of who's Heuron Dawn and who isn't, safer to ship the lot out."

Erik blinked.   "That'll make a mess of a lot of Spacer business operations out here.   They're going to be many hands short."   Which, as he could recently attest, was a real pain.

"They'll manage.   So who are you heading off to see?" Given that every senior person you'd like to see can't see you, she meant.

"Mitchell Klinger," said Erik.   "Debogande Enterprises CEO for Heuron."

"I know who he is," said Ritish.   "Is he family?"

Erik forced a smile.   "We don't *just* do nepotism," he said reproachfully.   "Just a company guy, but I hear he's good."

"What are you going to talk about?" Ritish asked.

Erik shrugged vaguely.   "Whatever there is to say.   This whole shit for one thing."   He indicated at the passing station outside.   "Gotta get a briefing from someone, may as well be him."

It was tempting to glance at Trace.   He didn't dare.   Clearly Ritish was suspicious.   Or more to the point, she'd been sent by people in High Command to talk to him personally, then report back. 'Check him out', they'd have said.   'Get some clues what that sneaky old man Pantillo's up to.'   Probably his eagerness to show her the hacksaw corpses had thrown her a little.   Those were very hard to come by, and proved the most unlikely part of his story was true.   And if that was true… but he knew better than to think her convinced.   None of her bosses trusted Pantillo, and Erik guessed that if they'd picked Captain Ritish for the task, they considered her reliable in a way they never would have considered the Captain.

The car arrived at the station hub, enfolded within the colossal metal bulk in a sudden rush of close steel and gantries, then halting with a gentle force that sent them swinging on their straps. Doors opened onto a near wall with more railings and handlines, and Erik pulled himself out, as Captain Ritish talked to some station hands on the point of entering. Several looked like medics, and all wore hazmat suits with the hoods currently down.

Trace gave Erik a concerned glance. "Captain?" Erik asked. "Are these guys heading out to *Phoenix*?"

"That's right," said Ritish.

"I'm sorry, we're sealed tight to all non-*Phoenix* personnel, Captain's orders."

"Lieutenant Commander," said Ritish with a frown, "you've been subject to a medical and possibly a chemical attack, and Fleet regulations say both should be attended by suitable personnel ASAP upon station arrival."

"Unless the vessel's captain declares his ship sealed," Erik countered. "I'm not aware of any external authority that can override a captain's command of entry to his own deck."

"Lieutenant Commander, I think that under the circumstances..."

And she stopped, as Trace interposed herself, drifting to Erik's side. "Don't fuck around," said Trace, "you know the regs as well as we do. Captain says we're sealed — we're sealed."

Ritish stared at her, clearly unaccustomed to being spoken to in that tone by anyone. And suffered perhaps a dawning flash of realisation, staring into that impassive, dark-visored gaze, exactly whom she was speaking to. And how that person might naturally feel about some *other* captain, telling *her* *C*aptain who should and should not step upon *Phoenix*'s deck. "Very well. But this will go on my report higher up."

"Good that something should," Trace said pointedly. "They know where to find us."

Ritish waved at her marines to leave, and the hazmat personnel went with her. The *Mercury* marine sergeant gave Trace a final glance that Erik half-expected to turn into an apology... but didn't. Then he turned and over-handed his way along a railing to the exit.

"They know," Erik murmured. "There's not a marine in Fleet who wouldn't love to get in your good books, but that guy just passed. They're not sure what they know, but they know something's not right."

"Major?" said Corporal Rael from nearby. "We're not gonna have to shoot at other marines, are we?"

Trace gave him a hard look. "You see a crystal ball anywhere on my person, Corporal?"

"No Major," said Rael in a small voice.

"Come on. Let's not keep the LC's rich and powerful buddy waiting."

Hoffen Station hub was one of the largest indoor microgravity environments Erik could recall moving through. Pressurised access from the personnel tubes lead past humming walls of machinery, and inset windows overlooked massive zero-G pumps feeding from fuel and coolant tanks. Handlines hummed, dragging strings of passengers along in rapid time, while station-hands flew independently on compressed air hand-thrusters or body rigs. There must have been a hundred thousand people in the hub at any time, Erik thought. Hoffen was not human of course — tavalai had built it several thousand years ago, taking nearly a century to complete. There was simply no way to do this scale of engineering quickly, but now Hoffen Station dominated and centralised the Heuron V system economy, creating a distribution hub for people and products to the hundreds of smaller stations and bases about the gas giant's moons and rings.

Main hub ring had two speeds of handlines, and the *Phoenix* party took the inner, faster line, flying about the huge, inner wall bundles of pipes and cabling as they overtook the slower traffic. The outer wall was a line of enormous magnetic railings, where the stationary hub wall met the rotating outer wheel, and millions of tonnes of mass whisked past each other for no friction or torque whatsoever. It did produce a sizeable magnetic field, however, and the hub rim was notorious for being the place where all kinds of electrical devices developed glitches. The side walls were lined with offices, restaurants and even hotels, stacked in three-dimensional space in a way they could never be down on the rim. Display signs flashed colour and graphics, and the odd massage parlour offered tricks to those who wanted a different kind of adventure in zero-G.

For all the life and colour, it was less lively than Erik recalled — many of the once-crowded facilities looked empty. And here passing the walls were a squad of station cops, grey uniforms with light armour and non-lethals — zap-batons in official parlance, but 'kidney sticks' to the locals. This group had sidearms holstered but moved with purpose, stopping now to talk forcefully to some shop owner floating in his circular hatchway. Some teenage kids holding to the inner piping, where no kids were supposed to hang, watched the cops sullenly. One saw Erik looking, and gave the passing crew the finger.

"I see everyone's real happy we won the war," Erik remarked.

"Which war?" said Trace.

"Yeah," Erik murmured. "Good question."

They dismounted opposite Registration — the dismount line ran close alongside the handline, and passengers simply took a plastic handle and let it run them at slow deceleration into the dismount station, alongside the mount queue waiting to get on. From there another handline ran wide up the wall to avoid tangling with traffic. Erik saw one of the shop glassfronts was broken, with no sign of impending repair. Several others were closed, lights off and dead. An office worker from an insurance shop watched them pass — insystem runners often liked face-to-face quotes, so insurance companies put reps up in the hub, one day a week so they didn't violate the heavy-time mandates. This rep looked bored and wary, watching the passing marines while sipping a sealed coffee flask. A Spacer, Erik guessed, personally unworried by the cops but unimpressed at the disruption to business.

Registration queues weren't long, automated gates checked IDs once they got inside, and scanned irises, while patrolling station security watched behind the gates with guns. Staff Sergeant Kono led them up the military queue, where a fast scan and a station guard let them through. All IDs heading from hub down to rim were registered, mostly to keep track of insystem traffic. Erik doubted the starship traffic was the main cause of station's security headaches here.

Beyond Registration, parallel passages emerged into one of the most amazing spaces Erik had ever seen. It looked like a steel canyon, with enormous magnetic railings along the walls, buzzing and crackling with incredible electricity charge. 'Above', the slowly moving canyon ceiling was the rotating outer hub, the outside part of Heuron System's largest wheel bearing. To either side of the canyon, capsule car rails ran alongside the mag-railings, curving up the endless horizon. These capsule cars were larger than those up in the station hub, and without near or far doors. People ahead floated into the near car, and it took off on humming rails while another took its place.

Kono led them on, and no following civilians tried to share it with them. They set off, shifting onto the outer lane and accelerating gently after the car ahead until they saw the huge stubby end of the station's five-arm elevator shaft running away from them within the massive space between canyon walls ahead. The first car paralleled it, people floating into the elevator car, then sealing as the empty capsule car pulled into the inner lane, and their own chased it.

A new elevator car arrived within the bulky double-shaft elevator, and passengers emptied onto the departure cars on the far side of the hub rim. Far doors closed, and near doors opened as the elevator car shifted from the ascent shaft to the descent, matching the open side of the marines' capsule car, and the *Phoenix* crew all pulled themselves in. A tight seal hissed, then a thud of movement and they were away, feeling as though they were moving 'up', into the ceiling between giant hub rails.

Information screens flashed on within the moving car, as shaft walls enfolded them at increasing speed. Kono's security ID would ensure it didn't stop for more passengers. *"Welcome to Hoffen Station,"* beamed a friendly female voice. *"Did you know that Hoffen is an old Earth word meaning 'hope'?"*

"It's German," said Private Terez, holding a support as station rotation pushed them sideways. "From Germany."

"No shit," said Arime.

"Where was Germany?" Van wondered.

"Europe," said Terez. "Where white people came from."

"Yeah I know that dumbass," Van retorted. On the information screen, the saleswoman continued to prattle about various tourist-friendly station statistics.

"Tavalai called it Kroptaptamian," said Trace. "It means a completed life's goal."

"Damn," said Rael. "Froggies got a word for everything, don't they?"

"Better than Hope," said Trace. "What the fuck is Hope? Hope for what? An icecream? A quick death?"

Bemusement on the faces of several marines. "Uh, isn't that kind of the point?" Arime asked. "That Hope can mean anything you want it to?"

"It means nothing," Trace said flatly. "I'm sick of happy bullshit that means nothing. Vacuous words for vacuous minds."

Kulina had no hope, Erik thought. Kulina accepted their karma. The universe had something in store for everyone, and for Kulina it was usually bad. Eventually.

"Kulina volunteer their lives, and their service, in the 'hope' that it will make a difference, surely?" he asked her.

Trace looked at him, as the sideways force translated to downward force, and they all slowly swung upon the pivots of their handholds, feet drifting toward the ceiling that now became the ground. "There is a necessity that someone should," Trace retorted. "Recognition of a necessity is not the same as hope."

"So you hold no hope for yourself," said Erik. "You're Kulina, you accept your fate, come what may. What about hope for the rest of us? Hope for *Phoenix*? For humanity?"

"Hope creates illusions," Trace said firmly. "People who hope only see what they wish to see. What you're talking about are my personal feelings. Of course I hope, I'm weak and human like everyone else. But I fight it every day, because wishful illusions get you killed."

"You hope it'll help," Erik offered.

Trace gave him a dry sideways look behind dark shades. It turned into a reluctant smile. "Don't be a smartass."

"I'll try," said Erik. "But I don't hold much hope."

Trace grinned. "Me neither."

"Evidently."

"Are you two flirting?" wondered Terez. And tried to shrink into his armour as both his superiors stared at him.

"No hope for this one," Erik deadpanned.

"I abandoned it long ago," Trace agreed.

The support arms on many wheel-stations were little more than transitions between hub and rim, but on Hoffen they had levels and levels, like a four kilometre high skyscraper, each level with progressively more gravity the closer it was to the rim. More hundreds of thousands of people in each arm, and this was just Hoffen-A — the entire station repeated, the second wheel of Hoffen-B, joined by the stationary axle and twin hubs. Seven million capacity per wheel, close to another million in the zero-G hub and axles, fifteen in total. The very first humans to see such things had had trouble getting their heads around the scale of it, and how it would be possible to fill such facilities with people. Now there was amazement that people had ever wondered, and talk of new facilities in the planning phase, to accommodate the growing boom.

The elevator whined to a halt at main rim dock, full gravity restored as the doors opened onto a high metal ceiling and relative open space. Simulated sunlight seemed bright, and Erik reached for his own glasses as they stepped out. The right-hand wall was the outer rim — First Rim in stationer talk, a hundred and ten berths all the way around, a hundred and ten more on Second Rim, two hundred and twenty on Hoffen-A and the same number on Hoffen-B. First Rim wall was a series of lighted displays all the way up the curving horizon in either direction, the ceiling heavy with piping for air and water, while cargo and fuel ran below-decks. The opposite wall was retail and accommodation, the station/city presenting a welcome face of bars, clubs, hotels and other entertainments to visiting spacers. Beyond that, through the hallways, the living and work spaces for all these people, layer upon layer about the rim.

Exiting the elevator, Private Kumar immediately swung left, indicating possible threat, and Kono followed. No rifles were raised, so Erik joined them and looked. Before them, standing by the elevator wall as though waiting for them, were three tall, robed, hooded figures. Their robes were various shades of grey and black, silvery in the synthetic sunlight and shimmering. Their faces were mostly veiled, save for jet black eyes with a bluish tint. Beneath the veils, the hint of wide nasal and mouth arrangement that made up most of the lower face, delicate and protected.

Alo. Three of them, and apparently waiting for them, as though they'd known precisely where to be.

"Greetings," said the one in the middle. Its voice was toneless, little more than a high-pitched series of clicks produced so rapidly it might have been mechanical. The hacksaw queen had been more expressive. "Crew of *Phoenix*. Welcome to Hoffen Station."

"Greetings to you," Erik said cautiously, stepping forward to Staff Sergeant Kono's side. "To whom am I speaking?"

"Aloish I am. That is enough. Your ship is damaged. We can repair." 'Alo don't answer questions,' Erik recalled the Captain telling him once. 'They'll walk all over you if you let them. Too much respect for alien customs is dangerous. Call them on it, or you'll find yourself dancing to their tune.'

"Without your name, your offer means nothing to me," Erik replied.

A short pause that might have been laughter. The dark eyes squinted a little behind the hood and veil. "Aloish. I am senior.

Phoenix is a grand vessel. One of our best. It pains us to see you mistreat her. Fix her we will."

A hand appeared from the robes, with a wise lack of urgency, wary of armed human reflexes. In the gloved fingertips was a white card. Kono reached for it, and the alo pulled it sharply out of reach, looking at Erik. Erik reached into his pocket, and pulled out a glove. Tugged it onto his bare hand, pointedly, then reached past his Staff Sergeant to take the card. Another light hiss from the alo, laughter again. With a gesture, it turned, and its two companions followed it away.

Erik looked at the card. On it was scrawled alo script, oddly scruffy looking, next to the alo's usual immaculate presentation. "Anyone read alo?"

He showed it to Trace. "Hang on." Presumably she activated some uplink function on her glasses back to *Phoenix*. "Torshik. That's an anglicised name, the original's untranslatable. Ambassador."

Erik frowned. "Ambassador to Hoffen Station? Or to Heuron V?"

"Ambassador to Heuron System. All of it. Database even gives me a match on the visual I got of his face. That's him, Ambassador Torshik. This is the alo's most important post in human space, so that's probably the most important Ambassador they have anywhere."

Offering to fix their ship? Erik watched the three robed figures vanish into a doorway, and felt a very nasty trepidation. Like somehow, they were all being watched, and Fleet command weren't the only people they had to worry about.

"Ask them why our dead hacksaws come back to life in proximity to their ship?" Kono growled. "Makes me wonder if we ran into those things by accident after all, or if our alo-built ship led us to them. I mean, what are the odds?"

Terez summarised everyone's feelings. "Fuck," he said.

Trace gave her Staff Sergeant a whack on the arm. "Don't scare the children," she said. "Come on, we'll be late."

There were a lot of station cops on the dock, and far less civilian traffic than Erik recalled from last time he was here. Or on any big, busy station, for that matter. Some bars were closed, flashing signs muted or turned off entirely. One hotel window was smashed, a big hole that looked like something, or someone, had been thrown out of it. Corporal Rael indicated some dark droplets on the steel deck as they passed — blood, it looked like. Some men stood nearby, and paused deep conversation to glance at the passing marines.

"Cops," said Kumar. "Plain clothes." The cops nodded. Erik nodded back.

"Bird can smell them," Van offered. "Cops that is."

"Never got along where I'm from," Private Anthony 'Bird' Kumar admitted. Many marines came from that sort of background, Erik knew. A few had been given ultimatums by judges — a long stretch in prison, or service. But only those who learned to control the aggressive impulse were any use.

Along the First Rim wall, occupied berths were either sealed firm, or watched by armed guards, or worse. Before one berth, another heated discussion — station officials in Immigration uniforms, arguing with freighter crew, while some worried-looking civvies watched on. One of the women held a small child, while the father clutched a suitcase. Either someone was being kicked off station, or had just arrived and was being denied entry.

Next up was a warship — *UFS Curzon*, the display read. Guarding the ramp were ten spacers with guns and light kit. They saw the *Phoenix* crew coming, with whispers and nods amongst themselves. They knew what ship these approaching marines were from. The officer amongst them saluted as they passed — technically outside the twenty meter limit for that formality, but spacers on dock always acknowledged other ships, and a salute passed as a greeting at distance. Erik returned it precisely, with a further nod, and kept walking.

"*Curzon?*" Trace asked him. As a spacer, he'd be more up to date on non-carrier ships than any marine.

344

"Sixth Fleet," said Erik. "Tiger-class I think. Nothing special."

Ahead, behind some decorative bushes before a hallway, was a disturbance, shouting and pushing. They got a clear view, grey uniformed cops in heavy gear were dragging some civilians, arms locked behind their backs while others shouted and yelled at them. Worlders, Erik guessed, as the marines silently formed up around him without needing to be told. Others were gathering, Spacers now grabbing those Worlders who were harassing the cops. More scuffles, and punches thrown. A wave of others rushing through, people flailing, screams and disorder.

More cops plunged in, buzz-sticks flying, and now people were falling. Erik saw a woman raise her arm to protect herself, then lost the use of it with a scream. A teenage boy broke from the mess, one wrist in cuffs but the other still loose as cops yelled and scrambled in pursuit. He tore straight for the *Phoenix* crew.

"Stop him!" the cops were yelling.

"Ware!" said Trace. "Let him go!" As the boy ran past them, two cursing cops behind, a third levelling his taser and looking for a dangerously proximate shot.

Kono half-raised his rifle, aiming just short of the cop's toes. "Hey asshole! Point that somewhere else!" The cop lowered the taser, wide-eyed, then turned to grapple with the fight behind. Kono steered them all carefully around it, as dock bystanders made way for them.

"Yeah thanks for nothing, marines," a watching plainclothes officer said sourly as they passed.

"You're fucking welcome," said Kumar. Because marines would only consider doing police-work when cops started leading combat assaults — which was never.

"*Phoenix!*" several others whispered as they saw the unit patches. "That's *Phoenix*! Hey that's Thakur, that's Major Thakur!" And muttered oaths besides. No mention of the famous Debogande, Erik thought. Again, a few weeks ago it would have bothered him, however stupid. Now it was a relief.

"What a mess," he muttered to Trace. By a dock ahead, civilians were clustered, holding various bags and cases. Many argued with station officials, looking dishevelled and short of sleep. A few were crying, or sat on the decking, head in hands. More Worlders, jobs lost, lives uprooted.

"How do they replace the workers?" Trace wondered. "If Spacer industry can't get enough workers, we all take a hit, Fleet included. You can't destroy the economic base our security's built on, it's madness."

"My mother told me that Worlders think money grows on trees," said Erik. "Get in debt, no problem, just go out back and pick a few billion more off the money tree. But she also said that Fleet's no better, they think money can be dug out of asteroids. She said that neither side truly understand that the real victory that humans won over the last thousand years wasn't military, it was economic. Turns out we're better at it than most other species out here, or at least we are when the experts are left to their own devices. But now here come the politics to fuck it all up properly."

CHAPTER 24

Debogande Inc security met them in the accommodation lobby, a wide lounge of comfortable chairs and expensive drinks, then crowding into a very large elevator. It was only a short ride, directly above the docks, then entrance onto a wide corridor with none of the bare steel of many working stations — here everything was carpets, potplants and polished panels.

The lobby walls were gleaming white, with inlays of abstract art. No one ever hung art on station walls — loose objects were not the hazard on stations that they were on ships, but regulations still discouraged too many things that weren't screwed down. Before the big dark doors stood a handsome man in a stylish suit, with two more security men to his sides. If he'd expected Erik to present himself immediately, he was disappointed, because Staff Sergeant Kono stood in his way, other marines facing the civvie guards, armoured, heavily armed and infinitely more dangerous.

"I'm Mitchell Klinger," said the handsome man, perhaps slightly offended that he had to address a mere Sergeant. "I'm the CEO of Debogande Incorporated in Heuron."

At which Kono stood aside, warily, and Erik approached with what he hoped was a disarming smile. "Mr Klinger." He extended his hand, which Klinger took. "I'm sorry about the security — in Fleet we have a protocol of doing things whenever a commander is on station in a less than entirely secure environment. No exceptions."

Klinger nodded, still serious. "That's fine Mr Debogande." His handshake was unnecessarily hard, as though he felt he had something to prove. "This is quite a situation, I agree."

"And this is Major Thakur," Erik added. "Commander, *Phoenix* marine company."

Klinger shook her hand too, stiffly. "An honour, Major." Erik had seen that look before. Klinger was a very important man, worth an enormous amount of money and accustomed to rank and respect within the civilian world. Trace in particular confronted such men with a vision of status and authority that lay completely outside their grasp. Many didn't like it.

"So you'll have been busy?" Erik suggested.

"In fact I'm extremely busy right now," Klinger admitted. "And so if you'll forgive me, I have to ask you precisely in what capacity this visit is taking place. Mr Debogande, I'm entirely aware that you are the son of my direct employers, and the ultimate owners of Debogande Incorporated. If you were visiting me solely in that capacity, then I would be quite delighted to invite you in and share all kinds of discussion with you..."

"But I'm wearing a Fleet uniform," Erik interrupted, "and you're currently having quite a tense relationship with Fleet Command. Or I'd imagine you are."

Klinger's smile was faintly relieved. "Exactly. In one capacity, there are many things I could discuss with you. In the other capacity, there are quite a few less, I'm afraid. And also there is the question of agency. You are third-in-command of *Phoenix*, and acting on the behalf of your Captain. He is well, I hope? We hear rumours he has taken ill?" Erik wondered where those had come from — the tall tale they'd concocted was for Fleet's ears only.

"He is ill, yes," Erik confirmed. "But he is recovering, as is Commander Huang, though neither can currently leave *Phoenix*. And yes, I am acting upon his authority."

"Ah," said Klinger. Erik was becoming very aware that he had not yet been welcomed inside. All these marines, plus him, standing in the lobby, had the makings of an uncomfortable standoff. "Then you'll be aware that Fleet Command seem quite disquieted at Captain Pantillo's arrival in Heuron. He was supposed to be at Homeworld, was he not? For the celebration?"

"We never made it," Erik explained. "I'm sorry, it's classified. We've explained our reasons to Fleet. But no, Fleet aren't happy to see us here." And now, he realised, he had to take the risk. "Captain Pantillo is not pleased to see these ordinances. Which I think gives him and you something in common."

Klinger considered him for a long moment. There was both fear and tension in his eyes. "What are you really doing here, Mr Debogande?"

"Captain Pantillo is concerned we are about to plunge from a foreign war, into a civil one," Erik said simply. "*Phoenix* would like to help. Whether we'll be allowed to is another question. As you say, Supreme Commander Chankow is not pleased to see us."

It smelt of treason. If this conversation were reported straight back to the Supreme Commander, they could all find themselves under arrest once more. Given how that worked out last time, Erik knew that he could not allow it.

Klinger nodded shortly. "Excuse me just one moment, Mr Debogande. I would invite you inside immediately, but first I have something else to attend to. My apologies."

He turned and went back inside. The door shut, the two guards standing firm before it. Trace glanced at her marines. They strolled back to the elevator, and took position by the second, further door. The guards looked nervous at that, but there wasn't much they could do. If you locked a group of marines in an enclosed room, they'd deploy aggressively to go explosively through those doors at the first sign of trouble, and kill everyone in sight. It was reflex, like what happened when you poked a venomous akrep with a stick and the claws and stinging tail deployed. One of the guards looked at Trace's impassive face, nervously. Erik couldn't believe anyone would be that stupid.

One of the guards received a signal, and opened the doors for them. Kono went in first with Terez and Van, then Trace behind. Erik followed, into a huge lounge with an oval, sunken middle about a central table. Beneath the table, shimmering light from the water display, and the flash of colourful fish. Beyond the far portholes, a slowly rotating view of open space — Heuron V's enormous red-brown girth, and the blinking lights of a passing runner.

A pretty female assistant greeted Kono with a disarming smile, and offered to take him on a security tour of the premises. Beyond them, coming into the room past the open bar and kitchen doorway, were other important looking men and women in suits.

Erik recognised several faces from his previous review of the local company board — these were all senior figures in Debogande Inc, Heuron branch. Trace recognised them too, and gave Kono a signal to accept the security tour. Any workable trap against a marine contingent would not place so many senior civvies in this proximity.

Introductions followed — there were seven company board members here, Erik suspected they'd all been waiting in the next room to see if it was safe to talk to the visiting Lieutenant Commander. All appeared various shades of nervous, and a wall display ran station news with the volume down, endless images of police action, protesting civilians and indignant talking heads.

Following introductions, all sat about the oval table in the room's central depression, Erik and Trace removing helmets, Trace placing her rifle carefully on the seat beside her, while Erik left his pistol holstered. The colourful fish beneath the false glass floor flittered and danced at the movement above them. Outside the porthole windows, night abruptly turned to day as Hoffen Station left the shadow of its moon. Several aides sat on the rim of the depression, watching portable displays, monitoring channels and ready to inform their VIP masters if something new and dramatic happened. Erik realised what this was — a crisis meeting. The local company arm was very alarmed, and hoped that he could shed some light on things... but did not wish to appear traitorous to Fleet in doing so.

"Mr Debogande," Klinger began, as tea arrived, and Kono reemerged from neighbouring rooms with an all-clear signal to Trace. "First of all, I'd hope that you could enlighten us all what the *hell* is going on?" Some smiles around the table at that, nervous energy escaping.

"Ah," said Erik, accepting tea and sipping. It was green tea, light and pleasant. "I was... *we* were, kind of hoping you could tell us. I mean, economically this is nuts, right?"

"Completely nuts," the older woman to Klinger's side agreed. "They're going to ruin us. We can't afford to lose that much Worlder investment, and we can't afford to lose all these workers. We spend the past few centuries accusing Worlders of thinking that money grows on trees, and now Fleet takes a very real chunk of that money, that we all need to keep the industry growing that provides all the money that Fleet needs to make ships and fight wars, and they flush it down the fucking disposal."

Her indignation was intense. Spacer industry always prided itself, relative to Worlder industry, on being left alone to do business. This was interference of the worst and highest order, and interference at gunpoint. It would make enemies not only of the Worlders it hurt, but the Spacers as well.

"Fleet aren't that stupid," a younger man insisted. "Supreme Commander Chankow is from an industry family himself. He's always been good on economic matters before, Chairmen Ali and Joseph too. If they've cooked this up between them, then they must have a plan of some kind..."

"Jorgensen," the older woman cut him off with a cynical shake of the head, "you have a very naive faith in the intelligence of our leaders..."

"They're not going to get us all killed!" Jorgensen retorted sternly. "Because those men know what's at stake, as much or more than anyone, they'll not just give all human industry a huge kick in the guts. They'll have something else planned!"

"Where?" retorted another man. "Where will they find these magical trillions? Like Tricia said we always lecture the Worlders, you can't just pluck that kind of money out of cold vacuum!"

"And so just give in to the Worlders?" someone else cut in. "They're a financial disaster, all of them! They'll have us bankrupt within a half-century if they're allowed to run human finances..."

"Whereas now," said Tricia, "we're bankrupt almost immediately."

"I think I know where the money's going to come from," said Erik. And said it again, when the ongoing argument drowned him out, to be shushed by others. Then silence, as everyone looked at him. Trace included, as he'd not shared this with her yet. He simply wasn't sure if it was feasible... but if there was ever an audience who could tell him if it was, it was this one.

"Please continue Mr Debogande," said Klinger.

"Um, first," said Erik with his best disarming smile, "if you wouldn't mind, it's Lieutenant Commander.   In uniform, 'Mister' just feels weird."   Usually he hated to pull rank on people, given his family, but the Captain had noticed his reluctance and warned him sternly against it.   'When meeting with powerful people about things that matter,' he'd said, 'never play yourself down.   It's unprofessional.'   Which from the Captain was serious criticism, and amongst these important civilians, 'Lieutenant Commander' of the famous *UFS Phoenix* went much further than 'Mr Debogande'.

"Of course," said Klinger.   "My mistake."

"Okay," said Erik.   "*Phoenix* has information, that we know to be accurate, about the actions of chah'nas ships in human space of late.   Particularly we know that a large force of them entered orbit about Merakis uncontested, and proceeded to execute... or let's call it murder... most of the tavalai still waiting there."

"Wait," said Klinger, frowning.   "How do you know this?"

"It's classified," said Erik.   "But completely reliable.   They destroyed the Temple of the Tenth Clan.   Wiped it out."   Big-eyed stares from around the table.   "There were no Fleet ships present to stop them.   Clearly a deal was done.   You all know the historic significance of Merakis and its temples to the chah'nas, and the tavalai.   Most species in fact aside from humans, given we're so recent in space.   And there has been some other chah'nas ship movement that I, and the Captain, consider suspiciously free from restraint.   Certainly very free from the kind of restraint most species place upon each other in sovereign territory.   Even allies in long wars.

"I suspect that somewhere, probably a century and a half ago or longer when the plan for the Triumvirate War was being hammered out, Fleet Command did a deal with the chah'nas."

"What kind of deal?" Tricia asked suspiciously.

"Shared sovereignty," said Erik.   "Theirs of our space, us of theirs.   Or something like it.   More than just trade — cross-investment, possibly even cross-habitation.   That's the only way I can see the investment shortfall being made back."

All looked astonished. Some looked horrified. "You mean we're about to be... fifteen percent owned by the *chah'nas?*" someone asked in disbelief.

"No no no, this doesn't work at all," said the one named Jorgensen. "Space assets are *strategic*. They're not just economic currency, they have political and military significance."

"I'm quite aware of that," Erik said drily.

"I mean *no one* shares strategic assets with alien species!" Jorgensen insisted. "Not just humans, no one in the Spiral! Not if they value their security, and... hell, why don't you tell *us,* Lieutenant Commander? Does anyone in Fleet truly trust the chah'nas that much?"

"Probably more than they trust the Worlders," Trace said calmly. "I've heard that said quite clearly, by people who meant it. I'm sure everyone else here has heard it also."

"It's the only thing that works," Erik insisted. "Money doesn't grow on trees, you're right. People make value, and currency measures it. The chah'nas have rather a lot of it, and no doubt the alo have even more, since they haven't actually had to spend that much on warships and fleets of their own. This way Fleet gets to put the Worlders back in their place, and force all Worlders who want to get influence in Spacer affairs to legally becomes Spacers first and abandon all Worlder benefits and affiliations. Spacers get to remain the sole human class with influence upon the grand affairs of humanity. The return is that we have to put up with direct interference in our affairs from the chah'nas, but we can balance that because presumably we'll now have direct interference in theirs'."

"It's actually damn clever," said Klinger. "If we get access to chah'nas space, and chah'nas industry. Imagine the opportunities."

"Wow," someone else added. Some of the disbelief began to fade, replaced by visions of vast awaiting fortunes.

"So why haven't they announced it yet?" Tricia said suspiciously. "Debogande Incorporated, and all the big Spacer conglomerates like us, are Fleet's greatest allies. Why get us all upset and doubting Fleet's intelligence? Why not just announce the whole deal first?"

"Well it looks suspicious," said Erik. "But then the Captain once told me 'never ascribe to malice what can be adequately explained by stupidity'." Some smiles from the executives. "Running this new empire we've acquired is difficult, every part is constantly moving under its own power and no part really knows what the other parts are doing until it's done. On the other hand, maybe inducing a bit of financial panic first is a good way to get everyone embracing the chah'nas with open arms when they come."

"God, can you imagine the futures markets?" someone said with awe. "Trading on chah'nas futures? Forecasting their results?"

"I've heard some crazy stories about their reserves, and the amount of tech they're still not sharing," said someone else. "If they were allowed to start investing *here,* in the kinds of sums we're talking about? I mean, we'd have to employ a whole other division of finance folks just to figure all the permutations…"

And they all started talking over each other with excited disbelief. Erik and Trace looked at each other. Trace smiled drily. "You're all missing the point," she said loudly. It cut through, and they turned to look at her. "You're all missing the point." More quietly, now they were all listening. "The Worlders, ninety percent of the human race, are about to become second class citizens in their own space."

"They already were," Klinger said bluntly. "Nothing's changed."

"Everything's changed," Trace corrected. "The war ended. Lots of Worlders told themselves they were only putting up with it because of the war. Once the war was finished, they'd stop putting up with Fleet kicking them in the balls, they'd take their place at the head of the table, finally. Now this.

"You all think you're going to make a lot of money from this, if the LC's correct. You may be right. I think you're also going to have to start spending a lot of that money on shooting our own people, because they're going to be pissed, and shooting at *you.*

354

They're already pissed.   Worlders are about to become *the tavalai*. During the Chah'nas Empire.   The second-class strugglers who did most of the work but were never allowed to make their own rules. And you know what the tavalai eventually did to the chah'nas."

"That's stretching it," one of the executives scoffed. "Worlders make all their own rules, on their worlds.   We don't tell them what to do down there, they shouldn't tell us what to do up here."

"We tell them to pay us six percent of everything they earn," Erik countered.   "That's not nothing."

"Aside from Fleet Tax, what they do down there barely affects us at all," said Trace.   "What we do up here could get all of them killed, or conscripted, or enslaved, or something else entirely. They may run planets, but Spacers run the empire.   And the empire just got a whole lot bigger, and a whole lot more dangerous."

"How could it be more dangerous?   The war's over."

Trace looked the speaker straight in the eye.   "That's what you think," she said grimly.

They stayed up and talked for a long time.   Dinner was served, then drinks, for executives, officers and enlisted alike. Somewhere in the middle of it, orders arrived on Erik's uplink — be at Supreme Commander Chankow's office, 0800 sharp.   Erik told Trace, and Trace said that in that case, she'd get some sleep.

The company quarters had three spare rooms for their *Phoenix* guests.   The marines organised a two-man nightwatch rotation, and pointedly informed their Major that it did *not* require her personal attention.   For once, Trace didn't argue the point.   Erik walked in on her now, sitting cross legged on the floor by the bed in her marine-issue underwear, eyes closed and utterly motionless, hair damp from the shower.

He walked softly past and into the bathroom, pondering that there was only one bed, a double, and damned if he was sleeping on the floor.   His father had raised him to be a gentleman on such things, but he'd start being a gentleman with Trace when she started being a lady. He was sure that everlasting peace would arrive in the galaxy first.

When he emerged from the shower, she hadn't moved a millimetre. He placed his boots by the bed, neatly lined up, and found a hanger for his jacket in the closet. Then the armour pieces had to be arranged on the floor for easy access if he needed to kit up in a hurry — he was nowhere near as fast at it as the marines, though he was sure Trace would help if needed...

"The left shoulder piece is a millimetre out of alignment," she said. He looked, and she still hadn't moved... but a corner of her mouth was twisted upward. "And if you're going to polish your boots before bed, could you do mine as well?"

Erik snorted. "Fuck you," he said, and got into bed. But he was smiling.

Ten minutes later he awoke as the mattress shifted. Trace was lying just opposite, her back turned. The sheet was not high, and he saw that she had tattoos, strange foreign symbols in a line down her spine. Or he assumed they went all the way down — he could see the top symbol above her singlet, and the bottom one at the base of her spine. An old Indian script, he thought. Kulina had their origins there, like many of the people, ethnically at least. One of those ethnic enclaves that had somehow survived two centuries of mixing, in the tight claustrophobia of humanity's living space following Earth's destruction, and had taken a liking to Sugauli and its rugged mountains following the krim's violent eviction.

Even with her back turned, he could see the hard muscle and power. Genetic enhancement meant Trace would have been athletic even before the combat augments that tripled the speed and power of her limbs. Add the micro-boosters that more than doubled the effect of exercise, and 'ripped' didn't begin to describe it. Erik didn't find it particularly attractive on a woman, but it was intriguing all the same. Where he'd grown up, pretty girls were soft. Trace was a pretty girl, yet she was soft like a freshly sharpened bayonet. Seeing that, at this range, changed the meaning of 'pretty'. And 'feminine', for that matter. His mother would have been appalled.

"We can't trust these people," said Trace. How she knew he was awake, he didn't know. Probably his breathing changed. He hoped he hadn't been snoring. "They're Spacer loyalists, ultimately. They'll be happy enough to see a partnership with the chah'nas, if it preserves Spacer dominance within humanity."

"And that's not our side?"

Trace rolled in bed and looked at him, face against the pillows. "You think it *is*?"

"No. I just think that you seem quite sure who is not our friend. Trace, I'm not even sure what side I'm on."

"We can't know whose side we're on because the divisions aren't all apparent yet," Trace said stubbornly. "But we can be damn sure who we're *against*, and that's all those at the top of Fleet Command who feel they can betray their oath to pursue their politics. *Whatever* their politics."

Erik sighed. Ran a hand over his face and rolled onto his back. It was easier than looking at her, at this range. She was too intense. And it was too odd, to see his legendary marine commander like this, in bed, and notably female in a way he'd managed to avoid truly noticing until now. "Trace, we're a renegade ship. We have no side. As its commanders, our first responsibility has to be the safety of our crew. How can we do that by continuing this fight?" He glanced at her.

"We bring them to justice," she said. "The ones who planned this. Fleet Admiral Anjo, if that's as far as it goes. Those above him if it goes that far."

"Justice for the Captain? We've seen far worse crimes committed here than just against the Captain. We've seen the murder of several thousand innocents — tavalai, for sure, but innocents all the same. We've seen the violation of human sovereignty in secret deals. We're seeing the subjugation of ninety percent of humanity in order to preserve the power of the dominant ten percent..."

Trace shook her head against the pillow. "I agree, but we can't spread ourselves that widely. We're just one ship. We expose what they did to the Captain, we let justice take care of the rest."

"You think they'll care?" He rolled his head to look at her. "Trace, the Captain was a known Worlder sympathiser. Fleet can make up stories. If those stories fit what people already want to believe, they'll believe it. What court will prosecute Fleet Admirals for the Captain's murder? A Fleet court-martial? What a joke. A Spacer civilian court? Fleet control those. A Worlder court? They have no jurisdiction."

Trace looked troubled. She did not have a ready reply. That was at once gratifying, that he could gain the upper hand in an argument against her, and frightening, because he relied so much upon her council. Except here, where he might be on his own.

"The Captain's murder was part of a larger war," he said. "How outraged people are by it will depend on which side they're on, not some abstract concept of justice. And even if we did bring some Admirals down, they'd just be replaced by others. Fleet is enormous, they've got no shortage of Admirals and wannabe Admirals."

"So what do we do?" she asked quietly.

He took a deep breath. "I don't know, Trace. I just... don't know." They lay in silence for a moment. Erik had not known the answers to things before. In those instances, his ignorance had not scared him particularly, because he'd known it was the ultimate responsibility of the smartest and wisest person he knew. Now it was all up to him, and that was both terrifying, and lonely beyond description.

"What do you believe?" she asked him. He frowned at her. "Why did you join Fleet? You could have stayed at home and enjoyed your riches. What motivated you to think you needed to risk your life out here? You personally, when millions of others could have done it?"

"You want the honest truth?" Because he didn't feel he'd been entirely honest with anyone about it, perhaps not even himself. But this seemed the time for honest truths. "I don't think it was concern for humanity. I mean, we've been winning clearly for fifty years. The only question was how much the tavalai were prepared to give up, and how much we were going to win by the final surrender. I think I came because I wanted to impress my parents. And because…" A deep breath. "And because when you grow up in a big, rich family where everything is given to you because you were lucky with your birth, you feel the need to have something that's yours. That you earned, and were not given. Or I did, anyhow. So I suppose it's ego. Self worth." He gave her a wry smile. "All the stuff you Kulina spend a lifetime beating out of yourself."

"Me too," Trace said simply. Erik blinked at her, astonished. "Oh we try to deny it. All Kulina do. But the more I think on it, the more inevitable the conclusion becomes. Even Kulina have ego. If you wish to live a quiet life, to exclude yourself from the events of the galaxy, to sit in a cave somewhere and meditate, then sure, you can probably divorce yourself of ego and desire.

"But Kulina *want.* It's unavoidable. We want to win. We want to achieve. And yes, we even want to survive, or at least for our comrades to survive. If you spend your life charging into gunfire, you have to want something out of it. I wanted to become Kulina, when I was a little girl. I wanted it so badly. And the instructors told me I should not want, and that became confusing. It's still confusing. So I suppose I'm a bundle of contradictions like everyone else.

"The question is *why* do we want it. And that's where I find my peace, as a good Kulina. I absolutely do not want a big house, fame and fortune. That's not ego talking, I'm quite sure — because some Kulina parade their lack of want around like a medal, as though it gives them pride, and makes them better than others. I just don't want it. Needless possessions give me anxiety. Fame is all garbage. Military fanboys and fangirls can't tell you who you are."

"Is it true you once locked a journalist in a toilet?" Erik asked.

Trace nodded. "Followed me in on a dock visit, while I was taking a pee. Tried to ask me questions from the neighbouring stall… this was just after I'd been awarded the Liberty Star. I slid out quietly without flushing so she didn't know I'd gone, then got the key from the janitor and locked her in. They stopped following me after that."

"How long was she stuck in there?"

"Don't know and don't care." Erik grinned. "The point, for me, is motivation. I love being Kulina. I love the idea that I matter. In this huge, endless expanse of a universe where countless beings live and die without notice — I matter. That's ego, there's no escaping it. But it doesn't bother me like it did, because the ego serves a greater selflessness. Humanity, and its protection and advancement. And I really have, I think. Objectively speaking."

"You have," Erik agreed. "Others might have done it also, but at a far greater cost. That, and winning formidable victories makes humanity look formidable, not just to present enemies but to possible future enemies. It all serves a purpose."

Trace nodded. "So there's no shame in doing this for ego. We all want self worth. If you save innocent lives because you want to feel good about yourself, well, innocent lives are still being saved. There's no shame in ego where ego is earned in a selfless cause. The question is, what is your cause?"

"Protect humanity," Erik said quietly. "Protect my family. Be one of *those* people. The ones who matter."

Trace nodded. "So. Look around you now. The Captain brought us here. He was one of those people who matter. What would he do?"

Erik gazed at her. Her intensity was catching. "The Spacer cause is corrupted," he said.

Trace nodded again. "Go on."

"They may be right that Worlders would make irresponsible leaders. They may even be right that humanity can't afford full democracy right now. But if they can only achieve their goals by murdering the likes of Captain Pantillo, and mortgaging humanity's future to chah'nas strategic interests, then they're taking humanity in an unacceptable and dangerous direction."

"And the Worlders?" Trace asked.   "Should we join with them instead?"

"The Captain was a Spacer.   He sympathised with Worlders, but he wasn't one of them.   I know Worlder politics, it's little better than Spacer politics.   I don't trust them either."

"So," said Trace.   "What's our role?"

Erik blinked at her.   "Fight for humanity," he said as it came to him.   "Be the one who stands up for everyone, not just some faction.   Don't be anyone's enemy, don't stand against this or that. Stand *for* something.   The entire species, whether they like it or not. And try to win as many people onto our side as will come, Spacer or Worlder, military or civilian."

Trace smiled at him.   "Now you're talking."

"I still don't know what that means, in terms of actual action."

Trace shook her head.   "Combat command rule number one; get the basics right.   You'll never be able to control the specifics in a fight anyway.   The number one basic is your objective, so get that right, and the details will fall into place."

Erik smiled back at her.   The responsibilities of the path before him were still frightening.   But it no longer looked so lonely.

CHAPTER 25

At 0645 Erik was woken by a blinking uplink icon on his retina. He opened his eyes and found Trace's side of the bed empty. But the uplink icon was for *Phoenix* command staff, so...

"Breakfast in the kitchen," came her voice in his inner ear. *"Get up, duty calls."* Which was the kind of thing she'd say to a junior officer known for late starts. Erik got up and dressed, wondering grumpily if she pressed his buttons on purpose, or if it was just a happy coincidence.

The kitchen was on the far side of the sunken lounge, and was guarded by Private Arime, still in light armour and kit but without the helmet. "Good morning Private," said Erik as he approached. "Get any sleep?"

Arime's reply was made unintelligible by a yawn. Erik smiled, entered the kitchen and found Trace there unarmored as he was, plain jacket and pants plus a pistol in the waist band. With her was an unshaven man, tall with an undercut around the sides, narrow face and suspicious eyes. Erik headed for the coffee machine with no more than a glance at the stranger.

"Coffee?" he asked them both.

"Don't drink it," said Trace. "You shouldn't either. Adjust your stimulant micros, Doc will tell you your response times will improve even on flight sims."

"Ever flown a starship?" Erik asked her, finding the loose grind and scooping. It smelt wonderful, a luxury you couldn't get on starships.

"No."

"Well let me tell you, neither self-flagellation, nor a bed of nails, nor coffee deprivation, helps me fly any better." Trace looked amused. "Going to tell me who your friend is?"

"That's probably not wise," said the man.

"Humour me," Erik insisted, pressing the button. The coffee machine burbled pleasantly. Erik turned.

"You can call him Linley," said Trace.   She was sipping some dreadful vegetable smoothie concoction that looked like minced caterpillars. "He's a journalist."

"What kind of journalist?"

"Newtown Investigator," said Linley.   Newtown was the biggest human city on Apilai, Erik knew.   "It's a newspaper.   I knew the Captain."

"Great," Erik said drily, with a glance at Trace.   "That's just great.   How'd he get in here?"   Which meant a bunch of things, mostly aimed at his marine commander.   Things like 'how'd you contact him?' and 'why didn't you tell me first?'... and others in that vein.   Though by now he was wondering if he should even bother. Journalists, in their present situation, were exactly what they didn't need.

"There's always unofficial ways in and out of big apartment quarters like this on stations," said Trace.   "You spend your life getting into firefights on stations, you learn the ins and outs."   And saw Erik's unimpressed expression.   "Linley was an army captain back when Fleet took Apilai.   Two month ground campaign, wasn't it?"

Linley nodded.   "The tavalai weren't much interested in fighting, but the sard left a couple of divisions on the surface to tie us down.   I was Army Intel, the biggest thing we had to deal with was resupply from the sard forces, which our Fleet couldn't always stop because they were spread too thin.   I talked to your Captain a few times about it, from orbit.   He remembered me.

"I came back after my term was up, set up in the colonial administration here for a while, getting the cities built.   That was a bit of a mess, like colonial administration always is — I took what I'd learned to the Newtown Investigator, had a good background to write about all kinds of stuff.   Got pretty involved in the local Congress, Apilai Congress has never been happy with lack of representation in Heuron Congress, but we put a lid on it because of the war.   Kind of."

Erik nodded.   Apilai Congress was the local Worlder Congress, Apilai being a Worlder population of 200 million plus.

Heuron Congress was the local Spacer Congress, representing maybe 30 million Spacers.

"Anyhow," Linley continued, leaning back on the kitchen bench. "About five years ago it got much worse. The war was ending, everyone could see it. There was a push... I still don't know who started it, but someone pushed to get Captain Pantillo to stand for Apilai in the Federal Worlder Congress, once the war ended. He got into talks with them — I understand he was talking with quite a few systems about the possibility — and that ambition changed to the Heuron seat in the Federal *Spacer* Congress."

Erik stared. The coffee machine's gurgling halted. Erik turned, and poured two cups. "You knew this Major?" Having his back turned forced her to say it aloud. He got some satisfaction from it, but only a little.

"Yes," she said. "He doesn't share it around." Present tense. Reminding him of the charade they had to maintain. "He wanted me to contact Linley. Couldn't tell you, the less people know the better."

'The man we talked about'. The message from the Captain's final recording. Was this him? This thin 'journalist'... what the hell kind of journalist kept secrets with a Fleet captain instead of writing them up for a story?

"Private Arime!" Erik called. "You take milk?"

Arime looked from the doorway in surprise. "Uh, yes sir." Erik poured, and took it to the grateful Private. "Thank you sir."

Erik returned, sipping his own. He looked at Trace without any particular accusation, just suspicion. She was unapologetic, as always. The Captain's message hadn't mentioned any particular system or destination. Trace had said she didn't know which man he'd meant — a lie, obviously. Had she helped steer them to Heuron? He couldn't recall her doing so, not even subtly... but then he supposed she didn't need to, if she'd thought they were obviously headed in this direction anyway. She was always first to know when he had an idea where they should go next — probably she'd wanted to come here immediately, but hadn't had to say so. Probably it had suited her to let him think *he'd* thought of it.

"Linley's got friends in Heuron Dawn," said Trace, meaningfully. "Lots of friends."

"Hmm," said Erik. A journalist who was a front for local Worlder extremists. But if rumours were correct, in Heuron they weren't so much extreme as mainstream. It made sense — Linley's military background, his administration connections, his current job in what was essentially a communications hub. A great place to hide in plain sight, for a Heuron Dawn organiser. "So basically we'd get shot for meeting with you. If they knew who you were."

"Oh they've some idea," Linley said grimly. "After the last few days I might have trouble staying out of prison. Be okay if I get back to the surface though, not many Spacer cops on Apilai." Of course not. On Apilai he could walk down Newtown main street unmolested. Down there, everyone was Worlder. Only up here it became a problem. The human race was becoming dangerously divided.

"The Captain bought them off," Trace continued. "They were going to get violent. It was going to spread to other systems. Apilai's the hub. Heuron is. It spreads a long way. But the Captain said he'd run for office once the war was over, in return for a promise they wouldn't resort to violence."

Oh dear god. "And let me guess," he growled. "Instead of supporting his effort to stop the violence, Fleet HQ called him a traitor." Trace nodded. Erik sipped coffee to smother a curse. And now the Captain was dead. If the local people found out... if their current *guest* found out...

Well. They would eventually. All hell would break loose, for sure. That was unavoidable at this point. The only question now was, how much could be done in the meantime?

"He'll want to know," Linley continued to Trace, urgently. "Stanislav Romki is here."

Trace's eyes widened slightly. "Where?"

"Crondike mining settlement, out on Faustino. I know the Captain wanted to speak to him again once he got the chance. Well, he's here now, there might not be another chance for a while."

"Who is Stanislav Romki?" Erik asked.

"He's a legend in xeno-sociology. Alien civilisations."

"Why haven't I heard of him?"

Linley smirked. "Because most of what he knows, he's not allowed to publish. It's classified — he works for Newtown University but he's funded by Fleet, and they censor everything. He doesn't have a choice but to accept their funding because Fleet blocks everyone else. He's not even allowed to give lectures or take students anymore, not for decades. Most of the academic community's forgotten about him, he's purely a security asset. Fleet's been trying to control him for years, but he goes rogue, wanders off, spends time with our 'enemies' and friends alike. Fleet love his research but are scared it'll give us poor, weak-minded civilians the 'wrong idea' about our allies or something. Tried to recruit him into Fleet Intelligence or some other Intel branch, offered him heaps of money... Romki always turns them down."

It was hardly Erik's area of knowledge, but it sounded all too plausible.

"The Captain's unable to leave the ship," said Trace. "I'll have to go. And right now."

Erik rode with Trace and Command Squad down the elevator on security override to outer rim dock. The time showed Erik only half an hour until his appointment with Supreme Commander Chankow. If Lieutenant Commander Debogande had a reputation for anything besides his famous name, it was for being immaculate and punctual. Being late to meet the senior commander of all human forces would be a good way to smash a few preconceptions, at least.

"So is Linley the guy the Captain spoke of?" asked Erik. "Or is Romki?"

"Either," said Trace. "Could be various people in Heuron. That was what he meant. Get to Heuron. Via Merakis."

"Could have told me," Erik suggested.   Trace gave him a look. 'You really want to have this discussion in front of Command Squad?' that look asked.

"Could have," Trace agreed.   "Didn't need to.   You were coming here anyway.   I'm the only person he ever really talked to with this stuff.   That habit's hard to break, and people in spacer crew were trying to kill you."

And she hadn't trusted him enough at the time to be entirely certain he wouldn't let something slip.   It was a fight once again not to take that personally, but a fight he was getting used to.   She'd known, ever since the Captain's death, that it meant Heuron was about to blow up, and that blow up would spread.   She'd been holding that in, all this time.   And not wanting to let it out for fear of what various people on *Phoenix*, with all their conflicting loyalties, might do with the information.

Erik decided he was tired of being angry with her.   And being hurt and betrayed at her lack of trust only made him feel like a child.   She was the big cheese in this relationship — he just flew the damn carrier, and it made him an irreplaceable skillset for her, the one vital thing she couldn't do herself.   The Captain had confided in her as he'd done with no one else on *Phoenix*, and that had been a huge burden for her.   He'd done so, it was obvious, because he knew it was a burden she alone could bear, even with him gone.

Erik nudged her on the shoulder armour.   "Pretty hard thing. Saving the galaxy all alone."

She glanced at him, and saw his wry smile.   And just for a moment, her defences dropped, as she realised she wasn't having to fight him again.   She smiled back, with the faintest touch of emotion.   "Nah," she said.   "Never really alone, see?"   Alongside in the elevator, Staff Sergeant Kono smiled.

The elevator stopped and the doors opened onto a wide steel floor, a small crowd of locals standing aside to let them off.   Down here everything was less glamorous, with low steel overheads, big exposed pipes and rows of cheap fluorescent lights.   Nearby generators hummed and the artificial breeze felt alternately hot and cold as they passed side passages off from the main dock.   A big, oval-shaped bulkhead through the floor announced each lower-rim dock, with lighted display boards announcing the berth number and the ship present — only small down here, shuttles with power enough to dock with the rotating outer rim, big atmospheric shuttles could do it, heavier insystemers or underpowered runners could not.

They filed through the crowds, watching and being watched by station techs, uniformed admin, bored passengers glancing at displays for departure times, and new arrivals clutching bags and looking around. Some grey uniformed station cops made way for the *Phoenix* crew with polite nods.

"*This is PH-1, now on final, ETA forty seconds. Berth G40, see you there.*"

"PH-1, Command Squad copies," Trace replied. "We're at G36, expect a two minute turn around for immediate departure."

"*PH-1 copies Major.*"

"Bet he scared a few people getting here so quick," said Kono.

"Hausler's the fastest shuttle pilot in Fleet," Van agreed.

They reached Berth G40 just as Lieutenant Dale and Alpha First Squad were coming up the stairs from below, flashing Fleet IDs at the doorway scanner. "Escort the LC to Supreme Commander Chankow's office immediately or he'll be late," Trace told Dale. "In Faustino's current position I'll only be a six hour trip to get there, I'll report back as soon as I've something to say. Expect *anything*. Trust no one. We've no dog in this fight between Worlders and Spacers and I don't trust Heuron Worlders anymore than I trust Supreme Commander Chankow."

"Aye Major," Dale agreed, and Trace descended the stairs past the last of Alpha First Squad on the way up, without a backward glance or a goodbye. Erik knew that shouldn't have bothered him, but it did. He *wasn't* feeling anything for her beyond any other female friend on *Phoenix*, he was pretty sure, whatever their recent night in the same bed. It was more that he ran on emotions in a way that she apparently didn't, or at least liked to pretend she didn't. He liked to feel close to the people he relied upon, and to know that they felt the same way back. This whole situation was fraught, and a final glance back, a little smile or simple eye contact, would have made all the difference. But then she was gone, and Command Squad with her.

"Rail's this way," said Erik, pointing down a cross passage, and Sergeant Forest led the way. Another squad to adjust to, Dale's boys and girls and as devoted to him as Command Squad were to their Major. "Fast ride down?" Erik remarked as they walked, Dale directly ahead, imposing in light armour and gear.

"Fucking Hausler flies like you do," said Dale. "Don't suppose we could up-skill him to backup for your seat?"

"Ideally it takes a year," said Erik. "Hard thing to learn, no shortcuts. How's *Phoenix*?"

"No place like home, sir." Meaning no troubles worth reciting here. Which was comforting, but Dale was a marine, and the things that bothered marines on *Phoenix* were not what currently bothered their LC. "Second Lieutenant Geish wanted me to tell you there's two new chah'nas ships insystem. Just jumped in, both Kulik Class, real high spectrum jump wave. Didn't want to tell you over coms, given who might be listening."

Damn right, Erik thought — *Phoenix* could easily talk to all *Phoenix* crew through station coms, but that would use Fleet encryption, meaning it would be indecipherable to everyone except Fleet Command. Who would be interested to know why newly arriving chah'nas ships worried them.

"Chah'nas aren't fast enough to be a worry," he said. They couldn't get here that fast with a message from Homeworld, that meant. "Probably."

"Probably," Dale muttered. "Aye to that."

They turned a corner into the transit station platform. Another flash of IDs at the scanner — Fleet rode free, of course. Back on Homeworld, Erik could have expected another dry observation from Dale about the mess Erik had gotten them into. He'd only been functional third-in-command back then, technically little higher in rank than Dale... and marines had a habit of not respecting many spacer ranks other than captain.

"I think we'll know as soon as we get there if it's a trap," Dale said on uplinks. *"Combat command can lay traps, I don't think these HQ bureaucrats could lay a convincing trap if their lives depended on it. And I don't think the bigwigs have the balls to make themselves a part of that trap."*

The rail was like mass transit anywhere, crowded coaches giving the armed marines cautious looks. At Red Sector Four they got off and caught the platform elevator to dock level, then a fast walk along a stretch of dock crawling with uniformed Fleet, spacers and marines both. With helmets on, Erik and Dale received salutes as they walked, and returned all — the station dock counted as 'outdoors' for formal purposes, where respect to rank would be given and received. A big open windowfront with multiple security checkpoints announced Hoffen Fleet HQ, and the security post let Erik and Dale through with a scan of each ID. They removed helmets, and walked across a wide, carpeted floor to a check-in desk, where a pretty Ensign gave Erik a big smile as he announced himself.

"Lieutenant Commander Debogande, you're three minutes early. If you'd like to just take a seat, I'll contact the Supreme Commander's office to let him know you've arrived. I'm afraid your marines will have to wait on the dock. Lieutenant, if you would announce yourself to the watch officer, I'm sure he'll be pleased to have the extra numbers on guard for the time that you're here."

Dale looked at Erik. And looked around, at the surrounding, open offices, the reception desks, the display screens, all busy and normal. Raised his eyebrows, meaningfully. No trap, that meant... or not that he could see. Dale returned outside, and Erik took a seat in the lobby, trying to repress the instinct to look around like a nervous herbivore in a carnivore jungle. Just in case someone was watching. Which someone probably was. Dale didn't think the bureaucracy could just keep functioning if some kind of kinetic action were planned. It was a marine's contempt for bureaucrats — bureaucracy was all they were good at, and if someone were about to start shooting, their nerves would show. Erik shared that prejudice, but didn't trust it. It didn't seem wise to just assume safety because you didn't respect the people who most immediately threatened you. Not long ago, Dale hadn't respected *him* much either.

There were displays on the walls — the squadron pennants of the Fleet formations that had fought for Heuron's 'liberation'... a euphemism of course, as Heuron had not been liberated but taken from the tavalai. Alongside the pennants, old-fashioned photographic stills of the Captains of those ships. Erik recognised several faces. Then his eyes settled upon Captain Pantillo. Not so old a man then, nearly ninety by Erik's reckoning, and looking decidedly younger than when Erik had known him. It was an informal image, caught at an unguarded moment on dock, as the Captain had turned to exchange a laugh with someone. That half-smile was just dawning on his face, and his jaw was unshaven, as though he'd just come off a long shift.

Erik recalled his surprise and alarm upon his first posting to *Phoenix*, discovering that neither the Captain, nor the ship, shared quite his degree of interest in presentation. The Captain's ops jacket was an antique, worn, scratched and repaired so many times it belonged in a museum... but he wore it with pride. And neither would the Captain allow others on the ship to make fun of their new LC to his face, and his insistence on polishing, aligning and brushing everything within reach. People were what they were, in the Captain's eyes, and while all may present differently, the quality beneath could come in all shades and styles. Erik had never known anyone who could discern that quality like the Captain had, and with care and attention, make it bloom.

Sitting in the waiting room, amidst passing staffer traffic and watchful guards, his eyes hurt, and he swallowed hard against the lump in his throat. You brought us here, Captain. I'm sure in my place, you'd get the job done, and everyone out of here safe. Let's just hope I'm as good at this as you seemed to think I am.

His uplink blinked and he looked up to see the pretty Ensign waving to him from the reception desk. "Sir, if you'll follow me?"

She led him through a security door, then down a corridor with offices everywhere, and the big air vents in the walls that were constant on stations.   Then a series of command rooms, with transparent walls and large displays showing Heuron system graphics — current planetary and lunar positions, ship movements. Concerned and serious officers stood and talked, or discussed on conference calls, watching ongoing intercepts in the near or outer system, or other actions on other stations.

It looked busy.   Given the sheer number of stations and facilities in the broader Heuron system, Erik didn't like their chances of achieving more than basic stasis in the security situation. 'Linley', or whatever his real name, was evidently still moving around okay, whatever his admissions that someone would likely try to arrest him.   No doubt there were plenty of others — Heuron Dawn affiliated or sympathetic.   God knew what they'd set up over the past few years of building tension, for release in a situation like this one.   Like finding out that the overly-decorated war hero who they'd thought would run for election in the Heuron seat for Federal Spacer Congress, and recommend their cause at the highest level, was now dead.

It occurred to him for the first time, walking these corridors, that the Heuron System Worlders would *not* automatically assume that Fleet's tale was correct.   No one on Apilai would believe that Lieutenant Commander Debogande had murdered his Captain — they'd all assume the opposite, that Fleet had murdered him, and framed *Phoenix*'s LC to kill two birds with one stone.   Worlder sympathisers everywhere would lean toward the same telling — most of humanity, in fact, when you added the raw numbers.   It was comforting, on the one hand, to know that so many humans would probably believe him innocent.   It would put huge pressure on Fleet as they tried to maintain their lies with a straight face.   Worlders might even make him into a hero if they could, lionise him for standing up to Fleet.   And yet, he remained far from convinced that he wanted to be on the Worlders' side.

The Ensign led him to some big doors off a wide, polished hall, scanned in her ID, then gestured Erik to enter as the door hummed open.   Within was a large office, displays on the walls all deactivated, and two big porthole views of the slowly rotating starfield outside.   Behind the table, Supreme Commander Chankow himself — broad, moustachioed, hair unnaturally dark for even the healthiest of older men.   About the same age as the Captain had been, Erik recalled, walking to the desk directly opposite the Supreme Commander and standing to attention, helmet under his right arm.   He'd been a carrier captain for ten years, followed by rapid promotion up the ranks of High Command.   Pantillo had no doubts of his abilities, and rarely spoke ill of higher ranks in front of lower ranks.   But if he had something good to say about a higher rank, based on personal experience, he'd never hesitate to offer it. Erik could not recall him ever saying anything good of Chankow.

"Lieutenant Commander Erik Debogande, *UFS Phoenix*, reporting as ordered sir."   To either side of Chankow, also seated, were two more bigwigs — both Rear Admirals.   The nametags read Ling and Iago.   Erik recognised neither — Rear Admirals in big HQ centres were like middle management in big corporations. Everyone had more than they knew what to do with, and no one knew what they were for.   Elsewhere about the room, four marines, all armed in light kit, helmets replaced with caps.   Guards, all enlisted, no officers.   That was odd.

"Lieutenant Commander," said Chankow.   "Please sit." Erik did so.   Chankow considered him for a moment.   Serious, but was there a faint trace of amusement beneath those dark brows. Erik's heart, which had been quite controlled, now began to thump unpleasantly.   "First of all, let's do away with this charade.   We know all about what happened on Homeworld.   Your Captain is dead.   You killed him.   You then violently escaped from lawful Fleet detention, killing another ten service personnel in the process, escaped to your warship, then ran from Homeworld System firing upon and damaging the warship *UFS Annalea*, thankfully with no further casualties."

The shock was like diving into freezing cold water.   But even as it hit him, Erik felt something else.   Hatred, pride, defiance... he wasn't sure what.   Only that if these men thought he was going to go down easy, they were about to learn differently.

"We have no record of your ship's activities after leaving Homeworld," Chankow continued. "I can only hope you haven't murdered more of your comrades in arms, from your ship or others. You've got quite the balls coming here in your very fast ship. But you don't have quite the monopoly on very fast ships that you thought you did."

Alo, Erik thought. It had to be the alo. He recalled the alo ambassador confronting them on the dock yesterday. Only alo ships could match *Phoenix* for speed — there must have been one at Homeworld that knew of the situation at Heuron, and came straight here. But what was the alo's stake in this? Were they invested with the chah'nas power-grab in human space? To what ends?

"And please, don't even think about making some stupid move for your weapon," Chankow continued. He nodded to one of the room's marines. "This here is Master Sergeant Afraz, off the combat carrier *Mercury*." No surprise there, thought Erik, recalling the *Mercury*'s Captain confronting them up at hub dock. "He's one of the best shots in the Fleet, and he'll see you dead before you unholster your weapon."

"I have no doubt," said Erik, with a respectful nod to Afraz. The veteran warrior's stare was impassive beneath his cap brim, his rifle easily in hand, ready to rise and fire in a split second. "But you're not the only one with marines, Commander. I did not violently escape from Fleet custody on Homeworld as you state — I'm not that good a soldier. That was Major Trace Thakur, Distinguished Service Star, Legion Medal, three Valorous Hearts, multiple Campaign Medals, Diamond Star and Liberty Star... and hear this, Master Sergeant," as Chankow opened his mouth as though to interrupt, "and tell this to every marine on *Mercury* and beyond — I was not the one who started shooting, she was. I was going to let the legal process play out, but she saw that Fleet HQ had stitched us up, had murdered her Captain and framed me with it, and she busted me out single handed. Find the security footage from those holding cells, that will confirm it."

"This is *not* a court room in which to argue your case!" Chankow barked. "You will drop this pretence at once!"

"Fuck you, you snivelling piece of shit," Erik snarled. "You want me to drop this pretence? Very well, let's drop it. Fleet Command murdered my Captain. That means you. I mean to see you killed. Make a move against me, or against *Phoenix* or any of my people, and they'll put a warhead through this portion of station rim and vacate it to space."

Deathly silence in the room. "You're a traitor!" exclaimed Rear Admiral Iago.

"I'm not the one who murdered Fleet's greatest hero in cold blood," said Erik. "For *politics*. Furthermore, you've made an enemy of one of the heirs to one of the greatest industrial empires in human space. You have *no idea* the shit you're about to be dropped in. I know for a fact there are senior Fleet captains on our side, they've told us so. Captains with powerful friends. Watch your backs, boys. Major Thakur told me all about karma, and you're about to get yours."

It was lies and bluster, but it seemed to have an effect. And there may well have been captains on *Phoenix*'s side, or about to be, given the chance — captains like Captain Lubeck of *UFS Chester* in Argitori who'd caused trouble by querying *Abigail,* trying to find out what the hell was going on in defiance of orders. And if the admirals thought that having marines in the room was a good idea… well, let the tales about Major Thakur spread through their ranks for a few weeks and months, and watch these bastards sweat, and watch their own marines nervously. Now he just had to live long enough to see that happen.

Chankow smiled humourlessly. "Erik," he said. First name, as though speaking to a child. A calculated insult. "Where do you think you'll go?" Erik said nothing. He wasn't about to give Chankow clues. "Firstly, you're nothing like the pilot and captain that Pantillo was. What chance do you think you'll have now? With our entire Fleet chasing you?"

"You think you can trust all your captains to chase me? Good luck."

Chankow snorted. "You think everyone loved Pantillo as much as you? Half of Fleet thought him a meddling fool. Fleet captains follow orders, but Pantillo? No boy, your Captain took liberties. He reinterpreted orders to suit himself and his crew, often he skipped orders he didn't like entirely. Only this... crazy media-inflamed status, this 'hero of the fleet' nonsense kept him from being busted back down to Lieutenant, or worse."

"I know you've got your cronies," Erik said coldly. "They're not the ones you should worry about. Plenty did like him, and if you keep all of them away from chasing me, they'll notice, and gossip and whisper behind your back. If you're going to chase me, you better catch me quick, because I'll spread the word about what you've done, and the longer you leave it, the more it will spread."

They couldn't take *Phoenix* here, Erik reckoned, thinking furiously. Shooting at a combat carrier with anything big enough to damage it meant a weapons lock first. *Phoenix* would sense it and fire back, leading to mayhem. Such engagements would certainly damage station and take collateral lives. And they had no way of knowing that his bluster about *Phoenix* being instructed to fire on this Fleet HQ section of the rim *was* bluster.

They could kill him here and *Phoenix* wouldn't know about it for a while at least... but if they couldn't take *Phoenix* quietly, it wouldn't advance their position. Boarding *Phoenix* by force was impossible. It would have to be from the dock, since assault shuttles would be quickly killed by close range defence, and good luck getting through *Phoenix*'s marines, with or without their Major. This here was a standoff.

"You haven't thought this through," said Chankow. "You speak of your family as though they're an asset to you. You don't understand the stakes here at all. Your mother is not the only voice that matters in the family company. She couldn't risk it all to save you even if she wanted to. She has a multitude of board members, executives, shareholders. They can overrule her if they have to. Most of that business comes through Fleet at some point. I can assure you boy, we have much more power over her than she has over us."

Erik smiled. "You think you can lecture me about my own mother? You have no idea how she operates. She doesn't posture and shout. If she moved against you in any way, you'd never know about it. And don't think for a second you can threaten me with my family's safety. They're better protected than you are, especially now."

"And yet," Chankow said drily, gesturing to the room. "Well protected as I am, here you sit. Sworn to kill me. Face to face. Things happen, Mr Debogande. To anyone."

Trace, Erik thought. Currently on PH-1, flying out to Faustino. He leaned forward. "Let me tell you what will happen if you put an intercept on Major Thakur, or shoot her down. Firstly, *Phoenix* marines will storm this station and kill you. Secondly, *Mercury* marines, perhaps even Master Sergeant Afraz here, will let them."

He looked pointedly at Afraz. Afraz's expression had changed, from hard purpose to a concerned frown. Thinking on it. And by no means denying the possibility. Seeing it, Erik felt his confidence soar. He'd only speculated before, how other marines would react to Trace's involvement. Now he saw it with his own eyes.

The Supreme Commander saw it too, then pointedly ignored it. But when he spoke again, he spoke a little too fast. "Major Thakur will be unmolested for now. As will you, and as will your ship. At least allow your objecting crew to deboard, if you will not see reason. Surely you have heart enough for that."

"I have no objecting crew," Erik retorted. He disliked this lie more than the others. Some lies were tactical, but this lie felt dishonourable.

"The Major is on her way to Faustino," said Chankow, eyes narrowed. "Why?" He didn't know about Stanislav Romki, Erik thought.

"Tell me," he said to change the subject. "Now that you've sold out the human race's security to chah'nas interests, will you send chah'nas after us too?" Chankow glared at him. Perhaps he'd expected a scared and spoiled young brat. Clearly he hadn't expected *this*. "When did you think to tell everyone? You've been sitting on this deal for over a century, haven't you? When did you agree to let them clean out Merakis for you? A world that *we* won, with *our* blood? What do they get next? Your balls in a jar? Liberties with your wife?"

Chankow got out of his chair and leaned on the table, his face like thunder. "You listen to me you pipsqueak," he said with menace. "You have no idea what you're playing with. This galaxy we've inherited is *nothing* like you've imagined, and if you threaten the plans we've made to keep humanity safe, forces beyond your dreams will crush everything in their path to get you and everyone you hold dear. Do you understand me?"

Erik got to his feet. "Perfectly, Commander." He turned his attention to Afraz. "Master Sergeant. I don't know if you've ever met Major Thakur. If not, ask after those who have. Ask them how likely it is that she's been led astray by some junior command officer with a rich family."

"That will be all, Mr Debogande!" Chankow insisted.

"Ask them how likely it is that she's lying," Erik continued. "Ask them if she's ever done anything for personal advantage, or served any cause but the human cause. And don't let these jumped up, spineless brass hats intimidate you into not asking more questions. And if you *do* ask more questions, watch your back. If they can murder my Captain, and thirty *Phoenix* crew at Homeworld, they won't stop at marine Master Sergeants."

He turned his back on them, opened the door, and left. And walked down the hallway outside, half expecting an alarm, or a crash tackle, or a thunder of running boots, but nothing came. He'd never before thought it good to be underestimated, but on this occasion it might have saved his life... and other lives besides. Now to get back to Lieutenant Dale, and hope like hell that someone didn't change their mind and blow Trace out of the sky.

CHAPTER 26

At any other orbital period, Faustino could have been up to a three day trip. But they were lucky, Faustino was on the near side of Heuron V, and at a constant 2-G acceleration and turnover, PH-1 was going to make it in just under six hours. It was a heck of a long time to run a shuttle's engines, and lying still for anything over an hour at even 2-G was difficult. At turnover, their speed was getting dangerously fast for a sub-light insystem run, and various vessels gave them non-verbal com-squawks, the sub-light version of two cars on a long distance highway flashing lights to warn of hazard. In this case, the hazard was them, but no one was going to reprimand one of *UFS Phoenix*'s shuttles verbally for violating lane regs.

Barely an hour out, *Phoenix* gave them a com burst of their own — no message, just a tight-beam alarm that suggested nothing good. Someone was listening, that meant. If they were listening so closely that they'd break *Phoenix* encryption, it meant HQ were onto them. Trace thought about it as she lay strapped to the seat, subconsciously flexing one muscle group after another against the ongoing strain. If HQ were onto them, it could only mean Erik was wrong, and word from Homeworld had beaten them here. That HQ hadn't shot them out of the sky suggested... well. She didn't know, and shouldn't jump to conclusions.

"Hausler," she said, putting both arms up, working the muscles against their double-weight. "Any Fleet ships heading for Faustino?" She could see PH-1's scan feed on her visor, but the pilots up front could see a lot more.

"Major, there's just the five civvie ships inbound," Ensign Yun answered for her pilot. As frontseater, she ran scan and weapons directly. *"You think it's a trap?"*

"I always think it's a trap. That's why I'm still alive."

"Supreme Commander Chankow has an appearance problem," said Hiro Uno. Lisbeth's ex-Intel bodyguard had joined PH-1 before departure, along with Second Section of Alpha's Second Squad — Lance Corporal Walker plus three more marines, giving them an even dozen including Trace. Hiro made thirteen, dressed only in civvies with a Phoenix jacket and whatever gear he'd brought from Homeworld. "If he's onto us, the only reason he hasn't moved is appearances. He can't share that information with many other people. If he moves against you Major, without a damn good reason, he could risk a mutiny of his own marines. And he can't let them in on that information."

"Why not?" asked Staff Sergeant Kono.

"Because the only ship that could get here that fast from Homeworld is an alo ship," said Hiro, his voice a little more strained against the Gs than the marines. "That implies a much closer working relationship between Fleet HQ and the alo than anyone knows. Alo don't run errands for anyone, not even Supreme Commander Chankow. Revealing the information also reveals the source."

Which was the kind of thing a spy would know, Trace thought. "You operated in Heuron before, Hiro?" she asked him.

"Yes. It's a ticking bomb."

"That might have been nice to know before we came here," Kono growled.

"A ticking bomb set to blow in about ten years," Hiro added. "We thought. We were wrong."

"If you've anything else to tell us that you haven't yet," Trace added. "Now would be the time."

"Fleet have had contingencies in case of Worlder uprisings for the past three decades at least," said Hiro. "What we're seeing here isn't rushed. But non-Fleet intelligence has told Fleet that they're not the only ones with contingencies."

"What did Fleet say to that?"

"They didn't listen. Fleet have their own Intel, they didn't trust us much. One reason why I left — Federal Intel is a dead end, no access to anything that matters. Fleet kept a lid on us."

"What do you expect to see happen here?"

"To judge from what your journalist friend told you? Could be nasty. I hope Fleet have fully inspected every non-Fleet vessel attached to all the stations. Wouldn't want a nuke to go off."

Silence in the shuttle, save the howl of engines and the rattle of restraints and armour. "That would be interesting," Kono deadpanned. "Faustino might actually be safer right now."

Soon Trace didn't need magnification to see Faustino clearly — a straight rear feed showed it huge and getting huger at an alarming speed, dull silver in the light of a distant sun. PH-1's engines roared and shook in their target's direction, blurring the visual with thrust, decelerating them down from a velocity that would have made a thermo-nuclear sized impact at its peak. It was the thing that Worlder civvies and new marines struggled to get their heads around about combat in space — velocity was energy, and velocity ate up distance at an exponentially accumulative rate. Warships put explosive heads in most ammunition only so armscomp could terminate misguided rounds — for killing targets the explosive was redundant, it was velocity that killed the target irrespective of armour. If your engines cut out at peak velocity in a 2-G push, after three hours of constant acceleration, *you* became the ammunition, travelling at speeds to give rifle bullets nightmares.

A quarter-orbit descent showed them various bases and settlements across the moon's broken ice-crust, lights gleaming far below. Hausler received clearance from a wary-sounding Crondike traffic controller, still approaching backward to wipe off the excess V. Doubtless some bureaucrats down there were already writing up the complaint to Fleet HQ about hotshot shuttle pilots. They were only five klicks out when Hausler finally turned them around, never having deviated from the 2-G decel, and let Faustino's low gravity arc them down toward the settlement ahead.

Crondike was a circular sprawl across the ice, like a dark island upon a fractured, silver sea. Somewhere beneath it, mining shafts descended to vast mineral deposits below. Buildings were low, squat and unglamorous, all pressurised and insulated against the airless cold. Landing lights blinked upon the periphery pads, and Hausler descended toward one, engines lightly humming in low-thrust relief after their long effort. Some big gas haulers sat upon neighbouring pads, bulbous tanks full from a maze of pressurised pipes and tanks beside them. Small bus shuttles arrived at a nearby pad, underside thrusters glowing faintly, all they needed for lift to carry passengers from one base across the frozen lunar surface to another.

They touched, feather light, and rolled to where pad workers were unhurriedly extending a docking arm to touch the dorsal port. *"Thank you for flying Phoenix Air,"* said Hausler. *"I know I can speak for all of my crew when I say that it has been an absolute contractual obligation to fly you here today, and I look forward to setting my ass on fire with you all again in the near future."*

"Jeez, can these pad guys work any slower?" his co-pilot wondered. *"Are they getting paid by the hour or what?"*

"Nice job guys," Trace told them. "Do me a favour and stay with the ship. Get some gas and stay alert."

"What, you mean we don't get to go and take in the stunning attractions of Crondike? 'Cause it looks like a peach."

When the access arm made a seal they climbed the dorsal hatch, then walked at a low crouch along the dingy, fluro-lit tube until they reached Embarkment. It was utilitarian like mining settlements everywhere, some pad workers operating the arm and peering out portholes, talking on coms. Beyond were offices, where bored workers paid little attention to comings and goings.

At the base of the steps from the tube stood an impatient woman in a working jumpsuit, red customs tabs on her shoulders. Beyond her, about twenty civvies with recording devices, and a few with notepads. About half were kids. Trace very rarely suffered outbursts of any kind, but she had to repress a bad word beneath her breath. It looked like a fanclub.

"Hello Staff Sergeant," said the customs woman to Kono as he lead the way. "Are you in charge here? I just need all your IDs for the log, if you wouldn't mind... thanks." As Kono flashed his on the reader. "Thank you Staff Sergeant Kono, thank you Private Kumar, thank you Private Arime." As they checked through one at a time. "Thank you Major..." and the customs lady's eyes bugged a little. "Major Thakur! Thank you very much!"

Gasps from the gathered fan club, who clustered not too close, recording devices activated and angling for a shot of Trace's face as she passed.   "Major Thakur!" called a couple of the kids. "Major Thakur!" As though hoping she'd wave and smile. If Trace resented anything about her Liberty Star, it was the celebrity that went with it. War was not a game show, and she absolutely refused to go along with this lunacy on any level.

And yet, in this situation, her celebrity could be an enormous help, eventually.   Marines weren't the only ones who would doubt Fleet's story about the Captain and the LC, with her standing against it.   It also made her an enormous inconvenience for Fleet.   Surely they'd like that inconvenience removed at the earliest.   But doing it in public would be problematic for them.

"Thank you Mr Toshi," said the customs lady as Hiro passed through, and Trace waited with the gathering group forming a ring to keep the fan club at bay.   A couple of the kids jumped to see more clearly — in the one-fifth-G they sailed nearly up to the ceiling.   A couple of her marines smiled. Trace did not. She beckoned Hiro to walk at her side, and they skipped lightly down the wide-spaced stairs, letting gravity sail them gently down.

"Nice inconspicuous entrance?" Hiro ventured.

"Manifest and flightplan security on mining bases is shit," said Trace.   "All the civvies hack it, see who's coming in.   Famous ships get a crowd."

Hiro nodded.   "Lucky they didn't know it was actually you — we'd have a hundred here. All these kids shouldn't be in low G."

"Local holiday," said Trace.   "They're down from the heavy station to see family."   Because Spacer kids had to spend a medically-mandated 96 percent of their time in full gravity. Anything down to 90 percent could be fixed, medically, but it was risky and expensive.   Less than 90 percent and kids got brittle bones, malformed heart and organs, all kinds of nastiness.   Every Spacer kid wore a 'heavy tab' somewhere that wouldn't come off, often a ring or bracelet, that recorded gravity levels at every moment and alerted someone if they weren't getting enough.   Station kids loved to mess around in the hub when parents and guardians weren't looking, and often got much less G than adults thought they were getting.   Twenty-percent-G here on Faustino wasn't technically any healthier than zero-G for kids over long periods, and bases like Crondike were usually child-free. Station rims on the other hand were often crowded with boarding schools, where parents from bases like this one would send their kids for medical and educational purposes equally.

The main walk through arrivals had a tall ceiling and some shops along one wall. Regular portholes overlooked pads to the right — spacesuited workers and runabout vehicles, various inspectors and machinery operators. Along the walk, passengers, crews, a lot of pads personnel, a few security. It always looked comical to the unaccustomed, because everyone skipped instead of walking — it was the far faster form of movement, with long, easy bounces along the corridor. Accidental collisions were common, as you couldn't change direction in mid-air if you saw you'd made a mistake. Carrying sharp objects in the transit halls was strictly prohibited.

"Who is Mr Toshi?" Trace asked Hiro as they bounced. The customs lady had read that name off his ID when he'd checked in.

"Debogande Inc employee," said Hiro, moving as well in micro-G as any well-travelled marine. "Performance Inspector, I made him up. He's a pretty nifty guy though, gets lots of places, high security clearance."

"I can imagine. You'd like to get a few places in here?"

Hiro nodded. "Crondike security aren't much worry, but Fleet have got others for emergency contingencies. Be nice to check it out while you're finding Mr Romki."

"Absolutely," Trace agreed. "Do your thing, just keep in touch." Hiro nodded, then skipped easily left and bounced off a wall down an adjoining corridor like a guy who'd spent quite a bit of time in this gravity. A well-travelled man indeed.

"You trust him?" Kono asked, taking Hiro's place at her side.

"Not yet. But the Debogande family has a habit of making all their inner circle feel like part of the family. It's not just a paycheque for guys like him, it's personal. I'm pretty sure he'd take a bullet for Lisbeth."

"Lisbeth's not here," Kono said dourly.

"We'll see," said Trace.

Erik walked with Lieutenant Dale and Alpha First Squad along a perimeter path of Blue Sector Park. The park was at the top of the Hoffen rim, and the high ceiling thirty meters above was a line of segmented, transparent panels presenting a spectacular upward view of the enormous hub and axle, huge support arms stretching away from the rim for kilometres. The park itself was central residential green space, long and rectangular, filled with plants and centred upon a series of winding ornamental lakes and a stream. The gardens were beautiful, in stark, natural relief to the grey steel of surrounding walls... though here the steel was broken by large windows overlooking at various levels, where expensive apartments looked onto the pretty view.

Ahead Erik spied the hotel he'd seen on schematic plans. Dale spied it also. "So long as we're not paying," he said. "And I doubt Fleet credit will take us at the moment."

"My treat," Erik said drily.

"What if they've blocked your account?"

"They don't know all my accounts." Even Fleet officers were allowed some secrets from Fleet Command. Most couldn't keep those secrets, if someone as high up as Erik's enemies were determined to discover them, but Erik's financials were Debogande Incorporated private accounts. Any bank that wanted to keep doing business with Debogande Inc would think twice about closing them, no matter who was asking.

They weren't headed back to *Phoenix* because Erik was concerned that while they waited for Trace, *Phoenix* was a sitting duck at hub dock. She couldn't go anywhere — vastly outnumbered she'd be out-positioned and out-gunned anywhere in the system, except at a full sprint for jump, which they couldn't do until Trace had finished her mission. If he returned to *Phoenix* now, Erik feared that she'd just become too tempting a target for someone who decided to just wear the nasty publicity, and kill two birds with one stone.   But if hitting *Phoenix* left LC Debogande still loose on station, it was less tempting.   Better to spread out for now, and hope that multiple assassinations was more than Fleet was prepared to wear, locked in a battle of public appearance as they were.

Private Lemar saw the running girl first, sprinting from a hallway adjoining the park and hurdling a flower bed.   "Ware right! Runner, two o'clock."   She was coming straight for them, short blonde hair, slim, not especially fast or graceful, but plenty scared. Then came the cops, four grey uniformed with light armour, another two plain clothes, guns and tasers out.   All the marines took a knee on the grass, rifles aimed without needing to be told... and Erik recalled to do the same before Dale planted him face down.

One cop aimed a taser, while a plainclothes aimed a pistol, yelling at her to stop.   She was just ten meters away when Dale sprang up and advanced on both her and the cops, rifle aimed and yelling.   "Put it down!   Put it down or I will fire on you!   Put it down now!"   Then other marines were joining in, and civvies in the near vicinity were running, freezing or falling for cover as some had been taught.

The cops backed up fast, and Erik caught the girl as she stopped and gasped.   Evidently she *had* been heading for them, not just passing through.

"Whoa whoa whoa!" yelled one plainclothes, both hands in the air.   "Chill, just chill!   That's a suspect, we just want our suspect!   Look, all guns are away, just cool it marines!"

"You do *not* point loaded firearms at the backs of running civilians!" Dale yelled back, his own weapon still aimed with deadly precision.   "And you *sure as hell* don't do it with armed marines in the line of fire!"

"Right, okay!" the plainclothes agreed.   "Lower the rifle, please!   We just want our suspect, that's all."

Erik looked at the gasping girl — she was maybe Lisbeth's age, maybe a bit older.   Pretty but for the bloody nose and swelling eye.   "Lieutenant Commander Debogande!" she gasped desperately. "Don't... I have to speak to you!   They know!   They know your Captain's dead, they all know!"

"Who knows?"

"I can't say!"   She stared at him with meaningful intensity. A civilian, in jeans, blouse and boots... too well dressed to be some street thug, and clearly white collar, not some blue collar dock grunt or engineering tech.   Who would the cops want so badly they'd point guns at her while she was running away? *Phoenix*! *Phoenix* is in danger!"

"Lieutenant!" he told Dale.   "We're taking her.   Fleet privilege, ship security comes first."

"Fleet privilege buddy," Dale snarled at the cops.   "Take a hike!"

"That's seriously not a good move," the plainclothes retorted.

"Arguing with *Phoenix* marines is seriously not a good move," Dale corrected.   "We matter, you don't.   Fuck off."   The cops didn't seem to take it well.   Where cops got the notion that Fleet marines were arrogant, Erik had no idea.

His Debogande Inc account was certainly still working at the hotel lobby.   The fact that the local banks owed maybe ten percent of their net capitalisation to Debogande Inc-related business probably had something to do with it.   The desk manager's eyes widened to see his ID-linked account appear on the screen.   Erik told him to skip the description of room services and specials — he'd stayed at such places before, and could fill in his marines.

In the big elevator riding up, Private Ricardo thought to check the blonde girl's handbag with apologies, as the girl held a cloth one of them had found to her nose.   In the handbag, a taser... recently used, Ricardo thought, as she sniffed the discharger. Powerful enough to do some proper damage, not just stun.

"Seriously boys," Ricardo told them all exasperatedly.   "It takes the girl to check the handbag?   'Cause this one's cute and pretty and couldn't possibly hurt you?"   Ricardo had a crewcut, tattoos and a granite jaw.   The look of displeasure suited her entirely.

"She was the LC's catch," said Dale.   "Good job LC."

"What part of 'personal protection for officers on station' do you find hard to understand?" Erik said sharply.   "Like what part of 'don't let one of our alien prisoners shoot another of our alien prisoners' don't you understand? Or 'don't let mutinous crew try to kill the LC?'" The marines in the elevator shifted uncomfortably. "I love my *Phoenix* marines, but you guys whine about non-standard duty worse than little girls forced to eat their vegetables." He took the taser off Ricardo and shoved it on Dale. "You take it. Try not to shoot yourself in the ass."

The silence that followed was oddly respectful. In truth he probably should have thought to check the girl's handbag in case she was armed... but as Private Ricardo had pointed out, the girl *was* slim and pretty, and scared and bloodied, and it hadn't occurred to him. But ultimately it was the marines' responsibility to correct for his oversights — they were the urban combat specialists, not him, and they were trained to expect judgement failures from less-trained spacers. If marines had a flaw, it was that they were trained to blow shit up, and disdained other duties as less important. He'd been wanting to point it out to them for a while now, but hadn't dared. Dale's jibe had seemed the perfect time... plus he was getting genuinely sick of it. But instead of resenting it, a few of the marines in the elevator were now almost smiling, like a sparring partner who'd just been caught with a good right hook, and appreciated it.

"You use that taser recently?" Dale asked the girl. She nodded. "On who?"

"Cop," she said, muffled by the cloth.

"He still alive?"

"She. Don't know."

Exasperation and rolled eyes from the marines. "Now we know why they were chasing her," someone remarked.

The girl pointed to her face. "She hit me first!" Indignantly. "Asking for it."

The elevator arrived at the high floor, and Gunnery Sergeant Forrest led them off with a cautious glance left and right, rifle ready. "Straight on," Erik instructed with a glance at wall signs, and they walked down the hotel hallway. "What's your name?" he asked the girl.

"Ivette. I'm from Apilai, I work for an insurance company, Allied Heuron. They're a Spacer company, I'm a Worlder. I got told yesterday I could stay if I changed to Spacer citizenship... so I'd have to give up property rights on Apilai, inheritance. I'd have to live up here half the year forever. Keep my money up here. No thanks."

Sergeant Forrest arrived at big double doors at the end of the hall, and looked at the keycard Erik had given him. "This the one?"

"Yep," said Erik. "Go in." Forrest opened the doors, onto a huge presidential suite, the far wall entirely glass, overlooking the park they'd just left, and the amazing upward view of the Hoffen Station hub. Marines whistled, staring around as they entered.

"Standard room for you LC?" one asked.

"You bet," said Erik. "Five adjoining bedrooms, three bathrooms, should do for all of us. View of the park in case anyone comes at us from there, you guys can check the rest of the layout for yourselves. Lieutenant Dale, security status is yours."

"Aye sir," said Dale, and went to do that. Erik escorted Ivette to the bathroom while she washed up in the sink. Her nose didn't appear broken, and her lip was cut. Her nose wouldn't stop bleeding, which seemed a first for her, so Erik wetted some tissue and put it firmly up her nostril.

"Thank you," she managed, still shaking a little from recent adrenaline. "I... I came to find you. I heard you were here, and I..." She looked uncertain how much more to say. Erik could guess. To know he was here, and where to find him, suggested eyes on the inside. Spies. People watching.

"Heuron Dawn," he said. Her eyes evaded him. "I'm not the police. I'm concerned for the safety of my ship. You said they think Captain Pantillo's actually dead?" Still playing along, just in case.

"They're sure of it. I don't know how they know." She looked at him questioningly. Erik said nothing. "He was going to run for office, you know. For Heuron, in Spacer Congress. Everyone thought he had the votes, when you put together Spacers and expat Worlders. They're saying that's why Fleet killed him, and why they're kicking all the expat Worlders out." Staring at him cautiously. No doubt she'd also heard what Fleet were saying, on Homeworld at least. That *he'd* killed Captain Pantillo. It was in her eyes, that fear. Erik was not accustomed to anyone being frightened of him. Tavalai maybe, but not humans. And he'd spent so much time lately around tough women with no physical fear of him at all, that he'd almost forgotten how he might appear to a young, slim civilian girl who now found herself very vulnerable in a strange hotel room with the big male commander of the legendary *UFS Phoenix*. And his heavily armed marine contingent.

"What are they going to do?" Erik asked her. "If the Captain was their saviour, what will they do now?"

She stared at him for a moment. "You should run," she said suddenly. "It's going to get nasty. Everyone here remembers *Phoenix*, *Phoenix* was one of the liberators of Heuron. We want you to get out, now."

"I can't leave Heuron, my marine commander is on Faustino doing important business." He felt his blood beginning to run cold, a chill prickling the hairs on the back of his neck.

"Then pick her up and leave!"

"Why? What's about to happen?"

Ivette took a deep breath. "I can't say. But it's about to become very unsafe for Fleet ships at Hoffen. Trust me. If you stay here, you won't be spared."

CHAPTER 27

Linley's direction had Trace ask the whereabouts of an engineering tech, whom she then asked about 'Mr Turner'. That brought her here, down a long tunnel walk between several habitats, occupied by huge pipes and the whine of great pumping engines. The air here was hot, generators throbbing in confined space, the huge pipes thudding rhythmically as they pulsed with liquids used in the extraction of minerals far beneath the surface.

The access gantry was a steel walkway along the pipes, lit by sodium yellow light. After ten minutes of low-G bouncing they emerged into the main pumping station, where pipes from five different directions converged into a massive tangle of machinery, pumps and engines. Workers examined controls, and shouted conversations above the noise amid the multi-level gantries. Trace climbed two flights to the top gantry level beneath the domed ceiling, and saw an office door built into the lower part of the dome.

She indicated to Kono, who indicated in turn to the marines. They spread across the gantries, weapons casually to hand and not threatening. A few struck up conversations with curious plant workers, who understandably wondered what was going on. She brought Kono with her to the office door, and considering there was no hope of her knock being heard above the noise, turned the handle.

Beyond was a makeshift office. The outer wall was curved to match the outer wall of the plant below, with several large portholes offering a wide view of the silver ice horizon, some near Crondike buildings alive with light, and Heuron V's huge gas hemisphere looming large beyond. The floor beside and behind the door arced upward, the ceiling of the domed plant behind, its irregular space lined with storage shelves and access steps. Crates filled the shelves, and some odd artefacts, clearly alien. Some long, decorated poles that might be weapons, a box on a frame that might be an instrument... and numerous other things Trace had never seen before, and could not guess at.

Down the sloping floor before her were chairs, tables and several large transparent display screens. Writing in alien text raced across each of them, and on a table in the middle, light scanners raced back and forth across the pages of a big, bound leather book. A little robotic manipulator turned the page, the light and screen writing paused, then raced on once more across the new page.

To one side, a man looked up from another small screen upon a table filled with odd screens, tables, even some scrambled paper files. Behind him, a small kitchen in an even more cramped corner, obviously far less important than all these big screens dominating the room, and the artefacts across the shelves behind. He looked up at Trace and Kono in alarm. "What do you want?" he growled at them.

"Stanislav Romki," said Trace. "Are you him?"

The man looked them up and down, eyes narrowed. His head was shaved, perhaps purposely. His stare was baleful, intense, with large dark eyes. "Who's asking?"

Kono circled left, rifle half raised. "If you're thinking about a weapon under that table, please don't," he said.

The bald man held both hands cautiously where they could be seen. "I'm not *quite* that stupid, Staff Sergeant. You're *Phoenix,* aren't you? Which would make you Major Thakur." Looking hard at Trace.

Trace nodded. "That's correct, Mr Romki."

He didn't dispute the identity. "How did you find me?"

"I won't reveal sources," said Trace. "But my Captain told me about you. He said he'd never met anyone who knew the things you knew."

"He's right," Romki said darkly. "No one else does." He got up, swinging his bodyweight easily from the chair in the low-G. Over his jumpsuit, he wore a leather vest with red and black markings. Chah'nas, Trace thought. With only two armholes. A custom made thing, and if it was anything like the real ones, it would have inlaid armour and hidden weapon sheathes. "Why is *Phoenix* in Heuron? Shouldn't you be at the parades?" Romki was middle height and not especially imposing, and had the smooth, educated tones of a sophisticate.   But from his manner, Trace got the impression of a man who spent his life studying aliens because humans didn't agree with him.

"There's quite a few people in Heuron at the moment who you'd think would be at the parades," said Trace.   "Yet somehow managed to end up here."

Romki considered her for a moment, some of the tension fading. An air of grim resignation crept into his expression. "Here, um..." he looked around at his cluttered kitchen. "Would you like a drink? Either of you? Coffee, beer, water?"

"Water please," said Trace, with a surreptitious gesture at Kono to lower the rifle.   "Staff Sergeant Kono has coffee, white, sugar if you've got it."

"Oh I've got sugar," said Romki, moving lightly to his kitchen.   "I know people who can get me real sugar, minus the inspections. Please, take a seat." Neither of them did. In low-G, standing was no burden anyway.   Trace strolled to the big leather books before the display screens. "They're chah'nas," said Romki, glancing her way. "I got them my last time in chah'nas space. The screen on the left is doing the literal translation, and then the other one is doing the contextual... you know the thing with chah'nas tongues, the grammar is all contextual, you need to know which frame-setting you're in or else you'll get the whole meaning wrong. So one for the literal, and one for the contextual, then I cross-reference them at the end and see what we can sort out. All my own design."

"You travel there a lot?" Trace asked.

"There, lots of places," said Romki with a shrug, as the coffee machine gurgled. "I'm supposed to be there now."

"Fleet don't know you're here?"

"Not today," said Romki, warily.   "They know about this little hidey-hole, of course, but I'm hardly ever here, and I wasn't supposed to be back for months yet. I come here so I don't have to put up with all the bullshit customs at Apilai — this way if I want to just pop in and out, I don't have to bother customs or Fleet or anyone. And these tough mining boys outside?"   He pointed at the door. "They're all unionised and they don't take shit from Fleet, so no spies. No surprise they let you guys through though, half of them have either family in the marines, or were marines themselves."

"Fleet command, and rank-and-file marines, are two very different things," Trace acknowledged.

Romki nodded knowingly. "And since you're not here to arrest me, I guess there's something else going on?" He leaned on his bench, waiting for the coffee machine. "Something to do with your Captain? Finally ended up in trouble with his own Fleet, has he?"

"You could say that," Trace conceded. The problem with someone who was not a people-person, getting a feel for where he stood on things could be like extracting teeth. And if she assumed he was somehow 'on her side', whatever her side was, and it turned out he wasn't... well she wasn't in the mood to start killing civvies just to shut them up.

"Smartest Fleet captain I ever met," said Romki. "That's not saying much, mind you. Pack of pole-climbing square heads, most of them. But Pantillo sought me out. Had lots of ideas about chah'nas and tavalai, about the empire and the uprisings... a lot of them wrong, but he was on the right track. And he actually listened when I corrected him — incredible how many smart people refuse to do that, even confronted with people who know a lot more than they do. We've kept in touch since, but we do it quietly. As you'd know, given you're here."

"So you're not allowed to talk to anyone?" Trace surmised.

Romki chuckled tiredly. "No. I'm not much of a conversationalist, apparently. I've been told I talk but don't listen."

"So why stay employed by Newtown University? If you can't take students, teach, lecture, publish, give interviews? Surely if your research is that secret, Fleet would just employ you in some Intel department?"

"You don't think they've offered?" Romki snorted. "They've offered all right, with all the generosity of a crime lord suggesting you do business together.   Or else, you know?"   He made the shape of a pistol with one hand.

"So why don't you?"

"Because fuck them," Romki snapped.   "Fuck all of them. They don't want me to work, they want to shut me up.   They'll disappear me into some little cubicle if they can, and that'll be the last anyone ever saw of Stanislav Romki.   Sixty years I've been doing this.   I've lived with chah'nas, I've even lived with tavalai, I speak the languages... I have five volumes of history on the Chah'nas Empire, two million words, all blocked from publication under the security laws.   Too sensitive, they say.   These people are scared of facts.   And there's nothing in all human space that scares me like human leadership scared of facts."

The coffee machine stopped gurgling, and Romki poured, controlling his anger with difficulty.   Then he came with coffee to Staff Sergeant Kono, and water for Trace.

"Thank you," said Kono, noticing a decoration on Romki's sleeve.   "You know the blades?"

Romki glanced at his sleeve.   "Yes.   Do you know *kon-dra-kis*?"

"I know a little.   I know you need four arms to do it properly."

Romki shook his head.   "There are many different forms, the good instructors make allowances."   He indicated his storage shelf. Up against the wall on a rack rested a pair of sheathed blades, above red-and-black body armour.   "It's an amazing art.   I'm not all that good but I hold my own against their kids.   Misunderstood people, the chah'nas.   I've many friends there, and I miss them whenever I'm here."

"We're about to be seeing a lot more of them," Trace suggested, watching him carefully.

Romki's eyes darted a little.   "Perhaps."

"You're hardly ever here, but you somehow managed to be here for this."   Trace indicated back toward Hoffen Station, and the unfolding mess of Fleet Command's ordinances.   "You knew it was coming, didn't you?   And you're a student of history, and you couldn't miss it.   Did your chah'nas friends tell you that humans were about to open their territory to chah'nas ships?"   Romki gazed at her, unblinking.   "I bet a lot of rank-and-file chah'nas aren't thrilled at having to open their territory to humans, either."

Romki folded his arms.   "Why don't you just tell me why you're here, Major?   What trouble is your Captain in?   I know Fleet High Command have never liked him.   I was given a list of people I'm *especially* not allowed to talk to, people they said flat out they'd *destroy* me if I was caught talking to them.   His name was right at the top."

"We've been in Merakis," said Trace.   "Chah'nas beat us there.   Unopposed by Fleet.   Bunch of tavalai historians and others were there waiting for humans to arrive, they got a face full of chah'nas instead.   All massacred."

Romki barely blinked.   "Well that was always going to happen.   What was *Phoenix* doing in Merakis?"

"On the way to Merakis," Trace added as she ignored the question, "we ran into a hacksaw nest.   We took some of their corpses for salvage."

Now Romki looked amazed.   "You destroyed a nest single-handed?"

"Just now we pulled up alongside an alo warship at Hoffen Station dock.   And wouldn't you know it, our hacksaw corpses reactivated and started moving, like some reanimated bodies from a horror movie."   Romki stared.   Not astonished at the revelation. Just stunned, Trace thought, that someone was confronting him with it.   "You knew," she said pointedly.   "There's a connection between hacksaws and alo, isn't there?   Is there also a connection between hacksaws and chah'nas?   Because I figure that if Fleet Command were going to threaten to shut you up over anything, that would just about do it."

Romki exhaled hard, eyes closed.   "Son of a bitch," he murmured. And took a deep breath. "Look, come and sit. Sit!" he insisted, beckoning them over to the kitchen.   He pulled a couple of chairs from the table, a low-weight skid on the floor, then took one and sat.   Kono sat on his sideways, while Trace turned hers backward and rested hands on the back, both seeking easier ways to stand up fast if necessary. Romki leaned forward intently.

"I've had this place scanned for bugs, I've revealed confidential information before and not been arrested for it, so it's clean." He took another deep breath. "You should understand. Half of Fleet don't want me shut up, they want me dead. The other half love my work and keep me funded, it's always a guessing game to know which half is in the ascendency at any time. But I've a civilian profile and I've told certain trusted journalists about it — it would be incredibly damaging for them if I mysteriously vanished, and they don't dare the publicity. Yet. You wanted to know why I stay employed by the university — that's why. Friends, contacts, public profile. Newtown has some of humanity's best scholars, they'd miss me if I vanished. Mostly I go there to cultivate contacts who'd make life difficult for Fleet if they killed me. I've also got little data bombs out on various worlds and stations. Trusted people will release that data if I go missing, and it will be... hideously embarrassing for Fleet if that happens. It's one big reason I was happy to talk to your Captain, he's yet another person who'd cause Fleet difficulty, thus making me safer."

"Why?" asked Trace. "What are you studying that could make you that much of a target?"

"How about," Romki said with methodical clarity, "a linguistic link between alo and hacksaws?" Trace blinked. "We're speaking English. Do you know where English came from?"

"Not my area of expertise," Trace admitted.

"Wasn't it, like, the regions around old England?" Kono suggested, frowning as he strove to remember something he'd read. All kids had some old Earth history thrown at them in school. A few even remembered it.

Romki looked encouragingly at the big Staff Sergeant. "Britain," he corrected. "Go on."

"Well there were the local English, then the... wasn't it the Vikings? And the French."

"The Angles, the Saxons and the Normans, yes," said Romki. "That language group used to be called 'Anglo-Saxon', a long time ago.   But there's an even older ancestor, because that whole European family, with both Latin in the south and the Scandinavian tongues, all actually have some common roots they shared as far south as India. Your people, Major."

"If you say so," Trace said mildly.

"An English fellow named Sir William Jones first postulated it in the seventeen hundreds, old Earth time. It was called the Proto-Indo-European language, and it explained why Latin, Ancient Greek and Sanskrit all had these intriguing commonalities. Now you have to go back... well, thousands and thousands of years to get to that common protolanguage, and back then, most humans weren't keeping very good records, so it all becomes very vague. But Spiral history has been recorded with modern computers for tens of thousands of years, the biggest loss of historical knowledge has been all the damn wars destroying records.

"Now there are records in chah'nas space that the chah'nas don't touch — for all their good points, the chah'nas are not curious like humans are, they like to leave established understandings alone and look to the future.   Another reason why they never got along with the tavalai, of course.   And these records are of the very first linguistic recordings of the alo, when they first made contact with the chah'nas. For a long time the chah'nas were the only race the alo talked to.   Since then, alo language has changed drastically — alo are not a static people, they're constantly transforming, and their current tongues are nothing like their old tongues. You almost can't make a transition map from old to new languages, they've changed that much... in humans you'd say it's like English turning into Chinese in just a thousand years.

"But I've found a treasure trove of the old stuff. It's safe, no one else knows where it is. And it has clear similarities to Ceenyne, which was the primary tongue of the deepynines, who were one of the main factions of the AIs, the hacksaws, who disappeared in the general direction of alo space during the AI civil wars, twenty five thousand years ago.   With the deepynines it was a machine language, it's based on numeric code but after a while they began expressing it audibly because direct data-transmission doesn't allow

398

time lag for group consideration, which was causing them to make poor decisions in complex scenarios.   The audible variants are similar to that early alo speech in the same way that Sanskrit, Greek and Latin were similar.   Suggesting a common ancestor.   And when I try to trace just *how* similar, and look at how fast alo language has changed between their present and their past speech, and I overlay that onto what the deepynines spoke twenty five thousand years ago... I get an almost precise match in the degree of expected variation."

And he gazed at the two marines, who stared at him, and tried to force their brains around all those unfamiliar concepts.

"Wait," said Kono.   "Are you saying the alo... *are* the deepynines?"

"I don't know," said Romki, with the amusement of an intellectual who could only laugh at the seriousness of it all. "Twenty five thousand years ago, one of the most vicious and devastating branches of the AI race disappears into what is now alo space.   Twenty three thousand years later, just one thousand before humans appear in space, the alo appear and become friends with the chah'nas and chah'nas only.   Alo today claim they killed all the deepynines.   But what kind of species adopts the language of its enemy?   Because they weren't just influenced by it, this isn't like the influence that American English or Indian English had on what we're speaking now — this is structural.

"How could the alo have wiped them out, given that they only got AI-level technology *after* they beat them?   Alo won't say. And we sure as hell aren't allowed in to look for ourselves, I know of at least three adventurous scholars who have tried and never been seen again, and the alo openly admit they'll fire on anyone not-alo whom they find in their space.   Maybe the deepynines *built* themselves an organic species from scratch.   Maybe they adopted one that they found, and altered it in various doubtless unpleasant ways.   All kinds of horrors present as possible.   Or maybe they're just friends, but you need an odd sense of humour to buy that one."

"You think the deepynines are still there," Trace breathed.

Romki smiled. "Oh certainly! And we're allied to them through the Triumvirate Alliance, on whose behalf we just fought a hundred and sixty year war and lost tens of millions of lives to secure."

"And are now about to welcome their chah'nas allies into our space as full partners," Kono muttered.

Romki made a grand gesture, as though proud of them. "Exactly! And now you know why Fleet wants me dead."

"Wants *us* dead," said Trace. "They killed Captain Pantillo on Homeworld."

Romki turned pale. "They *what?*"

"Court-martialled him with some trumped up nonsense, then murdered him when he wouldn't play along, and pinned it on our LC, Erik Debogande."

"Debogande," Romki murmured, aghast. "Of course!"

"We got him out, and ran here, via Merakis. We came here because word hadn't reached here yet. But we didn't count on the alo — there were no alo at Homeworld, we didn't think any other ship was fast enough to beat us here. But clearly there was an alo somewhere nearby, because Chankow apparently knows, and now we're screwed unless we can get the hell out of here soon."

"Well I was going to say," said Romki with alarm. "I wouldn't mind a lift, I had a ship arranged for tomorrow, but that schedule now looks a little too relaxed."

CHAPTER 28

Lieutenant Dale was not happy. "We can't just sit here and let some fucking Worlder lunatics do whatever the fuck they're planning to do to Hoffen," he said. They stood in the master bedroom, alone before the wide view of the park, and the vast hub-facing transparent ceiling above. "I don't care what our beef is with HQ — HQ is not Hoffen, and I didn't fight through thirty years of war to stop the Froggies blasting places like this one to just sit back now and let some local crazies do the same thing."

"I agree," said Erik. "What's your plan?"

Dale blinked at him. "*My* plan?"

"That's right, your plan. If I'm in charge of this boat, I don't just want criticisms, I want alternatives."

"We could question the girl harder. I'm sure she knows more."

"You going to break her fingers?"

Dale scowled. "If that's what it takes."

"Why not just hand her back to Hoffen cops? They'll do it for you. Be easier if you hadn't told them to fuck off."

"We don't need station cops to…"

Erik's uplink blinked, and he turned his back on Dale. "Go ahead *Phoenix*."

"*LC,*" came Shilu's voice. "*Transmission from the Major, ended ten seconds ago, no reply possible on this relay it's all one way.*"

"Copy *Phoenix*, send transmission."

"*Hello Phoenix, please transmit to the LC.*" It was Trace's voice, crackling with light static. From Faustino, it would be coming in at least a few seconds delayed, more with the com relays. "*We have who we came for, his information is dramatic. We're leaving now, could get hairy. Keep your eyes open.*"

Click, as Shilu came back on. "*That's it LC, did you get all of that?*"

"I got it *Phoenix*. The Major's last words apply to you too. LC out." He disconnected in frustration. None of them could say more with Fleet listening. He turned to Dale. "That's Trace, she's got Romki, says his information is dramatic, she's getting out now. Thinks it's about to blow up by the sound of it."

Thud! Something distant reverberated through the walls and floor. Thud! Thud! "Those are explosions," Dale said on coms to his squad. "Something's going down. Everyone defensive, I want one observer at the windows, everyone else keep the hell away from them." He disconnected, and strode for the main room. "LC, this way."

In the big suite, marines were refastening helmets, and moving away from the big observation windows. One of them took Ivette, looking bewildered as she went to stand by a bedroom doorway. Others opened the suite's big doors onto the hall, where two more marines were stationed, with another two up the hallway at the elevators and stairs. "*LT,*" said Lance Corporal Carponi on coms, "*I'm hacked into the elevators, but I've got no reading on those stairs.*"

"Just keep a door open and listen," said Dale, striding to Ivette. A main room screen showed station news feed, a reporter doing a hurried piece to camera, words scrolling across the screen, warning of multiple bombings and a code red. "Girl, what's happening? Are you in on this?"

"It's started," Ivette said breathlessly. Outside the observation windows, huge red lights began flashing, and a siren echoed across the park. Walls and floor began a low rumbling as blast covers rolled slowly across the transparent ceiling.

Dale grabbed her by the collar, threateningly. "Are you in on this?"

"No!" She pawed ineffectually at his fist. "No, I just... know the people who are." Thud. More distant this time, as Dale looked up, measuring this detonation in his mind from long experience of such things.

"What comes next?"

"I don't know!   This is just a distraction though, it's much bigger than this." Dale looked at Erik, who took his rifle from its shoulder strap, and wondered if he'd ever feel comfortable with its heavy weight.

"The security weakpoint is all the ships on the rim," Erik said grimly.   "Hoffen's security clearance hasn't been high enough to access all of them, especially not the big corporate freighters.   I think they've underestimated the threat.   If something big is still to come, that's where it'll come from."

"While all the security is responding to these explosions," Dale muttered.   "LC, the Major's moving, I say we go pick her up and get the hell out of this system."

"I agree," said Erik.   "But if we move immediately we could trigger a security response.   We're certainly being watched, if we dash now they'll assume we had something to do with it and hit us. Let's give it ten minutes and see what's unfolding in response to those explosions."

"That's a good thought," said Dale, "but I'm concerned we don't have ten minutes…"

"Get down!" yelled Private Tong by the main windows, as Dale grabbed Erik who was diving anyway.   An earsplitting crash as everything went sideways, and the air was full of flying glass and things breaking.

"Get in!" someone was yelling, hauling Erik up as he ran and dove into the ensuite bathroom adjoining this bedroom.   Other marines piled in, and Erik joined the armoured pile on the tiled floor as suddenly the walls were shaking with rapid, repeating impacts. Hands grabbed Erik and dumped him into the bathtub, then Ivette and Private Reddy piled on top, and someone elbowed Erik in the head.

"Down, stay down!" Dale was shouting, as walls thudded and more things broke.   A chain gun, he realised.   At least one, fired from somewhere across the park, through the main windows… that first shot had been an RPG of some kind.   It sounded like hailstones outside, but in these bedrooms and bathrooms away from the main window, bullets had to travel through multiple walls.

"Hallway!" Sergeant Forrest yelled, and the sound of shooting over coms. Forrest had been one of the four guarding the hall stairwell and elevators. *"Under fire!"* And in the background... *"Get him!" "Watch the corner!" "Masks! Masks!"* Meaning someone was using gas out there. They were trying to storm the suite, Erik realised. Who 'they' were, he had no idea.

Then Private Reddy was yanking his own facemask from its pouch, and Erik cursed as he realised the marines had theirs on already... he grabbed it, fastened over his nose and mouth, and flinched as a bullet broke tiles somewhere overhead. Even as he pulled it tight, cold, compressed air flowed into his lungs. Another tile smashed, and someone swore.

"Stay down!" Dale told them. "Let 'em spend ammo! Woody, status?"

"Lots of gas, can't see shit!" came Sergeant Forrest's reply. More gunfire. *"They're in the stairwell, and they tried explosive egress into the next apartment! Came out the door, we killed about..."* more gunfire, and some shouting. *"...killed about five! Ricky and Hap are clearing that room, we might have just got another way out!"*

"Let's go!" someone else snapped, and some hard breathing that sounded like several marines sprinting. *"LT, this is Kalo, I'm out the door with Buzz. Sarge, where to?"*

Wham! as something else hit the room outside, and the air itself seemed to gasp in shock. Another RPG, Erik reckoned. "Can't stay here all day LT," said Reddy against Erik's ear. "The LC's not that pretty."

"You just volunteered, Spots," Dale told him.

"Thank you sir," said Reddy as he rolled out of the tub and onto the tiles with a clatter of armour. The bullet impacts paused, and Reddy scrambled out of the doorway.

"You okay?" Erik asked the terrified girl in the tub with him. Ivette nodded wordlessly, her nose bleeding again.

"Got an exit," came Private Ricardo. *"Upstairs through the hole they made. Dumb fuckers didn't leave enough reserve, all dead now."*

Bullet impacts in the room outside resumed. Erik tried to get his rifle out from where he'd managed to get it wedged beneath him, lifting his head just enough as he shifted to see a round bullet hole in the tiles just above him. He stared. When the hell had that gotten there? Another loud crack!, and he flinched.

"LC!" said Dale. "You're next! Leave the girl!"

"I'm not leaving the fucking girl," Erik retorted. "They'll kill her." He got up to a crouch, expecting to get a hole in him any moment. It wasn't that he was *not* frightened, he thought, it was more that he didn't know *what* he felt. Everything was too fast and too intense, and if he didn't do exactly what his marines told him, he'd cause them an inconvenience that could get one or a number of them killed. And that scared him as badly as getting hit himself.

The bullet strikes paused again. "LC go!" Dale snapped, and Erik grabbed Ivette and leaped from the tub. Ivette was slow getting around the bathroom corner and he half carried her with his left arm, through smoke and debris from a barely recognisable presidential suite, everything aflame and shot to bits. As he made for the main hall doors the bullets started up again, and for the first time he felt real terror to hear their shrill staccato shweet-and-thud as they tore the air. Then he was out the door, and abruptly hit from behind as someone dragged him down and rolling on the hallway floor as bullets struck nearby. It was Dale, he realised, lying on top of him for protection as the bullets came, then hauling him up and shoving him on as he in turn collected Ivette and ran.

"You gotta leave her sir!" Private Tong yelled at him from the doorway opposite the elevators, catching his arm. "She'll slow us the fuck down!" As Erik stared at the hole in the ceiling of the room beyond, where attackers had blown the floor and come charging in. Their bodies lay sprawled about the room, the walls sprayed with blood. Evidently a marine had come in the door after the ceiling had blown, and shot them all as they jumped through the hole. Another of those things that might work against criminal gangs and terrorists, but weren't worth shit against Fleet marines who'd seen it all before.

And Erik saw Dale coming up behind Ivette as he paused in the doorway, and thought for a wild moment that Dale would just shoot her to save him the decision. "Go down the hall!" he yelled at the girl. "Get in one those rooms, hide, and surrender to the first security who enter!"

"I want to come with you!" Ivette protested.

"You can't!" Dale yelled, and shoved her down the hall. "Go!" Several other room doors had been kicked open by marines to save time at the next explosive entry from above. Then he shoved Erik into the room, and he went. Erik shouldered his rifle, found firm footing amidst the debris on the floor, and leaped. He was not marine-augmented, but he had enough of a vertical leap to grab an exposed rim even in armour, and haul himself up.

Above, he was in another hotel room, rolling on scorched carpet to find more armoured bodies against the walls, and a marine in a combat crouch by the doorway — Private Ricardo, he saw, and waving him past. She joined him as he ran up the hall, saw another armoured body on the ground, neck and face punctured by rifle fire. Then a T-junction, and a left turn to an engineering access door, god knew how the marines had found it, only it was their job to know these layouts, as Trace had told him, and then he was being hustled inside. A scramble along a narrow steel grating, ducking low pipes overhead, then a tight steel stairwell with another marine at the top, gesturing them to stop.

Barely ten seconds later, Dale and the remaining marines arrived behind, footsteps thundering on the steel grate. "That's it, we're all here?" Erik gasped. Dale ushered him on without an answer, and he went down the stairs fast. Another rushed and stupid Fleet HQ decision, he thought — both here and on Homeworld, Fleet made the same mistakes with them, making panicked, hasty decisions on the spot. They'd not used marines in this assault, probably fearing that marines would have refused, and couldn't have given this assault team much time to prepare. Attacking on short notice against marines the caliber of Alpha First Squad was always likely to end badly. He still didn't allow himself to believe they were all still alive until they reached the access to an adjoining hall outside of the hotel complex, and saw that Kalo, Chavez, Lauda and Reddy, the four he hadn't seen since the Presidential suite, were all waiting ahead and unhurt.

Lance Corporal Carponi shouldered past to take his place at the lead with Second Section — Ricardo, Halep and Yu. "Let's go," he said, and out into the corridor at a jog.

"LC," said Dale, and yanked him along with the rest of First Section, as Third Section brought up the rear. These corridors were residential, with lines of doors broken by shop windows and random offices. All lights were tinged red, and an alarm siren was sounding. Mostly there was no one else around, and the one civilian they passed seemed not alarmed to see marines doing what marines did in emergency alerts — running in formation with weapons.

"We need to call PH-4 for pickup," said Erik to Dale at his shoulder. He recalled not so long ago, jogging with Dale along the green and wealthy streets near his family home. So familiar, yet it seemed like another universe, and another age. "We're not getting back to *Phoenix* through the hub."

"Already done it," said Dale. "They won't leave yet, they'll want to make it as fast and direct as possible. We won't be at the pickup point for a while yet." And if they got held up on the way, PH-4 would be left waiting for someone to blow them out of the sky.

"If the girl's right, a whole bunch of shit might be about to break loose," said Erik. "Might make good cover."

"Yep," said Dale. "Watch this corner." They slowed as the marines ahead cleared it. "That girl could have been their target. Might have thought she was recruiting us to join the Worlders."

"Fuck no," said Erik, as they resumed a regular jog. "That's no reason to shoot up a nice hotel. That was a panic move — Fleet HQ panics a lot with this stuff, which might tell you something."

"Tells me they're a bunch of fucking fools," Dale growled.

"It has to be Trace. She's found something she wasn't supposed to find, and they don't want us to go get her. They're not up to shooting at *Phoenix* yet, but if they kill her commander they won't have to."

"That means the Major's about to get hammered next," said Dale.

"Go Hiro," said Trace as she bounced along one of the big service tunnels in the midst of her marines. Romki was right behind her, and thank god he wasn't one of those delicate academic types or he could have really slowed them down. Stanislav Romki was a traveller, a man accustomed to making his own way in all sorts of environments, and to judge from the way he moved, Trace reckoned he even had some physical augmentations of the high-performance variety. Doubtless it gave him a respectability among the chah'nas that would come in handy.

"Major you need to get out," said Hiro. *"I've run through local manifests for arrivals on the Crondike secure mainframe. I've got three local shuttles from nearby bases with no ID, and the local manifest refuses to query them, against all regulations."*

"We're moving now," said Trace. "ETA on those shuttles?"

"One in five minutes, all three in ten. I also can't find another thirty personnel who've arrived within the last two hours. I think they're already here… and we were in transit for six hours."

"Who, do you think?"

"Marines would be conspicuous, and loyalty could be a problem if they knew who their target was. At a guess I'd think Star Force commandos. Heuron's been a problem for a while, HQ has been building local elite security, far better than your usual cops. Not marine standard, but then this is their home ground."

"Copy Hiro, we'll make it fast."

"One more thing, I had to take out a couple of people to get access to the mainframe. I'll be fine once the other distractions start, but if you hear other alarms shortly, that'll be me."

Trace shortened her bounces a little, and let Romki draw up alongside. "What's your combat training?"

"Uh... chah'nas martial arts, some basic firearms." Nervously. "And I can curl up into a very small ball. Nothing that will be very useful in a firefight."

"Curling into a small ball is sometimes very useful. Basic first aid?"

Romki nodded. "Of course. Moderately advanced, actually."

"Good. If there's shooting, the non-shooter gets to treat the wounded. That means you." She flipped to coms, seeing the access tunnel ending ahead. "Guys, tunnel end ahead, watch for ambush."

Two more bounces, then, "Down!" yelled Corporal Rael up front, and marines in mid-jump caught rails and swung themselves violently down or to the sides as shots echoed ahead, seeking cover against the big pipes or beside and beneath the walkway. Trace bounced sideways under the pipes as Kono pulled Romki after them, and bullets cracked and whined off the steel. Rael and Second Section opened fire ahead, keeping heads down while Trace came up on the far side of the pipes, where there was no walkway, only a tangle of support struts, cables and air venting.

As soon as she put her head up she drew fire and ducked back. "Hello Hausler," she said calmly as other marines opened up around her. "We're under fire, it looks like Fleet didn't know Romki was here. Someone found out we're meeting him and flipped out." Hausler's reply was mostly static, snatches of words and no more. That was jamming. "Hausler?"

She rolled back under the pipes to where Kono had an arm around the alarmed academic. "We're being jammed," she told her Staff Sergeant. "I think we just lost our escape."

"Can't run on a shuttle anyway," said Kono. "They'd shoot us down."

"Maybe," said Trace. "But that's highly visible, everyone can see it. If they corner us down here with jammed coms, they can eliminate us quietly and make up some story." She flipped channels. "Hiro, can you hear me?"

"Hello Major, go ahead." That was much clearer. Given most spies' network skills, that wasn't surprising.

"Hiro we're under fire, they're blocking our return to the landing pads. What can you tell me?"

"Major get me your position, I'll try to get through to Hausler and get him to pick you up."

"Negative Hiro, we don't have suits, we're going to need a compatible airlock to get aboard. That means a proper landing pad or nothing. Hiro I want you to get me long range coms, either through PH-1 or through Crondike itself, I want to talk to *Phoenix*."

"Copy Major, I'll see what I can do."

She flipped back to local, bullets cracking by, but outgoing fire seemed further away. The lack of tacnet in light armour would have been infuriating if she'd let it be. Without tactical support, they'd have to do this the old fashioned way. "Cocky, talk to me, what's our range ahead?"

"Fifty meters," said Edward 'Cocky' Rael. *"Where the tunnel drops beneath the habitat ahead, into the basement. That's the bulkhead, they've got cover positions there."* A pause for more gunfire. *"I don't think they'll have anything heavier than this, too many utilities down here."*

"I'm hit!" Kumar said tersely. *"Left hand."*

"Hang on, I'm on it!" said Terez.

"This is what happens when you operate without full armour," Kono muttered.

"This is T-Bone," said Van, cool where others were shouting. *"I just killed my second, got a nice little fire position up here. Irfy, Leo, crawl up and push it another five meters."*

There wasn't a lot of fancy manoeuvring you could do, stuck in a tunnel. But Van was the best shot in Command Squad, and was wedged into a little cover between pipe and walkway up ahead. Once set, he could hit just about anything, and if the ambushers kept trying to fill the spot he had targeted, they'd keep losing men. That had to be disconcerting to the survivors.

"You fucking stay," Kono told Trace sternly, and crawled forward himself through the tight space. Meaning that she had a tendency to try to solve these problems by sticking her own neck out, and they weren't in that desperate a situation yet. But if the numbers of enemy were as large as Hiro's probing suggested, and if some of them came around behind, they'd be trapped.

"We're not going around?" Romki ventured, wincing every time a bullet hit near.

"If there's as many as we think," said Trace, "they'll just block us at every tunnel exit we get to." And gestured past him to Lance Corporal Walker, telling him and his four-man section to stay and watch the rear.

Another outgoing shot ahead. *"That's three,"* said Van. *"Dumb fuckers don't learn."*

Trace's uplink blinked. *"Major, it's Hiro. I have you a direct patch to Crondike antennae. On Phoenix encryption they'll hear it, but so will Fleet HQ."*

"Worst they can do is try to kill us," Trace said drily. "Put me through." A click, then a green visual signal. "Hello *Phoenix*, this is the Major. I have spoken to Mr Romki. This has made HQ unhappy and we are currently under fire and pinned down, they didn't know Romki was here and he's been under threat of elimination from Fleet Command for years.

"This is the situation. Romki says there is a common linguistic and technological ancestry between alo and hacksaws. He says alo may be the spawn of hacksaws. That may be the reason we're not allowed in their territory to see anything. This raises the very serious question of exactly on whose behalf we've been conquering this part of the galaxy for, the past hundred and sixty years. And who in Fleet High Command knew about it, and didn't care to share."

She glanced at Romki. His wide-eyed stare showed that he understood what she was doing. This was a secret he'd been instructed to guard with his life. Broadcasting this information, even on *Phoenix* encryption, would bring every Fleet ship in Heuron down on their heads. HQ could break *Phoenix* encryption, but there was no guarantee someone else might not find a way to do so. Anyone spreading this information was begging to be eliminated.

"When you get this message, reply and confirm that you have understood. I am not certain I can get out of here. I'll try, but even if I make it to PH-1, one shuttle alone in FTL space will be dead very quickly. Do *not* attempt a rescue. This information is too important, and you must live to make use of it. I repeat, do *not* attempt a rescue. This is why we came to Heuron, and it was worth it. If you attempt a rescue, every Fleet ship in Heuron will try to kill you and probably succeed. I'll try to find a way out, but if I can't, it's been an honour. Thakur out."

A flurry of gunfire ahead, and suddenly her marines ahead were out of cover and firing all at once. The lack of return fire suggested success. She gestured to Walker to take Romki, rolled out from under the pipes to the walkway and bounded forward. Ahead, as Rael had said, the tunnel dropped away beneath the bulkhead foundation of a habitat above. On those higher walkways were a number of bodies — light armoured like the marines, dark blue uniforms. Special police — Star Force — as Hiro had said. The rest had fled.

Kono was taping a bandage pad to Arime's jaw where a bullet had grazed him and removed an earlobe. Kumar's hand was a mess, but bound up tight. He wasn't going to be much of a shot one-handed, but he was still in the fight. Already Terez and Singer were on the upper walkways working on getting one of those doors open.

"You're guarding Romki," Trace told Kumar with a slap on his shoulder. "Shouldn't take two hands." And added, "Good job," to the impatient Arime, before jumping to the upper walkway. Accuracy under fire was one of those things you couldn't teach, and only acquired the hard way. Van's deadly sniping had allowed Arime and Rael to crawl close enough undetected to spring a surprise. Suddenly under fire at ranges where marines usually hit, and special forces cops usually missed, resistance had crumbled fast.

"The LC coming to get us Major?" Terez asked her.

"He'd have to fly through half of Fleet to get here," Trace said grimly. "And if he somehow survived all of that just to grab us, I'd shoot him myself."

CHAPTER 29

On Hoffen docks all hell was breaking loose. Sirens blared and emergency warning announcements echoed, telling all station residents to shelter in a secure, airtight environment. Engineering and security teams ran along the decking, with shouts and instructions. Nearby a section seal was coming down, a massive steel door closing off this portion of docks, everything rumbling and shaking as it descended.

On his uplink image of Hoffen general access, the public space available to any networked citizen, Hoffen-A wheel showed section seals down everywhere and all environmentals put into emergency reserve. Erik flipped to new connections as he crouched in the shadow of a shopfront by several marines. Ahead, at the dockfront express elevator, Lance Corporal Carponi and Private Yu were collaborating to hotwire the panel using marine tech that allowed it.

"It's taking too long," Gunnery Sergeant Forrest told Dale nearby. "They'll find us with the security cameras."

"I know," said Dale, staring across the pandemonium on the docks, rifle ready. "Another thirty seconds."

Erik found the local Hoffen traffic control. *"...no clearance to leave dock at this time,"* Control were telling someone sternly. *"Freighter Bluejay, I repeat, you have no clearance to leave dock at this time. Hold your position or you will be up on charges."* He could not access station scan, but audio traffic was busy all around the rim. Even as he listened, dock shuddered beneath him in a way that had nothing to do with the descending seals.

"Everyone's breaking dock," he told Dale. "Ships are defying Hoffen Control, they're busting grapples to get out of here."

"Could be someone's smuggled a nuke up to station?" Dale wondered.

"Too many sensor sniffers, they'd smell bomb residue," Erik disagreed. "If someone's going to commit suicide, cycling the jump engines in dock would do it."

"Fuck," Dale muttered. Jumping while still in dock would take a very large portion of Hoffen Station and stuff it into some place physics never intended. It wouldn't be nearly as catastrophic as a nuke, but it would be bad enough. If *several* Worlder-friendly or Worlder-controlled vessels did it at the same time...

Beside Carponi and Yu, Privates Ricardo and Halep knelt at guard. Now Ricardo raised her rifle, sighting something down the dock. "Yo!" she said loudly, which brought several others across to look at what she was seeing.

"Position!" Dale commanded, and several others darted to cover, seeking good angles down-spin along the dock. A shot rang out, and the marines replied in force, a deafening racket of automatic fire. Yells and shrieks down that way — Erik had no intention of getting out far enough to see, Dale had told him to stay in cover at all costs and his primary objective was not to get in anyone's way. Civvies on the docks fell flat, or ran frantically. Now fire came back, and marines pressed themselves down, Ricardo feeling herself too exposed near her Corporal fell and rolled behind a little bench-and-garden. Shots hit the wall right beside Carponi and Yu, who kept working oblivious.

"Carponi!" Dale yelled above the now-continuous shooting. "Status!"

"Nearly got it!"

"You said that three minutes ago! Are you any closer?"

"Another three will do it!" Yu shouted confidently. A bullet smacked just above his head.

Erik saw some running figures in light armour and weapons coming the other way up the dock — the direction he *could* see. "Watch out!" he yelled, as Chavez added a more useful, "Incoming contact, up-spin!" And marines turned the other way to fire on them. Erik saw them scatter, some rolling and slithering away, one running then falling, another lying still. And then they were under fire from two directions at once, as the others found cover and opened up. Erik didn't need to be a marine to see that very soon they'd get off the dock and surround them via the corridors and hallways of main-rim habitat.

"*LC this is Phoenix,*" came Shilu's voice in his ear. "*Priority message from the Major.*"

"Put her through." And he listened as Trace told him via a crackling connection that she'd found Romki, and... holy fuck. For a brief moment, he nearly forgot he was getting shot at. The crackling on Trace's transmission was more than just static — she was getting shot at as well.

"That's enough!" Dale yelled. "We're about to get cut off! Main service stairwell, we get down the hard way!"

Marines pulled off their fire positions and ran, partners staying behind to fire and cover with perfect coordination. Erik moved before Dale could grab him and ran at his side back into the corridors, dialling up the uplink volume so he could hear the last of Trace's transmission. Ahead, a warning yell and shooting, then he was running past a pair of police bodies, one only hit in the body armour and still moving.

Trace's message finished as they made a big down-stairway. The level below the dock was big and far more industrial, with heavy lighting and much less decor. Stationers got quickly out of their way, and several regular cops put their hands in the air as well, with real fear. So word was out on the police net — *Phoenix* marines were to be considered enemy combatants. Special security forces would act on that, while most regular cops very sensibly would not. Marines ran past them with barely a glance, knowing that Lance Corporal Kalo's Third Section in the rear would keep a much closer eye once they were all passed.

"*LC, what did the Major say?*" Dale asked on uplink to save the difficulty of talking while running.

"*Mr Romki suspects the alo aren't actually humanity's friends after all,*" Erik summarised. "*HQ's trying to kill her, she's outnumbered and outgunned on Crondike. Says we shouldn't try to rescue her.*"

"Girl's got a death wish," said Dale. "*Thinks she won't have fulfilled her purpose as Kulina if she doesn't die for her cause. We* are *going to rescue her.*" Even on uplink formulation, his tone suggested it might be dangerous for Erik to disagree.

"Phoenix leaves no one behind," said Erik. *"But you have to get me out of here alive first."*

There was more contact ahead, then they emerged into a big industrial space between huge steel supports and cross-beams. Across the floor were stacked storage shelves, tended by lumbering loaders, both the two-legged and four-wheeled kind, big lights glaring in compensation for dull ceiling illumination. Workers now pointed or ran as *Phoenix* marines smashed a secure gate and display warning of entry for station personnel only, and clattered down a big stairway at speed.

To Erik's left, empty space descended far into the depths below. On the next floor down, ceilings triple-height compared to residential floors, big workshop spaces where loaders were being fixed, a sprawling, organised tangle of station facilities and mobile machinery. Suddenly Dale stopped and fired upward, as return fire clanged and sparked off the steel around them. Erik kept running, descending stairs as fast as his shaky feet could take him, leaping now three at a time as he rounded the bend to the next flight.

He passed Ricardo as she stood and fired at someone shooting at them from amongst the machines, then Carponi was ahead and yelling at him to go past... and was hit, right before Erik's eyes, a sudden impact taking him left, then staggered... and Carponi fell as his legs gave way. Erik skidded in beside, as Ricardo was yelling "Yozzi's down! Yozzi's down!".

It had gone through his left hip, Erik saw, yanking out his first aid and fumbling for the tension bandage as even he knew how, though the only time he'd applied one before had been to a spacer with ship-board injuries. He somehow got the cover off as Ricardo skidded in beside him... "LC, I got it, leave him to me!"

"Give me some fucking cover, marine!" Erik snapped. "I carry, you shoot!" And Ricardo saw the logic, took up her rifle again and laid down fire. If a marine had to carry the wounded Corporal, that would be one good rifle out of the fight — far smarter that he did it. He got on the bandage, wrapped the tie awkwardly about Carponi's leg and yanked as tight as he could, recalling that instruction well and heedless of Carponi's scream. The hip was one of those spots that just couldn't be armoured effectively outside of full rigs. This one was bleeding a lot. Erik pulled the tag that activated the electro-chem overlay, which should have stilled the bleeding a little as it released micros directly into the bloodstream where they would propagate and attempt to fix damage synthetically. If the femoral artery was severed, even micros probably couldn't fix it quickly enough to stop Carponi from bleeding out.

"Corporal, on your feet!" Erik commanded, giving Carponi a heaving hand up, as more fire snapped by. Carponi complied just enough for Erik to get a shoulder into his middle and lifted in a combat carry. Erik was a big man, but so was Carponi, and in armour it felt like carrying a sack of concrete.

"Go, go!" Dale was yelling from behind, as Erik realised the Lieutenant had been just behind him the whole time, providing cover. Someone else swore in that loud, panicked way that told of another marine hit, but there was no stopping or further comment so Erik pressed on, concentrating on one stair at a time as fast as he dared, rifle in one hand and Carponi's leg in the other to keep his burden as balanced as possible. Aside from the scream when he'd pulled the bandage tight, Carponi had barely made a noise.

One advantage of having someone to carry, it focused the mind so much that Erik worried less about bullets and more about how many flights there were to go. Five hundred meters from main dock level down to outer rim dock, he recalled — Hoffen was a monster. That was the height of a very tall skyscraper, a very tough descent with a big, wounded man on your shoulder while under fire.

After a time it started to hurt very badly, despite his augments, high fitness levels and time in the gym. The shooting had paused to the odd, speculative shot, and distant yells gave the impression of pursuit from a safer range. At one turn in the stairs Private Yu was waiting for him, offering to take a turn beneath the load.

"Fuck off," Erik informed him and kept going. If they were ambushed again, which seemed likely, then Private Yu was going to be far more useful unencumbered than his LC. Having found the one thing he could do as well as any marine, Erik wasn't going to give it up short of collapsing.

When he reached rim level he was gasping with effort and covered in sweat. The industrial sector quickly turned into the rim docks from where Trace had departed for Faustino, where shuttles would dock with the rotating outer rim 'beneath' the relative direction of gravity. The concourse was nearly empty, stationers apparently warned that trouble was heading this way. But if stationers knew, security would know as well…

"Just one dock up," Dale told them as they moved. "PH-4 is in transit, ETA six minutes."

"Hang on Corporal," Erik gasped, struggling to keep up with the marines around him. "Almost there."

"*Phoenix*!" came a yell up ahead, and the marines on point took fast cover against the next bulkhead. "*Phoenix*! It's *Mercury*!"

Up ahead, Gunnery Sergeant Forrest peered quickly about the bulkhead. "*Mercury marines,*" he reported back. "*Plenty of them. We're cut off.*"

Dale swore, ushering Erik to a wall when Erik had trouble changing direction. "Fuck, we don't have time for this. We go through them, we're all dead." Because whatever the *Phoenix* bravado, they all knew that marines were marines, whatever their ship. These marines had defensive position, and dislodging them would be hell.

"*Mercury*!" Erik yelled. "This is *Phoenix*! Who is this?"

"This is Major Rennes! That you Debogande?"

"Fuck it," said Erik, and lowered Carponi as Dale and Reddy grabbed him. "Shooting won't solve it, gotta talk."

"Could tell PH-4 to get to another dock?" Dale suggested.

"With these guys on our ass, I don't think so," said Erik. "That's the *Mercury* company commander, that'll be his command squad, those guys don't quit."

Dale did not disagree. Erik strode forward, feeling suddenly light without the Lance Corporal's weight, and light headed too. He stepped past the disbelieving Gunnery Sergeant Forrest and into the open concourse, trusting that *Mercury* marines weren't so trigger happy that they'd shoot him dead on the spot. Several seconds after he'd had the thought, he was still alive, and the *Mercury* complement hadn't shot him yet. That meant it hadn't been their immediate intention.

"I got a shuttle inbound," Erik told the marines ahead, squeezed into tight cover behind ticket counters, bulkhead edges and railing supports. At least ten rifles that he could see, though only three of them aimed at him. At this range, three would be enough, and the others, with typical discipline, were watching the more dangerous targets behind him. "And I got a marine bleeding out who'll die if he doesn't get immediate attention. If you're gonna shoot, do it now and get it over with, or get out of our way and let us get back to *Phoenix*."

A thin, scarred marine with a lean face stepped forward. His rifle was cradled with that effortless balance of long-term veterans, and his armour was so scratched and worn it was a shade lighter colour than his comrades. On his shoulder, golden leaf insignia. "I'm Major Rennes. What's Major Thakur doing on Faustino?"

Of course he was interested in Trace. She was, as always, the key. "Talking to someone with a secret Fleet want kept at all costs," said Erik. "She's under fire right now. And you're keeping us from her."

Rennes studied him expressionlessly. His eyes trailed down. Erik realised he had Carponi's blood all over him. "What secret?"

"Alo and hacksaws," said Erik. "Same thing."

Rennes frowned. "Same thing?"

Erik nodded. "We ran into hacksaws a week back. The Major killed them. We had some dead ones on board. Or they were dead — until we pulled up alongside that alo cruiser in hub dock. And the damn things came back to life."

Renne's eyes went wide. It was a little dramatised for effect, but Erik was beyond caring. "HQ killed your Captain?"

"And pinned it on me," Erik agreed. "They had me in custody. The Major busted me out single-handedly. Pantillo told her what was going on, and her alone. If you've ever met her, or know anyone who has, you'll know she's everything they say."

Rennes shook his head. "She's more. I served with her on Ryda. She's exceptional."

"Yes she is." Erik took a deep breath. "And she's going to die if you don't let me get back to *Phoenix*."

Rennes stared for a moment longer. "I was there," Dale added from behind. Erik did not turn to look, but he could see at least two rifles swinging that way, as Dale stepped from cover. "I helped get the Major out after she busted the LC out of custody. It's all true, every word. I still live for Fleet every day, but not even Fleet Admirals can fuck with Fleet marines."

"Lieutenant Dale," said Rennes. "Been a long time."

"Yes sir."

Rennes took a deep breath, and stood aside. "Go," he said. "Before I change my mind."

"Major," said Erik, with a hard stare. "Spread it around. And watch your back. Marines know that there's no higher cause than the guy next to you, but these fuckers in charge, they think they've found one. And they will bury the lot of us to achieve it."

He looked back as the marines behind him moved, but Private Yu had Carponi on his shoulder, and waved him on ahead. With *Mercury*'s marines here too, Hoffen security wouldn't try anything more — probably they'd pulled back in relief, under the impression that Major Rennes would handle it for them. Erik fell in behind the forward guard, and they jogged through *Mercury*'s position. Cautious *Mercury* marines watched them with rifles partly lowered, perhaps uncertain exactly what was going on. Erik recalled Captain Ritish up in the hub, and wondered what would happen between her and Major Rennes after this. What Rennes had just done was treasonous, and Fleet could have him shot. But kill *another* marine company commander? One who though not nearly as famous among civilians, was just as respected among the marines who mattered most? That could get very tangled for High Command, very fast.

PH-4 made a hard dock with a crash of grapples through the concourse floor just as they reached the berth. This time Erik led, cycling the inner door, then onto the ladder and slid to make it fast, all the way down to the outer door above PH-4's dorsal hatch. Above the other marines copied — Yu and Carponi would be last, unable to balance on the ladder with them all piled into the tube and waiting for the inner door to close again so they could open the outer.

"Clear!" came the yell from high up the tube, and Erik cycled the door below, a faint pop of the ears as air pressure equalised, then the shuttle's dorsal hatch opened and Erik slid straight in and scrambled out of hatch access, down a level to the cockpit and stuck his head in on Lieutenant Toguchi in the pilot's seat. Outside the main view, the huge, curving underside of Hoffen's outer rim, studded with newly arrived shuttles, some leaving even now, other grapples left empty. Beyond that, more ship traffic than Erik had seen before in his life. Ships swarming, ships spinning, rotating, dodging, thrusting.

"Holy fuck," he said.

"No shit," said Toguchi, flipping switches and trimming engines. "Get everyone buckled in tight back there, it's a real mess. Got three freighters on the rim threatening to fire up jump engines, two on Hoffen-A, one on Hoffen-B. Everyone's getting the hell out while they still can, Fleet's threatening to blast those who don't comply with direction."

"Which will give us a nice big cloud of debris as well," said Erik. "Hostile contacts?"

"Not yet," said Toguchi. "But it's early." Something exploded to one side. "Fuck. Lee?"

"Cruiser *Far Reach* just fired on a freighter," said Ensign Lee from the front seat up the narrow cockpit. "Big hit, lots of debris. No idea why... there's five hundred different conversations going at once on different channels, lots of possible threats, lots of wires crossed."

"Damn, look at that com chatter spike," said Toguchi, and flipped channels. "Lieutenant Dale, how we doing?"

"One minute," said Dale. *"Locking down our wounded."*

"Another shot," said Lee. "That's… over by Hoffen-B, can't see that one, someone's shooting at Fleet I think."

"Whoa look at this fucker," Toguchi added. Ahead, a big freighter was rotating hard, nose and tail attitude thrusters blazing blue against the black sky. Her nose was missing station rim by half the length of the ship. "That's nuts. What the hell's he doing?" Erik was horrified by Fleet shooting at merchanters, but someone really ought to shoot this idiot on principle.

"Thirty seconds," said Dale down back.

"Better strap in LC."

Erik slapped Toguchi on the shoulder. "Better you than me, Chunky. Make sure you stick the dismount."

"All seals on," said Lee. "Station green, grapples green. Clear on your mark." As Erik moved quickly to the jumpseat directly behind the cockpit and strapped himself in with several fast, well-practised moves. It was far enough back that he could only hear the pilots on coms.

"Lieutenant Dale?"

"Five seconds." Pause. *"All sealed down back, you are clear to go."*

"PH-4 copies, we are leaving. All hands take hold." Wham! as the grapples released, and suddenly gravity was gone, hands and feet lifting to the ceiling, and blood rushing to the face as PH-4 fell away from the rim. *"Thrust on, here we…"*

WHAM! with an impact that made the grapple release feel like a tap, and everything was spinning sideways. That force did not let up, and the view up front was spinning madly, stars and station and ships, stars and station and ships… round and round. And then the decompression alarm was howling, an automated voice repeating, "Masks on! Masks on! Masks on!" as Erik scrambled to re-secure his infantry-mask and get the oxygen going…

"We're hit!" Ensign Lee was shouting. *"PH-4 is hit! We are taking fire! Toguchi? Chunky, what the fuck? Chunky!"* Looking back desperately over his shoulder.

Erik saw one of Toguchi's arms floating free, pulled outward by the centrifugal force. And blood spattering upon the forward screens. "Toguchi's hit!" Erik announced, and cut his straps. Immediately the force of the spin threw him forward at the back of Toguchi's seat. "Lieutenant Dale, get up here ASAP and help me remove the pilot!"

"On my way!"

As Erik reached about Toguchi's limp body, fumbling for straps and getting bloody fingers in the process. "Ensign Lee! Do you have control?" You could fly a combat shuttle from the co-pilot's seat, but the configuration wasn't ideal. Also, Ensign Lee was not as good as Lieutenant Toguchi, and that was not ideal either.

"Sir I think we've lost an engine! I can't get the spin to stop!"

"Just leave it Ensign, I'm taking control. If I can't get Toguchi out, you'll have to leave your seat." Click, as the harness finally came away, and Erik dragged at Toguchi's body... but the centrifugal force pushed him toward the nose, and Erik struggled to find the leverage...

"Here!" said Dale, arriving at his side with a thud, grabbing Toguchi under the shoulders and pulling. Erik fought to get the legs and arms clear of the loose harness, and suddenly he was out. Erik clambered awkwardly in, only now hearing the clear hissing noise from multiple holes along the right side of the cockpit.

"The seals aren't closing that leak!" said Lee. *"We'll start running out of air in fifteen!"*

"Unimportant," said Erik, getting his arms in the harness and finding the controls, eyes scanning multiple screens that showed red lights on attitude, engines, navigation frantically trying to get his attention as they spun out of control through the busiest shipping anyone had ever seen. "Reroute power to second gen, first is gone. Port engine is dead, run compensation through flightcomp..."

"Flightcomp is not responding."

"Just have to do it by sight then, hold on." As Dale reached around him to strap him in, seeing he hadn't had the time for it. Erik ignored the help, angling starboard engine offset twenty-five degrees, and rear thrust into the emerging direction of spin… he hit thrust, and they thundered, then the starfield began to slow. Trajectory began to emerge from navcomp.

"We are headed straight for that freighter!"

"I see it." As the straps snapped in and Dale pulled him tight with a hard shove. Erik wanted desperately to ask how Toguchi was, but just didn't have time. Something else snapped past them, lightning fast. "Manoeuvring!" he yelled and slammed on thrust, half expecting the engines to explode and solve their problems there and then. Instead he got an uneven kick that skidded them forward and sideways at once, and a grunt from Dale as he was flung backward off the chair and hit something down back.

More shots snapped by, and something blew up very bright to one side. "Full burn! PH-4 is under fire!" He angled thrust with three-Gs still pressing him back in his chair, somehow manufacturing a turn from unresponsive controls. Nav feed showed them curling around, out and beyond Hoffen-A's rim, into the heaviest adjacent traffic. At least it would be hard to hit them out here without hitting friendlies.

"PH-4, this is Phoenix," came Shahaim's voice in his ears. *"We've identified your incoming fire, it's a cruiser, UFS Starwind."*

"Phoenix, this is the LC," said Erik through gritted teeth. "Break dock and get farside of that alo bastard alongside you."

"Yes sir, do you want us to come and pick you up?"

"No, stay close to station or someone will take the opportunity of this chaos to shoot you. Station is cover. Get farside of the alo, watch him at all costs. Then kill that bitch *Starwind* for me."

"My pleasure sir."

"Sir," said Lee, *"I have Starwind's position on nav."* As the plot appeared on the HUD — it was an awful way to fly a shuttle in combat, he didn't have the helmet visor or the right uplinks and had to look from one side of the cockpit to the other to find everything, wasting precious time. There was a lot of traffic between *Starwind* and them, but it would be folly to assume there was only one Fleet ship aiming for them.

Erik cut thrust, spun them sideways, hit thrust again to take them curling past the side of an escaping freighter, cut and spun once more onto an approach vector past *Phoenix*'s end of the Hoffen-A hub. More grunts from down back as Dale and whoever else were flung about… but Erik hadn't the time to pay them attention either.

Another shot from *Starwind* — hitting an erratically moving shuttle with damaged engines in heavy traffic was proving hard for its armscomp. Then com crackled again. *"Hey Starwind! Greetings from Phoenix, you fucker."*

And *Starwind* smashed sideways like a car hit by a train at a level crossing, three heavy hits breaking it in multiple ways, then a bright flash and debris raining across the shipping confusion like summer rain. Unbidden, Erik recalled another of the Captain's lessons, 'when commanding a vessel in combat, you must never prioritise targets over threats.' Case in point, Captain, and correct as always.

"And *Phoenix*," Erik added. "Put a viper warhead through the outer wall of Fleet HQ on the Hoffen rim. Remote fuse, put it to Armscomp control."

"Aye LC. You want an open channel to HQ?"

You read my mind, Lieutenant Shahaim. "Yes please Lieutenant."

"Shilu, put the LC through." A pause, Erik firing them sideways on course-correction only, already carrying about five times the velocity he should be in this mess. *"LC, you have coms."*

"To Supreme Commander Chankow. Continuing to fire upon *Phoenix* or *Phoenix* support vessels will result in the destruction of Fleet HQ on Hoffen Station. Continuing to lead the attack upon Major Thakur on Faustino will lead to the destruction of Fleet HQ on Hoffen Station. In fact, you piss me off one more time, and I'll blow you up like we just did *UFS Starwind*. Your choice asshole."

There would have been about a hundred people on *Starwind*. There were considerably more in Hoffen Fleet HQ. That was sad, but he was becoming increasingly convinced that restraint, in this situation, would only lead to defeat… and the consequences of defeat would be astronomically worse than any damage he could do here. Trace had told him that when the stakes were high, he had to be prepared to do anything to ensure success. Only now was he coming to understand what that meant... and perhaps, why she'd been so insistent on making sure he understood. She'd guessed, no doubt, just how big this could get, and just the scale of opponents he'd face. This fight could not be won by half-measures.

Hoffen-A hub was rushing up, and he spun them awkwardly with what attitude control remained, pointed their tail at *Phoenix* and hit thrust. Everything thundered, and he got a burst of coms as Ensign Lee cycled through contacts — captains and coms operators yelling, directing, threatening. Small ships were leaving the hub, shuttles, insystem haulers, two nearby looked as though they'd had a low-V collision and were spinning apart amidst a spray of debris. He knew the only reason PH-4 was still alive was that most Fleet ships were positioning for angles to hit the three freighters on the rim threatening to cycle their jump engines. But they hadn't fired yet because they had to hit all three simultaneously, or else the survivor would cycle and kill much of Hoffen Station, and take several million people with it.

Then *Phoenix* was rushing up, hanging off the far side of the hub from the alo ship as he'd ordered, not further than fifty meters from the station's huge, curving side. Vector was drifting as the number three engine faded, and he adjusted, putting on more power and rotating them dorsal-up to face the approaching grapples. A final burst of braking, then an attitude push and slammed the damaged ship harder than intended against the grapples, but they were built for exactly this scenario and bounced them back down as the suspension recovered.

"Firm dock!" Erik yelled into intercom. "Dismount dismount! Move move move!" And fought to get his buckles undone, as Lee did the same before him, *Phoenix*'s huge hull filling the view overhead. He pushed out of the chair, and found Privates Tong and Reddy attending to Lieutenant Dale, who was out cold — that burst of thrust must have sent him into the cockpit door at 3-G, and lucky Tong and Reddy had come up too or he'd have bounced around even worse in what followed, that had been all the thumping and grunting he'd heard during manoeuvres. Lieutenant Toguchi they'd managed to strap into the rear observer's chair, limbs floating, blood pooling in surrounding droplets, eyes open and sightless.

But again Erik didn't have time, and powered himself straight past the marines, through the door now open in dismount and beat the first marine from main hold into the dorsal departure and up the tube. The hatch read green, equal pressure and he hit the release... a rush of air and the usual popping of ears, then up into Midships Operations, past the crew on the hatch and straight up the access to the core.

"Bridge, I am on my way and approaching core, ETA one minute ten." Because he'd timed himself, as they all had, and it was practised weekly by all, assuming they could find the time. When he'd first arrived on *Phoenix*, three years and several lifetimes ago, it had taken him closer to two minutes thirty. Behind him, some of the marines might make it to main hold, but most would stay here in Midships, as good a place to ride out a push as any — there were corpsmen standing by for the wounded, and Carponi couldn't get proper treatment in Medbay while they were manoeuvring anyway.

Up the fast running handline through the core, into the rotating main hold with its slowly spinning walls, then down gamma-b stairs with fast pulls, then leaps down the ladders to main corridor, then a sprint up to the bridge in what might have been his best time yet...

"LC on the bridge!" came the yell, and Shahaim was ditching straps and leaping from the chair, while Draper did the same in Shahaim's chair, then came fast to help Erik in. Everything secure, displays back in position, Draper began helping Erik out of his armour — neither the chair nor the all important armrests were shaped for it, and any physical misalignment could force piloting errors. Erik realised past his gasps for air that he was exhausted, muscles aching, his brain dead tired from endless stress and fear, and covered in Carponi and Toguchi's blood as well.

"LC has command!" Shahaim announced as she brought her own post to order.

"I have command," Erik confirmed, as his uplinks locked into familiar bridge frequencies, and the *Phoenix* HUD appeared on his inner retinas.   He reached quickly into the armrest pouch and pulled a stim tube, put it to his wrist and felt it sting.   Immediately his heart galloped and sounds came rushing, and he flexed his hands, then got a good grip of the sticks, arms free of armour as Draper got to work on the torso straps... and suddenly one of the bridge-guard marines was there to help him, and everything came unhooked in a rush.

"LC," said Shilu, "we've intercepted transmissions from Crondike, there's some serious action taking place out there. They're shooting the place up, the Major must be outnumbered like ten to one."

"Right," said Erik, holding his arms over his head as the torso armour was removed, "we're going to get her."   And was surprised that it was Kaspowitz who questioned.

"She gave us her information and told us not to die rescuing her," said the Nav Lieutenant.   "I'd love to rescue her too LC, but if we try it in this mess we won't make it three klicks."   Draper and the marine gathered the armour and disappeared to captain's quarters, the closest convenient location in which to ride out a push. Erik's legs were still armoured, but that wouldn't bother his flying.

"I'm not doing it for her," said Erik, "I'm doing it because I still don't know what I'm fucking doing out here compared to her. She's the only one who does, and she's worth more than her damned information, and so's the guy who provided her with it."   He was wasting time explaining himself, but he needed time to soak up the confusion on his screens, and gather his thoughts as the stim shot sent his brain into overdrive.

"Fleet HQ won't let them shoot us with that warhead embedded in the rim wall," Shahaim suggested without confidence.

"They will if five of them get a good shot all at once," said Karle from Arms.   "That'll kill us so fast we won't be able to trigger the warhead."

"Besides which they'll be evacuating and relocating," Erik said grimly. "Shouldn't take more than a few minutes for vital functions." He flipped channels. "Operations, who's on standby?"

"Lieutenant Crozier with Delta Platoon at combat dock," came the reply. *"Lieutenant Zhi with Echo at shuttle dock. We have just the civilian shuttle left with PH-4 damaged, and we have no qualified pilot — Ensign Lee is hurt as well, so we've no shuttle crew at all."*

Dammit, thought Erik. Lee must have been hit when Toguchi was, and not noticed at the time — with all the adrenaline pumping, it happened. And he noted more shooting on scan, as Fleet took out a merchanter they didn't like the look of. Another big flash. Without a functioning shuttle when they reached Faustino, recovering those marines would be all about hoping that PH-1 was still operational. If it was not, they had nothing to get down to Crondike with. Lieutenant Zhi had been thinking ahead to get Echo Platoon ready at shuttle dock adjacent to where PH-4 had arrived, but he'd been expecting to use PH-4 itself, and now both it and their last remaining shuttle pilot were incapacitated.

"LC... this is Ops, scratch that last, I have a volunteer just arrived here for shuttle pilot. No, scratch that, two volunteers." Almost immediately, Erik realised who. *"It's the kuhsi and... and your sister, sir..."*

As every pair of eyes on the bridge swung onto him. "Eyes on stations!" Erik snapped.

"Erik!" It was Lisbeth, down at Ops. *"Erik I'm a good co-pilot and Tif's got sixteen* years *as command pilot! She's really good, she can do it!"*

"Good, go!" he told them, not quite able to believe his own words as he spoke them.

"Go? You mean...?"

"Yes go! Get in the cockpit now, you won't be able to do it once we're underway. Lieutenant Zhi, that means you too."

"Echo Platoon copies LC."

"Yes!" Lisbeth agreed. And off-mike... *"Good, go Tif! Let's go!"* That would take another two minutes at least to get them

and all of Echo into the civvie shuttle, he calculated furiously. The most dangerous bit would just be getting to Faustino — on *Phoenix* or off *Phoenix*, the danger was about the same, and sometimes when ships were hit, their shuttle occupants were the only ones to survive and get clear. His subconscious had realised all that before the rest of him, and his mouth had given the order before his brain had properly caught up.

"Scan, who is this on the inner side of Hoffen-A hub?"

"That's *Adventurer*, D-class cruiser," Geish said immediately. "Looks like she's covering in case we cross the rim."

"D-class mass is 38K, right?"

"Yep, minus ten percent unloaded," said Shahaim. "*Adventurer's* manifest showed she was prepped for light duty, I'd guess mass 36K."

"Good," said Erik. "Ops, I want main docking grapple standby. Arms, all target on *Adventurer.* Lieutenant Crozier, do you copy?"

"Copy LC, this is Crozier."

"Lieutenant I want you to stand by for possible boarding. We are going to engage combat grapple and run with the target ship attached. You may need to go aboard at some point but I can't say when, just be ready."

"Oh holy fuck," Shahaim muttered, as across the bridge officers stared at each other, or swallowed hard in disbelief.

"Copy LC," said Crozier, with all the cool she'd learned under Trace. *"Sounds like fun."*

"Arms!" said Erik.

"Yes LC!" came Karle, young and anxious.

"We're going to come through the spoke arms of Hoffen-A and up alongside point blank and surprise them. I want weapons and engines disabled, tell me what you need."

"I… well LC, I think…"

"Come on kid, you are *Phoenix* Arms officer! It's your call, call it!"

"Aye LC! Two pairs of vipers in brackets for proximity burst, total surprise, blind their sensors and shrapnel damage on dorsal and belly emplacements.   If you can get us alongside within ten seconds of detonation, I'll have firing solution for a D-class in Armscomp and we'll take out remaining guns and engines with proximity cannon."

"Ten seconds is not enough time," Erik replied.   "I can get you there in fifteen.   Hold fire on the vipers for five seconds after I hit thrust, calculate your shot to miss the hub spoke and account for motion."

"Aye LC, five seconds after thrust, I copy."

UFS Adventurer was on the opposite side of Hoffen's hub, as well as on the far side of the huge, rotating wheel of Hoffen-A.   This was going to be some move.

"Erik we're in!" came Lisbeth's voice.   *"We're belting in, the marines are still securing."*   She probably didn't even know Lieutenant Zhi's name, let alone procedures for embarking and disembarking marines in any circumstance, let alone combat ops.

"Lisbeth, is Tif going to understand anything we say?"

"Probably not with all this static and noise, but I can translate."

Even better, Erik thought drily.   But spreading negativity before operations was not conducive to success.   "Good job Lis, now hold tight, it's going to get bumpy."   Ops would talk to her about the marines, and Lieutenant Zhi would be in her ear frequently — as co-pilot she was also load-monitor, though marines did their own load-mastering.   SLMs, shuttle and Ops personnel called marines, for Self-Loading Munitions.

And he took a moment to consider *Adventurer*, a much smaller ship with perhaps ninety crew, and no business being within *Phoenix*'s arc of fire really, given Phoenix could shoot down most of what came her way, and *Adventurer* couldn't.   Ninety lives and comrades for whom *Phoenix* in the war would have risked much under fire.   Now he was about to take a huge chance with all of them, and unlike *Starwind*, *Adventurer* hadn't yet done anything to earn it.

"This is Ops," came another call. *"Everyone from PH-4 is off and secure. Two fatalities, Carponi and Toguchi."* Erik saw red, and stopped caring about *Adventurer.*

"Lieutenant Geish," he said. "Highlight primary threats to priority please." Because it was such a mess out there, and his brain was still catching up with where everyone was. Red highlights flashed across his scan feed as Geish complied — several bigger Fleet cruisers holding off in cover-fire positions... and *UFS Mercury*, now undocking from the Hoffen-A rim with a hard reverse, spinning as Captain Ritish brought their main engines into clear space.

"*Mercury* is clear," Geish added, in case anyone had missed it. The one ship here they didn't outclass... although at these ranges and matching velocities, anyone was a threat.

"Scan," said Erik, running his final engine checks, "add all chah'nas and alo vessels to priority listing please." More red dots flared as Geish complied. Two chah'nas vessels still inbound from further out, but they could arrive real fast if they violated lanes and pulsed jump engines. And that blasted alo ship directly on the opposite side of the hub from them... plus one more on the rim of Hoffen-B. Still in place despite everyone else leaving around them, both of them. Did they know something? Or just playing possum?

Now or never. "All hands this is the LC. Prepare for combat. Visual report, all stations, give me a green." Green lights flashed across his vision, each of the stations reporting readiness — he didn't have time for audio reporting, visuals saved time. "All good, all green," he summarised. "We are going in five on my mark." Engines powered up to full, and he spared another thought for the jumplines. Second Lieutenant Rooke had been working feverishly as always while they'd been on Hoffen, continuing repairs and adjustments. But it didn't change the fact that the original repair in Argitori had been a patch-up. The enormous three-arm of Hoffen-A slowly swung to the 'vertical' before them, before continuing ponderously past.

"Mark," he said. Scan showed *Mercury* thrusting toward an overwatch position. More warning shots on the rim, a string of proximity detonations. "Five. Four. Three. Two. One." He hit thrust at 5-Gs, with a roar that undoubtedly scorched the Hoffen hub. His coms lit with automated screeches of alarm — thrust in excess of 1-G in any proximity to station was strictly forbidden outside of wartime.   Flying through the spokes of a station wheel was forbidden at any time.

He twisted the grips as the towering three-arm came up, angling toward it.   Thud!thud!thud! as Karle fired his missiles, rounds arcing up away from Hoffen hub, through the wheel and twisting around to the far side.   Erik dropped the stern to give *Phoenix* a shove into clearer space as they passed through the wheel, then kicked them around in a huge, swinging barrel roll, nose pointed to the hub all the way as the rear swung around in the direction of flight to slow them once more.

"Multiple hits!" shouted Karle as *Adventurer* came into view... trajectory was off a little so Erik increased thrust until his vision blurred.   "Proximity targeting, go Harris!"   Rapid thuds as *Phoenix*'s near-range cannon opened fire, and Erik caught a brief visual of the stricken cruiser, already yawing and stunned from the missile near misses, explosions now surgically removing its weapon emplacements before it could return fire.

"Good volley, good volley!" Harris added from Arms Two. "Lower emplacements disabled, engines disabled... sir he's rolling away, I have no angle on those dorsal emplacements!"

"Good enough, won't matter," said Erik, powering around to matching velocities, then hitting nose thrust to brake them right against the cruiser's belly.   Clangs and screeches of debris against the outer hull.

"We are being targeted!" shouted Geish.   "Two... three... five sources! *Mercury* has locked us!"

As Erik hit the final attitude burn and smashed the combat grapples into the much smaller vessel's mid-section.   Super-heated charges fired, burned into the thick mid-section armour, then the grapples smashed into those holes with a molecularly engineered grip.   Nose grapples got a lighter grip to make it steady, then Erik rolled them over with attitude thrusters to put *Adventurer* between them and *Mercury.*

"Good grip, good grip!" Ops was shouting. *"We got her!"* Coms were flashing, priority from *Mercury*, but Erik could guess what Captain Ritish would say. Their passenger was not big enough to obstruct fore or aft attitude thrusters, so Erik burned them into a hard rotation away from *Mercury.*

"Arms," he said. "If we receive warning shots, fire warning shots back. If we are fired upon directly, kill the offender."

"Aye Captain, kill the offender!" No one bothered to correct Karle's little mistake. It took twice as long to turn, but as soon as the aft was clear, Erik hit a 3-G burn and nosed down to put Hoffen's main axle between *Phoenix* and *Mercury.* The grapples held, so he increased that to 4-G, then to 5, frightening the life out of several small shuttles and station-close traffic who evaded wildly from the path of this over-powered alo-tech warship that came roaring past with its tail aflame, dragging a ruined smaller ship with it like small prey caught in a predator's talons.

"They're not firing!" Geish observed with desperate hope. "They're holding fire!" With *Adventurer* in their grasp, firing on *Phoenix* without hitting the small cruiser was nearly impossible. Just to be sure, Erik gave them a roll, rotating *Phoenix* and *Adventurer* around a common point of mass as he increased thrust to 6-G, increasing the difficulty for opposing armscomps from impossible to very impossible. *Phoenix* thundered and roared like the wild and hungry beast she was, only mildly troubled by the extra weight, her own weapons tracking targets as they moved across their individual patches of sky.

"*Mercury* is pursuing!" called Jiri from Scan Two.

"Arms!" said Erik. "One viper please, target *Mercury* directly and hit her."

"Aye Captain," said Karle. "One viper, targeting for a strike." Everyone knew what would happen when you fired one unsupported missile from matching initial-V at a combat carrier. It accelerated away from *Phoenix*, turning a sharp corner and charging straight at the fellow carrier at crazy acceleration... and abruptly vanished as *Mercury*'s defensive missiles blew it to very small pieces.

"She's backing off," said Jiri. "She's reducing thrust and steering wide." Erik skidded them past several fleeing freighters as, even burdened, *Phoenix* blew past them at a steady 6-Gs. To judge by the relative stress readings from grapples and engines both, Erik was sure the grapples would break before the engines maxed out — the sheer power of this ship was beyond belief, even for one who'd served on her for three years. Warning fire snapped by, and Karle returned fire, Erik slowing the roll to give his guns a longer look at the offender.

"Coms," Erik gasped past the heavy-Gs, "general frequency." Shilu flashed it up. "*Phoenix* to Fleet. *Phoenix* to Fleet. Stay clear or die. No more warnings."

"ETA on Faustino is sixty-three minutes on current thrust," said Kaspowitz. "Let's hope it's fast enough." Command Squad had to hold out for an hour then, plus whatever it took to get the shuttle down to them, if needed. Pulsing jump engines with a passenger was suicide, and even if they jettisoned the passenger they were still too close to Heuron V's mass. Besides which, if they lost their hostage, *Mercury* and others would be back after them at full speed, and would catch them as soon as they slowed into Faustino orbit. No, the hostage had to stay, and this was the fastest acceleration they dared. Major Thakur, and the units she commanded, were very hard to kill. He could only hope that they remained so for one more hour.

CHAPTER 30

Trace bounded down the engineering tunnel besides massive pressurised conveyors and siphon pipes, as Lance Corporal Walker's section fired in their rear to keep pursuit at bay. It was hot down here, generators thundering and steam venting, big industrial lights throwing a harsh glare onto working steel and gantries. Workers stared and ran as Staff Sergeant Kono and others yelled at them to 'get out or die'.

They'd tried to push for the landing pads, but the approach was hallways and open foyers like a shopping mall — the side approaches were sealed shut with doors they had no way to open, and the mall-space was now a killzone with zig-zag crossfires around every turn. In full armour and weapons her marines could have done it no trouble, but in light armour and no weapons larger than a rifle, she was facing a fifty percent chance of making the pads at all, at probably eighty percent casualties. From that point Hausler simply had to be there, and Hiro couldn't find him, as all of Crondike was in deep-static lockdown with jamming so intense even local civvie coms were crackling.

She couldn't get eighty percent of her guys hit or killed on a prayer, and all of them killed if that prayer wasn't answered, and so she'd opted for her next best-bet — find a well-defensible spot and force her attackers to come at her hard. That would create a localised firefight that could get Hausler's attention and tell him where they were. The pressure to kill them all before that happened could force the enemy to press harder than was wise, and if Command Squad had defensive position, that swung the odds back in their favour. If Hausler couldn't find them, they could still exhaust the enemy by killing a lot more of them than vice-versa, then charge and break out once they were vulnerable. And from there... find a shuttle, somewhere. Which would probably get shot down before they'd cleared Faustino, and certainly by some Fleet cruiser afterward. It was hopeless unless Hausler found them, and probably even then... unless some 'enemy' Fleet vessel had a change of heart and saved them, or joined *Phoenix*, futile straw-grasping hope that it was. She'd told Erik, in the elevator descending to the Hoffen rim, that Kulina didn't hope. But neither did they give up while still breathing.

She emerged into the target space — Crondike Wellhead Seven, the top of a nine kilometre deep shaft that burrowed into Faustino's ice crust. It was a tangled mass of pipes, pressure tanks and power units beneath a huge domed ceiling, and open to access tunnels from three directions only — one too many for Trace's liking, but a better bet for a defensible position than anywhere else accessible from where they were.

She took a running leap onto a circuit gantry three meters up, then bounced from there onto the one above that and skipped beside a huge blowout-preventer atop the wellhead to peer across that vantage. "Get out that way!" she yelled at some bewildered workers nearby, pointing down the further tunnel. "There's going to be shooting, if you stay here you'll die!" They ran.

"Walker," she said on coms, "your section has the tunnel you're in. Kono, you've got the one opposite, I've got the right-angles one with Rael. Is Romki still with us?"

"He's here Major," said Kumar. *"Just coming in now."*

"Put him in the middle, see if you can get him a better mask from one of these worker offices. And while you're at it, take a look for anything useful — explosive gas canisters would be nice, we seem to have left our grenades on *Phoenix*."

"Major," said Kono. *"I'm sure you're aware, but some of these big tanks are explosive."*

"And heavily armoured," Trace added. "They might not use anything heavy on us for a while at least, this place is expensive. Someone check for the outer airlock, do we have a landing pad here?" Because access to Crondike schematic was blocked, but many wellheads had shuttle landing pads and direct-access airlocks so that visiting engineers and miners could get to the business end of operations directly.

Someone was climbing up to her right — she looked, and found a big workman heading her way in heavy protective clothes, dangling mask and fixed helmet. He looked more grim than scared, one look and Trace knew better than to warn him to get lost.

He stopped short, respectful of her weapon. "Major I'm Chief Stanton!" he shouted over the generator noise. "I run this wellhead! I was a marine sergeant, in for nine years! You're from *Phoenix*, right?"

"That's right!"

"Then that makes you Major Thakur! What's this all about?"

"I don't have time to explain, but local security and Fleet HQ want us all dead!" Stanton stared. Up the tunnel they'd come from, more firing broke out, Corporal Walker's section in defensive position, shooting up the way they'd come. "Does this place have a landing pad?"

Stanton considered for a moment longer. Then pointed at the far wall of the domed wellhead complex, where a fourth access tunnel would be if they'd been symmetrical. "Just out there! Do you need it operational? I can prep it for you!"

"Is there any way you can visually signal our shuttle? We can't talk to him but I'd guess he's looking for us!" And she took the Chief's arm and pulled him down to a crouch as more shooting rang out from Rael's position up the next tunnel.

"You know that Crondike has air defences?" the Chief shouted back. "I doubt he'll be anywhere in visual range, but I can get out there and signal in case he makes a visual pass! That'll save you a rifle at least!"

Trace gripped his arm with a thankful stare. "Buddy, Fleet HQ is rotten at the top. They murdered Captain Pantillo." A shocked look, but not entirely surprised. Trace was certain that offers of heartfelt assistance, in situations like these, deserved at least that much truth. "I'm Kulina, you know I don't lie."

"I'll do it," the Chief said grimly. "Heard bad stories about Chankow, the guy's a prick. Good to serve with you finally!" And he scampered back to the railing and took a calculated jump off the edge, sailing down as the gravity took him.

Trace did the same off her end, bounced off the top of a pressure tank, then off a gantry rail and down to tunnel level. *"Major,"* came Hiro's voice in her ear. *"Big commotion at Hoffen, local coms are jammed but I've got access to main Heuron feed. Phoenix has broken loose, the whole station's in chaos, some Worlder ships at dock are threatening to cycle jump engines."*

Well that would do it, Trace thought, bounding up to where Rael, Terez and Van were pressed to walls or lying flat behind big pipe braces. And it would provide an excellent opportunity for *Phoenix* to get clear and run. "Are they getting out?"

"No Major, Phoenix is coming this way. Faustino."

"Oh that fucking *fool!*" Trace yelled, braced by Rael's corner, then rolled across to Terez. "He can't fight off the whole Fleet, he's going to get everyone killed!" All that effort, riding the kid hard, kicking his butt and ignoring the poor hurt puppy look of betrayal when she did it — all so he wouldn't make the soft and lethally sentimental call when the moment arrived. Because he was basically a nice kid, emotive and caring where he needed to be hard and ruthless, and exactly the kind of kid who caused disasters by trying to do what was 'right'. And now all that effort was wasted.

"Major, he's ambushed and grappled a small Fleet cruiser. He's carrying it with *him. As a hostage. So far it's working."*

Only several times in combat had Trace been so astonished at something another officer did. All of those times had been with Captain Pantillo. Until now. Opposite her, Corporal Rael had heard, and laughed wildly. "Fucking LC! That guy's insane!" From a marine, who typically thought spacers soft and feckless, there was no greater compliment.

Fire snapped by, and Trace raised briefly from her cover to fire back. "Guys!" she shouted over coms. "Hold positions and fight! The LC's on his way with *Phoenix!*"

After mid-way turnover, Erik became worried about the stress readings on the grapples. "Ops, what about those grapples?"

"I dunno LC! It'll hold another ten minutes, but beyond that we'll be pushing it!" With thrust thundering directly at Faustino's approaching icy sphere to slow them, ETA was reading fifteen minutes. But if they dumped *Adventurer*, the nine Fleet ships trailing them at a safer distance would pulse jump engines and open fire with a vengeance. Exactly what would happen if the grapples snapped, Erik didn't know — probably no one had done the sims on a 6-G run while hauling a smaller ship because they didn't want to give crazy captains ideas. He supposed they'd lose the load unevenly, it would tumble and probably hit their engines aft as it fell, for bad news all around. But they were screwed either way, so the only option was to proceed as planned, and hope. Trace's favourite word again, and boy was she going to kill him if he saw her again.

"Captain! I've got Lieutenant Hausler from Crondike!" Even Shilu was making that mistake now.

"Put him through."

Click, in his ear, then, *"Phoenix this is PH-1. Crondike communications are completely jammed, I can't contact the Major. They have defensive emplacements active and I have seen several lower capacity military shuttles in proximity, they appear to be bringing troops from other bases to Crondike, but they're sticking around and they're armed. I have withdrawn from Crondike landing pads, I'm on a blind spot from their scans so I'm safe for now unless someone gets a visual on me. If you're sending a shuttle, it will take at least two armed shuttles to take out defences and make distractions on the way in. In the meantime we have to find out where the Major is, because right now I've no idea. Awaiting further instruction, PH-1 out."*

Erik blinked on his own icon to reply. "PH-1 this is *Phoenix*. PH-4 is damaged and not operational. We're sending the remaining civilian shuttle, our kuhsi friend is piloting, Lisbeth is co-pilot, both are qualified but civilian. Echo Platoon is aboard, Lieutenant Zhi is in the loop and will have a better idea than me where the Major may be defending from in Crondike. At this velocity we're going to have to make a full orbit of Faustino — that's seventeen minutes if we hurry it along, I can elongate that to extend or shorten, but your time frame will be twenty minutes plus or minus. Communication with the civilian shuttle will be through the co-pilot, the pilot's English is poor. *Phoenix* out."

And he tried not to think of Hausler's expression upon hearing all of that. It was like asking a pilot to fly combat ops while juggling one-handed and singing the Homeworld anthem. A few seconds later, Hausler replied.

"PH-1 copies, Phoenix. Piece of cake." Erik grinned. And the grin vanished as it finally registered what Hausler had said — Crondike had surface defences, and armed shuttles present. And Lisbeth was co-piloting an unarmed civvie shuttle down into it, flown by an alien who had quite recently tried to slit the throats of those sent to help her, and whose actual qualifications everyone was dubious of to say the least, and who didn't speak the language. Trace had warned him about hard calls, and he didn't think they came any harder than this. But as she'd also said — when there was no choice, there was no choice.

If the attackers stuck to small arms, Trace knew she could hold them off indefinitely — even if they cut the air supply, her marines had personal supplies for hours yet, and more if they salvaged emergency systems from the miners' supplies. But when the heavy rounds started incoming, she knew they were in trouble.

"Pull back!" she yelled as the first round hit the ceiling of the first tunnel. "Walker, second line of defence now!" As Lance Corporal Walker and his three marines scrambled back into the maze of gantries, pipes and heavy machinery surrounding the enormous wellhead. Another grenade spat past them and hit a pressure tank, showering all with shrapnel as they fell flat.

About her, Rael and Terez fired as a new target presented, and the shooter's grenade hit the ceiling twenty meters short with a blast that brought small pipes and debris crashing and twisting down. "Think I got him first," Rael suggested.

"Pull back," Trace told them. "Displace in pairs, go." Rael and Terez went first as Trace put down fire, then she left as Arime fired, rolling on the exposed decking, then running for a good cover position on a higher walkway by a big generator that also gave her a flanking look at Walker's first tunnel. Problem was, from here neither she nor her marines had anywhere near as good a view up the tunnel. It allowed the attackers to advance to the tunnel mouth, right on top of them... if they were prepared to risk marines at close quarters.

"Guess they've been told to trash the wellhead to get us," Rael remarked from his new cover.

"What's in these damn pipes anyway?" Terez wondered.

"Bunch of things," said Trace. "Most of them flammable."

"Great."

"Big enough rupture here would endanger this whole part of Crondike. It's a big bomb, if these guys set it off they'll be dead too. This steel is tough."

"Major," said Private Singer from Walker's section. The reception on local coms was crackling with static, but the jamming wasn't so intense in here that the marines couldn't talk to each other. And if they could talk, the enemy attacking from three different tunnels at once could talk also. *"I'm hit, shrapnel in the arm from that fucking grenade. I'm still in the fight, Parker's patching it."* That was three hurt out of twelve, though Arime's injury was just cosmetic. It was going to get worse.

Two more big explosions rocked the second tunnel entry, followed by lots and lots of smoke. Even with her targeting glasses, Trace couldn't see anything up the tunnel. She did some fast calculation. "Give it fifteen seconds," she told her marines, sighting along her rifle into the smoke. "Could be a big push. Kono, anything up..."

A grenade explosion cut her off. *"Is now,"* said Kono. *"Everyone pull back."* Three tunnels out of three now with heavy weapons, but still not quite in synch...

Grenades sailed out of the smoke, flying long and slow in the low gravity. Trace saw nothing heading close enough for trouble, though Arime swore and ducked for cover as one came too close. Big flashbangs, shrapnel cracking all around, Trace felt something smack her armour and barely flinched. Several armoured figures rushed through the smoke, flanking left and right... she was angled for the left side, shot the first one in the neck as Terez shot the second. Whatever had been about to follow them, didn't. Trace could distantly hear someone talking on coms up the tunnel, no doubt asking those two runners of their status... there was cover in gantry platforms and pipes just meters in that direction, those grenades were intended to buy them enough time to make cover. But all the smoke had obscured the attackers' vision also, and the grenades hadn't been accurate enough to put off the marines' aim.

"Nice try!" Rael shouted at them. "Why don't you try that again, that was fun!" Shouting things at the enemy was new for all of them. Previously their opponents hadn't spoken much English. And also, it was disconcerting, to be targeting humans, and being targeted by them.

"Clear on this side," said Trace for everyone else's benefit. "One attempt failed, two enemy down. Hold a moment." Because the opportunity it presented was too good to miss, and she rolled from cover, slipped gently down off the gantry and bounded to the wall beside the tunnel, and flattened herself there. Before her, the bodies of the two dead soldiers had several throwing grenades, so she scooped two quickly. The thing with smoke thick enough to stop IR penetration, it worked both ways.

The grenades were cylindrical, two fit in a hand if you practised it. She put the rifle briefly beneath her armpit, pulled both pins, then released the handles. Counted to one-and-a-half, then lobbed them high and gently about the corner into the tunnel and smoke. Then flattened herself to the wall once more and waited.

They exploded near simultaneously, still high as everything in low-G took a long time to fall, and rained shrapnel onto those in the smoke below. Screams and yells, and Trace rounded the corner, moving swiftly into the smoke and confusion. Several dark shadows were down, others assisting them. She shot the assistants first, point blank, having the advantage of knowing that anyone she saw was enemy. By the time they figured what she was, they were already dead. She put five more down, execution style at zero range, sidestepping one who did figure her for an enemy at the last moment, simply wrenching her head out of the way and shooting him from an angle. Then she knelt amongst the corpses as their comrades yelled for clarification further up the tunnel, and collected more grenades.

By now the smoke was thinning, but not knowing who was who, those further up the tunnel would be reluctant to shoot. She primed and threw a couple of spare grenades in their direction, took a com headset off one bloodied head, then ducked out of the tunnel and back up to her cover on the gantry.

"Here," she told Arime calmly, and tossed across a pair of grenades, then another for Rael. Then activated the headset and put it on over her own earpiece and mike.

"You going to talk to them?" Rael asked wide-eyed. Trace shook her head and gestured silence, a finger to her lips, not knowing if the mike was activated. Now the smoke was clearing, exposing many bloody corpses lying sprawled across the walk and gantry beside the big pipes. Several were still moving, one of those screaming — grenade casualties she'd left alive. It took healthy troops to move the wounded, and would limit incoming fire from up the tunnels, fearful of hitting their own.

"Holy fuck," Arime murmured.

"Stone cold killer," said Terez. And yelled up the tunnel, "That's courtesy of Major Trace Thakur, *UFS Phoenix* you pricks! Try again!" Which was met with a volley of automatic fire, but none of the marines' positions were directly in line of sight from further down the tunnel. They were silenced by yells, no doubt to be careful of the wounded.

"Sir!" Trace heard on the captured headset. *"Sir it's Thakur. She just killed a bunch of my guys."*

"Get a grip soldier! She's just one marine!"

"Yessir… sir, I'm pretty sure that was her…"

"I'm sending up more heavies. Get it done Commander! You're running out of time!"

"Yessir."

Trace removed and deactivated the headset. "Okay guys," she said on coms. "I think we've got a pause for a bit while they send up more heavies. They're got a commander on scene, I figure probably a major equivalent. These guys just figured they're outclassed on quality, so they'll resort to blasting with brute force. That's exactly the correct tactic for them, it's about to get serious."

"Not a Major equivalent," Walker said pointedly.

"Fuck no," Kono agreed.

CHAPTER 31

Lisbeth didn't know the Ops officer's name... but in action it seemed *Phoenix* crew called each other by their post, not name or rank. *"AT-7, this is Ops, twenty seconds to release. Can you confirm systems green?"*

"Um..." Lisbeth tried to focus on her controls, breathing in the little, short gasps of breath she'd become accustomed to in steady 6-G thrust. She was already exhausted, and had no idea how she'd manage more stress to come. "Yes Ops, all systems green. Tif? Tif, all good yes?"

"Good yes," Tif agreed in that odd little growl of an accent she had. She'd refused a helmet, Lisbeth still had no idea how kuhsi ever used helmets over those ears. Instead she wore a headset that she'd had to twist to fit in one ear, and a little mike protruding down to her mouth. Lisbeth's own helmet felt far too big and bulky on her head, and she had no idea how to use the visor HUD that sprawled across and interfered with her vision of the controls. On a civilian flight you never had to worry about taking a few extra seconds to find and read the correct display. Military pilots had to take short cuts, because every wasted second put you at risk.

"Ten seconds," said Ops. Lisbeth was incredibly scared. Her heart was hammering so fast it threatened to burst out of her chest. With the Gs and dizziness, she thought she might faint. And then thought again that it was just as well she was so physically distracted, because otherwise she might burst into tears. Fear was an exciting thing to contemplate in the movies or in books, but real terror was like a crushing weight from some heavy object that had fallen on you. You could wriggle and strain and try to free yourself from it, but escape was impossible as it slowly crushed the air from your lungs and the sense from your brain. She didn't want to die young, and she certainly didn't want to die painfully, and if she'd learned one thing in the past few weeks, it was that death in combat was rarely quick and painless. She tried to recall the things the Major had told her about fear, about battling and conquering it, but

she was flat on her back in a 6-G burn in an unarmed shuttle about to plunge toward a moon base where people would almost certainly shoot at her with intention of blasting her shuttle into a scorching ball of flame. And there was no rational thought to be comforted by.

"Four," said Ops. *"Three, two, one, release."* With a crash, and then they were free, and Lisbeth gasped for air as for a brief moment the crushing pressure on her chest was gone. Then Tif kicked the shuttle thrust in once more, and the pressure resumed... but not as bad. Four-Gs, the relevant screen showed her after a search... and then she noted the same figure on her visor HUD. Maybe useful after all, she thought.

Ahead now she could see *Phoenix*, her tail ablaze with bright blue light, the damaged wreck of *Adventurer* dangling bits of wreckage that flapped helplessly in the bigger ship's talons. Tif murmured something that might have been an oath. Tif certainly understood their situation or she wouldn't have volunteered... probably she knew just enough to know how crazy-good a ship and its commander had to be to pull off a move like that. And her loyalty in this situation was without question — her little boy was still on *Phoenix*. Why Tif thought that this risk was worth taking, with those odds in the balance, Lisbeth couldn't begin to guess.

"Altitude one-fifty klicks," she announced off the screen. If she glanced back, she could see the huge, silver horizon of Faustino arcing off to one side. No atmosphere plus low gravity, which made approach easier. And also dramatically extended the range of surface defensive weaponry, she figured. Dear god, what was she doing here?

"Hello ladies!" came a cheerful voice in her ears. *"This is Lieutenant Trey Hausler on the Phoenix assault shuttle PH-1! I see you have dropped into what I'll be calling Hausler-controlled-airspace and are about to commence your run into Crondike... you'll be pleased to know that I'm about to shoot the crap out of the Crondike communications tower, which ought to lighten up some of this jamming they're doing and give us a better idea where the Major is currently located.*

"In the meantime, please commence descent on the co-ordinates my lovely co-pilot will be forwarding to your screens shortly, it will bring you down just over the weapons horizon of Crondike's defences where you will maintain an orbit and await my further instruction to come and pick up our marines.   For this run, since I have the weapons, I'll do the shooting and you'll do the carrying.   If you have any difficulties with this plan of attack, please lodge your complaint at the Office of Lieutenant Hausler affairs, courtesy of Kiss My Ass, Shiwon Homeworld and have a nice day."

Lisbeth could barely stop grinning, despite the Gs.   The fear was far from gone, but far more manageable.   She'd never actually met Lieutenant Hausler face to face, but she wanted desperately to hug him.

"What say?" Tif asked.   It had of course been far too much for her.

"My pilot barely got a word of that," Lisbeth told Hausler, teasingly.   "Don't worry, I'll fill her in.   Just remember that she doesn't speak English, and I don't speak military."

"AT-7 I will try to remember.   PH-1 out."

"Tif, navigation coordinates.   Nav computer Tif..." a flash as they came through from PH-1 onto Lisbeth's screen.   She transferred to the pilot's screen, and felt much better for having something to do.   "Follow course, Tif.   Do you have it?"

"Have got," said Tif, quite calmly.   *"Nice shuttuw.   Debo-gand nake good, yes?"*

Actually Debogande Inc didn't make these shuttles, just used them.   "Debogande make good, yes Tif.   Altitude one-ten klicks, ETA to surface orbit four point three minutes."

Heavy grenade fire came down Kono's third tunnel first, and big explosions rocked the wellhead.   The other two tunnels followed, with little warning now that someone had figured she might be listening.   Trace pressed flat, eyes closed and held her breath with long experience as blasts pounded her skull and chest like body blows.   Secondary explosions blew a pipe, then flames were roaring near, screams and yells as gunfire and attackers darted in.

She primed and lobbed one captured grenade, knelt and aimed with bloody-minded focus despite her ringing ears and head, and put one running figure down, as others hit their near cover and dove.   Incoming fire came from the tunnel mouth cover and she ducked back as shots snapped past, then dropped off the gantry and slid in a low-G fall behind the pressure tank.   Warning lights flashed red and sirens howled, machinery shutting down with emergency overrides as she bounced down and scampered low amidst the thicket of pipes and supports at ground level, hot air blasting up from the grille floor below, malfunctions in the pipes kilometres deep feeding the backwash up to the surface.

Her move put her immediately in position to target the covered, attacking soldiers' next move, and she shot one more through the side of the head as they broke.   More fire roared above and to her side, her other marines returning fire, and she heard Singer yelling that Walker was dead.   That put first tunnel under pressure on her left, so she rolled and scampered that way, lobbed her remaining grenade behind the most obvious cover on that side — a big pipe relay — and shot two more as they ran to avoid the explosion.

Another big explosion nearby sent metallic debris crashing around her, then fire from near cover where attackers had gathered. A shot hit steel beside her head, another clipped her body armour as she rolled for better shelter... and found Private Singer on the deck where that last explosion had blown him, face half-shredded and arterial blood jetting.   He screamed and writhed, and Trace grabbed him, hauled behind some machinery yelling, "Singer and Walker are both down! We are weak on Tunnel One!   We are weak on Tunnel One!"

Tension bandage on in as fast as she could, pressed it down, then grabbed up the rifle to lay down fire on movement beyond the immediate tangle of pipes.   "Hang on Sing, hang on buddy."   As his eyes rolled back in his head, insensible with pain.   Fingers on his left hand were missing too. She couldn't stay here and tend him, she had to fight or they'd be overrun.

"Major!" came Romki's voice behind her, and she looked to find the bald academic crawling toward her, a pistol someone had given him in one hand, looking terrified but still coming. "Major go and fight, I'll move him back! The gravity's only low, I can move him!"

"You got first aid?"

"Yes yes, I have it back there…"

"Good, keep your head down." And she darted away, leaped to a new walkway level, and found Private Teale from Walker's section pressed by a feeder pipe and firing, one leg bloody. "Heading left Gigi," she said as she went, neither of them with time to patch the leg, and swung under another railing to where she figured the big left flanking manoeuvre would have gone… and sure enough, here was more shooting on the First Tunnel flank, a marine was wedged into the gantries behind smoking, sparking generator pumps, holding the attackers back or the whole flank might have fallen.

Several of them made a low-G sprint or leap to the far side of a pressure tank, and Trace refrained from firing so as not to give away her position. Suddenly her uplink crackled; *"Major Thakur, this is Lieutenant Hausler PH-1, requesting your position for immediate extraction."*

Trace ducked back so they wouldn't hear her talking either… though with the racket of gunfire, yells and explosions beneath the low, echoing ceiling, that didn't seem likely. "PH-1, immediate extraction requested from Crondike Wellhead Seven. A landing pad is on east-side proximity."

"Crondike Wellhead Seven, landing pad on east-side proximity, roger that Major. Extraction will be by AT-7, PH-1 will be flying cover, ETA four minutes and counting. We are now taking special requests."

"We will attempt to keep an airlock clear for you, request immediate fire support once inside, severe firefight in progress." 'Special request' meant fire support, but masks alone were not enough to save her marines from explosive decompression, and that was the only way a combat shuttle could give direct fire support in here. They'd have to land and get in through the airlock to cover their retreat... assuming they could survive the ground fire to get here in the first place. Hausler must have blasted the Crondike coms tower to cut the jamming, she thought.

"PH-1 copies Major, hang tight. If you haven't heard from us in five minutes, we're dead." Which was not flippant, but professional. If the rescue couldn't reach that airlock, then no point hanging around waiting for it, that meant. Trace didn't think it would make much difference — there was no getting out of this wellhead. If the shuttles died trying, she and her marines would die right here.

Wellhead Seven showed as a red mark on Lisbeth's navscreen as PH-1 relayed it, and Lisbeth had it on direct relay to Tif. "Tif? Red mark. Target, you see it?"

"See," said Tif, as they arced in a low, clockwise turn about Crondike. The mining settlement formed a low cluster of dull metal buildings on the near horizon. Faustino itself looked like a sea of cold and dirty ice, cracked like broken porcelain and sliced by the occasional dead-straight pipeline. In low-G with no atmosphere the shuttle was barely using engines at all — without drag all thrust accumulated as V, making airless worlds a V-hazard to approach. Atmosphere made for hot reentries and sometimes poor visibility, but at least it slowed you down without thrust. Tif turned them now by tipping them ninety-degrees right and applying gentle thrust, careful not to add more V until they needed it.

"Lieutenant Zhi, you have that position?" Lisbeth asked.

"I've got it," Zhi confirmed. *"If you come under fire on the pad, the priority is to dispatch all marines into Crondike. With combined firepower we could take over the entire base and take whatever ship we need by force to get back to Phoenix."* If this shuttle was lost, he meant. Lisbeth was no soldier, but she could see

numerous problems with that scenario, including delays that could get *Phoenix* killed while waiting. And herself, off-ship, in ground combat. The flightsuit she'd pulled on before departure could become pressurised enough to keep her alive for a few minutes in vacuum, but if they came down any further from a Crondike airlock the walk would be fatal even if the crash wasn't. And behind her, Tif hadn't been able to find any helmet that fit.

"AT-7 this is PH-1. Crondike have four defensive magfire emplacements that I can see, and there are at least four more armed flyers of some description that are staying hidden for now. On my signal I want you to come in on a heading of 290 degrees on the Crondike compass, past those big habitat buildings, and put it down on the landing pad outside Wellhead Seven. Make certain you land in contact with the airlock extension arm, it's a tough thing and it can take damage, Lieutenant Zhi can get aboard from there."

"I've got it," said Lisbeth. "I mean I copy. Tif, Crondike compass 360. Compass 360, understand? Our heading, 290."

"Unnstan," Tiff agreed.

"290 to target..."

"Welled Sefen," Tif interrupted. *"Good, got."* No doubt she'd absorbed a little of what else Hausler had said as well. Two-ninety degrees on the compass was coming around fast, and scan showed PH-1 make a hard cut from its orbit opposite them, and come racing in low. Lisbeth's heart hammered — she'd thought she still had thirty seconds!

"AT-7, commence run now!"

"Go Tif!" But Tif was already going, a sudden, slamming roar that crushed Lisbeth into her seat, and sustained as Crondike's position on the silver horizon moved across, and finally lay before them. Tif kept the thrust on for a moment, then eased off until they were skimming the silvery ice at barely fifty meters. It was breathtaking and surreal, for the speed made no noise, just enough thrust to hold steady altitude. A pressurised vehicle flashed beneath them, a thin line of tire tracks on the ice behind... possibly a scout? Or just a civilian miner minding his business?

Ahead, a bright flash, then some terse chatter from PH-1 that Lisbeth missed.   Another flash, then the terrifying sight of silver streaks shooting high away from Crondike at scary speed, arcing into the black and starry sky.   Magfire, aimed upward from the surface at something flying over.   Another bright flash, and another line of fire, hosing the sky.   Closer now, Lisbeth saw pieces rising from the explosion, tumbling over and over.   Then the deadly arrowhead-shape of an assault-shuttle, low and fast across the ice, turning belly-out and thrusters flaming as it came around for another pass.   Then the buildings were rushing up, and it was their turn.

"Brace for manoeuvres!" Lisbeth thought to say... and then suffered the anti-climax of ongoing silence as Tif dropped even lower, buildings zooming past left and right, then an abrupt right bank and a big roaring kick in the pants as she dodged an upcoming obstruction.   A connecting skyway forced them to climb, and Tif rolled straight upside down and roared thrust again.   For a heart-stopping moment Lisbeth thought they were going to power straight into the ground, but Tif flipped them again and nudged more power to flatten them out barely thirty meters from the surface, then edged the thrusters forward and slowed them with a roaring burn that slammed Lisbeth painfully forward against her straps.

Around another low, pressurised structure, skidding and turning left while slowing... and suddenly before them was a shuttle, barely half their size and ugly-industrial, but clearly armed and rotating their way with bursts of attitude thrust to acquire them.   Tif dropped the right side and hit full thrust, powering them sideways and around as the enemy shuttle fired and missed, then looped them upside down again as she rolled for opposite thrust and came around behind it... a bright flash, and Lisbeth saw the shuttle explode. Then a streak on scan as PH-1 came by.

"Nice move AT-7, I got him.   Proceed to target and keep your eyes peeled, these bastards are tricky."   Lisbeth tried to process that people had just died back there, but couldn't.   She was too pleased it hadn't been her to care.

A slide across some open ice, then big steel passages like great pipelines on the icy surface, three of them culminating on a central, low domed hub. Scan read that as Wellhead Seven, and sure enough, the fourth side with no tunnel attachment had a hard steel landing pad alongside, with an extension arm waiting for them. And most incredible of all, the light above the extension arm was flashing, meaning someone was waiting for them.   Someone friendly, Lisbeth hoped.   Though given their payload, it wasn't her who needed to worry about that.

Tif somehow came out of the move directly on course, angled them straight to the pad then kicked forward thrust hard and dropped them near-motionless onto the pad.   Skid wheels brought them straight to the extension arm, and then it was reaching above the cockpit toward the dorsal hatch — a big, worn and dirty thing that looked like it could handle four marines abreast in full armour.

"We're down!" she shouted for everyone's benefit, and Lieutenant Zhi in particular.   "The extension arm is coming, dismount, dismount!"   Suddenly she was gasping, as though she'd suddenly remembered to breathe, and could hear Zhi and his men speaking in short, fast grabs down back as they clattered and moved. And then her breathing tightened once more as she realised how exposed they were here, sitting on a pad atop a blank expanse of ice, with enemy shuttles around playing hide and seek with PH-1 and looking to kill them both.

If she survived, Trace was certain this would be the last time she operated in light armour.   She leaped across a yawning gap between gantries, across the blaze of burning generators below, smoke choking her lungs and accumulating below the domed overhead where the air filters were no longer clearing it. And hit the opposing railing just as the latest grenade exploded behind her, and something smacked her back armour and thudded her leg with a hideous pain.

But the leg still worked, and she swung herself over, rolled low through an exposed patch as fire smacked the steel around her, then slithered the last bit on her belly beneath a red-hot pipe that hissed and steamed. Her move exposed the four who'd been trying to flank between the big east-side slurry processors — two saw her and fired, but she took more time and snapped one's head back, then the others dove and covered. Another grenade, predictably, and she rolled off the gantry and held on beneath it, using the walkway as a shield. It exploded too far away — throws under fire in low-G were hard to judge, nothing dropped where you'd intended, but still she had about six shrapnel injuries and was losing blood, though not enough yet to slow her.

She dropped to the floor and pressed to a steel side amongst the tangled machinery, there was shooting to her left where Kono's section were still fighting, less to the right where Walker's section had once been, but had now fallen back with only one left and fighting. Movement as an attacker tried to get a shot at her from the right, then was slammed into pipes and slid as someone else shot him. The attackers had them surrounded in the steel maze, but were having trouble closing the deal, as every time they squeezed, several of them died.   Hurt and exhausted, marines kept fighting, point blank, outgunned and hopeless, they didn't care. Just hold position and make the attackers leave their cover if they wanted to win.

Suddenly Kono was peering at her past gantry supports, bloodied as she was but alert.   Trace held up three fingers, indicating the slurry processors… then snapped her rifle up straight at Kono.   Kono ducked and she shot the man who'd appeared behind him. Something exploded, Kono lost his rifle, then tackled the next man at him before he could fire. Trace leapt behind a pipe as two more fired on her point blank, hitting only steel… and at the first pause she put her pistol over the edge for more accurate close range fire and knocked one off his feet. The other covered, and tried to shoot Kono as he wrestled, then a grenade hit the wall next to Trace, and she leaped on the shooter as his gun came back to her.

She swung around the support pylon he used for cover, converted her grip into a headlock and unleashed full power to slam him over backward.   His buddy who she'd knocked down was getting back up — she broke his friend's neck, then flattened as the grenade exploded and blew the other off his feet.   Kono threw off his wrestling opponent, got on top and punched him until his skull broke open. Trace grabbed a grenade off some webbing, pulled and threw it at the slurry processors, then tossed two more to Kono.

Boom! as the grenade she'd thrown exploded, but no screams — those guys had gone. "They just committed a section to this charge," she said hoarsely to Kono. "They're exposed now — we take some grenades and see who we can flank. You ready?"

Kono nodded grimly, one eye swollen closed, an arm dangling, but determined. "Let's do it."

Suddenly a crash above the echoing racket of rifle fire, then her ears popped badly. "Airlock!" she yelled, yawning hard behind her oxygen mask. "Crash entry!"

Wind was rushing, then warning yells, followed by the unmistakable whine and howl of a chain gun spitting devastation. Past the tangle, Trace glimpsed some armoured figures bounding away at high speed... then the hail of bullets hit and sent them kicking and spinning through the air. She crawled past the latest corpses and peered through a visible gap between machinery, and saw the big, armoured figures of Echo Platoon Heavy Squad, stomping in with big armoured rigs braced for extra loadout, chain guns and rapid cannon blazing.

"Echo Platoon this is the Major!" she shouted. "Flank and flank hard! Get around the walls and watch for surprises! Soak those tunnels!"

Corporal Barry complied, Echo heavy commander splitting his two sections and sending four each way around the walls — they must have come in with local radio silence, Trace thought, so the enemy didn't know they were here. No atmosphere outside meant the shuttle's approach was silent, and Chief Stanton in the pad airlock must have let them in. And here behind them, she saw, was the rest of Echo Platoon, in full armour and moving fast. Any surviving special forces soldier who saw that coming would be wise to run.

Trace got up and limped to where she thought Kono's section might be scattered. On a high walkway she found Kumar, bloody hand now accompanied by a bloody side and torn face, but alive and until recently, fighting. She gave him a hand-up whether he wanted one or not. "Move Private, we're leaving! Sergeant Kono, make sure you get Romki! He was taking care of Singer last I saw him!" As gunfire and explosions rapidly retreated around the wellhead dome. Marine Heavy Squads were scary enough against full armour — against light armour, and with low gravity allowing maximum loadout, they were carnage.

Suddenly there were marines jumping gantries alongside her, and someone took Kumar off her hands, then simply picked him up and jumped with him, powered armour making that comfortable even in full gravity. She ignored the offered help and jumped from a gantry down to the floor — there were marines everywhere, she guessed Echo had brought two regular squads plus the heavies, one squad staying behind to make room.

"We are thirteen in the room!" she told the room as she hopped one legged for the airlock. "Twelve marines including myself, plus Mr Romki who has been helping us!" And added on coms, "Hiro! Hiro, where are you? We're leaving!"

"Major your leg," said the marine alongside, hovering anxiously. "Let me take a look at…"

"Not now." She waited by the big, scarred steel doors of the airlock, two marines plus Chief Stanton working to equalise pressure — with a connection to AT-7 at the other end, they should be able to open both airlock doors now without major decompression… but old beat-up airlocks like this one weren't always obliging. The doors opened and she waited alongside as they came back — a number of her marines limp as they were carried, but she couldn't look too hard, there were too many troops still moving, counter-attack or violent decompression still not impossible, and her job now was to make sure no one got left behind.

Kono waited with her as finally everyone started pouring back in. "Giddy," she told him. "Get."

"After you," said Kono.

"Get!" she shouted, and he went. She went to Chief Stanton by the airlock panel. "Sky will fall on your head if you stay here," she told him. "We've room if you want to come."

"I got friends here," he said grimly. "Friends who need to hear this. Do your cause more good that way."

Trace nodded and slapped his arm. "Hiro!" she tried again on coms.

"Hi Major," said Hiro right alongside her, and she nearly jumped. "You're hurt, you should get in." He wore a miner's jumpsuit, helmet and breather mask, no doubt how he'd been sneaking around. But how the hell...?

"Major go!" yelled Lieutenant Zhi as he and the last of Heavy Squad came running for the airlock, and Trace went, stubbornness serving no further purpose. Hiro tried to take her arm down the ugly, pressurised tube beyond, and she shook him off, one leg was all she needed in this gravity.

Then the floor seal to the dorsal airlock, only big enough for one fully armoured marine at a time and taking great discipline and practice to get everyone out of it in a deployable hurry. She hopped and sailed down it, shaking off more assistance at the bottom to get down to her command chair in the main hold beneath the dorsal level. She locked in, slammed the restraint bar down and heard a crash from above as the airlock arm disengaged. Again her ears popped, AT-7's life support pumping in the extra air she'd lost in the docking. A thunder of engines, and they were lifting.

Opposite her in the restraints, Private Van, head lolling, his neck torn by shrapnel. Marines had put bandages on it, but the blood was no longer pumping. One kept his head still as they powered and swung through manoeuvres. All looked morose. Van's eyes saw nothing.

"T-Bone?" called Trace. She knew he was gone, but she couldn't help herself. He'd been with her for three years, having joined Command Squad about the same time as Erik had arrived on *Phoenix*. He liked loud music and funny movies, and wanted to make apple cider once the war was over, a product for which he insisted the market was drastically underserved. She'd even broken her strict no-alcohol rule for a small sip, just to learn what he was talking about. He'd been so pleased that she'd do that for him. "T-Bone. Oh no my friend. Oh no."

With nothing left to do, and no commands left to give, she was blinded most of the way up by tears.

CHAPTER 32

With *UFS Mercury* chasing them, it took two jumps clear of Heuron to be sure they weren't being followed. There, drifting mid-system at an unsettled dwarf binary romantically named AG-41, Erik finally unhooked himself from the command chair after a half-hour's systems review.

Exhausted didn't begin to describe it, and he limped down the main corridor with utter unconcern for crew threats, and headed for the medical bays. Even now, two marines posted to guard the bridge accompanied him, but the only crew they encountered down the corridor were exhausted themselves.

In Medbay Three, Erik found a most expected sight — Major Trace Thakur in singlet and shorts, holding a crutch while standing on one leg, various bandages wrapped around her while a corpsman treated her standing up and pleaded with her to at least take a seat. But Trace was talking to her wounded, and until she'd made her rounds, rest and shrapnel holes alike would have to wait. She turned to look at Erik, her hair flattened by her helmet, marks about her eyes and cheeks where glasses and breather mask had dug into her face. Looking at her now, Erik understood truly for perhaps the first time why she was like she was. Anything less would crumble, mentally if not physically. Even most toughened combat veterans couldn't do it, not like she did. And for this, her marines loved her — she was rare like diamond, and nearly as hard.

Erik pulled his pistol in full view of everyone, and with some theatricality checked the magazine, then handed it to her. "I hear you told Staff Sergeant Kono that you'd shoot me if I came to get you." He gestured for her to do it. "So go ahead."

Trace nearly smiled. She pocketed the pistol, and hugged him hard. Erik hugged her back, though carefully. "Captain didn't pick you because you're a Debogande," she said against his shoulder. "He picked you because you're a fucking freak. I'm not sure even he could have pulled that off."

"He could," Erik said confidently. "I'd actually discussed it with him — full power with a captive warship. He said it was possible, with *Phoenix*, though he'd never had to do it. Without that discussion, I'd never have tried it."

Trace pulled back and looked at him with those deep, dark eyes. "Knowing it's possible, and actually doing it, are two different things. Our friend kuhsi's a gun too. You hear stories about kuhsi reflexes but Hausler says her one evasive move on approach was beyond computation, navcomp review won't classify it as evasive because the software won't accept her reaction time."

Erik nodded. "I'm sorry about your guys. Van, Walker and Singer." It was the first time he'd dared to give condolences. It was the first time he'd been sure they'd be welcome. "Carponi too. He was hit right in front of me. I carried him, but…"

Trace looked down at his blood-stained jacket and pants. She smiled tightly, and patted his cheek. "You did good, Erik."

"He was protecting me."

"It's what we do," said Trace. "We try to protect each other. But bullets are dangerous. It doesn't always work. And we lost Toguchi."

"Right in front of me again."

"And just as well or you'd never have gotten PH-4 back. See, both times? You were right where you were supposed to be. First to carry Carponi, and second to save PH-4 and Alpha First Squad. Not bad karma at all. Good karma. Something's going right with you." Erik frowned at her. "What, you're surprised a Kulina believes in karma?"

"No, it's just that the karma you believe in's a bitch."

"Karma is a bitch," Trace agreed. "But if she was a bitch all the time, nothing would work. Speaking of bitches, Dale's over there, he's okay. You go there, we'll work our way around."

She was inviting him to talk to her wounded marines, as though they'd actually be pleased to see him. A little while ago, Erik would have been pleased. Now he was realising, as he'd probably never realised before, that it really wasn't all about him.

461

"What would happen if I ordered you to get off your feet?" he suggested.

"Very little," said Trace, and swung on her crutch to the bedside of Private Arime, who'd been shot through the arm and shoulder, and now lay half-asleep amidst tangled fluid tubes and monitors, but struggling to stay awake to talk to the Major.

"Hey LT," said Erik, sitting on Dale's bedside. The big marine's head was wrapped so he could only see out of one eye. "How's the head?"

Dale clasped his hand with a crooked smile. "Few days in bed, Doc says. You finally got sick of me enough to knock me out."

"If you hadn't buckled me in I would have knocked myself out and crashed the shuttle. I'm sorry about Carponi."

"Yeah." Quietly. "Yeah, me too. Toguchi too. Too many good people, LC."

"Far too many." He looked Dale firmly in his one visible eye. "And it's not over yet."

Two jumps later, and they were at Gogi. Yet another red dwarf, duller than usual with several huge gas giants in close orbit leading to frequent partial-eclipses along its equatorial plane. But Gogi's outer system was glorious for fortune-seeking free rangers, here beyond the official administrative zone of human or sard administered space. There were ice chunks aplenty, and rare metalloids in compact, near-sun rings that would have made rock and atmosphere worlds uninhabitable from constant strikes, but co-existed fine with mining settlements and stations against whom impacts remained statistically improbable.

Phoenix came in slowly from zenith, selecting the asteroid base of Leechi for approach. Leechi was a Barabo base, in that barabo were the dominant species aboard. But barabo were such anarchic administrators that few systems in their 'possession' were ever strictly considered to be 'theirs'. They'd not had their possessions taken from them by virtue of their location out beyond the established rim of Spiral civilisation, and because until recently, they'd enjoyed the protection of the tavalai. But now that protection was faded if not yet gone entirely. Barabo territories rimmed up against sard space as well, and listening to com traffic upon their arrival, and not yet aware of *Phoenix*'s presence, Erik was not surprised to hear a quiet tension in communications.

"Never thought I'd find myself out here," Lisbeth murmured by Erik's chair, with a firm grasp of a chair arm, and gazing on the forward scan. A chaos of rocks and small bases and little ships, interspersed with a few larger ones. No warships that they could see. With this many rocks, that meant little. Systems like Gogi were places where those who did not wish to be found came to hide.

"Leechi's got repair facilities," said Erik. "Big enough for us, I think."

"What if they refuse?" Lisbeth asked.

"Would you refuse?" Erik asked with a faint smile. "Looking at us?"

"So what... we're going to go around the outer rim territories intimidating everyone into helping us?" A few curious glances their way from the other bridge crew.

"Well first," said Erik, "it's not the 'outer rim', that's just what humans call any place beyond where we're most interested. Technically it's neutral space that would actually be barabo space if the barabo actually had the balls and firepower to ever claim anything."

"Now that the tavalai are pulling back," Kaspowitz added, "it'll probably end up sard space."

"Oh I think Fleet will have a thing or two to say about that," Erik added. "More likely it'll end up human space. But not for a while. And secondly, 'we' are not going to go around doing anything. 'You' are going home to Mother as soon as we can find a reliable transport."

"Many of those out here?" Shahaim asked cautiously, looking up from the transponder transmissions she was scrolling through.

"Given what Mother will pay them when they deliver the cargo at the other end," said Erik. "Probably quite a few."

"Yeah, I know," Lisbeth said calmly.   Erik was almost surprised.   "If you're going to survive out here for a while, you'll need Mother's help.   Someone's going to have to get back to her and tell her what's going on.   Probably should be me."

The click of bridge-guards standing to attention told Erik that Trace had entered the bridge.   It didn't warrant a vocal announcement because up here, technically she wasn't that important.   Erik glanced, and saw her walking on light exo-legs, secured tight about her waist and keeping the weight off her bad leg. Otherwise she wore the usual black marine casuals, that gave no outward sign of other injuries.

"What does the Doc think of you moving around?" Erik asked her.

"Didn't ask," said Trace, taking a hold of his chair on the other side.   "Do they know we're here yet?"

"About half an hour ago," said Erik.   "They went very quiet."   No one out this way would have heard of events on Heuron or Homeworld yet.   But a human combat carrier out this far from primary human concerns, on its own with no support, was odd indeed.   Particularly *this* combat carrier, which was known the length and depth of Spiral space.   A lot of folk up to things that Fleet might disapprove of would suddenly be very nervous.   "Who's on standby, with you and Dale sidelined?"   With an edge to his question, just in case Trace hadn't yet realised that she *was* sidelined.

"Crozier," said Trace.   "She's still pissed she didn't get a capture on *Adventurer.*"

"Tell her that if she wants to take pointless risks to pad her personal resume, she should join the chah'nas.   At the very least we'll need port security on Leechi, it's not very big so one platoon should do it."

"So do we know who's staying and going yet?" Trace asked.

"You'd know better than me," Erik retorted.   "I know a couple I'm booting off personally."

"Seriously?" Kaspowitz asked. "You're not going to punish a bunch of mutinous wannabe assassins?"

"Not this time. Conflicted loyalties after what happened can be expected. Sides were not fully declared because we didn't know what the sides were. Besides, getting abandoned out here without funds could be punishment enough. If anyone tries it *after* we've given them a chance to get off, it'll be the airlock for them."

"So how many *will* get off?" asked Lisbeth.

"From what I hear, I think about fifteen percent of spacer crew. No more."

"And marines?"

"None," said Trace. Erik gave her a sideways look. Trace shrugged. "I think a lot of us now take this fight more personally than the war. We know a lot of the corps will support us when they hear. That's real trouble for Fleet Command. Can't dull that impression by jumping ship now."

"We're hell short of crew as it is," Shahaim muttered. "Another fifteen percent will put us down to a skeleton crew."

"Can you survive out here?" Lisbeth asked quietly.

"Sure," said Erik. "Piece of cake."

"Sard will try and kill us," said Trace.

"Tavalai remnants still hiding out here will try and kill us," Kaspowitz added.

"Pirates and privateers after the price Fleet will put on our heads will try and kill us," Shahaim added.

"And Fleet themselves will try and kill us," Geish said dourly.

"Like I said," said Erik. "Piece of cake. Besides, we're not out here to just survive. Humanity needs a safe zone where those who don't like the growing polarisation can come to talk it out. This is as good a spot as any."

"I think you're thinking too big," Trace said calmly. "That may follow eventually, but for now, let's set small, achievable goals. Like put Supreme Commander Chankow's nuts in a vice, and squeeze. It may be that in gathering all the people who don't like him together, you'll achieve some kind of peace process as well.

Hating Chankow, Anjo and company might be the only big thing that Spacers and Worlders all have in common."

"Mother will help," said Lisbeth. "I know she will. I know she doesn't like Chankow."

"Mother is a businesswoman," Erik disagreed. "First and foremost. She employs several million people. She takes their welfare very seriously. Don't expect too much from her Lis, and don't push too hard when you get back."

"She'll help," Lisbeth repeated confidently. "You'll see."

Erik found that train of thought opened up whole new avenues of fear. Family Debogande was powerful, but that power was nothing compared to Fleet. If push came to shove, Debogande Inc needed Fleet a lot more than Fleet needed Debogande Inc. Ultimately Fleet had all the guns, and could make its own rules.

"Is Leechi very pretty?" Lisbeth asked, gazing at the forward scan.

"I doubt it," said Erik. "Barabo mining station, they're not the tidiest people."

"Sell you some good weed though," Kaspowitz volunteered. Erik gave him a stern look.

"I'd like to buy a few things," Lisbeth said wistfully. "Before I go home."

"A new spaceship wouldn't count?" Trace suggested.

"Oh shush," Lisbeth retorted. "*I'm* not that rich, it's the family."

"I'm sure I don't see the distinction."

"Envy," Erik cautioned his marine commander, holding up a warning finger in her face. Amused, Trace swatted it.

"Besides, I'm sure they don't take human currency out here," said Lisbeth. And blinked. "Gosh, how are you going to *pay* for anything?"

"Charge the aliens money to come and stare at Kaspo," said Shahaim. Nav made a rude gesture at her.

"We'll think of something," said Erik. "You can go shopping Lis. It'll be a nice vacation stop for you, strolling down a barabo mining station market, just you and Delta Platoon and a thousand weed-chewing barabo miners."

Lisbeth smiled at him. "That actually sounds like fun. You forget, I wanted to join Fleet, but Mother wouldn't let me. I'm finally here."

"No I remember," Erik said tiredly, examining a new incoming jump track that appeared on scan. "You're living the dream, Lis."

"We're all living the dream," Kaspowitz echoed. It had been the kind of thing they'd said in the war, echoing the corny Fleet recruitment ads, full of cheerful, brave and patriotic young people off to do their duty in the great adventure. "The Major especially. She's not cut out for peacetime."

"I dunno," Trace said quietly. "I hear there's money to be made making apple cider. I might have opened a brewery."

"You might still!" Lisbeth said cheerfully.

Trace smiled at her sadly. "Yes," she said. "Sure I might." Erik gazed at the scan, thinking of Private 'T-Bone' Van, whose plans for post-war cider were known even to him. And thinking of the Kulina hunting party that would even now be gathering to join the hunt for the *UFS Phoenix*, centring upon one of its officers in particular. Luckily Kulina didn't produce warship pilots, just marines and the occasional special forces soldier. If Fleet could not catch them, the Kulina wouldn't either. He hoped.

"LC," said Shilu. "Leechi's calling. The English is bad, but fluent enough — sounds like a person, not a machine. He sounds nervous."

Erik sighed. "I'll take it." He glanced at Kaspowitz. "Any ideas how to sound reassuring to a frightened barabo? It's my first experience with them."

"Just don't mention the Shuhai campaign, where we destroyed about thirty of their ships for minimal loss, killed ten thousand of them and single-handedly set back their civilisational confidence by a hundred years," said Kaspowitz. "You know — we come in peace, please ignore the bloodstains, that kind of thing."

"Was *Phoenix* there for that?" Karle wondered.

"Fraid so kid," said Shahaim. "And so was I."

"Me too," said Kaspowitz.

"Great," said Erik. "Thank you Kaspo, helpful as always."

"Don't mention it."

'We come in peace, please ignore the bloodstains'. That might become *Phoenix*'s catch cry out here, Erik thought. After so many hundreds, and previous thousands of years of war, he wondered if it was possible to ignore this much blood. He gazed at the forward scan for a moment longer. Station broadcast was showing a lane-buoy visual, a small mining station, only a single wheel with sixty berths, more than half of them empty. Positively catatonic compared to most human systems. It looked old and battered, and from what little he could see of the ships nestled along the rim, they were nothing impressive, mostly old freighters with barely a defensive weapon amongst them. No wonder they were nervous, seeing this alo-powered killing machine looming on the scan-horizon.

It would be nice to make friends here, he thought. To not have to terrify anyone, let alone kill anyone. Perhaps it would be possible. Perhaps. But given what was following, and what would soon be hunting from numerous directions, it didn't seem likely to last.

He took a deep breath, and opened a channel. "Hello Leechi Station. This is *UFS Phoenix,* requesting lane placement and berth assignment. We are displacing 120K, hauling standard military cargo, and will be requiring block accommodation in the vicinity of our berth. Our intentions are entirely peaceful, and I look forward to greeting the Stationmaster in person, *UFS Phoenix* out."

He glanced askance at Kaspowitz. Kaspowitz shrugged. "Not bad LC. You may get the knack of this job yet."

ABOUT THE AUTHOR

Joel Shepherd is the author of 12 Science Fiction and Fantasy novels, including 'The Cassandra Kresnov Series', 'A Trial of Blood and Steel', and 'The Spiral Wars'. He has a degree in International Relations, and lives in Australia.